HUMAN

Also by AG Claymore:

Humanity Ascendant

Human

Humans

Humanity

Ragnarok

Rebels and Patriots

Rebels and Patriots

Beyond the Rim

The Gray matter

The Black Ships

The Black Ships

The Dark Defiance

The Orphan Alliance

Counterweight

Asymmetry

Firebringer

Terra Cryptica

Prometheus Bound

Human

Published by A.G. Claymore
Edited by Beryl MacFadyen
Copyright 2018 A.G. Claymore

ISBN: 9798727847909

Get Free e-Novellas

free stories

When you sign up for my new-release mail list!

Follow this link to get started:
http://eepurl.com/ZCP-z

Property

Surrender

"We're gonna surrender?" Ethdu blurted. Caught off-guard by a sudden swerve, he stumbled against the side of the co-pilot's chair.

"Full stop," Abdu told the pilot, using the change in the shuttle's momentum to pivot his body around a ceiling handhold. He came to rest gazing at his protégé, one eyebrow raised, orange emergency lights pulsing across his face from the Chironian security vehicle in front of them.

Ethdu's expression smoldered with self-anger. He was tired of constantly being on the back foot with his mentor. Abdu's 'see if you can figure out what I'm up to' style of instruction might have been a compliment to Ethdu's expensive genetics but, in reality, it felt more like a never-ending series of slights. He had to learn to control his surprise. His outburst revealed a tendency to ask before thinking, a habit he'd thought was long past.

He forced a shrug, though anger and nonchalance were poor bedfellows. He had to get himself under control and the outward displays often helped to bolster the inner efforts.

"Of *course* we're not actually surrendering," he continued.

"You're just buying time."

Abdu's eyebrow took a break, much to Ethdu's relief. "Our team was sent here for some serious interplanetary shenanigans," the older

1

man said, nodding out the window at the Chironian security vehicle, whose lights had stopped flashing orange, now that the shuttle had come to a halt. Green and white lights now pulsed as a warning to other traffic as it slid around to come alongside.

"*We're* just the sort of folks who *wouldn't* meekly pull over for a routine traffic stop." He grinned at Ethdu. "Pretty cunning, don'tcha think?"

Now it was Ethdu's turn to raise an eyebrow. "Routine traffic stop?"

Abdu inclined his head in acknowledgement. "Fair enough. The flatfoot probably scanned us, so he'll know we're Humans and, therefore, as unaccompanied slaves, we're contraband."

Ethdu treated himself to an eye-roll at this understatement. "His scan will have also told him about the combat focus in our genomes, which is probably a bigger concern for him than our being contraband."

Both men looked aft at the sound of the security vehicle's warbling alarm. Abdu chuckled, leading the way into the cargo compartment where the rest of the Human team waited, weapons stashed out of sight. They still looked somewhat dangerous, due to their armored EVA suits, but civilian and military variants were almost indistinguishable.

"That can easily work in our favor," the older man continued. "That domestic security officer is going to be a bundle of nerves, going up against purpose-designed killers like us, but he'll be damned before he calls in backup and dilutes the credit for this catch. He could get promoted over this."

Abdu waved Ethdu aft of the wide side hatch. "So stand over there and attract no attention until you see a chance to throw him off his game." He reached for the hatch release but stopped, frowning. "The current unrest-index in this city is below a four, right?"

"Three," Ethdu confirmed. "He won't even have a patrol-mate on that vehicle, let alone troops."

Human

The older man chuckled. "That could have been embarrassing for us!" He hit the large release button and adopted a casual pose as the hatch swung down to turn itself into a boarding ramp.

The Chironian domestic security officer slid the side of his own vehicle open and reached out to attach a heavy-duty safety line to one of the rings at his end of the Human vehicle's boarding ramp. The line retracted, pulling the DSO's vehicle tight to the end of the ramp and he crossed over, ignoring the two-thousand-meter drop.

Those long arms gave Chironians decent balance so railings were rare enough on their world. Their heavy forearms gave them a strong grip, making them a dominant force in the empire's professional grappling circuit.

It tended to make them a very confrontational species and this one clearly thought he'd be able to handle a few runaway slaves. "What do we have here?" he rumbled, stepping through the hatch and rounding on Abdu. "A pack of runaway slaves without your thieving master to make excuses for you!"

It was a known fact that Mishak, the Quailu lord who owned the Kish system, was prone to economic raids on his neighbors but it was still unwise for this Chironian native to speak ill of any member of the imperial master-race. It had to be nerves talking. This DSO was twitchy, running on the ragged ends of his courage.

And it was the perfect opening.

Ethdu pitched his voice low, imagining that he was trying to gargle a throat-full of rough gravel. At the same time, he wove in a slightly higher tone. "And what gave you the impression that I wasn't here to make excuses?" he demanded.

The security officer spun around or, rather, started spinning. His heavy forearms made him unwieldy in quick turns – not a problem in the grappling ring, if he could get his hands on his opponent, but this wasn't the ring.

"My Lord!" he stammered. "I meant no…" He stopped in mid-apology, realizing that there was no Quailu standing there. There *was* another Human and the dratted creature had taken his gun away in a fluid, lightning-fast motion.

"Disarmed by a mere slave," Ethdu mused, shaking his head in mock commiseration. "We'll be borrowing your patrol vehicle as well." He glanced at Olivdu who was holding her right hand behind her back. He gave her a quick wink. "I assume you still have a sizeable armory on board? Those food riots were only a few cycles ago, so I imagine you're still carrying backup weapons for the foot patrols…"

"You filthy thieving little pricks!" the cop roared, launching himself at Ethdu.

Ethdu skipped nimbly out of the way and Olivdu jammed a stun stick into the Chironian's side.

The hulking creature let out a strange, warbling shriek and fell, twitching, to the deck of the shuttle.

"His patrol vehicle is shielded against scanners," Ethdu suggested, glancing up at Abdu, "and it's designed to carry a full platoon…"

Abdu was looking at the twitching Chironian but not really seeing him. He was running the probabilities through his head. How often would the cop need to call in to central?

The Chironian, unable to control his body, let out a massive, burbling fart.

"Into the patrol vehicle," Abdu shouted over the chorus of groans. "He can have the damn shuttle, stinking bastard!"

They piled into the police vehicle and cast off the safety line. Hendu shoved his way through the crowded passenger compartment and claimed the pilot's seat.

"Get us to the lab, Hendy," Abdu said, opening a weapons locker that formed the bulkhead between the flight deck and the small two-by-six-meter 'cargo' area.

Abdu whistled. "Would you just look at all this? They must have been shooting a hell of a lot of protesters."

"Mostly Mushkenu population here," Ethdu said.

The Holy Quailu Empire had three classes. The ruling Awilu, the lower-class Mushkenu and the Wardu or slave class, which included all Humans. Kish had been too backward, at the time of annexation, to support a free Mushkenu class.

"They don't have to worry about reimbursing owners for dead slaves, do they?" Olivdu said, stating more than asking. "Mushkenu like that DSO can sneer at me all they want, but you don't hear of Humans getting killed in a riot response."

Not for the first time, Ethdu wondered who that argument was intended for. His people liked to brag that they were too expensive to kill out of hand. In an empire where the lower class accepted that they could be killed by almost anyone in a uniform for the slightest of reasons, that argument carried some weight.

So why did he envy the perils of the free class?

He took a pulse rifle from the rack and looked over the controls. It was a nasty weapon, designed to frighten the public. You didn't just take a flesh-wound from a pulse weapon, you scattered yourself, and those nearby, all over the immediate area.

It fired a crystalline, metallic hydrogen round that was just barely in the solid state. A containment field, projected by a nano-emitter in the round itself, kept it from sublimating directly to a gaseous state. Once fired, the field emitter went into impact-disarm mode, with a pre-programmable delay that allowed the user to select for surface or sub-surface detonation.

Ethdu almost dropped the weapon when the deck angled, shifting hard to port. The distinctive whine of kinetic rounds came from starboard.

"I think they might be on to us," Hendu shouted over his shoulder. "I can't return fire unless I turn us around. These things are built for shooting citizens, not for dogfighting."

Ethdu pulled a line from his chest-plate and snapped it to a tie rail running along the side door. Abdu slapped the opening button before securing his own line.

"Keep heading for the lab, Hendy," Abdu shouted. He leaned out, trusting his line to save him and trusting Ethdu not to lean any farther than needed to fire from in front of him – a compliment his protégé appreciated.

Both men aimed aft to where another domestic security vehicle was trying to match Hendu's wild maneuvers.

Eth resisted the urge to duck back inside to avoid a stream of tracers, knowing the craft's flimsy airframe was no protection. He took careful aim and selected for sub-surface penetration.

The five-round burst impacted low on the craft's nose, a meter to the right of Abdu's rounds. The field holding the dense crystals in the solid state collapsed before the rounds had passed more than a few centimeters beyond the outer shell and then converted directly to gaseous hydrogen.

The entire front of the cockpit disintegrated and the back half slammed back into the fuselage. With a dead pilot and the entire control system destroyed, the craft corkscrewed wildly in an expanding pattern until it crashed into the side of a glazed commercial tower, its engines still thrusting the wreckage until it passed out the other side, along with at least twenty office workers.

"No wonder they only use kinetic in their vehicle cannons," Abdu shouted over the wind. "Spectacular crashes like that cause a lot of property damage."

"At least we bought ourselves..." Ethdu stopped mid-shout, frowning past Abdu, "... about eight seconds of freedom from pursuit. Hang on!"

He grabbed a stanchion, anticipating Hendu's evasive reaction to the three new DS vehicles approaching them from ahead. Abdu grabbed a handhold just in time to avoid dangling out the hatch from his safety line.

"Those guys have a grav-lock on us," Hendu yelled, throwing the small vehicle into a hard turn to port.

Ethdu looked aft to where one of the pursuing vehicles was swinging out of view behind the fuselage. *Those cops must have missiles if they're bothering with gravity signatures.*

"Missiles in the air!" Hendu's shout came as no surprise. "Do those Chironian weapons you're using have prox settings?"

"Not unless you count proximity to the layer they just penetrated," Abdu shouted back.

"Hammurabi's hairy balls!" the pilot cursed. "I'll just take care of everything, then, shall I? Oh fornication…" There was a pause and then the shuttle swung hard to starboard and put her nose down. "Yeah, actually, that should do nicely!"

Ethdu and Abdu looked forward and both let out wordless exclamations of surprise.

"Are you insane?" Abdu shouted. "That DS carrier will have point-defense systems. They'll shred us the instant we enter their engagement envelope!"

"Not with three of their own on our tail," Hendu shot back. "Well… probably not…"

Eth's armored fingers were starting to bend the stanchion but he didn't notice. He was staring fixedly as the carrier grew to fill his entire field of vision. He was about to shout a warning to the pilot but stopped, laughing, as he realized what Hendy intended.

Purely out of showmanship, the pilot threw the small DS craft into a barrel roll as they flew in the port side of the huge carrier. Docked security vehicles and their startled ground-crewmen blurred past dizzily and then they were rocketing out the other side.

The pursuing missiles, spiraling around each other in imitation of Hendu's roll, lost track of the original gravitational signature they'd been assigned to. They decided, from the mass of the carrier all around them, that they were near enough and, rather than lose the target entirely, it would be best to detonate now and see what happened.

After all, they'd had a good run…

The carrier had plenty of wide open space on either side to vent the explosion but that didn't mean it came out unscathed. She took heavy damage from the inside out and the docked DS vehicles were either smashed or, in the case of the Human team's newest problem, tossed out the side like a paper model.

"Oh sh…" Ethdu was cut off as the tumbling vehicle struck their tail assembly with a glancing blow. It rushed past in a hail of debris, some of which had just been torn loose from their own craft.

"Good news is we're near the labs," Hendu shouted, his voice slightly higher than usual. "Bad news is that nobody'll ever call what happens next a 'landing'. Grab something and hope it doesn't come loose!"

As if to prove him right, the small vehicle, having lost half of its tail, started to spin. Of all the buildings flying past the hatch, one seemed to be coming inexorably closer.

Ethdu and his mentor were trapped at the hatch. The rotational inertia was too great by now for them to make it to the seats. They both closed the helms on their suits.

Ethdu punched his arm through the outer hull so he could wrap his arm around the whole hatch frame. He did it just in time.

A hail of glazing and framework invaded the craft slightly ahead of the sound of the impact. They slid to a halt, throwing up desks and chairs in what appeared to be an office. The lights, those that still remained in operation, were at half illumination so the place was probably off shift, except for the guard who sat behind a desk near a glazed entry vestibule.

Human

Ethdu activated the team heads-up display and breathed a sigh of relief when everybody came up green.

Abdu must have done the same because he was grinning as his helm opened. "All right, everybody, get your shit together. Security'll be all over this site in a matter of minutes."

"I think I peed in my armor," Noadu said, "just a little…"

Abdu hopped down to the tiled floor and sauntered over to the security guard who still had a mug halfway to his mouth. He didn't even appear to have noticed the large wet stain on his shirt.

It went without saying that it would be best if the guard didn't get a chance to call this incident in to his supervisors.

"Hey, Bud," Abdu began, giving the Chironian a casual nod.

The guard nodded back slowly.

Abdu leaned in. "Parking up here in the two-thousand block is *so* expensive. Do you validate?"

The guard's eyes narrowed at this but then he twitched and fell over, stunned by the contact plates on the older Human's armored gloves.

"Grab a weapon and let's go!" Abdu growled.

Ethdu decided to keep his Chironian weapon. The locals weren't fond of the domestic security officers and carrying a captured DSO weapon might earn him some points with the disaffected population if he used it on the authorities. One way or the other, it should discourage the general public from interfering.

"We're eight levels up from the lab," Hendu advised, checking the ammunition state on his assault weapon. "Icon is green-alpha-one."

Ethdu brought up the overlay as they walked. The green icon was almost directly below them. It seemed deceptively easy, if you could forget about the hostile security forces.

"There's a three-floor drop-shaft over there," Noadu said.

"Good," Abdu replied. "Everybody, follow Noa."

Ethdu stepped into the quarter-grav opening in the floor, following the systems specialist down past two sets of exit railings but he cursed in annoyance. "Get out of the way, Noa!" He angled his legs back so he'd slide down behind the techie who'd failed to clear out of the drop-shaft's base.

Basic shaft etiquette, he thought. *What does he think...* *Fornication!*

Oliv slammed into them, forcing all three of them to stumble out into an open-air café surrounding the drop exit.

It figured, of course. Higher traffic areas, like shafts that connected several levels, were ideal spots for quick-transaction businesses like cafés. Like cafés on any planet, really...

"Hello, officers!" Eth said with friendly enthusiasm, grinning like a long-lost pal.

There were eight of them, sitting at tables, standing in line or just about to leave. All of them watched the growing group of Humans, not failing to notice how heavily armed they were. They kept their hands on their drinks.

The civilians cleared out.

"The Goddess of Luck is sure stacking the bones against us today," Abdu said quietly. "Every damn throw turns out a draw at best. Let's just back off. There's a ramp behind the shaft and we can probably get a good head start before they decide to escalate..."

A ninth DSO stepped out of the washroom, adjusting the seals on his light armor. He saw the Humans and his hand went to his sidearm. He froze then, realizing he was intruding on an already shaky détente.

"This might be the last throw for us," Noa groused, watching the DSOs all put their hands on their weapons before the situation stabilized again, "and all we have is a lousy knave for a pivot bone." He slid a high explosives grenade-disc from the dispenser on his chest-plate and tossed it to the DSO who'd escalated the situation.

"Tip for the dealer," he quipped. The grenade was roughly the size of the usual gambling chip found in bone houses so it was mildly amusing. More importantly, the pending explosion should help cover the team's withdrawal.

The grenade went off, spraying the café with bits of the cop as well as fragments of a sign advertising for new franchisees. Apparently, a new franchise was opening somewhere in the empire every thirteen minutes.

Noa, standing on the right of the group, was closest to the blast. "Dammit!" he yelled, slapping a hand over his cheek. "I'm alright," he grumbled, turning to follow the team. "Just caught a fragment from that damn sign."

Ethdu followed but walking backwards to cover the café. The grenade's effect on the lightly armored officers was more than he expected but it wouldn't last.

They descended the ramp to the next floor. Ethdu stepped off the incline, lowering his weapon as he moved around a support column. He was about to start sprinting for the top of the next ramp when a Quailu passed him, heading the other way.

Judging by his clothing, he was clearly not from the ruling Awilu class but he was still a Quailu and, therefore, above any petty dispute between intruders and the local natives of the security force.

The alien must have realized he was allowing his curiosity to show because he sniffed dismissively, turning his gaze away from the hurried Humans as he headed for the ramp.

Where at least eight DSOs, angry and disoriented, would soon be appearing with revenge on their minds.

Too late, the danger of the situation gelled for Ethdu. He turned to go after the Quailu but Abdu pushed past him, cursing like a cargo handler.

The older man stepped into a blocking position just as the Quailu rounded the column at the base of the ramp. He grunted in pain, stumbling but remaining on his feet as three rounds slammed into his armored back.

Abdu grabbed the now-protesting Quailu and forced him back around the corner of the column to safety. He sank to his knees as the angry alien stormed off.

Eth rushed to Abdu, pulling the older man's arm over his shoulder and helping him to the next ramp but the rest of the team wasn't advancing.

"We got a huge force of DSOs down there," Olivdu warned.

Eth noticed she'd split up the team, three to one side of the ramp and four to the other. They only had to fire the occasional burst to keep the DSOs suppressed but they'd soon call in backup. An aerial unit would change the situation drastically.

"News of our presence would have been… filtering up the chain since… we got here," Abdu wheezed, spitting up blood with every painful word. "Bound to have reached… someone who knows about the Chironian raid on Heimdall's labs."

"So they'll know where we're headed," Ethdu finished angrily. He looked at his mentor. "How bad is it, Ab?"

"One of… my lungs… at least, so…" His eyes went wide, mouth open in a silent scream as he arched his back, nearly falling from his protégé's grasp. "Suit just injected… stabilizing foam," he whispered. "Hurts like buggery!"

Eth felt a cold chill down his spine. If the suit was injecting foam in a wound, it meant the injury was beyond Ab's genetically enhanced healing abilities.

All of the combat slaves in their team were designed with strength, endurance and healing in mind. They could recover from wounds that would kill the average Human.

But there were limits.

"We can't go back," Noa said quietly in Eth's ear, "and we can't get to the labs." He nodded over his shoulder. "So we need to hold this area long enough for me to crack my way in through that public node over there."

Eth looked over to the node, twenty meters away in what looked like a dead end. It was open to the left, verging on a drop so high that you'd work your way through the entire seven stages of grief before you impacted the ground.

There were just enough planters scattered around the area to make it defensible. "You can get in through a public node?" he asked.

Noa nodded. "Take a lot longer than accessing a terminal in the labs but that option's off the table, I'd say."

Eth nodded at Ab, still hanging from his shoulder. "Help me get him over there and then get started. Oliv, start pulling back before the DSOs upstairs get over the shock of nearly killing a Quailu and come down to flank us. Take up positions behind those planters."

It could be worse, Eth mused. *Not by a lot, but it could be worse.* Ab was out of commission for the duration and they'd lost their chance to smash into the lab and grab the data the 'easy' way but they still had a plan.

There wasn't really a plan for exfiltration and it was a safe bet that the locals would call in air support on the Humans, exposed as they were on the open-air platform.

Sometimes your problems were just answers in disguise.

He would almost have laughed if not for the state his mentor was in. Ab was the closest thing to a parent Eth had ever known, closer than most Humans ever knew.

When every one of your kind came from a maturation tube, parenting was pretty much a lost art. Only intense assignments like combat and, especially, combat leadership led to the kind of close relationship that existed between Eth and his mentor.

Whistleblower

It was a fashionable corner of the galaxy. The Grannazian stellar nursery was a common dropout point for dozens of shipping lanes. Customers actually paid more for the longer voyages that dropped from path-shaping and loitered here for a day or two.

Just the sort of place where you wouldn't expect to die in a hastily planned government cover-up.

There was a lot of fear among the other Quailu passengers. Allamu could feel it despite his remote location in the ship's gardens. He lurched forward, tripping on an exposed root and falling on top of Z'zedthenu's thorax.

He scrambled off the insectoid's leathery, chitinous plates in revulsion – not the best timing for a stomach already unsettled by the sudden shift in their vessel's motion.

If Z'zedthenu had been discomfited by the emergency dropout from path-shaping, he wouldn't show it on his… face and his species didn't appear to have emotions in the normal sense. Allamu, like all Quailu, was strongly empathic but the Zeartekka were a blank slate to him.

He wasn't the only Quailu to feel it was like dealing with a living corpse.

"What was that?" Allamu looked away from the insectoid with a shudder, feeling the guilt at his revulsion but unable to do anything about it.

"We've stopped shaping path," Z'zedthenu rattled in reply.

Allamu could feel consternation and fear filtering down from the bridge crew now, passing through the Quailu passengers like the flow of a river, intensifying the existing mood. He looked back to Z'zedthenu, a new worry replacing his dislike for insectoids. "This was not done by the crew. They're as confused as the rest of us. We're nowhere near Goodhaven-7 and the express isn't supposed to stop at Grannazian."

Z'zedthenu turned his dull black, multifaceted gaze toward the shielding above. He sprang to his feet with unnatural speed.

They had agreed to meet in the ship's 'night garden', a small collection of nocturnal plant-life from around the empire. It was a four-hundred-square-meter area recessed into the ship's upper surface and the atmosphere was held in by energy shielding.

Allamu had arranged to meet the rogue intelligence officer before their arrival at Goodhaven 7 in the hopes of getting a head start on all the other news-shapers who'd be waiting there. It might have turned his career around.

What he wanted and what he got were rarely related. At best, the two concepts might be described as mildly antagonistic acquaintances.

Still, this felt worse than usual. The fear filtering down from the bridge was intensifying. He took a step back, leg muscles tensing.

The insectoid officer pointed upward. "There," he rattled. "Do you see the disruption in the star-field? They blur at the edges and N'Cheb 419 is entirely missing. It should be at the center of that dark patch."

Allamu crouched in alarm as the Zeartekka emitted a loud, deeper rattling noise. He realized it was laughter and came back to a full standing posture.

"They have a sense of drama," the imperial officer croaked, "blocking any view of my home-world before they make their next move." He turned his unreadable face back to Allamu. "There can be no doubt. They came for us. This is the only vessel currently underway from Throne World to Goodhaven 7. If they learned of my plans to meet the press, this ship is my most likely choice of transportation."

"They came for you," Allamu corrected. "I'm nobody to them, unless I can publish whatever it is you wish to reveal." He brushed the dead leaves from his tunic. "You should give me whatever information you have while you still can," he urged, waving a hand up at the distortion. "Once they have you in custody, the secrets you carry will disappear."

The laugh startled him again.

"You misunderstand the situation, Allamu." Z'zedthenu waggled his head to accentuate his amusement. "I said they've come for us – all of us." He spread his upper forearms to indicate the ship that carried them. "They will leave no evidence. They never leave evidence and twelve thousand passengers telling of a covert team boarding this ship and carrying away an imperial officer would certainly count as evidence."

Allamu stared, his skin crawling. His mouth moved but no sound came out. He tried again but his mind was already dangerously distracted by the fear flowing through the ship. He looked up as the insectoid gestured toward the menacing shadow in the stars.

A haze of glittering points had appeared but they weren't stars. They were moving, separating into even more tiny points of brilliant danger.

"An anti-ship spread," the officer said, chittering meditatively.

"No!" Allamu blurted, his mouth taking matters into its own… lips... Then his brain valiantly tried to take control again. "They wouldn't wipe out an entire passenger liner just to stop one person."

Z'zedthenu tilted his head back a few degrees. "And who is better suited to know what they're capable of, an imperial intelligence officer or a second-rate news-shaper?"

Allamu felt rage building and he encouraged it as a preferable alternative to gut-churning fear. This creature from a subject species dared to insult a Quailu? It might hold an officer's commission and exercise the devolved authority of the Quailu Emperor himself, but that was no excuse for such insolence!

He cast about for a suitable rejoinder, wanting to put this arrogant *bug* in its place.

"They will fail, of course," the officer rattled calmly. "I've already prepared for this eventuality."

Allamu's sense of anger evaporated in an instant. "You have?" He looked around the garden, sure he'd spot a pre-arranged escape craft of some sort.

Of course, this was why the Zeartekka had chosen the night garden for their meeting. They would escape together, thumbing their noses, or whatever the Zeartekka thumbed, at their attackers. The relief was swamping out the fear he still felt from the crew.

"I've stored the evidence on multiple public-access nodes," the insectoid said. "When this ship is destroyed, their communications link with my office on Throne World will expire. The dead-man signal that I've piggy-backed on their beacon will cease and every news-shaper in the empire will receive the data."

"But…" Allamu stared at the creature in shock. He shook his head. There was no escape pod? Damn all insectoids to the corpse ripper! "That's your fornicating plan?" he screamed. "They kill us and you call it a victory?"

That haughty look again. "My spirit will return to our queen," he rattled. "I will be reborn."

"It'll have a long damned trip ahead of it," Allamu yelled, "getting released all the way out here…"

"Distance is of no importance when you are freed from your corporeal…"

The sub-munitions swirled in an evasive pattern as they approached but the two people in the night-garden never noticed the intricate dance. Allamu screamed in incoherent rage as he launched himself at Z'zedthenu, wrapping his hands around the narrow neck.

He was still trying, ineffectually, to strangle the insectoid when the weapons vaporized the ship and its inhabitants.

Op Center

"Sir, we have a signal coming in. Matching the code-pairs now."

Marduk sat up in his chair, waving off a med-tech and his stimulant injector. He wouldn't need it after all, not when they were finally about to learn how the operation had gone. He only used stims in emergencies.

He allowed himself a moment of satisfaction. When you served as Chief-of-Staff to Tir Uttur, the four hundred twenty-ninth emperor of the Uttur restoration, every day brought new emergencies.

This latest one, brought about by one of the emperor's more pedestrian imagined emergencies, was all too real. If they'd managed to stop the traitor while he still represented a single threat-vector, then the real emergency would be over and Marduk could return to dealing with the demons under the emperor's bed.

"Pairs match," the comm-tech confirmed, his positive feelings preceding his next announcement. "The captain of the *Nightsider* reports his mission is accomplished."

Marduk let out his breath. The traitor was eliminated. He'd still have to pay a visit to the intercept group. Some fool had allowed an insectoid analyst to access an intelligence compartment containing intercept-data on the Zeartekka hive-worlds.

They made excellent analysts, but there would never be an insectoid who placed empire before the hive. Whoever had cleared the traitor to work on Project Wardrobe would soon be coming down with an acute case of decapitation.

"Send the packet." He turned to the media officer. "We want it fully embedded in the public nodes before nightfall."

"Sir…" The com-tech's head tilted to the side as he stared at his displays. "We're getting an *inbound* packet." He leaned in slightly. "Open-source origin. It's working its way through the scrubbers now."

Intrigued, Marduk got out of his seat and walked over to get a better view of the com-tech's screen. This operations center, deep beneath the imperial palace, was widely rumored to exist but few knew how to route a message *directly* to the access points that stood guard over all communications with the outside world.

Confusion.

"Sir, it's from the *target*!"

Marduk drew back so far he had to shift his left foot to avoid falling over. A flow of data scrolled past his eyes, proof that the emperor had not only been using the intercept group to spy on prominent nobles, he'd also shown no qualms about using the information to keep them all fighting amongst themselves.

It revealed an emperor, already advanced in years and degraded in health, seeing enemies in every ally. It showed him as a leader who felt insecure in his position and unsure of the succession.

If this data were released, the succession would be up for grabs. Many of the nobles being manipulated by the emperor were electors and they would not look kindly on his interference.

The Holy Quailu Empire was an elective monarchy. Twenty-six nobles currently held elector status and few of them would remain willing to vote for Tashmitum, the emperor's daughter, if they knew what her father was doing to them.

Marduk fumed, his anger causing the com-tech to hunch down over his controls. He was certain Z'zedthenu was dead but, perhaps, he had a co-conspirator or an arrangement to send this message if he'd died.

A holo image of the traitor appeared and Marduk felt the usual revulsion, though it was mild. Somehow, the Zeartekka were less unsettling on holo. No species was readable in a holo recording.

"I am, or *was*, an intelligence officer in his majesty's service," the image croaked. "If you are watching this, I am almost certainly dead at the hands of our government. The data accompanying this transmission proves that our monarch has been using military assets to spy on leading members of the Awilu class as well as the royal persons of the Zeartekka Hive. I have doubtless been killed in an attempt to prevent the release of this information.

"I have programmed this release server to search for a media-shaping packet from the palace. It will mention some deplorable incident, most likely a terrorist attack that explains the event in which I will be, or *was*, killed."

Oblivious to what else might be said, Marduk reached out to grasp the com-tech's shoulder. "Was this sent anywhere other than here?"

Hopelessness.

"Everywhere…" The tech quailed at the waves of anger washing over him.

Marduk wheeled on the media officer. "The packet went out?"

"It's already into the tertiary repeaters," the officer shrugged. "There's no pulling it back now."

Marduk's shoulders slumped. It was ironic that the emperor's illegal spying program had been unnecessary but, in being discovered, created a need it could no longer fulfill. The great houses would take measures to prevent further surveillance and they would use the incident to justify a wide range of aggressive actions.

He'd argued against it from the start. He'd watched his childhood friend grow increasingly paranoid over the years and he'd managed to prevent any number of ill-advised schemes but he'd failed to stop Project Wardrobe.

The emperor was becoming increasingly reclusive. He'd long ago replaced the palace staff with non-Quailu personnel. It had been portrayed as an imperial effort to reach out – to be more inclusive toward the ruled species. In reality, the native peoples of the subject worlds were brought in because of their inability to read his emotions.

Marduk knew that Tir Uttur had never quite felt up to the job of ruling an empire and those feelings of inadequacy were behind his deep-seated desire to keep his emotions to himself – at least at night, when official business was at a minimum.

The Emperor had been unwilling to do it Marduk's way – a diplomatically phrased warning here, an offer to use imperial prestige to close a negotiation there... The office of the Holy Quailu Emperor was a potent force, when used to the best advantage, but the emperor was too convinced his nobles were plotting to vote a new dynasty into power.

Marduk would have to go back up to the palace and tell his oldest friend that an imagined danger had now become very real.

He squared his shoulders. "Start tracking the response to this data in the open streams," he ordered. He nodded at the media officer. "Take charge. I'll be in the residence."

He didn't need to add that he'd be closeted with the emperor till suns-up.

Promotion

Too soon, Ethdu thought. *I'm nowhere near ready for this.*

He looked down at the indicator on his assault rifle – one hundred forty-eight rounds left. A few drops of blood spattered across the readout from the man coughing next to him.

"I'm a dead man," Abdu insisted. "Too much damage to heal…"

"Shut the hell up. This is *your* fault for breaking cover." He had to use a harsh tone or, he knew, his voice would break. *Is this what it's like for a mushkennu when they lose family?*

"That damned Quailu got in the way. Someone had to save him or we'd all be terminated when we got back to Kish." Abdu coughed again, frothy pink blood from his lungs dribbling down his chin. "Did I ever tell you about the ceremony they put me through to take over this platoon?"

Ethdu didn't answer, disturbed by Abdu's sudden willingness to open up about his past. He took a couple of deep breaths before pushing away from the low graphene planter they were covering behind. He came up on one knee and fired three bursts in the direction of the enemy's security forces, certain a round would impact his skull at any moment. "Noadu!" he shouted as he took cover again. "You said you could get this done through any public node. What's taking so fornicating long?"

"I could make a list," Noadu shouted back, "and right up there, at the top, would be the need to answer dumbass questions. It takes as long as it takes."

Funny how a firefight makes you feel the need to yell to a guy who's almost within reach, Ethdu thought irrelevantly. He noticed the blood drying on Noadu's face. A jagged scar on his cheek was rapidly closing – genetically enhanced healing abilities pushed even farther by medical nanites.

"That all your blood?"

An irritated shake of the head. "Mostly from that Chironian security officer I gave that grenade to. Silly bastard exploded all over me."

Everything had gone wrong. The original plan had been to land on Chiron as commercial passengers and proceed to the lab where the local government ran research on stolen tech. They would use Noadu's skills to gain entry during off-shift hours and steal a data module that the Chiron government had already stolen from Heimdall 4.

The only problem with the whole plan was that it was a *plan*, and plans never survive contact with real-world variables. Halfway to the lab they'd been caught up in a routine traffic stop at eight thousand feet. The team had still been unarmed but the scanners on the security vehicle picked up the combat focus in their genomes.

Things had deteriorated rapidly from there and now they were trying to hold on long enough for Noa to make Plan-B work.

If some random event throws your plan out the window, it's probably a surprise to both sides and a prepared operator can usually gain some kind of advantage out of it. There was no reaching the labs now, but they wouldn't want to, not with a small horde of DSOs on their tail. They'd end up trapped inside.

Far better to seize a piece of territory they could actually exfiltrate from.

And speaking of exfiltration… "Oliv, take nine men and get behind that big planter to the south. Our ride will be here in a moment so make sure you only use stun grenades on it, no frags." He chopped his hand toward the large collection of trees and bushes in the dead end, just beyond where Noa was working. "Take Hendu," he added.

He fired another burst toward the DSO's who were unwilling to push forward from the ramps. Their own weapons were a pretty effective deterrent when they had to face them.

No sane species wanted a metallic hydrogen crystal converting directly to a gaseous state inside their armor or their bodies.

"They set up a table," Abdu wheezed, "on the flight-line, right in front of the drop-ships and the platoon watched while Geddu and I drank shots of expensive whiskey and talked about all the crazy shit we got into over the years. He was an old man but, Gods, he could soak up the sauce!"

"You're still talking about that?" Ethdu looked over as his leader broke into a painful coughing fit. The blood was all over his tunic, plastering it to the light armor underneath.

"Lord before the horde," Abdu croaked, a sad chuckle turning into another coughing fit. "We finished the last drop in the bottle and then I put a ceremonial bullet through the middle of his forehead." A tear welled up and shook loose with another round of wet coughing.

Ethdu fired four more bursts at the security forces, preferring the raw fear of combat to the dull ache of having to kill his mentor. He dropped back against the low wall, pulse racing, breath shuddering. Chiron was a hot world, but he felt cold, nonetheless.

"Loyalty… must be affirmed," Abdu said weakly. He tried to reach for the pistol in his belt but he was too weak and his hand flapped down onto the graphene floor. "Lord before the horde…"

A conventional round fired by one of the DSOs hit the top of Ab's planter, spraying graphene fragments between them.

"No, Gods-dammit!" Ethdu flared. "I've seen men survive worse."

"Bullshit. I might survive long enough to do a ceremony but I'll never fight again after this. I'm not going all the way back to Kish just to wait for a bullet. I'm in a bad way. They'd have to strap me into the chair." A gasp. "I'm not going out like a damned invalid. Shoot me."

Ethdu flinched as a flurry of rounds glanced off the top of the low wall. He controlled his breathing and popped up to return fire. He ducked back into cover, feeling the rush – holding onto it rather than face what needed to be done.

"I trained you better than this, boy!" Some of his old sternness emerged through the frothing blood. "You always knew you'd be taking over our unit. You were grown for this."

No answer.

His voice deepened. "Well, now the gods have made it easier on you…" Abdu spit out a large bloody mass. "I could never imitate Quailu the way you do," he admitted with a chuckle that quickly turned into a bloody cough. "Look here. You can take casualties trying to drag my dying ass back to the extraction point, just to put a bullet in my head a week… later, or you can end my pain now."

"Got it!" Noadu shouted, waving his left hand, the data chip pulsing green through his skin.

Ethdu nodded then pushed himself up to a kneeling position, firing over the low wall as Noadu broke the cover of the heavy data-glass terminal and raced across the open space. He slammed down into cover next to Abdu and pulled out a capsule of wound-sealant but Abdu waved it away.

"You got the process data?" Ethdu demanded.

"Got it all," Noadu said. "Also, interesting tidbit, they have Human genomes on file, those naughty Chironians. I burned them out, but we have a copy of their file roots, so we have some leverage on them if they try to complain about this raid.

He looked at Abdu. "Been an honor to serve with you…" His voice faltered. "You'll be missed, you cranky old bastard!"

They clasped hands just as a deep whining sound announced an armored transport some fifteen meters south of their position, sidling in close to the walkway.

The front bore the symbol of the Chironian security forces. It was out of sight from the enemies currently shooting at Ethdu's small group, but the DSOs it carried would easily flank the Humans. There would be no place left to take cover.

Ethdu looked at the hovering vehicle, his face unreadable. "I was starting to wonder if they'd ever notice how easily our position can be flanked." He looked down at Abdu's suddenly firm grip on his right arm.

"Don't let them take me." Abdu handed him a plasma grenade. "Let me take a few of them with me."

Ethdu took the weapon.

Abdu broke into a series of weak coughs, bringing up more blood but with little force. He sighed. "I had a good run," he whispered.

"I wish it could have been a little longer." Ethdu took his hand, looking him in the eye. He returned his mentor's nod, took a deep breath, brought his pistol up and fired a round into his forehead, killing the closest thing he had to family.

He shifted to the right, setting down his rifle and transferring the grenade to his right hand. Before he could activate it, he heard the distinctive crack-whine of a sublimation round hitting one of the massive carbon beams above him.

Damn it! They're not complete idiots after all…

The crystalline metallic-hydrogen round converted directly from a solid to a gaseous state, the newly released gas expanded rapidly, slamming Eth against the floor and tossing Noa back toward the armored DSO shuttle.

Their armor saved them but Eth could swear he'd actually felt his brain collide with his skull and half of his sensors were now flashing warnings in his HUD. There may have been alarms sounding in his helmet as well, but they were over-ridden by the high-pitched tone his ears were already sending to his brain.

He could see that one of his team icons had gone red. He rolled over onto his right side. Fredu was there, head up against one of the planters at an impossible angle to his body. His head must have been partially over the planter when the blast slammed him down onto the floor.

Only in charge for a few seconds and he'd already lost someone.

"Noa!" he shouted, trying to compensate for how garbled his voice sounded in his own ears. "Get ready to withdraw!"

Noa waved groggily. Eth heard something garbled in his helmet.

He looked down at his hand – he still held the grenade. He set it for bio-proximity detonation and slid it behind Abdu's back. A series of faint lights flashed out from under the body, growing increasingly fast as it calibrated for the current bio-signatures in the immediate area. It melded into a continuous glow and then shut off.

The weapon was armed and they were out of time. The shuttle would disgorge more armed officers and the Humans would be rolled up.

At least, that was the plan from the Chironian side.

He grabbed his rifle. Ten meters to his right, the armored shuttle dropped a ramp in the side of the fuselage, bridging the three-meter gap between ship and sidewalk. A slip on the ramp would result in a fourteen-hundred meter drop to the city's ground level.

A split second before the ramp made contact with the sidewalk, a stun grenade sailed out from the small collection of decorative hydroponic trees where he'd sent Oliv and her small team. It flew into the transport and detonated, overloading the occupants with noise and light.

Oliv's fire-team broke from the cover of the foliage and raced up the ramp. The fight was short and tightly controlled and Ethdu had no way of knowing whether the Humans – his responsibility now – were winning or losing against the armored security troops.

He had to proceed as if they were winning or all was lost.

He looked to Noadu, relieved to see that he was now covering behind another planter and watching for signals. The ringing in Eth's ears was starting to attenuate but this was no time to take chances with orders.

Eth made a fist, then splayed his fingers to indicate a grenade, waggling his hand to denote the stun variant. He and Noadu both pulled small flat disks from dispensers on their chest plates. They were roughly half the size of a man's palm and half the thickness of a finger. They set them to stun, wanting their witnesses half dazed but still lucid enough to think no further pursuit was needed. Both men dropped two more disks at their feet, set to smoke.

Noadu threw his overhand from a position of cover. The instant it detonated, Ethdu came to a kneeling position and tossed his deeper, reaching a point where it could incapacitate the security forces covering behind the five-meter-wide support column at the corner of the ramp they'd descended earlier.

Noa rose and tossed his next stun grenade just over the lip of the ramp leading down to where another team of DSO's were stalled. The detonations would easily overpower the sound attenuation of the cheap security armor.

His inner ear was still in a mischievous mood, after the sublimation blast, and it let his body keep rotating after releasing the grenade. Eth nearly spur a full circle before his body dropped, arms flailing for balance. He bounced off the side of the planter with a grunt and he landed on his back, looking up at the brilliantly pulsing light of his grenade washing across the ceiling above him.

At least he'd been planning on taking cover anyway.

Seconds after the detonation, the armored vehicle slid forward until it was directly opposite the two remaining Humans. Ethdu stayed on his back, raising his hands in surrender as figures in orange and white Chironian security armor emerged through the swirling white smoke.

They grabbed him and Noadu, dragging them into the vehicle and dumping them into seats against the portside wall. The ramp swung shut as they pulled away, and Ethdu leaned back, blowing out an explosive breath. "You look like something from a puppet show," he told Olivdu who was loosely encased in Chironian armor. It wouldn't stand up to a review of the security footage, but it should buy them enough time to get away.

"Where's the boss?" Olivdu asked voice slightly muffled. She tossed a Chironian arm-brace to the back of the craft and started unlatching the breastplate.

Noadu waved a hand. "Eth is the new boss," he yelled, causing her to pull her head back.

She grimaced. Tossing the breastplate aside, she came over to place a hand on Eth's shoulder. "Sorry," she said. "They don't make many like old Ab."

"That's 'cause his genome's so damned expensive," Noadu shouted, digging at one of his ears with a finger.

"Twice what it cost to make us," she agreed. She took her hand from Ethdu's shoulder and gave it a light punch. "Alright, Boss, how are you and your expensive genes gonna get us out of this ass-pounded mess?"

"Well, I…"

"They're hailing us," Hendu shouted back from the cockpit. "Get Ab up here immediately. We're gonna have to tell 'em something if we want to reach orbit in one piece."

Ethdu was glad of the interruption. He didn't have an answer for Olivdu and he needed a chance to get his head in the game. Being in charge of a team like this was a terrifying prospect.

He raised an eyebrow at her – a vague enough gesture for the moment. It would help if they had Mishak with them. He turned and headed for the short corridor to the cockpit his path weaving only slightly, enhanced healing abilities making short work of his injury.

Mishak.

Having a member of the ruling race would give them the ability to bullshit their way out of atmosphere but Mishak wasn't just any Quailu; he was the governor of Kish. He sent teams like this out on economic raids. He could hardly run a planet *and* play soldier at the same time.

And the political impact, should he be captured in a situation like this, made it improbable that any off-world Quailu noble would ever be involved.

He stopped, one foot inside the cockpit hatch.

A local Quailu might conceivably be aboard this craft, if it was carrying out an important mission.

He stepped in, grinning as he leaned past the pilot, who looked over at him in surprise before assuming the expression that Ethdu was quickly coming to hate – that mix of personal loss as well as sympathy for what he'd obviously had to do to his mentor.

Lord before the horde. Eth tapped the synch icon on the control board.

He dropped into the co-pilot seat and linked his auditory implant.

"*...deviation from your assigned transit corridor. Please advise, over.*"

He looked to the center console, grabbing a holy relic of some sort and yanking it from its gold chain. He tossed it back down the corridor before reading the call number that had been hidden behind the religious object.

He took a deep breath, holding his diaphragm tight and forcing his throat to constrict. "Control, this is Chel-Ineth-four-five-eight-two," he rumbled. "Explain yourself."

There was a long pause and he could imagine the consternation in the control room. He didn't need to look over at Hendu to know the pilot was grinning in amusement.

"Sire," the voice replied, alarmed. "I apologize but your current trajectory..."

"We are taking the prisoners to orbital detention," Ethdu told him, his deep gravelly voice dripping with confidence.

"But there's no detention facility in..."

30

"I would strongly advise you to stop talking," Ethdu snapped. "You don't wish to draw further attention to our flight path, do you?"

"Certainly not, sire," the controller squeaked. "I will erase the records immed…."

Ethdu cut the link. He leaned back in the seat and closed his eyes.

"The sooner we get aboard the *Coronado*, the better," the pilot muttered.

"Why aren't they shooting us down?" Noadu almost sounded as though he were complaining. He poked his head into the small cockpit. "We should be dodging or weaving or something, shouldn't we? Maybe at least drift lazily to the left?"

"Wow!" Hendu glanced up at the tech specialist. "You know a few moves, huh?" He chuckled, turning back to the instruments. "Eth convinced them we got a local Quailu lord running the show," the pilot replied.

"You're daft as a cabbage, Hendy." He shook his head sadly. "Don't you realize the trouble we're in for impersonating a Quailu? They'll probably tack on an extra death-penalty for that. You don't want to be shot twice, do you?"

"Is it just me," Hendu asked, "or is the air traffic starting to divert from our path?"

Noadu shrugged. "If you say so. I never get to sit in the front, so I couldn't say."

"You scared 'em good, Eth." The pilot grinned over at him. "Now we just need to figure out how to get aboard the *Coronado* without drawing attention. This DSO cruiser doesn't much look like our old shuttle and we don't have time for Noa to reprogram its nanites."

"Screw it," Ethdu blurted out before he even realized he'd come to a decision. "We'll just fly right into the aft cargo bay. I like this little flying turd. I'm gonna keep it."

The other two men shared a concerned look.

"Look, Eth," Noadu began reasonably, "we just got out of the shit. No reason to jump right back into it…"

"You got proof they had Human genomes in storage?" Ethdu interrupted.

"Well, yeah, but… Oh!"

"'Oh' is right." Ethdu confirmed, face grim. "Sure, they'll file an official complaint with Throne World over our incursion, but we have proof they're violating the Meleke Company's charter by holding unauthorized genomes."

"Or the Meleke Company violated it themselves," Noadu suggested, "by selling them Human sequences on the sly."

"Either way, they can't afford to bring the complaint to adjudication without exposing themselves…"

"And not in a good way," Noadu interjected with a grin.

"…so they'll end up having to withdraw the complaint, which will cost them favors at court," Ethdu finished. "So, not only have we stolen what we came for, but we've managed to weaken the Chironians and, unless I'm mistaken, bolster the prestige of our own lord as a bonus."

"Might be a half-assed idea but it sure beats trying to jump the gap to the *Coronado*. Hard to look nonchalant while you're abandoning a stolen vehicle." Noadu gave him a thump on the shoulder. "Looks like you've got this, Boss. Maybe I'll head back and let the gang in on the plan."

The pilot glanced back at Noadu as he left. "You know he's probably planning to mention folks exposing themselves," he said as he looked back at his instruments.

Ethdu nodded. "And he'll make sure he's looking at Oliv when he does." He watched Noadu's departing back.

"She certainly likes the direct approach," the pilot agreed.

The Meleke Company owned the rights to all wardu-class genomes by imperial charter. Slaves emerged from the maturation chambers already sterile. Nature would not get in the way of quarterly profits.

Consequentially, sex among the wardu class was no biggie.

With no risk of pregnancy, it came to be looked upon more as interpersonal recreation. Emotional attachments still formed, but they tended to shift frequently.

"Let's just hope they wait till we get off this crate first," Ethdu said, forcing a chuckle.

Some things are best left unseen, especially when your *own* genome is designed to prevent fraternization…

A.G. Claymore

Bottom of a New Heap

The Elector

"He was a good unit leader," Mishak said. He stood up from the governor's throne and walked down to where Ethdu stood, placing a hand on the Human's shoulder, pretending not to notice the mild surprise in his mind. Until now, Abdu had always been the primary contact with the very hands-on Mishak.

He liked to keep a very close circle on his tech-espionage operations; often discussing target selection and operational considerations with the Human team leaders and only a limited group of intelligence specialists from his family's military.

"He was the best of my wardu fighters. When he said something could be done, I listened and I made sure he got the chance to prove himself right." Mishak took his hand from Ethdu's shoulder, gesturing that they should move toward the terrace door.

He led the way out of the governor's throne room and into the warm sunlight of a spring afternoon. The terrace was as large as the throne room but it ended abruptly with a three-hundred-fifty-story drop. The Quailu considered railings to be an offense to natural selection.

A sunken, circular gathering-space had a fire-pit burning in the center, the obligatory Quailu hearth that one could find in any noble's hall.

Mishak waved away the Human attendants and sat facing the fire, gesturing for Ethdu to join him.

It was unusual, to say the least, for a Quailu to join a wardu at hearth, especially for the governor of a planet and the son of Sandrak, ruler of 19 systems and an elector in the Holy Quailu Empire. As the eldest son, Mishak would inherit his father's holdings as well as his right to vote on the next emperor.

Mishak knew it was odd, but he felt comfortable among his subjects, even those who hated him, because they couldn't sense his moods. He also envied his off-world raiders, Humans like Abdu and his young protégé, who now sat across from him. They had a swaggering confidence, despite their slave status, and they didn't care what others thought of them.

He envied them and so he sought their company, reveling in any hint of approval. He authorized them for advanced training modules in tactics, strategy and technology and, though he'd originally done it to please Abdu, he had come to appreciate the differences it made in their performance. Their operations in neighboring systems had advanced the state of Kish's economy by leaps and bounds, bringing back technology and processes researched by rival lords.

Kish's position, at the far end of an isolated corner of Sandrak's holdings, meant they were surrounded on almost all sides by unfriendly noble houses. Mishak had turned that to an advantage by robbing them at every opportunity, though his noble father sneered at his 'brigandage'.

Mishak realized he was clenching his fists. It had been a long time since he'd slept fully and his emotions were getting the better of him.

The Quailu could rest their minds by alternating hemispheres. One side of their brain could be asleep while the other remained active. It wasn't a good idea where detailed analytical thought was required but it had given his species an evolutionary advantage and it still had its uses.

He forced his hands open and waved to the lone Human guarding a door to one of the terrace waiting rooms.

The rest of Ethdu's team filed in and Mishak casually gestured to the seating around the fire. He reached into his tunic and drew out a long strip of fermented bison fat, one of Kish's most popular exports. He took a bite of the intoxicant and handed it to Olivdu as she sat.

"So," he began as the Humans settled in, "I've seen the holo of your report. You found proof of Human genomes on Chiron?" He looked first at Noadu, then to Ethdu, showing that he knew who had actually found the data.

Ethdu nodded. "That's right. Noa found the files while pursuing our main objective."

"Excellent!" Mishak said warmly. He was gratified to see this new team leader already felt comfortable using diminutive names for his people in front of their lord. It had taken Ab more than a year to get there. Legally, they could be terminated for failing to use the 'du' suffix. It was a mark of their trust that they would speak so freely in front of him.

Many other Quailu lords would have killed them all on the spot.

He turned to Noa. "Do you think they're aware of what you found?"

Noa shook his head. "No, Lord. They'd have to compare the transit keys between the data itself and the node that accessed it to realize it even happened. We fried that node when we set off the stun grenades. They're not hardened against combat conditions."

Mishak leaned forward. "And none of you have talked about this to anyone outside your team?"

"No, Lord," Eth insisted. "We kept to ourselves while aboard the *Coronado,* as usual, and came straight here."

"And not a word to each other while in transit," Noa added, nodding at Eth. "Eth explained, during our flight out of Chironian atmo, how this can hurt the Chironians at court. After that, we kept our pie-holes shut."

Mishak nodded approvingly. "It's even better than you think," he told them.

Again, few Quailu lords would condescend to explain the implications but he knew his operatives worked best when they were well-informed.

"You weren't the only visitors to Chiron," he hinted. "Hendrikwilu of Gliese, Selatwilu of Irridani, Mosettawilu of Tau Ceti and a collection of one-system minor representatives were all there during your shenanigans."

He leaned back, enjoying their astonishment. Eth, however, was looking at him with a keen expression.

"So," the Human leader mused, "they've finally started to pull a coalition together?"

"Coalition," Mishak confirmed. "The pile of flaming turds that has haunted me since I came out here fifteen years ago. A coalition of small and minor houses, intent on taking Kish and capturing the only son and heir to Sandrakwilu. All they need is for someone to have the will to lead it and a suitable inciting incident to mobilize it.

"By now, they're drafting the necessary forms for transmission to Throne World. I expect the imperial demand for my response within the week."

Eth laughed. "We can safely assume that Chiron, as the strongest partner, will be the coalition leader, yes?"

Mishak grinned back, though the gesture lost something on his less-mobile, Quailu face. "You can also safely assume that I will choose direct, un-mediated negotiation with Chiron. Your evidence," he pointed to Noa, "would cause the Meleke Company to cut them off and their economy is heavily dependent on their wardu class."

"So when the coalition leader renounces their grievance…" Eth paused to take a bite of the fermented fat, "…the coalition is dissolved, ending the threat for the next decade and seriously damaging their credibility at court."

"While burnishing my own family's reputation," Mishak added, leaning back into the cushions. "I'm trying to find the negatives in this – the balancing kick in the gonads that the Universe usually insists on adding in – but I'm not seeing it."

A shadow passed. He frowned up at an opulent shuttlecraft. Just as it disappeared past the parapet of his rooftop landing pad, he saw the crossed encryption keys emblazoned on the underside of the wings.

The sigil of his great house. *There's the kick.*

He stifled the curse that came to mind, sighing in nervous frustration. He was glad the Humans around him couldn't feel his apprehension. He sat up.

"Look, this was nearly an absolute disaster with you stirring up a coalition but it was my decision to run the risk and it would have been my fault alone. You turned it into a huge victory for my house and I won't be forgetting that."

He looked over at the sound of approaching feet. A page came up to him, eyes wide with the enormity of the moment.

"Your lord-father, sire," he said hoarsely. "He wishes to meet you in your throne room."

Mishak stood. "I will think of some way to thank you all properly," he told them. He followed the page back to his official audience chamber.

What in all seven hells is the old bastard doing here? Mishak was more than content to sit here in obscurity while he waited for Sandrak to show a little good sense and just die already. He couldn't remember a single encounter with his father that didn't provide less pleasure than having his groin ravaged by wild canines.

Of course, he thought as he walked into the large room, *the old hump would be sitting on my throne.* It was a standard right of any overlord when visiting one of his retainers, but Sandrak always managed to convey an element of insult with the gesture.

At least Mishak had been out on the terrace, saving himself the need to step down for his father.

He came to the base of the steps, looked up at his father and gave him a formal bow. "My Lord, to what do I owe this great honor?"

"Shut your mouth," Sandrak snapped. "Your job is to listen, not to talk." He waved the Human attendants out of the room, his anger at their presence clearly open to Mishak. "I have heard of your mess on Chiron. I left you out here to limit the harm you can do to our family and now I learn from sources on Gliese that you've stirred up a coalition against us with your petty thievery."

Usually, this would be the point where Mishak would wilt in shame, confused, hurt and angry all at once and Sandrak would sense it and revel in the power it gave him over his son. There was no concealing a Quailu's disdain for another of his own species. It tended to form a vicious feedback loop.

Dueling, understandably, was one of the leading causes of death among their race.

This time it was different and Mishak held his tongue, enjoying this new feeling of being right while his father was spectacularly wrong. He knew who he owed for this situation and he vowed anew to find a way to thank them properly.

Sandrak's eye ridges lowered in the middle. He could feel that his son was not properly cowed by his outburst and it disturbed him. "Perhaps you're not taking this seriously?" he suggested darkly. "Do you understand what a coalition means at a time like this?"

What does he mean by 'a time like this'? Mishak wondered. "I know what a coalition is, Father; it's a threat I've lived under since arriving out here. Perhaps *you* don't understand how useful it can be to trigger a coalition when you possess enough evidence to squash it in preliminary registration."

Sandrak leaned so far forward, he nearly fell from the throne. This was unprecedented. Never before had Mishak responded in such a fashion. "What are you talking about?" he demanded. "Just what evidence do you have?"

Mishak re-opened the holo report he'd been reviewing with Eth earlier. He brought up the genomic data and slid the image over to face his father. "The Chironians would undoubtedly be the leader of any coalition against us," he said mildly, "and here you see evidence that they've violated the Meleke charter, section five, sub-section twenty-three, if I'm not mistaken."

He was tempted to continue, but it was best to show Sandrak he understood the implications by leaving them unsaid. To lay them out explicitly would imply that Mishak thought he'd been particularly clever. Far better to act as though the subsequent chain of reasoning was completely obvious.

Sandrak scanned the data before waving it aside. There was a new look in his eyes and a feeling Mishak couldn't quite identify emanated from the old goat.

"Direct negotiation?" he asked.

Mishak offered a negligent gesture, as if to suggest the question need not even be asked. "Un-mediated," he said.

Sandrak drew back in surprise. "But we can crush the Chironian economy completely if a mediator sees the evidence," he protested.

"Their products don't compete with ours," Mishak replied, "and the longer we can keep this from involving the Meleke Company, the longer we'll be able to exert leverage over Chiron."

Surprise. Consideration.

Mishak frowned. There it was again. He was picking up some strange feelings from the old meat-bag but he couldn't quite put his finger on it.

Now amusement.

Mishak's fists were clenched again. He didn't care for this mockery, especially now that he'd finally gotten the better of the great Sandrakwilu. He'd…

"It would seem you've done well, son," Sandrak grudged. He held up a warding hand. "I know, I know… I'm as surprised as you are."

He stood, coming down to stand near his son, something Mishak would never have expected. "And the timing couldn't have been better. You've heard about the emperor's meddling ways?"

"Who hasn't?"

"Well, it's damaged his authority considerably. Throughout the empire, dodgy claims and old grudges are being dragged out for a fresh airing and we've got our fair share of enemies. We didn't get to be one of the largest houses by our good looks alone."

"Then we'll be fighting soon?"

"Very soon," Sandrak confirmed. "I thought I'd come here and fix your mistakes, allowing me to draw off most of your military forces for use in our higher-value systems."

"And now?"

That odd new feeling again.

"And now I think I'll be taking you as well. Our holdings can be split in two if someone takes the Heiropolis system. If that happens, I'll need someone with sense in the smaller half to watch over our holdings."

He held up his hand again. "That *someone* is your uncle, but I want you to attach your forces to his and learn all you can."

"We're at half strength as it is," Mishak reminded him. "We can barely leave orbit right now and I'd need to get updated configurations if I want those ships to be combat effective."

Annoyance.

"I'll have the latest ship configurations transferred from the data banks on my shuttle. Start re-growing your fleet immediately. We can worry about crew numbers while the ships update."

"I can crew my ships as soon as they're ready, if you give me a free hand."

His father looked at him for a few moments. "What do you have in mind?"

"My native forces have been remarkably effective in local skirmishes. It was one of my Humans that found our dirt on the Chironians. I'd like to recruit and train them for duty on our ships."

"Wardu serving with our house military?" Sandrak exploded. "If we field slave-troops against our enemies, we'd be the laughing stock of the entire empire!"

"Which is why we'll give mushkenu status to those who serve," Mishak replied calmly, forcing his mind to ignore the astonishment he should be feeling at his own outrageous suggestion.

Resignation, reluctant acceptance.

"It's a dangerous precedent," the old bastard grumbled. "Once you create the first free Human, you open the floodgates. One of our ancestors did that, eight thousand years ago, and a handful of mushkenu had their sterilization reversed. A century later, they were breeding free Humans like a plague. We had to ship them off to a new colony just to halt the spread."

"Yes," Mishak interjected dryly, "a shame the colony ship was lost en route."

"Go ahead and do it," Sandrak jabbed a finger at his son's chest, "but make sure your *free* Humans don't make it home again."

Sandrak started walking toward the elevator. Clearly, his visit was at an end. The door opened as he approached, revealing two Quailu security operatives. He walked in, ordering the top floor as he turned.

"Don't embarrass our house," he growled as the doors slid shut.

Mishak walked back toward the terrace door, relieved to lose contact with his father's mind. To hells with the old man, he'd bring his Humans home. The economy of his world needed a shake-up if they were to keep up with the rest of the empire. He wanted his fief to have the kind of economy that only a free population could support.

The leverage he now had over Chiron would have been useless if they weren't so dependent on the Meleke Corporation. Chiron's economy was based on slaves and they could only get them from one place.

Yet again, luck seemed to have come to his aid. The idea of using freed Humans had only come to him on the spot, just as the unexpected proof from Chiron had saved his ass in the most literal sense.

And now he had a way to reward Eth and his team for their efforts.

He waved the page over as he reached the door. "Bring us a tray of the aged fat, the stuff with the blue mold." He had a celebration to begin and he knew the newly freed Humans on his terrace were going to get royally drunk.

He strode out to the fire-pit, reaching down to accept the last remnant of the bison fat he'd passed around earlier, nodding his thanks to Noa. He looked around the fire.

"Who here is interested in joining our house forces," he asked them. "Who will volunteer to come and fight with me, to help defend our house against its enemies?"

To his immense gratification, after a moment of surprise, every one of them stood. He could feel their pride at receiving the offer, alien though it was, and he could feel loyalty. He raised the strip.

"A toast to you," he said. "To you, Ethkenu and to you Noakenu…" He continued in that vein, naming each of the Humans, relying on the neural interface for most of the names. He reveled in the feelings of confusion, astonishment and barely acknowledged hope as his use of the lower-class suffix sunk in.

"You've volunteered to fight with our house forces," he explained. "We can't have slaves serving in our regular military, so we have no choice but to make you all into mushkenu." He grinned. "I said I'd find a way to reward you, didn't I?" He popped the last of the fermented fat into his mouth.

The silence drew out; amazement and elation washing over Mishak. Finally, Noa chuckled and slapped Eth on the back. "Mushkenu! Didn't expect *that* when you woke up this morning, did you?

Eth shook his head, still in shock.

Hendy cuffed at his cheek and stared into the fire.

A steward arrived and passed out the premium, blue-mold fermented fat, a product that was never offered to slaves. They each held up a piece, joining their governor in his toast, eyes sliding to their compatriots.

Could it be real?

Induction

Eth stepped out of the ground vehicle and looked at the entrance to the 405th Transport Wing's main terminal. He'd walked through those doors hundreds of times but today was different. He took a sip of his coffee.

One of his world's greatest gifts to the empire, coffee was cheap enough here that even the slave population could get their hands on it, though he was a slave no longer.

He looked behind to Noa. "Everybody here, Noakenu?"

His second in command grinned at hearing his free name. The novelty was still new. "Thirty-two heads. All accounted for and ready to go!"

He moved away to stand where they could all hear him. He hadn't planned to say anything but it had suddenly struck him as the right thing to do. He realized things might get difficult and he wanted them ready for that but, more importantly, he wanted them to realize that *he* wasn't just leading them blindly into a tense situation.

Much of that came from observing Abdu's leadership, but the rest was programmed right into his genome. He wished his mentor was here to see this day.

He also wished Ab was here to run the show.

He still didn't want to be responsible for the whole team but it wasn't as if he had a choice. He'd been designed for this, so he might as well do it to the best of his abilities.

"This… is a day our people will never forget," he began. There were smiles at that and a few shared glances, quiet comments…

"But you need to keep in mind that making history is never easy," he said, bringing them back into focus. "There are going to be those who don't approve of free Humans. He nodded up to the sky. "The Quailu and other mushkenu species up there in our defense fleet have known us only as wardu and some will resent serving alongside former slaves.

"Keep your spirits up, and don't let them provoke you. Don't let them prove we're unready for this." He grinned. "But let's not stand around, overthinking it." He turned and led the way inside. They approached the security checkpoint, the same one they'd used every time they left on an operation. Just in front of the wide arch used by free citizens, a guard stepped in front of Eth, like he always did, and waved his hand-scanner at him.

Same old deal, as far as the guard knew. Confirm their identity and then divert them into the body scanning cubicles to search them for smuggled items.

Eth dropped his pistol onto a conveyer belt and it slid into a scanner. "Morning Erndu." Though he knew the guard well enough, he couldn't leave off the suffix, not in an area under constant surveillance.

The guard shook his handheld and then scanned him again.

"Something's wrong with your property tag," the guard told him. "Just wait here for a second." He tried to scan Oliv, then Noa – no luck there either. Frowning, he worked his way through the entire unit.

"What the hell is…" Erndu trailed off as he finally noticed they'd traded their gray uniforms for the dark blue of the house-military. Eth himself wore the insignia of a warrant officer.

"What the hells are you playing at?" he hissed. "Disabling your prop-chips, masquerading as house-military?" He looked around at the small group of curious Humans who worked in the terminal. One of them had noticed the hiccup in the normal scanning procedure and wandered over, his reaction drawing the attention of several others. A crowd would quickly start to form.

The guard pulled out his weapon. "Did you really think I'd just let you pass?" he demanded helplessly. "I have no choice but to arrest you for servile insurrection!"

Eth felt a moment of cold shock. He'd expected resistance from the mushkenu but he'd failed to anticipate the same from his own species. Not for the first time, he questioned his fitness to lead his small unit.

He forced his doubts aside. Fit or not, he was what they had for the moment and he wasn't going to let them down on their first day in the house-military. "Easy Erndu." He waved to the growing crowd, mostly Humans with the occasional alien. "You're causing a disturbance."

The guard, predictably, turned his head to look and Ethkenu stepped in, grasping his weapon and turning it downward and toward the guard's middle. The pistol came away from his fingers cleanly.

A murmur of surprise and alarm came from the crowd and they surged back but Ethkenu reversed the weapon, handing it back, grip-first, to its owner. "We've got our chips, Erndu, but you're using the wrong scanner." He nodded toward the arch.

The guard was flabbergasted. He took the weapon back but let his arm drop to his side. Haradu, the guard supervisor, came hurrying out from an office behind the scanning cubicles, his face an unreadable riot. He came to a halt near Erndu and stared at Eth's team.

He shook his head, ever so slightly, incredulous. Finally he shrugged to himself before gesturing toward the arch. "Through there," he said, sounding as though he'd been told something while in his office but still didn't quite believe it. He moved over to get a better look at the readout over the arch as Eth approached.

Eth walked up to the arch, took a deep breath and stepped through.

And nothing happened.

It hadn't chimed. He'd half expected to set off an alarm but nothing was happening. Then he realized that his next breath was only his second since passing through. Had so little time passed? It seemed like an eternity and…

The gate gave a friendly chime and the crowd gasped as one.

He looked up at the top of the arch.

Ethkenu – Warrant Officer, provisional grade.

There was a pause and then a buzz of chatter erupted. One of their own had made that incredible, impossible leap to mushkenu status. Something that hadn't happened in thousands of years.

Freddadu, the elderly guard that checked the weapons, walked over to Eth to return his sidearm. He beamed up at Eth, his cheeks glistening with moisture. "I've seen some amazing things, over the years, but I don't think I'll ever top this," he said, voice trembling.

Eth put a friendly hand on the man's shoulder, not trusting his own voice at the moment. He took his weapon and moved over to the flight-line door to wait for the rest of his team.

Cheers were breaking out as the rest of the unit passed through the arch, each recognized as mushkenu citizens of the empire. Some of them gave Old Freddy a hug as he brought them their weapons.

"That felt better than I expected," Noa admitted as he came to stand with Eth. "Almost teared up when Fred gave me my weapon. Poor old fella's ready to burst!"

"And you're not?" Eth asked, a catch in his voice.

"What, me?" the older man looked away. "There's just some dust in my eye. That's all."

"Really? You're standing here, right in the middle of history, and you're nothing but a stone?"

"Can't last," Noa said gloomily. "You think the Meleke Company are gonna let you undo your sterilization? All of our genomes are expensive, but *yours* cost more than a couple dozen of those ordnance-men over there." He nodded toward the red-vested Humans cheering the unit through the arch, one by one.

"You start giving out free samples for recreational purposes," he shrugged, "the price they can charge our governor will plummet. A minute-and-a-half of fun for you represents hundreds of thousands in lost ducats."

Eth tuned out the room. Noa was right, though not about the minute-and-a-half. As mushkenu, it was their right to take back their reproductive abilities. The idea was terrifying. They'd all seen mushkenu children but no Human child had existed in nearly twenty centuries. Wardu were all brought out of the maturation chambers as physical adults with language and basic skills already implanted.

How do you even keep such a helpless creature alive? Eth couldn't even keep a potted plant alive, let alone a complex and highly demanding infant.

And Noa was right about the Meleke. He represented a serious threat to their balance sheets. They weren't going to be pleased with Mishak.

"All here," Noa said quietly.

Eth squared his shoulders. "Let's get moving." He looked back at the crowd and instantly wished he hadn't. He knew he couldn't just turn away from them. They were expecting some kind of gesture, now that he was looking their way. He gave them a quick wave, feeling like an idiot, and they broke into applause.

His ears felt hot as the blast doors snapped open in front of him.

The ground crew, already informed by the flight crew as to whom they were carrying up to the fleet, were clustered together, staring silently at the approaching team.

Eth stifled a curse. The prolonged scrutiny had made him conscious of how he walked, a personality trait he believed was due to some genetic engineer's sense of humor. He was reasonably certain he didn't walk strangely, but being stared at always made him feel awkward. It either made him strut like a peacock or trip over his own feet, sometimes both.

His arms were starting to come out of synch with his legs and he put his right hand on the grip of his sidearm. He knew he probably looked like a bandit but at least it stabilized his stride.

He let go of the weapon as they walked up the rear ramp and filed into the long rows of seats. The hum of worm-gears announced the closing of the ramp and he leaned back, closing his eyes and putting his feet up against the stack of footlockers they'd sent aboard earlier.

It was tough enough stepping into Ab's shoes, though that was what he'd been made for, but having to lead his team into a new social status and hold their own among the house-forces was beyond his design parameters.

They all remained quiet as the shuttle lifted off. The usual banter was suppressed by the knowledge of their destination. They'd done this ride hundreds of times but it had always ended up at some fast freighter. Now they'd be entering the fleet's exclusion-zone.

They accelerated to the standard velocity. The weather, relatively mild at lower velocities, hammered at the fuselage until suddenly easing off to nothingness, the light blue outside quickly turning to black. The scents of metal, oil and sweat grew thin in the colder air as the shuttle bled off excess heat.

They all leaned again as the shuttle accelerated toward the fleet. Eth looked around, wondering if they were as nervous as he was. Noa leaned over to say something to Oliv and she laughed before giving him a lengthy reply. They seemed calm enough, but everyone had their own way of coping.

The shuttle slowed and a flash out the window announced the arrival of their escort. A fighter, loaded with missiles, would follow the civilian shuttle in. If they misbehaved in the slightest, they'd become a problem for a salvage crew.

"Look at that!" Noa called out, gazing through the portal behind his head.

Eth released his restraint bar and moved over to get a look.

A ship, one of the obsolete old frigates, was melting before their eyes. The new specs had come in already and the nanites making up the old warship were migrating to where a newer design was being grown. Only the core, with the specialized composites and superconductive lines, would remain from one ship to the next.

"I've programmed mods for shuttles," Noa said, "but an entire warship? Can you just imagine watching a frigate or even a heavy cruiser growing right before your eyes from a design you came up with?"

The blackness turned into light again, cutting off their view as they passed through the nav-shield on the *Dibbarra* and into her forward bay.

Already out of his seat, Eth moved toward the ramp as they settled onto the deck. The loadmaster, one of the mushkenu Quailu who called Kish home, hit the controls to open up. He was a decent fellow who'd opened the ramp for this particular group of Humans many times. He offered them what passed for a Quailu grin.

Before the ramp got halfway down, a Quailu, wearing the insignia of a petty officer; 3rd class, jumped up onto the ramp. "What do we have here?" he jeered as he strutted up the ramp. "Slave-soldiers? Well, don't get comfortable. We don't want your kind on this ship."

Eth moved to stand between him and his people but the Quailu kept coming, putting out a hand to shove him away.

The Quailu, even those of the lower class, were never to be harmed by any other species. Even the lowliest of them was still the same race as the emperor himself. Abdu had died to prevent the death of some lower-class Quailu. It was a matter of fact rather than a fear of punishment. No formal laws even existed on the matter.

You just didn't harm a member of the ruling species.

But this one was intent on mistreating Eth's people. Even worse, a petty officer was about to assault a warrant officer – a violation of the Uniform Code of Conduct that now resided in his expensive brain. If he let this happen, his authority would be in tatters before he even stepped off the shuttle. It occurred to him that it might have been this Quailu's intended goal.

It made him angry.

There were subtle variations but most species were hurt in the same ways. He grasped the offending hand before it made contact and bent it in towards the elbow. The gasp of pain came with gratifying quickness and he increased the pressure, leaving his opponent with no choice but to drop to his knees or face increased agony.

'Release me at once, you filthy savage! I'll… Ahh…" He stopped in mid-threat as Eth increased the pressure on his wrist joint.

He twisted the hand, forcing the Quailu to move to the right, and looked down at the symbols on his sleeve. "Handler, 1st class, perhaps you'd care to explain why you assaulted a superior in front of witnesses?"

The petty officer glared at the watching Humans, clearly not considering them to be credible witnesses. He noticed the loadmaster but, whatever mood he was sensing, he saw no allies there either. "Let me go!" he raged. "Giving a warrant to a Human! It's ridiculous – you'll be turning to drink within a single lunar!"

Eth pressed a little harder. "If you persist," he explained, "I'll have no choice but to pursue charges. I might pull some flak for it but you'll definitely have regrets. Your superiors won't appreciate your lack of tact, brought up on charges by someone who was a slave only hours before…"

He leaned down, close to the Quailu's left ear. "You should know that I'm somewhat of an enthusiast when it comes to preventative violence. If you cross my path again, you'd better remember that or I might not be this pleasant." He pushed a little harder on the hand to punctuate his warning, bringing out a breathless gasp.

He stood, letting go of the hand. "You're a cargo handler?"

The Quailu came to his feet, holding his wrist and refusing to meet Eth's gaze or answer his question.

Eth leaned in, deliberately letting himself feel the urge to commit further violence. "I asked you a question, petty officer."

The creature took a hurried step back. "Yes." Then, as Eth took a step closer… "Yes Warrant!"

Eth waved a hand at the footlockers. "Then *handle*. Get our dunnage off the shuttle. Our pilot doesn't have all day."

He brushed past and headed down the ramp, desperately hoping he could keep his breakfast down. The encounter had spun out of control so quickly he hadn't even had time to assess his options and he was filled with adrenaline and more than a little fear. He forced himself through the breathing-control exercises programmed into him by the maturation chamber.

He was oblivious to his surroundings. The almost-gothic structure of the hangar bay was far more ornate than that of the *Coronado,* but the metal arches were functional in the decorative way common to Quailu design philosophy.

He decided he'd acted correctly. He could see the apprehension and respect on Noa's face as he came to stand next to him.

This, too, was covered under Ab's endless lessons. If you need to stand up for your people, it's always better for morale if they actually *see* you doing it.

"What happened to taking it easy, Boss?"

"You think they'll be upset?"

"Nah!" Noa turned to count heads. "If anything comes of it, they'll likely let you off with decapitation."

"You figure?" Eth smiled.

A shrug. "Sure, there's extenuating circumstances…" He turned back. "All here. Looks like nobody fell out on the way up. Watch left," he suddenly hissed. "Button merchant."

He looked left. A senior officer with eight rows of battle-citations was inbound. "Silence on deck!" Eth commanded as the officer approached to within ten meters, the required distance for paying respects in an open space. They kept movement to a minimum and refrained from communicating by voice or gesture, observing the standard imperial custom for house-militaries.

The officer stopped in front of them, gazing impassively at the thirty-three Humans. His right eye-ridge twitched up ever so slightly, perhaps in annoyance that they weren't sufficiently nervous for a pack of recently freed slaves.

"I don't know what command was thinking," he suddenly admitted, "sending me a barely-civilized pack of simians and expecting me to make 'em into crewmen, but we don't always have the luxury of sensible orders, so I'll just have to pretend along with the top brass for now."

That facial tic again. Eth knew he wasn't the only one amused by this speech and the officer had to feel it.

"My name is Ashurabel, and I'm the XO of the *Dibbarra*. She's the flagship of our master, Mishakwilu, only son of the great Sandrakwilu, and I'll thank you filthy beasts to stay out of our lord's path when he's aboard."

Eth tilted his head to the side, making direct eye contact.

"Yes, Warrant?"

"Sir, what will our roles be aboard the *Dibbarra*?"

There was a grudging pause. "You may have come at an opportune time," he admitted. "We're just drawing up a new watch-bill after re-growing the old girl to a new heavy-cruiser pattern. We'll be spreading you throughout the divisions, assuming you stay aboard, and you," he added, pointing at Eth, "will report directly to the master's mate and he'll assign you a station on the bridge. You'll also be responsible for this lot," he added, waving at the Humans, "through the mate as well."

Eth tilted his head again but didn't wait for the acknowledgement, seeing as they were already conversing. "Shouldn't each department head be responsible for his or her own crewmembers? I'm not complaining, sir, but it sounds as though this creates a secondary reporting structure."

"Hmmm…" The XO looked at Eth for a moment. "Perhaps they did more than just shave your hides and teach you to speak. Yes – it's a grade-A cluster-hump but it's what command wants so it's what we're going to do. Understand?"

"Yes, sir."

A nod. "Good. Now shut your noodle-holes and stay put. We're supposed to wait on the lord-commander's arrival before dispersing you, so keep your paws down and act respectful. You might have been hot shit as interplanetary thieves but you're on a real warship now and you'll gods-damned well act like it or I'll have your livers for lunch." He wheeled around to face the open middle of the landing deck.

An honor guard was rushing to form in the middle of the hangar in response to a flashing orange light above the main hangar exit doors.

Eth had a pretty good idea of what the XO was hoping for. Mishak would come aboard to take command of their small fleet, see the Humans standing there and flip a gasket. With any luck, they'd be back on Kish before the end of the current watch.

He just smiled, completely unconcerned. Ahead, he could see the XO's neck turning red, no doubt in reaction to the lack of fear in the new crewmen.

The shuttle that slid in through the nav-shields couldn't have been Mishak's. It bore the bright red glyph of Chiron on its nose and it gave Eth a sneaking suspicion. There was a reason for the Humans to be left standing on the deck but it wasn't going to be what the XO thought.

Human

Mishak's hand darted out to grasp a stanchion as the shuttle lifted off the landing-bay deck of the *Haldita*. The Chironians must have arrived. He'd only have a few more seconds to re-hash potential approaches to the pending meeting, though he knew how it was going to go.

He was a bundle of nerves but it was nothing like he used to feel when summoned into his father's presence. Something had changed during their last meeting and it was a change that Mishak liked.

Under his father's close supervision, he'd never been able to do anything to satisfaction. His years at court, fostered to the Emperor's household for experience, had been a pleasant change but everything had gone back to the old ways as soon as he'd returned home.

This time had been different. This time he'd shown competence and he'd so surprised the old bastard that he'd forgotten to dismiss it as insignificant or somehow wrong. He had no intention of letting things backslide this time and, though he was nervous, he was looking forward to being on the *giving* side of a good thumping for a change.

The shuttle slid into his flagship's hangar and settled in front of the Chironian craft, only a little later than was polite to keep them waiting. He popped the side door and hopped down to the deck, striding over to a point between the two shuttles.

The other shuttle lowered a forward ramp, revealing its passengers standing at the forward edge. They stepped off as it touched the deck, the Chironian representative leading the contingent of minor houses.

This was a big moment for Chiron.

Their ambassador held out a hand and one of his attendants placed a sealed papyrus scroll in it. "Mishak, son of Sandrak," he began in a low, clear voice, "we have had enough of your aggression and thievery. We have registered a coalition against this quadrant of your family's holdings. You have selected un-mediated response. Though you have this opportunity to reason with us, I warn you: we will not be put off."

Mishak took the proffered scroll and, imitating the Chironian ambassador, handed it back to a non-existent servant. It fell to the deck. If that imaginary servant had been real, he'd have been in for a good beating.

The visiting nobles gasped at his cavalier treatment of their rare, hard-copy document.

Surprise, confusion, anger. It felt good and Mishak knew it would feel even better before they were done. "I accept," he said cheerfully.

Confusion and, now, *a little fear.*

Acceptance of a coalition notice was almost always deferred to the maximum of two weeks. The rules were intended to give the target a fair chance to mobilize his defenses. The empire had always frowned on sneak attacks, ever since the seventh emperor had doubled the size of his dominion through a sneak attack of his own.

Mishak's two-word response meant that an immediate state of war now existed between him and the coalition. Sandrak would not have been named in the document and the ambassador had taken care to single out this particular quadrant. If Sandrak were to intervene, he'd be disavowed, open to attack by any who dared.

It should have left young Mishak terrified.

Apprehension.

They were apparently now coming to the realization that they hadn't approached under a flag of truce. How could they, when the state of war had only just come into effect. It was a minor loophole in the rules of civilized conflict but one that could have serious implications for the individuals standing in front of him, nonetheless.

"I commend your bravery," Mishak said, bowing so deep as to make a mockery of his own words. "To make such a declaration, to put your own world at such risk…"

Anger growing. Belligerence now.

The Chironian waved to his fellow Quailu. "As you can plainly see," he blustered, "I have not come alone to make this declaration."

"Haven't you?" Mishak prompted helpfully. He turned to take a few strides to his left, and then, turning to walk back, he contrived to notice Eth and his team. He gave them a friendly nod. Turning back he saw the Ambassador glaring at them. Mishak continued. "What will your allies do when our troops land in their cities? Will they stand fast after we learn *their* secrets?"

He suddenly stepped in close, lowering his voice. "What if we find they're holding contraband data? Genomes, perhaps?"

Blank confusion.

It's possible that he doesn't know. Probable, even. He handed him a dataset. "I'd advise you to keep that angled so nobody else can see it."

The ambassador raised his voice. "We Chironians have nothing to hide!" he flared.

"Oh, but you do, my dear fellow." Mishak gestured for the angry Quailu to turn. "You'll thank me – well, you won't thank me but you'll be glad that you listened."

The ambassador turned, pressing a control and a two-dimensional, polarized display sprang up in front of him. It was only visible in a narrow arc but Mishak had already seen the proof and knew what would happen to Chiron if the Meleke Corp. ever got wind of it.

Even if they'd sold Chiron the Human data on the sly, they'd never be stupid enough to leave evidence. They'd deny everything and cut off all further sales of native Chironian genomes because that was what an *innocent* party would do.

Concern, deepening to outright alarm as the understanding set in. The Chironian turned even farther away from the rest of his delegation.

"It might be wise of you to make immediate contact with your superiors," Mishak advised indulgently. "Please feel free to make use of our communications suite. You know the old saying: '*your* ship is *my* ship'."

"I will use the facilities on my own ship," the ambassador retorted.

"Perhaps you weren't listening," Mishak replied, a slight edge now in his voice. "I said your ship is *my* ship."

Disbelief.

Mishak stepped in closer, invading the quarter-meter of personal space that defined the comfort zone of the average Quailu. "As a courtesy," he explained quietly, as though confiding a secret, "I'm according your party diplomatic status, even though there's ample precedent to justify a very different approach. Your ship and its crew, however, are not covered under the conventions. As there was never any truce in play, they count as having been caught in enemy territory at the outbreak of hostilities."

He gestured to the aft exit portal. "Shall we?" He led the way, savoring the gut-churning sense of failure in his opponent.

"Stay here!" the ambassador snapped.

A muddle of confused minds.

Mishak turned to see the minor representatives strung out behind their Chironian leader and chuckled. The last thing this situation needed was for these minors to learn the truth. There'd be a race to gain leverage over Chiron, ending, ultimately, in the collapse of all their economies.

A secret like that could never be kept by so many potential enemies and it was a valuable secret for Mishak to hold over Chiron.

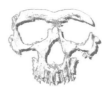

Eth watched in amusement as Mishak led the Chironian past them. The ambassador turned a look of pure malevolence on them and the executive officer at their front must have felt it as they passed.

Eth bowed in response and the Chironian flushed red, turning to fix his gaze on the middle of Mishak's back.

The officer turned to look at him, eye ridges raised in the center. He'd probably sensed the human's triumphant mood but Eth merely gave him a polite nod, nothing out of the ordinary between two officers in a Quailu warship.

Dark Days

Marduk kept the smile plastered to his face until the representative from the Lady Bau was out of his office and the door was sealed. He blew out a deep breath and leaned back in his chair. Bau controlled nine systems and she'd turned them around in short order after the death of her husband, Nin-girsu.

She'd taken over a mostly agricultural fief and the worlds had been heavily specialized to the point of ecological failure. Her first order of business had been to forcibly transplant elements between the worlds, creating a system where plant and animal cultivation could be rotated. In a matter of years, she'd reclaimed vast swaths of former farmland from the deserts, turning her holdings into a food-producing powerhouse.

Five decades later, she controlled the empire's bread-basket and she had no qualms about using that to get her way. She wasn't one for false outrage. She'd laid out her position much as a mathematician would. The emperor had damaged his prestige with the latest spying scandal.

He had lost some of his ability to project authority among the nobles. Clearly, a state of violent unrest would soon break out to *help* everybody forget the whole mess. If they wanted her food, she wanted two specific systems added to her domain and she'd appreciate if His Royal Highness kept his disgraced nose out of the matter.

After all, there'd be a lot of small wars going on. It's not hard to grab a few planets here and there…

He had to admire the old gal. The two systems belonged to a minor lord who'd been known to pledge support to the Imperial household only to turn on them once he had what he wanted. Far better for all concerned if those systems went to a reliable ally and an electress at that.

The steward arrived, gratifyingly late, with Marduk's morning coffee and set it on the desk.

Mild anger, answered with indulgent tolerance.

Marduk was glad the rest of the empire didn't know him as well as did this young Quailu. He took the proffered cup, looking down at the dark liquid. It was a shame there was no legal loophole allowing coffee to be grown on one of Bau's worlds. He shrugged to himself and took his first drink.

Leave it to Sandrak. He gets his hand on some backward dunghole of a world in the very cloaca of the empire and he still develops a product that nobody can do without. He was a great deal like Bau, just more aggressive. Both were successful because they identified what they wanted, then worked out how to get it. Many thought him to be lucky but Marduk knew it was just Sandrak's habit of being prepared for success.

He took another sip and sighed. He could feel his brain coming back to life.

He turned his attention back to the holo-screens that projected in front of his office walls. They were constantly tuned to newsfeeds from around the empire. A bank of them also presented an intelligence feed that would switch to news outlets when visitors entered.

He set down his coffee and selected one of the intelligence feeds, enlarging it over his desk. Sandrak would soon find himself in the midst of scorched grazing. Marduk didn't want to do it, believing him to be more or less loyal as long as he was given no provocation.

Sandrak had even fostered his only son to the imperial court. Young Mishak had been a decent lad but he'd been reserved and reluctant to take chances.

Nonetheless, the emperor feared his power and influence more than any other lord. He was certain that Sandrak would come to take his throne and so he would have to be dealt with.

A lucky stroke had come in the form of the Chironian-led coalition. Though Sandrak wouldn't be able to intervene, he'd still be distracted by the certain knowledge that his only heir would fall into unfriendly hands.

Meanwhile, a plan was about to go into action that would separate him from half his holdings before he could react. He began to assess the display in front of him as the coffee took hold. He stretched it out into a three-dimensional display and began moving his head from side to side in order to get the full picture of the map-sector in question.

The Quailu were descended from omnivorous grazers. They'd mostly eaten plants throughout their history but didn't turn their noses up at the occasional slow animal. This was a major factor in their limited depth-perception. They could see everywhere except for a six-degree arc directly behind their heads and they could only perceive depth in a six degree arc at the front where their vision overlapped.

They didn't entirely disdain the benefits of 3D displays, but they had to work a little harder to get the most out of them.

He began drawing in force vectors from the various neighboring fiefs, factoring in deployment times and current political stance as well. He could have had the AI do this in a heartbeat but he felt there were too many variables left out of an AI interpretation. It was all too easy to take such an analysis as fact and form an entire plan based on a lie. He had to consider the personal factors.

He leaned back in his chair, cradling his coffee as he stared up at the display. *One fleet.* He decided. Any more would look like the whole thing had been planned by his office. Just one fleet of Imperial Varangian Guards would be sufficient to deter interference. Even Sandrak knew better than to attack such a force.

He could destroy a small Varangian force easily, of course, but not quickly and not quietly. The Varangians were known for their luck even more so than Sandrak. It all sounded like mystical hyrak-turds to the uninformed, but the Varangian race had some kind of special ability where expected outcomes were concerned.

Many xenobiologists had tried to study the phenomenon but few had ever come back from Varangria-3 alive. Varangians were willing to fight for their emperor but they didn't care for busy-bodies.

And they would savage any force sent against them. Sandrak would be able to destroy a single fleet, but the forces sent to do it would be severely weakened and surrounded by hostile fiefs, all of them let off the hook by Sandrak's attack on imperial guardsmen. He nodded in satisfaction and drained his mug.

All it would take is a few words in the right ears. A few promises and a few threats.

He accessed his assistant's workstation and asked for his next guest to be sent in.

The door opened and Kuri, one of his dark-operatives, waiting in the outer office, got out of his chair but, before he took a single step, another Quailu rushed into Marduk's office, the assistant following him in a rage.

The young fellow didn't go so far as to place hands on the intruder because he was an accredited court diplomat, but he looked as though he'd like to punch him below the third stomach.

"I apologize, My Lord," the assistant said. "I had no idea he'd do such an un… that he'd rush in like this." He seemed slightly mollified by Marduk's mood.

Anger at the representative from Chiron but approval that the assistant had stopped himself from insulting a diplomat.

Marduk waved the assistant out before looking back to his display. There was a three-dimensional newsfeed now hovering over his desk. He hadn't saved his work…

New anger.

The Chironian seemed to shrink slightly but then he composed himself. "My Lord, I am pleased to announce that we are ready to dissolve our coalition against Mishak, Governor of the Kish system."

Cosmetic paint on a sack of fresh droppings.

Marduk didn't need empathic senses to read this fool. He was presenting a dry savannah as a lush paradise. He let his anger reach out.

The Chironian's gaze darted nervously away and back again several times. He lifted his heels as if to move back but mastered the reflex. He seemed to realize that his position was stronger if he could keep his mouth shut but he didn't have Marduk's experience.

"We have managed to negotiate a settlement with our enemy," he offered. "In doing so, we have spared countless lives on both sides!"

More cosmetics.

Marduk stared right through the fool. The Chironians were supposed to tie up Sandrak's attention for months while he schemed at the other end of his holdings. Still, if they'd won so quickly, perhaps they still held leverage over their opponents. "What concessions did you win? Have you taken hostages to secure their compliance?"

Having young Mishak in their clutches might work very well although...

Consternation, embarrassment.

The ambassador flapped his hands helplessly. "A ship."

"A ship?" he asked darkly. "No hostages? Just promises and a ship?"

"No promises, My Lord... just a ship. The ship that carried our delegation to Kish."

Humiliation, shame.

Marduk came out of his chair and the ambassador took two steps back in the face of the anger that radiated from the imperial chief of staff. "You mean that your people went there, and, though you possess twenty-five times the force of your opponent, you let him take *your* ship? By Aralu's divine gonads! Mishak's broken the code of civilized conduct and you come here pretending otherwise?"

Perhaps he was wrong about Sandrak's son. He certainly seems to have developed a taste for risk.

"No, sire," the ambassador insisted desperately, hands reaching out across the desk. "The forms were observed."

Marduk leaned forward, fists on his desk, the news display coloring his face. "Did the little prick accept on the spot?"

Affirmation.

Then Mishak had used some unexpected weapon. He must have remembered his tutoring sessions at Marduk's knee. He had something on the Chironians; something big enough to terrify them. Would they be foolish enough to give that secret to this halfwit?

"What does Mishak know that frightens your lord so much?"

Helpless ignorance.

"The coalition will be struck from the imperial roll of conflict," he grated, waving a hand at the door, "now get out!"

Alone again, he began to pace. This would, of course, change the equations in his plans. Perhaps it was just as well he'd lost his earlier work. He turned back to his desk and re-opened the base map of his targeted region. He had to admit his anger at this turn of events was tempered somewhat by feelings of almost-paternal pride.

Whatever his former student had done, he'd done it well.

The Learning Curve

Eth stepped back from the damage control workstation and turned to Kinziru, the master's mate. Like Eth, he held a warrant rather than a commission. It was the highest rank-plateau open to citizens of the mushkenu class.

In the various Quailu house-forces, the master's mates were responsible primarily for navigation but also for the training of new crewmen. Kinziru, a mushkenu, could eventually become a master, ranking among the junior officers, though he'd always be at the bottom of that particular ladder unless his master, in this case Mishak, registered a patent of dispensation so he could hold a full commission.

It rarely ended well. A non-noble, cut off from his lower-class familiars and forced to associate with the upper class usually ended up disgracing himself in one way or another.

Kinziru brought up a holo-projection in front of his left eye, calling a halt to the exercise. "So," he growled, "let's recap. You've managed to isolate the coolant breach in engineering, you've stabilized the decaying orbit and you rigged the ship for combat, opening the outer hull shunts and venting the ship before the expanding coolant could blow out half the ship's belly…"

Eth was no empath, but he could sense a trap in the relatively impassive master's mate. "Yes, sir."

Kinziru leaned in slightly. "Where did the volley of missiles strike us? Where exactly?"

Eth frowned, thinking back to the hectic rush of the exercise. "Engineering-6-ventral…" He suddenly shook his head. "Fornication!"

The master's mate scratched at a long shrapnel scar that ran from his forehead, down across his nasal ridges, all the way to the tip of his chin. "You and your Humans would be the only ones doing any fornicating," he said calmly. "The computer estimates a ninety-eight percent probability that the modules controlling the hull/suit interlock were knocked out.

"Sure, all our suits closed up as they reacted to the simulated pressure differential, but opening the shunts makes for a very quickly-growing differential, wouldn't you agree?"

"Yes, sir," Eth responded miserably.

"And stop calling me 'sir', you ape! We both hold warrants. I don't give a pile of droppings what species you are as long as you don't get me killed!

"And I might wish myself dead," he ground on, "after my auditory membranes and eyeballs burst. I'd rather freeze out than sit here in the dark waiting for you to sort out your next step."

It was the closest Eth had heard to an admission that Humans were better at anything. The Quailu had evolved on the coastal savannahs of their world, rarely venturing to the higher elevations.

Their eyes had very thin corneas. They were fine for normal atmospheric use but vulnerable to any changes in pressure. Likewise, their ears relied on gas diffusion to equalize pressures and didn't fare well in rapid pressure fluctuation.

He took care to avoid any feelings of satisfaction over this, as Kinziru would have felt it as plainly as if he'd spoken it aloud. He forced himself to focus on his own performance. "I failed to fully assess the damage properly," he admitted. "I should transmit a suit-close imperative before rigging the hull for combat in a situation like this…"

"Or you could have vented only the affected section," the master's mate offered. "With the coolant vaporizing, you'd hardly have done any further damage to the Quailu crewmen caught in there."

Eth nodded diplomatically. "Of course, we were under attack at the time. The next salvo might have breached a central corridor or a hangar bay. The resulting explosive venting would have blown valuable crew out through the breach."

Kinziru grunted.

Eth had screwed up; there was no denying it, but so had the master's mate in suggesting a course of action more in keeping with a peacetime accident than a hostile attack.

"Let's go review your people before we stand down from the drill." He waved Eth toward the aft hatch.

Eth shuddered at the sight of a PLC team in the corridor. They were working out the kinks that accompany any ship's regrowth but it disturbed him to know they were working aboard a ship that might suddenly separate into its components. He didn't like being reminded that almost all of this heavy cruiser, aside from the warheads and the main power bus, was composed of microscopic robots.

They made the rounds, med bay, weapons; Humans were dispersed throughout the ship and many were standing by to fight fires or repair critical systems. The hatch to Engineering-6-v snapped open in front of them with a speed that Eth still wasn't quite used to. The hatches on the old *Coronado* were far more leisurely, but then she hadn't been built with combat in mind.

The engineering team, six Quailu and four Humans, were sitting on the deck next to the 'patch' they'd put on the coolant leak.

"How'd they do?" Kinziru asked the team leader, a petty officer, 1st class.

"Well enough," the old Quailu allowed. "Though this one here's full of ideas for a raw hand." He waved a hand toward Noa.

Eth looked at Kinziru but he looked as though he intended to leave the compartment and call it a day. Noa was looking intently at Eth, clearly itching for a chance to speak.

Eth decided to give him an opening. "What's on your mind?"

"I've already told him to keep it to himself," the petty officer snapped.

Eth turned to him, slowly enough to get a quick look at the master's mate. Kinziru looked mildly annoyed, though whether it was at Eth or at his fellow Quailu wasn't clear.

Screw it. No sense having a rank if you let someone piss on it. "Don't interrupt my conversations, if you please, petty officer." He turned back to Noa, who was clearly fighting to suppress a grin. That might work among Humans, but the underlying emotions would cost him after Eth left the compartment.

"Sir," Noa began pointing a thumb over his shoulder, "that module over there is responsible for closing up suits when we rig for combat. Seeing as it got taken out in the attack, we'd have lost half our crewmates to blindness and hearing loss."

Eth already knew this and it wasn't helping him much to hear it again, especially in front of that now-smirking PO. *Laugh it up, pal. You'd be unable to hear your own laughter.*

"It would be a simple matter to set up a redundant module on the other side of the ship somewhere, so we have a backup."

Eth forgot all about the PO. "And you can program that?"

"Sure," Noa shrugged. "We have a copy of the whole ship's plan up on the bridge in the damage control station, but we also have local copies in each individual module."

"Sheckter droppings!" the PO exclaimed. "Check your pattern manuals, sonny. They keep the data under strict copyright control. One copy per ship and it's at damage control where there's always a record of all activity."

"And if the main bus takes a hit?" Noa demanded. "You think a damaged module is going to regrow without pattern access?"

"No," the PO insisted, "it won't and we'd all be properly dead because there are no local copies on modules."

"And how much demand will there be for your ship patterns," Noa asked as he got up and walked over to the interlock unit, "if they're always on the losing side?" He pressed a control and the front panel slid open. "See this little bump?" he pointed.

The PO got up and walked over, squinting into the opening.

Noa dragged a holo screen into existence between his hands and pulled a search link down from it to the area of the small bump. Seventeen returns appeared and number seven had no label, just a blank space. He selected it and a long string of programmable logic controls began scrolling across the interface.

"Simple risk management, PO," he said with a mildly apologetic shrug. "The programmers would have seen the possibility of a breach in the connection between the bridge pattern and the rest of the ship. If it can't regenerate, it gets destroyed, like you said, so they risk hiding local copies for each module, allowing the ship can repair itself. They weigh the risk to their copyrights against the potential gains from having a design that wins more fights."

"You've seen this before?" the master's mate demanded.

"No, sir, but when you're a student of programming, you hear a lot of surprising stuff." Noa closed out the interface. "I've met a few ship designers through prog-net that gave me the inside loop on how they really work. In fact, we still have some PLC boys aboard. If we bring this idea to them, they'll do it for us, nice and legal, and they'll pass it back to the designers so it can be sold to other customers."

"Customers we might have to fight," Kinziru mused. "You can do this yourself and not get found out?"

"Well, sure, sir." Noa closed the panel. "We'd have to wait until the contractors are gone and we'd need to put together a mining unit, down on the surface, to provide the extra material. If you can get me an old shuttle or something, I can crank out the instructions for a mineral extractor and handle the reconfig from up here."

"Good, get started on everything you can do while the contractors are still here and I want this done for the whole fleet after they've been regrown." Kinziru jabbed a finger at Noa. "Make sure those nodes are grown somewhere they won't be noticed if anyone comes aboard for a quick code adjustment or inspection. We don't want to get caught and we don't want our advantages sold to our enemies."

"Yes, sir!"

"Any other ideas about improving our combat effectiveness, you talk it over with the PO and then bring it to me or to Warrant Eth. Understood?"

Eth noticed that the PO had nodded his agreement while Noa was responding. Clearly, the master's mate had recognized the resistance at play within this department and he'd aimed his message at *all* present.

"Excellent!" Kinziru rubbed his hands. "I think we can call an end to a very useful drill!"

He started turning away but stopped and looked back at Noa. "What is it?"

"Well, sir, I…" Noa suddenly grinned and held up a hand, asking for a moment. He turned to his supervisor. "PO, as ordered, I should mention to you that I was thinking we could put in a few ladder chutes to speed movement between decks."

"What the devils is a ladder?" the petty officer asked peevishly.

"They have them on arboreal vessels," Kinziru said. "Tree-climbers. Useless for Quailu."

The Quailu weren't big on climbing. Their leg joints were adapted for migrating across their ancestral plains rather than for life among trees. They tended to look at arboreal tendencies with disdain.

"Are we even keeping these monkeys?" The petty officer asked Kinziru. "Why should we change the ship to accommodate them?"

Noa scrambled atop a large condenser housing. "We *monkeys* can get into place to do a repair pretty quickly," he countered. "If I have to follow a long ramp to route around a disabled lift, I might not get there in time. Getting a repair quickly can mean the difference between life and death in a battle."

A.G. Claymore

The master's mate looked slightly disgusted. "It makes enough sense to go ahead with," he admitted. He started for the forward hatch but wheeled around before he reached it. "Make very sure no outsiders hear of this either," he ordered. "I don't want us becoming a laughing stock."

Eth was having a hard time holding in his resentment. Changes to make the best use of Human crewmen shouldn't be an embarrassment. When the master's mate turned left in the main companionway, he turned right, moving quickly to get out of his range.

His path took him to the senior NCO's mess without his even realizing it. It wasn't his favorite place on the ship by a long shot. A surgeon's mate stuck out a heavy foot to trip him up as he steered toward the bar and he shifted his gait enough to step heavily on the fool's primary tarsal tendon.

The mate hissed with pain. "Watch where you're going, ape!"

Eth spun around, letting his feelings have full sway and the NCO backed away, hands coming up in the universal gesture for peace. A willingness to do harm could be far more effective than a verbal threat.

He stopped at the bar, the steward, 3rd class, clearly wanting to defy him despite the massive difference in rank.

Eth held up two fingers. "Malted," he demanded.

Now faced with the direct attention of the Human, the steward suddenly lost interest in defiance. He sliced off a strip of the high-quality alcoholic fat and handed it over.

Eth looked down at it, suddenly remembering the words of the handler who'd accosted him when they'd arrived on board. One moment of stress and here he was, ordering intoxicants. He picked it up, nodding to the steward, and turned for the exit. He passed the surgeon's mate, handing him the fat. "Next time, I'll be more careful," he growled on his way out the hatch.

The Money

Marduk shaded his eyes. The suns, penetrating the glazed ceiling of the throne room, shone directly in his face and the coxswain corrected his lapse of attention at once, turning the barge to place its awnings between the chief of staff and the suns.

They were almost a kilometer from the nearest side of the huge room and several from either end. The floor of the chamber, some two hundred meters below, was a lush green and orange savannah.

Marduk lowered his hand and watched the stately ballet of imperial court politics. Other barges, usually five by ten meters in size, were continuously coalescing into small groups as their diplomatic passengers crossed extendable gangways to confer.

The flocks of hovering craft faded away into the hazy distance. Wars were being plotted, revenge sworn, promises given of assistance that might well turn out to be sneak attacks. Such things were the coin of the imperial court but there'd been a sharp upswing since the leak.

With the emperor's prestige damaged by his own paranoia, the noble houses were emboldened. It was far less likely that Tir Uttur would attempt to intervene in a conflict now, knowing that he might well be ignored.

Not that it presented a problem, of course. The crown could remain officially aloof, while secretly maneuvering to their own advantage. Minor lords who stood on the verge of becoming electors could be nurtured, nudged and then incited into action.

The emperor would most likely come out of this mess with more votes than ever but Marduk would be kept very busy. The current electors would need reassurances, perhaps even concessions, and potentially friendly candidates would need support while opponents needed to be destabilized.

It would be a busy year in the Holy Quailu Empire.

A dark shadow played across his face. A large, ornate barge lowered down on his port side, matching course and speed.

Marduk nodded to the coxswain who set a straight leisurely course, one that was easy for the newcomer to replicate.

He hated the banking guild. No imperial court in ten thousand years had been able to govern without their consent. Perhaps it was because of this hatred, instead of cold calculation, that he refused to cross to their barge.

He knew the arguments they would present in an attempt to gain further powers and it was largely a pile of fresh droppings.

Instead, he turned his seat to face out through the glazed gunwale. He watched an artificial river in the savannah below. It sparkled in the suns, diminishing to a dull ribbon as it flowed toward the emperor's security-exclusion zone.

With the court in damage-control mode, the accursed bankers would expect Marduk to play the role of supplicant. As far as they were concerned, he'd made the first move in coming to the throne room and cruising aimlessly about.

They were correct, of course, but he'd be damned if he would admit it. He tapped the table on his left and the steward brought over a carafe of coffee, pouring him a mug of the brown liquid. "Leave it here," he said quietly, and the steward set down the carafe before moving away.

Calm concentration, guild conditioned. Nothing given away.

"I sometimes forget we're indoors," the guild representative said, coming to stand on Marduk's right.

Marduk waved him to a seat. "Will you take coffee, Namtar?"

"Thank-you, no, it makes me sneeze, I'm afraid." Namtar eased into the chair. "Your emperor has been naughty," he chided.

Marduk remained calm. "*My* emperor? Are you suggesting the Banker's Guild has seceded from the empire?"

"Certainly not," Namtar remained unruffled. "Perhaps a subconscious slip, an attempt to distance myself from recent imperial actions?"

"And perhaps the matter is simple enough that we can dispense with the fencing and get straight to the heart." Marduk offered mildly. "You feel the recent leaks about imperial spying will threaten cash flow, yes?"

Namtar inclined his head in acknowledgement.

"I've run the projections a number of times," Marduk said, "and the threat to current commitments is less than two percent."

"Two percent," Namtar interjected, "given the scale involved, is more than the GDP of most one-system minor holdings. If we have to accept such a risk…" He looked up as another barge, even more ornate than his own, suddenly blocked his view.

A row of Varangian guards lined both sides of the barge, weapons primed, wispy tendrils of incense framing their deadly bulk. A pair of them crossed over to Marduk's barge as the two vehicles linked up.

A Quailu, solid and gracefully beautiful, stood up behind the row of Varangians and was quickly obscured by a half-dozen scensors who stood to surround her. It was the Princess Tashmitum, only child of the emperor.

She'd never been one for imperial trappings but she seemed to be more willing, now that the family's prestige was in jeopardy. Marduk approved of the scensors. Natives of the Moksh system, the scensors had chitinous protrusions on their skulls that could be slowly burned to produce a fragrant smoke.

The heady scent took him back to the glory days of the previous reign. The empress had been a force to be reckoned with and she'd understood the power of the olfactory senses. A cheaper version of the same incense was publicly available (on sticks rather than in humanoid form) and anyone who'd been in her presence would immediately recall her splendor if exposed to the scent.

Marduk and Namtar came to their feet as Tashmitum crossed over and both bowed deeply before her. "Your Highness," Marduk said to the decking at his feet, "you honor us!" He shivered at the emotions evoked by the scensors.

"Please, Uncle!" she replied, according him the honorific due to an old friend of her family, "there's no need to stand on ceremony between us!"

Marduk allowed his curiosity to emanate. It was natural, after all, to wonder at the purpose for this unexpected visit and it helped him to conceal from Namtar the affection that a real uncle might have felt.

He'd known the princess since her birth. She'd gone from a wild brat, digging holes in the throne room savannah, to the graceful aristocrat now standing before him.

She nodded at the banker. "Namtar, isn't it?"

Surprise and pleasure leaking past the conditioning.

Bankers were a barely tolerated class and they were usually kept at arm's length from the nobles by intermediaries. Sometimes, with great lords or monarchs, a noble such as Marduk *was* that intermediary and, usually, he was the limit of the guild's direct interaction with the upper class of the HQE.

And here was the second-highest-ranking Quailu in the entire empire, addressing him by name.

"You come with concerns, yes?' she asked.

Namtar nodded in assent, apparently unsure whether he was meant to explain those concerns to the princess.

"As I'm sure Marduk has already explained," Tashmitum continued before he could speak, "risks to current engagements are minimal and more than offset by all this…" She waved to indicate the flow of barges.

"Wars are brewing out there," she assured him, "and that means new ships, devastated planets, new administrations, infrastructure restoration contracts…" She smiled at Namtar. "Regime changes don't come cheap. You'll have half the lords of the empire in your debt before the dust finally settles."

"Indeed, Highness." Namtar inclined his head.

Slight consternation. Had something been inadvertently conceded by his agreement?

Marduk forced himself to focus on the cost of post-war reconstruction. He couldn't dwell on how easily she'd slipped past the guild's emotional conditioning. "I'm glad to hear we're all in agreement!"

Before Namtar could respond, Tashmitum stepped forward, linking her arm into Marduk's. "I apologize for my rudeness," she said to the banker, "but I have an urgent personal matter to discuss with my uncle. Would you please excuse us?"

The banker bowed deeply before returning, slowly, to his barge. One didn't move quickly when a royal and her Varangians were nearby.

The guild barge pulled away and Marduk relaxed his mind. "That saved me an hour of uncomfortable conversation."

She smiled, feeling his approval. "It's time I started earning my keep. I'd come here looking for you because I want to take a more active role at court. I saw the guild representative and assumed, correctly I hope, that you'd like to see him off."

"You assumed correctly," he assured her, "but this is a dangerous time to be stepping into court politics."

"It's exactly the *right* time to step in," she countered. "You need someone to represent the imperial family and my father, if we could even drag him out of seclusion, would likely prove counterproductive. I understand the subtext of what's happening right now, without his… preconceptions.

"Your efforts, after all, concentrate on nurturing enough votes to secure my ascension to the throne. I need to be a known quantity. The other nobles need to have confidence in my abilities if they're going to elect me."

"You're right," he admitted with a sigh. It was a day he knew would come, but he didn't relish the idea of putting her at risk.

She could feel that and she put a hand on his arm. "Don't worry, Uncle. I'll avoid unnecessary risks."

He prayed, fervently, that she would.

Damage Control

Eth stifled a yawn. They'd been up all night supervising the growing of a ladder column between the engineering levels and they'd still need to run an isolated damage-control exercise before sacking out.

He didn't notice the engineering petty officer until he was talking in his ear.

"We'll be putting all this back the way it should be," the PO hissed, "as soon as we get you off the ship, which will be sooner than you think!" He gave Eth a shove sideways.

The Quailu may not be good runners or climbers but they had a heavy base and a low center of gravity. They excelled at wrestling and Eth was easily thrown off balance.

That didn't mean his reflexes were on vacation. He rebounded off a stanchion and drove back in, hammering the heel of his palm against the upper right side of his opponent's abdomen.

The petty officer vomited explosively, his primary stomach chamber compressed by the sudden impact to its governing nerve cluster.

And then Mishak walked into the compartment with the master and his mate.

The PO drew painfully erect, wiping at his mouth with his sleeve but he still looked very pleased with himself.

So this was the plan.

Eth should have paid closer attention to the heightened tensions between the two species in the engineering department. If the PO felt the Humans were only temporary, then his Quailu subordinates would pick up on his attitude and echo his hostility.

Taking a punch in the gut probably wasn't what he'd had in mind, though. He'd probably just intended to put Eth into an angry, unstable state of mind before Mishak arrived, showing their lord how unsuitable

Humans were for 'proper' military service. That should have put an end to this farce.

Should…

"Warrant Eth," Mishak gave him a friendly nod. "You look like a walking corpse! How long have you been awake?"

"Just long enough, I hope, Lord."

Mishak looked over to the petty officer. "Whenever you're ready, PO."

The engineering NCO was thoroughly thrown off course. He'd picked up on the easy familiarity between the Human and his lord and it was more than enough to scare and confuse him.

He composed himself and activated two test-screens. Each corresponded to one of the Humans working in engineering and to their likenesses in a small holographic display of the course.

"Why is this test only being run with Humans?" Mishak asked, startling the petty officer who'd been about to initiate the alarm.

"Sire?"

"Have one of your Quailu crewmembers line up as well. Let's see what the real differences are, if there actually are any, that is."

Eth didn't need Quailu empathic abilities to see how uncomfortable the PO was getting.

"Allatu!" He opened another tracking screen as the female Quailu stepped forward.

"Oh, hells no!" Oliv turned to Noa. "Switch places. I want a piece of her. She's been stealing my calibrators…"

"Quiet!" the PO snapped, a little louder than one might expect.

Without another word, he activated the exercise and an alarm sounded, indicating a shunt rupture, two decks above. A secondary chime underplayed the alarm, identifying it as a drill.

Allatu was the first to start moving, shoving Noa to the side as she raced for the exit. With a curse, Oliv bounded over to the ladder, stopping to shoot a glare at Noa before scrambling up and out of sight.

Noa was running before his Quailu crewmate was out of the compartment but he'd have a tough race.

The Quailu might not be built for climbing but they had an extra joint in their legs. Allatu had roughly twenty centimeters more leg than Noa and it gave her more speed in the long run. Noa was pulling up on her, but Allatu would quickly reach full speed and then she'd start to out-distance him as they made their way around the wide, corkscrewing companionway that linked the decks.

They were just a quarter of the way through the first circle when Oliv passed the first deck. Noa had almost caught up to his opponent. By the time they'd made it half-way to the first deck, Allatu was beginning to pull away from Noa but Oliv was already stepping off the ladder and onto the target deck. She raced over to the affected module, located suspiciously far from the ladder but very close to the ramp, and touched the control panel, locking in her time.

It seemed to take forever for Noa and Allatu to reach their destination.

"Unless I'm missing something, the idea of using ladders on ships with Human crewmembers has already proven itself." Mishak turned an innocently inquiring gaze on the petty officer. "Oliv would have effected the necessary repairs while others are still rushing to reach the damage. In combat, the ability to get our weapons back online or restore maneuver means the difference between victory and defeat."

Noa and Allatu reached Oliv and it looked as though Allatu gave Noa another shove. A light shove, which could mean either aggression or joking around. Eth wasn't sure which.

"Pass the coding for these ladder columns to our other ships," Mishak told the master. "I have a similar contingent of Humans for each vessel undergoing the necessary memory implants. This represents a potential advantage for us, so keep it quiet."

He nodded to Eth, a very Human gesture, and then tilted his head, looking at him intently for a moment.

Eth felt mildly guilty. He'd been thinking 0f how he missed the freedom of his old raiding life. The walls of this ship were starting to close in on him and he was pretty sure his fellow Humans felt the same.

He didn't want Mishak to sense his feelings and think he was ungrateful for all he'd done.

Mishak made no comment. He simply led the master and master's mate out of the compartment, leaving Eth and the PO.

Eth turned to the confused petty officer. "Who did you think signed my warrant?" he asked. "Only a noble of the first rank can do that and we only have one here at Kish. Did you really think he was unaware he'd freed us and given me my rank?"

He stepped in closer, quickly and without warning, backing the engineering team-leader up against a bulkhead. He jabbed a finger into the still-tender abdomen. "That's nothing compared to the beating I'll give you if you harass my people," he hissed.

"You can't..." he stopped in shock as Eth slapped him hard, rattling all three rows of teeth.

"You're thinking of complaining," Eth continued. "I don't need your abilities to see that. Let me walk you through how that's going to work out for you. First – you'll be the laughing stock of the empire for claiming a native, your superior, has been slapping you around. Second – no military codes have been breached so our lord will simply laugh at you, assuming he doesn't have you removed for incompetence."

He pointed a finger in his face, causing the Quailu to flinch backwards, bumping his head against the carbon bulkhead with a dull thud. "I'd better not hear about any problems from your team. Is that clear?"

"You won't." The reply was sullen but at least it was an affirmative.

Without another word, Eth turned and left the compartment. He took a series of deep breaths as he walked. His fingers were flexing repeatedly.

Despite being reasonably certain how his aggressive display would be received, he'd been up against forty-thousand years of tradition and conditioning. To threaten a Quailu was almost unthinkable and, yet, he'd done deliberate harm to three of them since coming aboard. He knew there had been no other alternative but that still didn't mitigate the adrenaline racing through his veins or the almost supernatural fear of retribution.

If he merely knuckled under to every Quailu he met, he would prove his team incapable of effectively serving on this ship. He didn't want to repay Mishak's confidence with failure.

He stopped walking, staring down the curving hallway in surprise. Hiding deep inside, under all the fear, was something else, something exciting and disturbing.

He'd enjoyed dominating the handler. He'd enjoyed the fear in the PO's eyes. A rush of power suddenly washed over him, drowning the fears.

He resumed walking, a grin ghosting his features.

The Old Goat

Mishak led the way into the ready-room, heading for the seat where he'd left several unclassified projections up. It was clearly his seat but it was exactly like the other nineteen seats around the large oval table.

He waved the projections away and waited for his father to choose a seat. Mishak had made it clear where he'd been sitting but Sandrak frowned at the oval of chairs.

Ordinarily, he'd take Mishak's place in accordance with an overlord's prerogative. It was often waived between father and son but Sandrak would never dream of such a courtesy. He took every chance to remind his son who was in command.

To make him give up one of twenty identical seats simply because he'd been using it would have simply looked petty. He dropped into the nearest chair and Mishak sat as well, carefully ignoring the small triumph lest it be picked up by his father.

"When will you be ready to depart for your uncle's holdings?"

"Soon, Lord. I'm receiving the last group of Humans from the training center in two days."

"How many in total?"

Mishak resisted the urge to confirm the number on a screen. His father had a way of making him doubt his grasp of any situation. "A little under three thousand."

His father glared at him. "You'd better keep an eye on how they add up because they're damn good at *multiplying*.

"You can leave in two days?" he pressed.

Mishak nodded. "The modifications to our ships should be done before the last Humans report aboard."

Sandrak nodded. "The PLC teams are still working out the glitches?"

86

"A few," Mishak agreed, "but we're also adding in some redundant systems and a few ladder chutes for the Humans."

Sudden anger.

"You're modifying our ships for the slaves?" Sandrak thundered. "I said you could fill the ranks with them, not change our whole damn military to accommodate them!"

Mishak calmly opened a holo recording of the test in engineering. "Watch this," he said simply.

Uncertainty, some of it a result of Mishak's calm demeanor. He'd noticed a facial tic that a friend had taught him to recognize as annoyance.

The holo was impossible to dispute.

"Do you see, now, why the Susai are so successful in combat?" he asked respectfully.

The Susai ruled nine systems containing twelve inhabited planets. Three of their native species were arboreal and two of those had been mushkenu for millennia.

"They let their free natives serve…," Sandrak mused.

"And we all laugh at them for it, despite their combat record." Mishak froze the display, just as Oliv reached the target. "It's not much of a secret," he admitted, "but it's an easy one to hide in a society that doesn't *want* to see it.

"These free Humans will give us an edge," he insisted.

"We could replace the ladders with elevators…"

"We already have elevators, but they're still slower than ladders and you have to wait for the damned things to arrive. What if you have a hull breach on the ventral side but the elevator is taking a damage control team to fix a dorsal shield emitter? If you replace that elevator with a shaft that multiple crewmen can use, you get both problems fixed faster."

"The bleed on grav-plating?"

Mishak nodded. "We looked into that as well. Five meters for standard plating. You'd need at least a twelve-meter hole in the deck to get a two-meter-squared hole in the gravity. That's one hundred forty-four square meters of lost deck-space per deck per hole and we'd need them in multiple locations."

"Which takes as much space as sixteen elevators…"

"Or we just do a meter-squared hole for a ladder," Mishak countered. "Believe me, I've done the math. This will give us an edge without having to sacrifice secondary systems. All that's really needed is a willingness to help the Humans work at their peak efficiency."

"And what do we do when the fighting calms down and we're stuck with free Humans? If we don't get them all killed off, Kish will be flooded with a mushkenu Human population in five decades. You can't very well eliminate them without losing valuable ships." Sandrak waved his hand at the far wall. "This is the latest design, very expensive."

He looked sharply at his Mishak, who'd been wondering if there might be another son that he didn't know about. His concern had been entirely over the loss of the ships and not the loss of his 'only' heir.

"I have an idea about that," Mishak said. "One of the Humans on this ship is a highly trained coder. He's the one who penetrated the system on Chiron."

"That was a valuable strike," Sandrak allowed, "though you might have easily ended up in their hands by now, if it had gone backwards on you."

"It was a risk," Mishak admitted, "but a risk never taken is an opportunity lost.

Sandrak sighed, another physical 'tell' that his friend had told him to watch for in his fellow Quailu. "It gave us an edge in this region at a moment when we needed it most."

Mishak could feel how hard it was for his father to say that. He let his annoyance escape.

Sandrak glanced at him. "You said you have an idea involving your native programmer?"

There was no need to fake his enthusiasm though it wasn't necessarily directed toward the death of his freed Humans. "He's the one making the improvements in our fleet. I've been thinking of challenging him with a new idea while we shape space for Ur."

He opened a holo between them. "A small scout-ship. We can build it entirely for Humans, so we save space by eliminating ramps. We can make them very stealthy, give them minimal armament to reduce the heat signature…"

"And they reveal an approaching enemy by exploding?" Sandrak raised an eyeridge. "It sounds like a good start. We'll need time to find enough Quailu recruits to replace them," he warned, "so don't start killing them off right away."

"I'll try to restrain myself."

"Hmph!" Sandrak leaned forward. "I've entered negotiations with Dagan."

"For recruits?"

"Don't be absurd! It's time you were married. You should at least be up to the task of providing an heir, assuming you can tear yourself away from your Humans long enough!"

Mishak felt the color coming into his skin. He needed to avoid following the new trend of thought before his father picked up on it. Sudden mention of a mate naturally let to thoughts of other… activities. "Mot?" he said, incredulous.

"She's a fine young female, very intelligent, good tactician…"

"And my first cousin!"

"The chromo match is clear; there's no genetic risk."

"She's vile! I once watched her torture a wardu Keevan to death, just because she was bored."

"I don't care," Sandrak snapped. He stood, leaning forward to place his hands on the table. "At the earliest possible moment, you will find yourselves in a bed-chamber in front of accredited witnesses. Our houses will be joined."

"We're already joined too closely for my comfort."

Sandrak ignored this, stepping back from the table. "Signal me when you leave orbit."

Without waiting for an answer, he turned and left.

"So," Mishak mused, "I've got *that* to look forward to."

Mot was an attractive Quailu by any physical standards you wanted to apply but she was a vicious creature. Raised by Sandrak's youngest brother who was also fostering uncle Uktannu's son – so perhaps her disposition was no surprise – Mishak's skin always crawled when he was near her.

The idea of being her mate, sharing her emotions, horrified him. He didn't want her in his head, not even as a hypothetical exercise.

The door snapped open and he looked up in alarm, thinking he'd missed sensing Sandrak's return, but then he smiled.

"The old prick is gone?" Oliv asked from the door.

He nodded and she gave him a sympathetic smile, sauntering over to where he sat.

It amazed Mishak how she could read him better than most members of his own species and she didn't even have empathic abilities.

She swung her leg over him, sitting on his thighs, facing him. "You held your own," she declared, looking at his face with approval. "He didn't manipulate you the way he usually does."

"I think that pisses him off."

"No doubt, but he's probably a little pleased as well. No father wants his son to be a complete pushback."

"Thanks ever so much…"

"Hah!" She leaned forward, placing her hands on his waist. "You gave him a reason to feel proud, so what's got your face so twisted?"

Body language was a dark art to the Quailu, thanks to their reliance on empathic communication. That didn't mean they were devoid of any physical cues. Faces the universe over tended to react to feelings but the Quailu were terrible at understanding them or at noticing that they even had them. Why waste time on micro-expressions and gestures when you could simply feel someone's mood directly?

Of course, as Oliv had already taught him, all Quailu learn to exert control over their emotions before they could be read, but none were adept at concealing the physical expressions. They always showed up, even if only for a brief moment, but they were enough to read.

It often came as a shock when Humans could sense his moods, but it still felt far less invasive than his own species.

"He wants to marry me off to my cousin."

"So? It's time you had a mate."

"She's pure evil."

Oliv laughed, sliding up his lap. "So just go to her homeworld," she whispered in his ear, grinding against him, "and do your noble duty until you're both dehydrated." She glanced down in pleased amusement. "Rinse and repeat until you have an heir or two and then just forget she exists. I'm sure that's her plan already."

"Thanks. You sure know how to seduce a fellah…"

"You've met her?"

"Many times."

"Then she already knows how you feel about her. Don't you think she's looking forward to getting rid of you so she can enjoy a little freedom?"

He reached for the front of her crew-suit, only to find it already open. His hands slid inside to her waist. "Can we talk about this later?"

This old habit of theirs had even more spice to it, now that she was no longer a wardu.

He wondered how long she'd be interested in continuing it.

The Meeting that Never Was

"Not in there, you fool!" Kuri took a longer step forward and slapped the chamberlain on the back of his head, hard enough to rattle his third row. The hapless Quailu nearly stumbled through the door into his lord's throne room.

He recovered his footing and wheeled on Kuri in outrage but his threat turned to a squawk as the imperial envoy grabbed his tunic and dragged him away from the entrance and into a side hall.

"Has there been any announcement made or schedule notes regarding my presence here?" Kuri growled. "Am I actually expected in your master's *throne room*?"

Fear, confusion, uncertainty.

"Well, I…"

Kuri cursed quietly. Despite clear instructions, this moron had scheduled him for a formal presentation, no doubt unable to resist the prestige of receiving an imperial envoy. If he walked in there, he wouldn't be able to have the necessary conversation, not with hundreds of witnesses. If he simply avoided walking in there, suspicion would be aroused.

He hadn't spent eight days in path-space just to turn around and go home. The only way to avoid walking into a public meeting was to make everyone forget about it in the first place. They'd need something more important to worry about. Nodding to himself, he pulled out the ceremonial sidearm that all diplomatic personnel carried.

The chamberlain's eyes grew wide.

Kuri gave him an apologetic smile. "Can't afford to take any chances. Sorry…"

The chamberlain squealed in terror, hiding his face in his hands as Kuri fired up at the ceiling. He shuddered, then peeked out from between his fingers.

Kuri waved his weapon to clear some of the acrid smell from the launch rails and shoved it back into its holster just as the first alarm started blaring.

Apparently, weapons fire had been detected in the governor's palace.

Kuri turned his attention back to the chamberlain. "Where do they take him during a weapons alert?"

The chamberlain radiated fear but he at least had some small measure of courage. "No! I can't…"

Kuri decided to kill him if he wouldn't be of use. He could hardly leave him here to rally the security forces. He let that resolve flow through his conscious mind.

The chamberlain flinched as though he'd been slapped again. He looked down the hallway they stood in.

"That way?" Kuri demanded.

A nod. "But the anteroom is unbreachable during a lockdown. You'll never get in."

Perhaps that thought allowed him to think he wasn't really betraying his lord. Kuri grabbed him and shoved him along the hallway.

They came to an ornately decorated round door at the end of the hall.

"It's eight thousand kilos of advanced composite armor," the chamberlain advised, clearly still terrified of Kuri's wrath, especially now that he'd be thwarted. "It would take a warship to blast through it."

Which of course would destroy the entire room along with it. Kuri grunted in amusement. He kept his left hand on the collar of the chamberlain's tunic and grabbed a fistful of cloth nearer his lower back.

With a shove, he propelled him forward, gaining speed as he veered to the right. He slammed the poor fellow into the carbon wall panels to the right of the door and the chamberlain crashed through the relatively flimsy wall to sprawl at his lord's feet, covered in acoustical batting.

Kuri stepped through the newly made opening, shooting the two guards who were training their weapons on the chamberlain, shuddering at their surprise and pain. "Sorry I'm late, My Lord," he offered mildly, "but we could hardly have a meeting like this in a crowded throne room." He glanced down at the chamberlain who now had a dark stain spreading out from his groin.

"Thank you for conducting me here." He smiled down at him. "I think we can carry on without your assistance." He gestured toward the hole they'd just come in through.

The chamberlain wasted no time in scrambling to his feet and scuttling out of the room.

"You shot my guards," the lord chided.

"And I could easily have done the same to you," Kuri replied, unruffled. He holstered his weapon. "Seeing as they've failed in their primary duty, I can only assume you'd have had them executed for dereliction anyway. I've saved us all some bother."

"Well, you certainly have my attention." The lord stepped over a dead guard and moved to a couch. "What message does your master send?"

"He finds it interesting that your overlord keeps you on the verge of becoming an elector."

Intrigued.

"My duty is to my overlord," the lord replied carefully.

Kuri sat in a chair facing him. "Loyalty is one of the most admirable qualities, but it's a binary system. If it's not reciprocated, it eventually decays. A wise overlord realizes that a grateful colleague is far better than a disgruntled subordinate."

Betrayal is best eased into. One must first portray it as a normal, even natural thing. Outline the root cause, blame it on the victim, and then promise open approval and support.

The lord waved off Kuri's words and leaned forward. "Let's come straight to it. You said 'elector'. That means the imperial court would like for me to seize a system and not out of any concern for my status. What is this proposed target that will give me my eighth system and why are we discussing this?"

For once, the personality modeler was correct. Kuri leaned in as well. "Heiropolis."

The lord drew back. "Your master has spent too much time at court and not enough in the real universe. I would rather bide my time and hope my overlord changes his mind. Do you really think Sandrak would smile upon such an endeavor? I'd be splitting his holdings in half!

"Given the recent scandal, he'd also expect a free hand in dealing with me."

"And if he didn't have that free hand?"

"Don't offer me hints and riddles! If you want me to risk my neck, then you'd better lay your pieces on the board – all of them!"

"Taking Heiropolis is contentious, to say the least," Kuri admitted. "We would have to dispatch a force of Imperial Varangians with an adjudicator who would, of course, find your claim to be valid. You should put something together, before you launch your assault – perhaps the cousin of a long-lost uncle who once ruled there…"

"Where will this force be staged," the lord demanded, "and how quickly can it arrive?"

"A neighboring system. Not here, obviously. We don't want to arouse suspicion."

"And the court will confirm me as an elector?"

"They will," Kuri confirmed, "but there's more to the bargain…"

"There always is, isn't there?"

New doubts growing. Too good to be true…

Kuri held up a hand. "It all comes *before* you take the system. When you seize Heiropolis, everything will have to move very quickly, including your elevation to elector, or the entire enterprise will unravel."

"Then what's missing from this puzzle?"

"You need to conduct false-flag operations in Sandrak's territory, in the half that's farthest from Throne World."

"You want to draw off his forces from the closer half, then cut them off?" The lord shuddered. "If any part of this rump-ravaged enterprise should happen to go awry, I'll not only lose my current systems, I'll lose my skin as well!"

Kuri smiled. "Then we have an agreement?"

A.G. Claymore

Playing to Strengths

Scouts

Eth walked into the forward hanger and over to the cluttered corner where Noa, Hendy and Oliv were staring at a large hologram. Behind them was a row of seven old shuttle cores, just the main bus conduits, control linkages and propulsion systems. Next to each sat a neat, black cube of the nanites that had formed the hulls of the shuttles.

Mishak had ordered the small craft brought up from the surface before they left Kish. His explanation had been exciting, to say the least. Eth would be given command of a small scout-ship, one with an entirely Human crew. If all went well, they'd become the core of the fleet's security picket.

First, of course, they had to design the ship.

Noa shook his head, reaching out to drag a block of code from the main program. The entire aft section of the holographic ship disappeared. "It doesn't need to end there, Hendy," he insisted. "The shuttle's propulsion is pitch-based – no shaping involved. It can project the pitch field effectively out to fifty meters before it loses focus."

"I keep forgetting about the pitch-drive," the pilot admitted, scratching at the back of his head. "I'd still rather have the ability to shape a path. If the fleet shapes away in a fight, we'll be left behind if we just have a pitch-drive to run away with."

"So why not use two?" Eth asked.

Noa looked at him in surprise. "We only have seven cores!"

Eth shrugged. "So we only make three scout-ships at first and hold one core as a backup. We don't have enough Humans to man all seven anyway, not without leaving the fleet shorthanded."

Noa tilted his head, looking at the hologram, or through it. "The pitch-drives emit waves," he mused. "We could do interesting things with them if we can calibrate the controls for it." He looked over at Hendkenu. "Get it right and we can have the waves reinforce…"

"Screw it up," the pilot countered, "and someone has to scrape us off the bulkheads!"

Eth chuckled. "I have it on good authority, Hendy, that our job is already high-risk. What's a little more? We could almost match a shaped path at short to medium ranges."

Noa had already doubled the coding for the second core and now he was getting his fingers into the three dimensional representation. He dragged out the hull diameter until the core-mounts snapped into place.

"I'd be a lot happier if we had weapons on the damn thing," Oliv muttered.

"Me too," Noa admitted, "but I doubt our shipmates will want to give up any warheads for an expendable scout."

"Mass driver?" Hendy suggested.

Eth nodded. "Last-ditch weapon. Something this small won't likely get detected until they're right on top of us. If that happens, we smash something heavy into their ass and run for it."

"We could use nanites for the projectiles," Noa looked over to the matte black cubes on the deck.

"Would they even survive the acceleration of a railgun?" Eth asked. "If they break apart into a cloud, they won't even have enough concentration to overcome nav-shields, let alone combat shielding."

"Gotta use the head," Hendy said, trotting over to a hatch on the starboard side of the hangar.

"They can handle it," Noa replied confidently. "And they can be set to change shape once they're inside an enemy ship."

"Change shape?" Eth gave him a blank look.

"Sure, like anchoring to the nearest structural element and then sending out long spikes in random directions. Retract, rinse, repeat…"

"Continued random damage." Oliv's eyes gleamed. "The gift that keeps on giving!"

"How would they even stop something like that?" Eth wondered.

Noa was already back at the code screen. "Focused EM beam should do it," he said over his shoulder, "but I'd like to see them think of that in an emergency and it risks damaging their own nanites as well.

"We don't have a lot of mass to play with, so I'd have to identify expendable parts of the ship like storage compartments and privacy bulkheads."

"So you wouldn't be able to sneak your new girlfriend aboard," Oliv teased him, "because the walls might disappear in a fight…"

"Wait a minute." Eth stepped closer, noticing the red hue of Noa's ears. He looked at Oliv. "Girlfriend?"

"I'd hardly call her a girlfriend," Noa demurred, pretending to be absorbed in his work.

"She was groping you in the shower compartment," Oliv countered gleefully.

Noa sighed. "She was just curious." He abandoned the coding and turned to face them. "We've been talking at work, so she felt comfortable asking questions."

The shocked silence might have dragged out if Oliv hadn't been there. "What was she asking you?"

"Wanted to know if it was always… you know… external."

"And that required a physical inspection?" Oliv raised an eyebrow.

"Well… she also asked how it would go into a female when it was so… soft."

"And she soon found out how to make it change shape," she told Eth, "which is when I decided I was clean enough and left them to their *explorations.*"

"Hey! Nothing happened after you left," Noa protested. "Anyway, is it even possible?"

"Of course it is," she scoffed. "There've been cases throughout the centuries."

"Those could all be nothing but wild stories," Noa argued half-heartedly.

"Will you listen to him?" Oliv was laughing. "He's arguing against his own will. Would it make you feel any better if I told you I've had the occasional tumble with a Quailu male?"

Noa and Eth stared at her, mouths hanging open. "You... You um..." Noa stammered. "Anybody we know?"

"Nobody you'll know *about,*" she shot back. "But take it from me, their retractable part does the job just fine so I can't imagine you'd leave Allatu disappointed."

"Allatu?" Eth nearly shouted in shock. "Oliv, I thought you hated her!"

"I did," she admitted, "but since she's taken an *interest* in our boy Noa, here, she's been a lot easier to get along with.

"You should go for it," she advised Noa. "Just remember, she didn't grow up wardu like us, so it means more to her. Don't be an ass about it."

"I still don't even know if I want to..."

"I saw you in the shower, Noa, and I'm having a hard time un-seeing it. You definitely showed her that you want to."

Eth wondered what he'd have to do to stumble into a situation like that. He couldn't fraternize with one of the Humans that he might have to order into danger. None of the Quailu females aboard the *Dibbarra* fell under that restriction.

Perhaps some of them were curious as well?

Noa turned back to the screen. "Can we please get back to designing the ship that we're all going to die in?"

Hendy wandered back, frowning at the silent group, noticing the smiles on Eth and Oliv and the red face on Noa. "What did I miss?"

Noa let out an exaggerated sigh.

Family Reunion

Mishak looked over at the communications officer. "Say that again."

"Sir, the Lord Uktannu is aboard his own flagship. He's waiting for you to report to him there."

Mishak vacated his chair. "Captain, I'd be obliged if you could have a shuttle readied for me."

"Right away My Lord."

Mishak left the bridge. *What could he be up to?* His uncle Uktannu was very much Sandrak's brother. Mishak had been to Dur nine times and his uncle had always received him while seated on his throne. What military emergency would cause him to forgo a chance to lord it over the nephew who might one day inherit his service?

Arriving at the launch bay, he smiled at the growing scout-ship in the forward hangar. According to Eth, it was nearly ready to launch.

The shuttle ride was brief as was his reunion with his uncle.

He was ushered into the flagships ready-room, just off the bridge and Uktannu, not entirely above the family games, made Mishak wait while he completed a consult with his house-oracle, a consultation which could be heard through the open hatch.

"Your endeavors will bring about the destruction of a noble house," the holographic figure advised, "and a great opportunity will be seized."

Mishak felt the skin tighten at the back of his neck. Though he usually placed less stock in the mysticism of the older generation, the oracle's words aroused a sudden sense of unavoidable destiny.

Would they bring down the Emperor himself?

Uktannu stepped through the door.

Mild surprise at finding Mishak already there and... something else...

"Nephew," he grunted, waving a display into life over the table. "Let's see how you handle independent command. I need someone to hold down the Kwharaz region. We've had problems with the neighbors so step lightly unless someone needs a good punch in the primary gut."

If brevity was what Uktannu had in mind, then Mishak could play along. No doubt his uncle expected him to burst into a flurry of panicked questions about the situation in Kwharaz but he'd form his own opinions.

He'd most likely own the region someday, along with the rest of Sandrak's dominion, unless Uktannu managed to kill him off.

"Very well, uncle." He stood. "If we have nothing else to cover, I'll be getting underway immediately."

He detected no emotions – Uktannu was always a reserved one – but he did notice a slight facial tic that might indicate nervousness. He wished he could have brought Oliv along. She would probably have taken one look and warned Mishak that his uncle had unsavory plans against him.

Was this Sandrak's idea of a test by fire? If so, it seemed an unreasonable risk to take if you only had one heir.

He rode back to the *Dibbarra* in silence, though his pulse quickened at the sight of Oliv working under the new scout-ship. He returned her decorous nod and went straight to the bridge.

He settled into the force-commander's chair. "Captain Rimush, we'll be shaping space for the Kwharaz sector at your earliest convenience."

"Very good, sir," the fleet captain replied. "Communications officer, notify the fleet. We'll be passing coordinates for the Kwharaz sector within the hour. Navigation, set our course for the Chohot system and pass it to the rest of the fleet."

Mishak sank back into his thoughts as the bridge crew prepared for departure. Was he really here to protect his uncle's systems? Was he really Sandrak's only son? He frowned. Was Uktannu really Sandrak's brother or was he a son from some illicit encounter? Maybe Mishak's succession was less certain than he'd thought.

It made a twisted kind of sense, given that it involved Sandrak. It sounded like the kind of thing he'd do to simplify a complicated inheritance. Put both sons in the same area and see who survives.

He shook his head. That was crazy… probably.

The ship vibrated as it built up a compression of space-time in front of the bow and a dilation behind. The powerful engines were shifting the Universe past them.

He left the chair and headed for the forward bay. He wasn't going to unravel his relatives' motives any time soon so he might as well distract himself with the new scout-ship.

He smiled. Definitely the ship.

He saw nobody around the small craft when he entered the hangar bay, so he walked around to the back and climbed in through a large hole in the hull that they hadn't grown shut yet. He figured there were boarding hatches somewhere, but he hadn't been keeping close tabs on the project.

He could hear voices coming from the engine compartment so he walked in, finding Noa and, to his surprise, one of the Quailu crewmembers. Noa gave him a friendly nod but the Quailu looked nervous to find the fleet commander standing in front of her. He could feel it from her. She looked recently familiar for some reason.

"Almost ready for a shakedown run, Noa?"

"Nearly there, sir." Noa gestured at the Quailu. "Allatu was just helping me sort out a few glitches in field calibration. Get that wrong and we end up tearing the ship in half."

That was it. "You did well in that competition," he told her. "Even though it was only this lazy-ass Human, you still showed him not to challenge a Quailu to a race!"

She relaxed, both from picking up his sense of humor and from Noa's chuckle. "Oliv still got there first," she admitted, "and that was the goal of the whole test in the first place."

"Your accent," he mused. "You're not originally from Kish, are you?"

"I grew up on Prakha, sir. Came out to Kish with my aunt five years ago."

That explained why she didn't seem to mind working with Humans. She hadn't grown up with the idea of them being slaves. He sensed they wanted to get back to work.

And he wondered whether Oliv might be staking out his suite. Their encounters had always been on *her* initiative and he knew she wasn't in this small craft. She might be waiting to pounce. "I'm going to rest in my suite. You two enjoy yourselves."

He left, but not before catching mild alarm from Allatu at his parting remark.

Why the hells did everyone stop making sense all of a sudden?

The Shakedown

"Why didn't we bring cleaning supplies?" Glen grumbled. He was alone in the communications cubicle.

"You should at least be glad I made the consoles splash-proof," Noa shouted from the engineering compartment which dominated the middle of the scout-ship. "It's hardly our fault you decided to eat two servings of khled before coming along on a shakedown run. You'd better clean every nook and cranny up there. I don't want my baby smelling like stomach acid.

"That ought to do it, Eth," he added.

Eth came out of his deep breathing exercise. A lot of Quailu were probably watching them and most would already be laughing at their attempt to run with tandem pitch-drives. They could laugh, as far as he was concerned. None of them had ever bothered to try it because they just used the commercially available patterns and the Quailu weren't keen on small craft in fleet operations.

Perhaps it was some atavistic herd mentality but they liked to just hammer their way in and win by sheer brute force. Mishak was more open to new things, perhaps because he'd spent so much time slumming with his Humans, but he'd still be inclined to fight in the old way.

Nonetheless, he'd brought Humans aboard his ships and he usually used them in stealthy operations, stealing information or technology. It wasn't much of a leap for him to look for a finesse role that they could fill. The Quailu did make efforts to secure their flanks and provide early warning but that work usually fell to the frigates. It drew off useful combat power from the main body so, if they could prove the scout-ship concept, it would give Mishak more hitting power, allowing him to concentrate his ships.

"Give it another try, Hendy."

"Roger that. Initiating a lateral shift."

The ship lurched sideways, the fleet blurring past them beyond the front windows. Kwharaz-3, the namesake for the entire sector, flashed by. Eth could feel his upper torso pulled to port a lot more than his lower body. His inner ear gave it up for a bad job and left his stomach to its own devices. It decided it had had enough and tried to climb out through his throat. "Belay!"

He kept his eyes closed but he could tell they'd stopped.

"Hammurabi's balls!" Henku gasped. "I'd forgotten I was the one flying this bucket till you told me to stop!"

Eth lurched out of his seat, not bothering to answer the sweat-soaked pilot. He stood, facing aft, until his stomach settled down and then he started for engineering. Glen was retching in his cubicle but his stomach was already empty from before.

"At least you're not making any more mess," Eth offered. "Good man!"

Glen didn't look up but he managed to give him the finger.

Eth chuckled, his stomach making him regret it immediately. If his people could still show some attitude after a ride like that, they'd learn to handle space-combat.

"You have that container," he said, pointing. "You can come out of there after you've cleaned up the mess." He shut the door on him.

"Hey!" Glen yelled through the panel.

Oliv poked her head out of the tactical cubicle, opposite Glen's communications room. "*Thank-you!*" she said in an exaggerated tone. "That was just nasty! Ruining the new ship smell."

A muffled "screw you!" came from behind Glen's door.

"It's sweet of you to offer," she shouted back, "but I'm all set for partners right now."

Eth continued back to engineering. He found Noa sitting in front of a code window. "Noa, the inertial dampening is way off."

"You're telling *me*? I was almost scrubbing my teeth with my stomach lining. I think we need to double up on the emitters." He chewed his right cheek meditatively, glancing up at the swarm of piping and lines above. "Yep. Ceiling's just the spot for 'em. The dampening field has a slight fall-off, starting right at the emitters, but you never notice on a capital ship. They maneuver so slowly you don't feel any differences. At the speeds we're trying, it could cause internal injuries or even worse."

He got up and walked to the starboard side, looking up at the spaces between the lines. "With a second set above us, aimed down, we can complement that falloff. It'll take a little tweaking, but we can test it out easily enough."

"How long?"

Noa held up a hand to stall him and walked back to his screen. He moved a few lines of code, copied a couple of blocks, pasting them into new locations and then typed in a few extra lines.

"Ready, but some of the emitters will grow pretty close to the pressure hull. The compiler always prioritizes some systems over others. Inertial dampening is critical for a number of reasons and it's way higher up the decision-tree than the pressure hull, especially since the source code was written by a species that removes atmo from their ships before a fight to prevent catastrophic breaches."

"So... you're saying?"

Noa waved at the ceiling. "I'm saying the system will cannibalize the hull to grow the new emitters, then it'll use our spare nanites to repair the hull."

"Can't you tell it not to do that?"

"Sure," Noa shrugged, "but you don't want to monkey around with that stuff. If you forget to set one little trigger back to normal, you end up with a damage controller algorithm that'll get you killed.

"Believe me, you don't want the ship to prioritize the hull over inertial dampening. You'll end up with a nice shiny hull full of squashed crewmen."

"So, we need to close up our suits for this?"

"Just say the word when we're all ready, Boss." Noa activated his helmet and gloves.

Eth walked back to comms and opened the door.

Glen glared at him. "You guys are assholes!"

"We are. Thanks for noticing!" Eth responded cheerfully. "And what kind of ass are you?"

Glen frowned at him. He'd heard the question from old Ab a thousand times. Whenever he wanted to drive a lesson home with one of his fighters, he'd use it. "A dumbass?"

As an answer, Eth leaned forward and touched the emergency close button on Glen's suit. A spherical shell enveloped his head and then shrank down to proper size as the nanite-based helmet flowed into place.

"Smells better now, doesn't it?" Eth asked. He tapped the side of Glen's helmet. "Never accept the situation. There's always a better way."

"Yeah," Glen admitted, "the stink is gone."

Oliv laughed.

Glen gave her a mock-angry look. "That offer still stands…"

She made a face. "No, thanks, Retch!"

"Oh, hells no! That is not gonna be my call sign on this bucket…"

"Alright, knock it off you numbskulls!" Eth climbed into his seat next to Hendy. "Everybody close up. We might have hull breaches while the new emitters grow." He waited till all suits read as closed and operating in his heads-up display before pumping the air into storage.

He opened a channel to all the suits. "Noa, you're clear to go ahead and make the changes."

Eth looked up and, sure enough, small sections of hull above him were dissolving away and flowing in to form the new emitters. It took less than two minutes to finish the new nodes and then the hull flowed forward to close the gaps. He got up to look in the back and found that one large hole had been left above the cube of spare nanites in the cargo area, just aft of engineering.

Rather than bringing the new replacement material forward to seal each individual breach, the hull shifted sections forward to seal the breaches, leaving one collected hole at the back where the new material wouldn't have as far to travel.

The hole closed up as he watched.

"Repressurizing," Noa advised.

A faint hiss slowly grew in volume as it created the atmosphere to carry it. Eth's HUD gave him a green indicator and he opened up again.

That first breath after a re-press always had a slightly oily taste.

"We're ready to try again?"

"Yeah, but take it easy this time. Let's do a one gee acceleration and I'll get some data. We might want to do a little more adjusting to make sure nobody suddenly loses their eighth vertebra through their chest or anything."

"Y'know, that might have been a more sensible way for us to have run our last few attempts," Eth muttered.

"Maybe," Noa conceded, "but they implanted us with crew skills not with ship design and testing. I'd say we're doing pretty damn well so far."

Eth returned to his seat. "Keep it to one gravity this time, OK?"

Hendy grinned. "Fine with me."

"Anytime you're ready, Hendy."

"We're already moving," the pilot replied, grinning. "One gee forward."

"Huh!" He kept quiet for a few minutes, half expecting another gut-wrenching evolution.

Noa came up to kneel between them. "Found a few trouble-spots but they should all be gone now. Wanna try something more fun?"

The three men shared a look.

"Set up an attack run on the *Dibbarra*, Hendy." Eth tightened his restraints, though he was certain this attempt would succeed.

"You're not gonna need those," Noa scoffed, "because, if you *do* end up needing them, they ain't gonna save you at high gee. The recovery team will be scraping pasta sauce off the bulkheads for days." He saw the pilot's look. "Just kidding, Hendy."

The pilot's shoulders relaxed slightly as he finished setting up his run.

Noa grinned. "Because they'd probably just dissolve the ship back into a cube and then hose off the hangar deck."

Frowning, Hendy's finger stabbed at the control panel.

The entire fleet suddenly snapped back into view with brutal speed. The ships appeared to spread, rapidly growing until only the hull of the *Dibbarra* was visible through the windows.

Eth grabbed his armrests, his knuckles turning white, and even Noa was holding onto the back of Eth's chair.

They stopped so suddenly that the three men twitched in alarm.

"Whew!" Eth shuddered. "That was intense!"

"Why'd we stop here?" Noa was looking out the windows above the front seats. The large circular armature that generated the spatial distortion of the *Dibbarra's* shaping drive loomed overhead like a planetary ring.

"Blind spot in their sensor suite," the pilot said quietly. "They'll be wondering where we went." He wiped a hand across his forehead. "That seemed a lot less horrifying when I laid it into the helm!"

Who's laughing now? Eth thought. *Still the Quailu, but now they're laughing at their own instead of at us.* The other ships would know where they were because the only blind spot they were in was the *Dibbarra's*. They'd know the sensor team aboard their flagship was scrambling to figure out what had just happened.

Oliv came forward, stopping next to Noa. "It still stinks back there," she declared. "When are we gonna try moving this bucket? I wanna get back aboard the flagship and spend an hour in the shower-hall getting this smell off me."

The three men looked at each other, hardly believing she'd been completely unaware while they were scaring themselves half to death. After that kind of strain, there was no stopping it. They all broke out laughing.

"What?" she demanded, but they just laughed harder. Her skin flushed and, given her comment about taking a shower, she was probably interpreting their reaction all wrong. "Glen was right." She stormed off. "You guys *are* assholes!"

Shore Leave

Eth passed through an open airlock onto the station's main concourse. From the looks of the undisturbed corrosion on the huge doorframe, it hadn't even been test-closed in a few centuries.

He forgot about the door and stopped walking, his mouth hanging open. The space in front of him was immense.

The station orbiting Kwharaz was the size of a small shepherd moon and the middle was an open space that could have swallowed up the entire fleet without even noticing.

He had no real plan, but he had four hours before he needed to be back on the ship and the chance to get away from everything was impossible to pass up. He never realized what a luxury it had been to serve under Ab. With Ab dead, his entire unit looked to him for answers.

He walked across the busy surface-street, stepping around a patch of bird droppings beneath a lamp-post. He approached the railing on the far side. Looking down, he thought he saw the bottom but it was kilometers away. The ceiling, if that word applied to something so large, curved away into the hazy distance.

A roughly spherical conglomeration floated in the middle and he'd been told it contained the majority of the station's commercial and entertainment districts. It also served as a transit node for people and goods travelling from one side to the other. He had no specific destination in mind so he headed for one of the barge docks.

There was a toll-gate but he just jumped the railing and dropped into the barge, knowing he wouldn't get caught. He took a seat just as another alien did the same thing. He was slightly taller than Eth but built more lightly. A single, heavy plate of flat horn, triangular in shape, descended between wide-set eyes that stayed on Eth as he sat across from him.

The forehead plate was Eth's first clue.

The barge pulled away from the dock and turned for the central globe. When they left the bleed edge of the station decking, he noticed that the gravity didn't extend above the gunwales of the barge. A good jump could send you floating off into the empty space. He let his arms float free to confirm it, then dropped them back into the gravity, feeling like a yokel.

He shrugged at the tall alien, who was still watching him, but the creature made no attempt to reciprocate the gesture.

Screw you, buddy.

About a half kilometer into the trip, they ran into moist air. Droplets of increasing size were coalescing all around them. With no gravity out here, atmospheric water had nowhere to go unless it was picked up by one of the small orange and white collector ships that plied the damp weather.

He leaned forward, which finally seemed to elicit a reaction from his new companion, but it was mastered quickly. Curious, Eth sat back again, just missing a large lump of water that undulated past where his head had been. He gave up on the alien and concentrated on avoiding the water.

He could see now why the grav field only reached as far as the gunwales. Any higher and it would be pulling a torrent of rain down on the passengers. He noticed they were all leaning down with their heads between their knees or, if space permitted, laying on their sides on the benches to avoid the water.

Why can't they just put a shield out front? He lay over on his side, noticing the other creature merely sat upright, making no effort to avoid the water.

It seemed completely improbable, but not a single drop touched him. Eth could have called this his second clue, but why waste time. That kind of luck was confirmation enough.

He'd never seen a Varangian before.

The water seemed to have passed or, rather, they'd passed the water, so he sat up again. The globe was closer now and he could make out a steady stream of cargo vehicles on flight paths that led to the arms radiating from the outside surface of the station where freighters docked. The interiors of the arms were hollow to allow fast access from the receiving docks to the commercial zones deep inside the station.

They pulled up to wait for their turn at a dock and he could smell the place. Spices, hot food, garbage and the sweat of a thousand races all mingled in an exotic brew. It made a surprisingly pleasant change from the musky odor of his Quailu crewmates.

These were people who didn't automatically think of Humans as slaves and they didn't have any expectations of him either.

Nobody out here gave any thought to a backwater like Kish.

The barge ahead of them finally backed away and they slid into place. He hopped off and set a course for the center, not as a result of any particular logic; he was just letting his feet choose while he enjoyed the new environment.

Centuries of grunge had accumulated in every corner. Cooking-grease smoke from the myriad hole-in-the-wall cook-shops had settled onto every surface and, where it didn't get ground away by shoes, it trapped dirt, building up a crust, spattered here and there with droppings from the birds and small pests that infested every station in the empire.

His stomach growled and he turned down a side alley, narrowly avoiding a small delivery vehicle that careened around a corner. The smells were promising good food. He stepped over the extended legs of a Vegan youngster who sat outside a noodle shop, scrubbing sensory hairs from the back of some kind of arachnid they'd be featuring in that night's menu. Another Vegan, probably his little brother, was rinsing small cups in a trickle of water that ran along the curb.

Eth made a mental note to observe the plumbing arrangements of any place he decided to eat at.

He picked a shop at random but their menu was one of those annoying holo screens that kept changing every time you thought you'd spotted something you might like to try.

He moved on, finding a shop with an interactive holo-menu and bought some kind of dead animal on a stick. He had no idea what it was or where it came from but it had a great sauce on it. The meat was cooked to a crisp so it was probably safe. By the third bite, the salt content was making itself unmistakably obvious. He continued along in search of something to drink.

The alley opened up on a small urban crevasse of sorts and he stopped at a small bar that was little more than a walk-up counter where the bartender stood with his back to the railing. It gave a great view of the open space and, more importantly, the bartender was washing something in a sink that had suds in it.

Eth ordered an orange-hued ale. He took a deep drink, then set it down to take another bite.

The hairs on the back of his neck sprang up and he looked to his right. The Varangian was standing next to him. He was annoyed but did his best to pretend the creature wasn't there.

"You're a Human, aren't you?"

Eth finished chewing his last bite of… whatever… and tossed the stick in a collection bin behind the bar. "Yes." He took another drink.

"I've never seen a Human before," the Varangian said. "I thought they all had to stay in their sector. Aren't all of your people wardu?"

"Not all of us," Eth grunted. "Not anymore."

"Ah." He nodded. "Lots of native species filling out the ranks lately, given all the excitement." He looked over at Eth. "Not many arboreals, though."

"You have a problem with that?"

"Why should I?" The Varangian sounded mildly amused. "My species is arboreal as well. Something about leaping for branches and not missing… It opens evolutionary paths – sometimes."

"We're certainly rare, you and I," Eth admitted, turning to look at the creature. His face was mildly unsettling. The hard plate on his forehead gave him a fierce appearance. "What stroke of wild luck brought the two of us to this conversation?"

"Luck is a deliberate thing, Human. Some of us may be more deliberate than others, but never mistake luck for mere numeric chance."

"Ok, my deliberate, arboreal *brother* – what deliberate stroke of luck put us here together?"

The Varangian gazed back at him for a heartbeat. "That toll collector, back at the barge dock – he works on commission. He'd slit his own mother's throat before he'd let her ride free… Well, mother-in-law, at least.

"There's a fair amount of money lost through rail-jumpers, so he employs a couple of urchins to watch the rail for him. They get paid every time they catch someone and the little brats are hungry. They don't lose focus."

"So?"

"So, how did you know you'd get away with jumping the toll?"

"You with the transit police?"

"I'm a forensic accountant."

"Then why all the questions?"

Another pause. "Because you seem very lucky, my arboreal acquaintance." He'd somehow managed to make it sound almost like an accusation.

Eth was getting tired of talking about himself. "You're really an accountant?"

"Why not?"

"I guess I thought you'd turn out to be an imperial guardsman."

"I get that a lot. Would it surprise you to know that my world has an entire economy of its own? We have soldiers, cops, politicians, accountants, welders, washroom attendants…"

"You mean those guys that sit by the hand-washers, handing out mints? They creep me out and, given what you were just doing, where do they expect you to put the mints?"

"You're changing the topic…"

"Yes, I am. That's what you do in a conversation. It's frowned upon, however, in an interrogation, so piss off." He turned back to his ale and took another drink.

The Varangian inclined his head. "As you wish. I'll…"

Eth looked over, intrigued by the pause and frowned. The mug he was setting down on the counter missed and tumbled down onto the barman's shelf, splashing ale everywhere.

The young Human female they were both staring at turned to them and went immediately into a slight crouch, eyes wide in shock.

Before Eth could say anything, her expression went blank and she turned to sprint away, her dirty orange jumpsuit still advertising her progress until she ducked down a side alley.

"One of your crew?" the Varangian asked.

"No."

Without another word, the alien raced off after the woman.

Eth stood there, frowning until the barman's complaints finally registered. With an irritated glance at the ale-soaked creature, he waved his wrist over a scanner to pay for his drink and then set off after the Varangian.

Why would an accountant take such an interest in some random Human? Why would he take an even greater interest in the wild-looking woman they'd just seen?

More to the point – who the hells *was* she?

He jumped, sailing over a trashcan knocked over by a drunk, and landed lightly, swerving right to head down a side alley parallel to the one she and the Varangian had disappeared into. He raced through the startled crowd, fending off elbows and protrusions as he approached the outer end, facing onto the massive open space of the station.

A deep thrumming noise vibrated his gut just before he rounded the corner to find the woman lying on the ground with the Varangian jogging over to her.

"Thought you were just an accountant," Eth commented, nodding at the small stun emitter in the other's hand.

"Well…" The Varangian shrugged. "… Not *just*." He knelt beside the woman.

"I'm trying to decide what to ask first –" Eth admitted. "Why you were following me, why you chased that woman or why you *shot* her with a stun weapon."

"We've been curious about you Humans for a long time now," the Varangian explained as he slid his weapon into a pocket. He leaned forward to gently open one of the woman's eyelids. Apparently satisfied with what he saw there, he stood again, turning to face Eth.

"As for her, she ran." He grinned at Eth. "It seemed churlish of me to simply ignore the gesture and, as I've said, we're curious about you."

"So why stun her instead of me?"

"You're mushkenu." He nodded down at the woman. "She's wardu and, from the look of her, she's been on the run from her owners for a long time. That makes her contraband."

Eth's right hand came to rest on his holstered weapon. That word didn't sit well with him. He'd been a member of her class a few short weeks ago but he was surprised at how angry he now felt at hearing one of his own kind referred to as contraband.

A major part of coming to terms with his own freedom involved a re-definition of his views on Humanity in general. Comments that would have passed unremarked now had new impact for him. You couldn't insult a slave.

But you *could* insult a mushkenu.

The Varangian seemed to read some of this in Eth's facial expressions, or perhaps simply from his hand moving to his weapon. "I mean no insult to your species," he asserted. "You have no need to fear for her safety, assuming, of course, you don't intend to claim custody." His tone pitched the last part of his statement as a question.

Eth was on the verge of challenging the need for custody at all but remembered that she was, technically, a wardu and, therefore, contraband. "What do you intend to do with her?"

"Nothing untoward, I assure you," he replied sincerely. "No harm will come to her, but we *will* test her. We *will* have our answers."

"Answers to what?"

The Varangian grinned, holding out his right arm in formal greeting. "When we have our answers, Human, *you* will know the question."

Eth waved his own right forearm over the alien's, exchanging contact data. *Hjalmar,* his implant whispered to his consciousness and he shuddered at the sudden intrusion. This was his first formal introduction as a free citizen. Slaves didn't get social implants.

The Varangians, though they had, eventually and at massive cost, been conquered and incorporated into the HQE, had never been enslaved. Their uncanny prowess as warriors had earned them the right, not only to avoid enslavement, but also to remain outside the class conventions of the empire. They had kept their naming conventions unsullied by the tags of the lower and slave classes.

"Eth," the Varangian nodded his head, deliberately omitting any reference to class, which was probably meant as a courtesy. "We will meet again, when we have more to discuss."

Eth knew he was being told to bugger 0ff but, to be honest, it was done far more politely than he'd done only moments earlier at the bar. Something told him to trust this person, despite his own questions about the unconscious mystery woman. "Very well, Hjalmar," he replied, finally removing his hand from his sidearm. "I'll find you next time we're here."

Human

He turned and walked away, in no way certain that he'd done the right thing but he didn't know what else he could have done.

And he was burning to know why the Varangians were so interested in his kind.

What Was That?

"Mmm!" Eth made a show of sniffing the pellet he'd just dropped onto his platter. "Mystery protein!" He put it into one of the three small ovens that sat between engineering and the bunks. Their little scout ship was finally complete.

Almost.

The oven's sensors scanned the pellet and emitted a brief blue flash, giving it just the right amount of moisture and energy to reconstitute.

He pulled it out. "Steak!" It resembled a normal steak, which it *had* been before it got collapsed, except for the half that looked like it had been buried with one of the ancient emperors for use in the afterlife.

He put the plate back in the cycler and, using the desiccated half as a handle took a bite as he walked forward. He stuck his head in the engineering space. "Oven's still a bit off, Noa."

"Hey! Is that steak?"

"Some of it is…" Eth carried on up to the bridge. "Anything change in the last eight hours, Edku?"

"Hendy thought he saw a reflection. Was that when you were on with him?" the backup pilot asked.

"No, must have been the second half of his shift." He stepped back to the tactical cubicle. "You got any data on Hendy's mystery sighting?"

Oliv brought up a recorded projection. "It was only for a few seconds and then it was gone. It's consistent with a sizeable vessel but there's no way to be sure. It's faint enough to be a glitch but…"

"But it could also be a screen-frigate running picket for a hostile force," Eth finished for her.

"Has a conflict been declared?"

"Not to my knowledge but, out here, we wouldn't hear anything until we had warheads inbound anyway." He took another bite and chewed while staring at the replay.

It could be nothing but he wouldn't keep his crew alive very long trusting to that kind of assumption. He needed more information.

There were three minor lords out that way with direct borders on the Kwharaz sector. Any one of them might consider probing for weaknesses. Still, the suspected ships were moving the wrong way if they wanted to penetrate the sector.

The trace they had was minimal, almost too close to the margin of error to even call it a vector, but it still looked to be moving along the border between the Kwharaz sector and its unfriendly neighbors.

"Assuming it's a real vector, extend it for me so we can see where it's headed."

Oliv selected the icon for the contact and extended a line along its estimated path. "I wouldn't want to bet on being able to intercept using this," she warned.

"That's fine, Oliv. I just want to get us close enough for a better look. You listening, Ed?"

"I got nothing else to entertain me."

"I want us to stay between that projected course and the local star. Start moving us in closer."

"Won't we be easy to spot if the sun's behind us?"

"If we were a frigate or a cruiser, sure." Eth nodded toward the stern. "This gal's not much bigger than a shuttle. The algorithms in their sensors'll scrub us out, assuming we're just random noise."

"Eth," Glen spoke up, "should I signal the fleet and let them know we're gonna move off-station?"

"Not yet. Even with a narrow beam, we risk some of it bouncing off one of our ships and getting picked up. We'll see what's out there first."

Ed pushed them forward at ninety percent acceleration. With no visible frame of reference, they might have been sitting still. The boredom set back in. The mild excitement of having maybe seen something soon faded as they got farther and farther from their assigned station.

And then it paid off.

Eth thought he saw faint twinkles of light.

"Multiple contacts!" Oliv called out. "Ninety-eight by fifteen by point six-seven – holding station at those coordinates. I'm getting a main body of five larger ships and six smaller contacts around them. Estimate as a squadron-size raiding force – cruisers with a frigate screen. That initial contact must have been on picket."

"Check the Orbat," Eth told her, trying not to lean over her shoulder. He was going to talk to Noa about getting rid of these cubicles. He couldn't even remember why they'd decided to partition the bridge crew like this. It was probably just left in some old coding.

"No friendlies in the area," she confirmed from the order-of-battle list.

"Sound general quarters," Eth told the system. "Glen, *now* we contact the *Dibbarra*. Get the summary from Oliv and fire it off as fast as you can. We need to bring our force into contact with these guys."

Mishak had eighteen ships at his disposal. With surprise on his side, he should be able to make short work of the interlopers.

Mishak walked onto the bridge to find Captain Rimush moving sideways past the tactical holo. "Report."

"Sire, a scouting report indicates a five-cruiser force with a six-frigate screen sitting in our territory. We have no friendlies in the area."

126

"Then they need a kick in the teeth!" Mishak rubbed his hands together. "Which captain found them?"

"Not a captain, Sire, a warrant officer." He had no need to say more. Most of their scouts were frigates – a captain's command. The one exception was Eth and his Human-designed scout-ship.

"It would seem our experiment was a success," Mishak observed. "You've been fighting for a long time, Captain," he continued in a low voice. "My father speaks very highly of your abilities so I have no qualms about leaning on your experience. What would you recommend?"

Rimush's posture, usually a picture of military correctness, somehow managed to draw him up by at least another inch in height at this statement. "Immediate attack, Sire. We bring the cruisers straight down their throat in a reverse-hemi formation and coordinate the path-shift to put our frigates on their starboard beam. Catch 'em in a crossfire."

"Sounds good." Mishak's eyes glinted. He could feel Rimush's enthusiasm for the coming fight and it was infectious. "Perhaps we can get in close enough so we come out of path with our guns charged. Hit 'em with slugs *and* warheads!"

"Aye, Sire!" Rimush's approval wasn't feigned. "We can get some much-needed experience for our crews out of this." He turned to his staff, ensuring the plan was being coordinated with the other captains.

"That'd be the fleet," Eth said, seeing all the twinkling lights as their ships dropped out of path around the enemy. "Move us in, Ed. Let's see if we can help."

"Oh, sure," Oliv chimed in. "Our dinky little pop-gun oughta scare the hells out of... Who are we fighting, anyway?"

"Don't know," Eth replied calmly, "and I don't care. They shouldn't be sitting out there so we're gonna shoot at them."

There was a bright flash of plasma. None of the eye-searing brilliance one sees after a drop out from a long path. It was a short jump.

"Two of the enemy contacts have broken off and micro-pathed to get behind our fleet," Oliv warned. "One cruiser and one frigate."

They could just sit and wait, he knew. They'd done what they were supposed to do. They'd found an enemy force and they'd guided the main body into combat with it. In the after-battle assessment, there would be a nod from Mishak for doing exactly as expected.

Eth frowned, watching the two ships grow larger in their cockpit windows. Nobody ever lasted in this business by doing what was *expected*.

"Oliv, rig for combat and lock your pop-gun on that cruiser."

"Rigging for combat," she replied, and all the helmets snapped shut, "but you realize our first shot will light us up. They'll have their secondaries firing at us in half a heartbeat. That's assuming they don't pick up the initial heat-loss from our reconfig before we fire."

The last of their air was pumped into storage and hatches along the sides grew open to space.

"That's why this is Ed's great moment!" Eth grinned, slapping the pilot on the shoulder. "He's going to show those douche-nozzles what maneuverability can do for close-in combat."

Hendy came forward with a block of nanites. He slapped it onto the front of Eth's suit and it flowed into place across the bottom of the breastplate. "Congratulations," he said. "You're now an official damage-control auxiliary." He climbed into the co-pilot seat.

"We're close enough for gunnery," Oliv advised. "If you can even call it that with only one gun… What the hells took you so long?" The last was directed to Lil, her second-shift counterpart. They'd decided that, during combat, both shifts should report to duty stations rather than stand around waiting to repair damage.

"Let's get in a little closer." Eth gripped a stanchion, as though expecting the ship to lurch out of the way of fire at any moment. "I don't want them getting any more warning of an incoming round than absolutely necessary."

"It'll also leave us less time to fret over their return fire as well." Oliv chuckled darkly. "So we've also got that going for us! No, I'll stay on weapons," she told Lil. "You take sensors."

"Speaking of sensors," Lil said, looking up to catch Eth's eye, "we're a stealthy little ship, but even *we* can't stay hidden much longer at this range. They're bound to pick up the gravitational signature of our drives any second now."

"Alright, Oliv." Eth turned to look out the front. "Give 'em an ass-full of nanites!"

"Firing on the cruiser!"

Eth shuddered as the railgun howled. Its frequency never failed to elicit a sliver of primal fear. Even Oliv refrained from comment, other than to report rounds-complete.

"Emergency evasive!" he shouted at the pilot and the two enemy ships immediately slipped out of view.

"Some inbound secondary rounds now," shouted Lil, "and I'm reading a spike in both ships... It's not for their guns." She shook her head. "They're charging their main engines!"

"They're running?" Eth couldn't believe it. "Must be another micropath..." No, he knew they were leaving. They were all leaving.

"Firing!" Oliv shouted.

"Impact from our first round!" Liv announced. "The nanite mass penetrated and it's active. I'm reading... Holy hells!" She pounded the bulkhead beside her output screen. "The energy spike just dissipated throughout the ship! It looks like one of those nanite spears cut into the main bus. That ship's dead in the black!"

"Their secondaries are still active." Eth leaned toward the pilot. "Ed, better..."

"Mass-separation!" Lil shouted. "Mass-sep from the frigate. Possible warheads showing on the trace!"

Eth's blood ran cold. They may have an advantage over the single, micro-sized pitch-drive in a warhead but a brace of warheads had the combined hive-computing power to box them in and wipe them out. Oddly, Eth remembered the order he'd been about to give Ed but now it was for a new reason and not the obvious one.

"Ed, back us off from the targets, fast as she'll move!"

He wasn't concerned about their ability to evade the limited event-horizon of the warheads. He was worried about secondary explosions from their target.

"The warheads are converging on the cruiser." Lil cast a quick glance at Oliv. "They're shifting. The frigate is in-path. They're gone!"

A dark sphere seemed to appear in the cruiser's bow, the hull and supporting structure crumpling and shredding into the darkness. A second and third sphere appeared farther back and the center of the ship was gone in the blink of an eye. The last two spheres joined, their combined effect also pulling the first sphere aft.

Eth and the crew watched in silence. Though they'd been shooting at the cruiser only a few seconds ago, they shared all crewmen's universal hatred of singularity weapons. Being thrown from a shattered hull to die in the void was nothing compared to the soul-sucking beast currently devouring the enemy ship.

The three spheres had joined into one large malevolent rift and the remainder of the enemy cruiser fell into it. A threshold was passed and the inbound mass destabilized the artificially created phenomenon. With the shaky equilibrium gone, the contents were released as energy.

"Brace!" Eth shouted.

The expanding front hit them, but there were few parts of the original ship that hadn't already been consumed. A few small pieces pattered against their hull and most of the radiation was easily handled by the bow, though some bled in through the open sides. Eth felt a mild vibration and he looked down to find that he still held the remains of his steak. It was sizzling silently in the deadly energy. He dropped it with a shudder.

Fortunately, he'd thought to back away. Doubling their distance from the origin of the blast cut the radiation levels to a quarter of the original total and they'd already quadrupled their original distance, cutting exposure to just over six percent of the original.

He watched his steak curling up on the floor between the pilots. The radiation levels would have been more than enough to overpower their suits if they hadn't backed off. They'd have left nothing more than charred remains and an empty ship for a *new* Human crew to inhabit.

"Main body of the enemy fleet's bugged out as well," Lil announced. "Flagship's demanding a status report and they signal no severe damage to the fleet."

"Why'd they do that?" Hendy turned to look up at Eth. "They killed their own guys. Are they that reluctant to surrender to Humans?"

"They don't know we're Humans," Ed countered.

"We could've scavenged a ton of useful gear from their ships," Oliv groused. "We would have observed the forms regarding the crew."

"Maybe that's the problem," Eth said before he realized he was thinking it. Still, it explained a lot. "Maybe they don't want us talking to that crew and finding out where they came from or, more damning, who gave them their orders."

Oliv cursed. "Is it just me, or is this just the same job we used to do, except on a larger scale?"

Eth gave her a wan smile. "Welcome to politics in the HQE!"

"You figure they were sent here to make it look like the neighbors are getting frisky?" She frowned. "Seems a little too convoluted."

"In this case," he countered, "it's the simplest explanation. They destroyed that cruiser to maintain secrecy. If it really was the neighboring lords, they wouldn't screw around with secrecy, they'd attack outright and seize what they could. If you want to turn us against them, then you try to give an *impression* of an attack."

"Yeah," Noa interrupted, stepping into the crowded cockpit, "that's all great stuff, but we have bigger fish to fry."

Everyone turned in alarm.

"Our ship just saved our collective hides," Noa went on, "and she still doesn't have a name. That's just bad joss."

A few muttered insults were thrown as they visibly relaxed but they were all said with smiles.

"How about the *Crispy Lunch Platter*?" Ed offered, picking up the tiny black curl that used to be Eth's steak.

"The *Snitch*," Glen insisted.

"I got it," Oliv announced, stepping out of her cubicle. "*Your Last Chance*!"

Ed was the first to get it. "Imagine hailing some dumb bastard! *Unidentified vessel, this is* Your Last Chance*!* They'd be so damned confused!"

They all laughed, glad of the release after the adrenaline rush of the last few moments. It trailed off into chuckles and the occasional snort. A few heads tilted, thoughtful.

"Hmm," Eth looked at Oliv. "That works for me."

"That's gonna get confusing," Noa grumbled.

"Not within a friendly fleet," Eth countered. "We'd be in the ORBAT files and who gives a pile of fresh droppings about an enemy being confused?"

Noa stumped off back to his engines. "Should've left well enough alone…"

After Action

Eth stopped just outside the door to the *Dibbarra's* ready room and turned to two of the Human petty officers who'd been recruited, along with their teams, to shore up the crews of Mishak's fleet.

After triggering a coalition war, the Lord of Kish had decided to ease off on the raiding, so he had a few extra teams, all grown at great expense, with nothing left to do. Eth had helped him select crews for the second and third scout-ships from among the many Humans now serving in the fleet.

They had off-world combat experience but they were still green at running ships of their own, except for the shuttles they'd used on raids. "This is a captains meeting," he told them, "so you all qualify for entry. Don't let any of those guys in there back you down. You give them a single opening and they'll be all over you."

He grinned at their alarmed faces. "But try to have fun!" He turned and led them inside.

The large oval table had been sunk down flush with the floor and a holographic projection of the enemy force was filling the middle of the room.

The buzz of argument stopped as they all turned to look at the three Humans. Eth forced himself to keep walking as though he weren't doing this for the first time. His legs felt as like they were made of lead and he was certain that he was now overcompensating by putting too much roll in his gait.

He came to a stop and gazed up at the projected fleet. It was far better to ignore the Quailu captains before they got a chance to ignore him. The two Humans with him followed his example.

His discomfort faded as the image grabbed his attention. *Why were they just sitting there?* He'd assumed they were on their way to attack one of Uktannu's systems, but this behavior made no sense.

134

They'd been in the border zone but it was a foolish place to assemble an attack on Mishak's uncle.

Mishak came in, nodding to his assembled captains, Flag Captain Rimush in tow. "Gentlemen, we can all congratulate ourselves on an excellent first skirmish! We've given our foes a rough handling, costing them a cruiser, and we've validated the concept of a dedicated scout-ship design."

Eth kept his eyes on Mishak but he knew he was back to being the center of attention.

"Our new scout crew however," Rimush interjected, "moved off-station without notifying fleet command."

"That's right," Mishak confirmed. "Perhaps the warrant officer commanding that ship can clarify why."

"We had a possible contact," Eth explained. "It needed further investigation. I decided there was too much risk in sending a signal back to the fleet until we knew what was out there. If our signal bounced back their way and got intercepted, we'd have found nothing out there."

"Are you suggesting this should be added into the standard operating procedures for scouts?" Rimush asked.

"Not quite, sir. I think it should be tolerated on a case by case basis. It does carry a risk of the scout being destroyed and leaving the fleet blind."

"How fortunate for you that we're still alive to agree with your actions!" Mishak grinned. "On to the next matter. Who in the seven layers of hell did we fight and what were they thinking, sitting in the Kwharaz sector?"

Eth had been savoring the relief at not being sanctioned over his decisions but Mishak's question yanked him back to the present. "Repairs, My Lord?"

"They showed light battle damage," Mishak confirmed. "Nothing severe."

Eth stepped closer to the projection. "We assumed they were on their way to some black-flag operation, trying to implicate us…"

"Looks like they were on their way back instead," Mishak finished for him.

Eth nodded absently. "I suppose, if you've just shot up an objective while pretending to be someone you're not, you don't run straight home, you run to an enemy's territory."

"How do you know they're trying to conceal their identity?" one of the captains asked.

Eth looked at Mishak.

Mishak reached into the display. "We haven't shown everyone the full picture yet," he explained. With both hands facing palm-outward, he pushed the display back and *Your Last Chance* came into view. He set the display to begin the playback and stepped out of the way.

There were a few chuckles as the tiny little scout-ship began her attack run on the enemy cruiser. The chuckles turned to surprise as their first round stopped the cruiser from powering her main drives.

"What exactly did you do there?" Rimush demanded.

"We fired a nanite slug, sir."

"That's damned expensive!"

"It is, Captain, but we couldn't get our hands on warheads. Our engineer programmed them to stay together and send out spikes in random directions. We got a lucky penetration."

"They're firing on one of their own ships!" a captain exclaimed.

"That's why we believe they were trying to remain anonymous," Mishak explained. "They didn't want us talking to that crew or downloading their nav records."

"You were damned lucky you backed off just before those warheads went off," one of the Humans said in awe. "Damn near got sucked into the event horizon."

Horizon.

Eth grabbed the display and pulled it back to the main enemy fleet. "We don't need their nav records."

Mishak turned to face him. "You know where they were?"

"Not yet, My Lord, but I know how to find out." He stepped back. "Computer, give me a sphere around the enemy force, just big enough to contain all of the ships."

The projection system added in the sphere.

"Did the BDA team assess the existing enemy damage?"

"They did," Rimush confirmed.

"How long were they working on repairs before we arrived?"

"No more than four hours."

"System, back up the display to the starting time of the battle, then back up another four hours."

The collection of enemy icons coalesced into a single unit icon in the absence of individual ship data. This was before Mishak's force had made contact.

"Now, based on your best estimate of a standard raiding force's path-speed, expand the sphere while reversing the clock accordingly. Overlay any sub-dimensional messages with emergency tags that coincide with the outer surface of the sphere. Give it a fifteen percent margin of error in terms of when the surface passes the source of any signal."

He stepped back and watched as the sphere grew. The projection had to keep zooming out to keep up with the expanding orb. Signal indicators began appearing at the surface but they were mostly single-ship distress calls – a freighter that lost power or a courier ship that passed too close to a black hole and fell out of path.

The viewable area now included all of his uncle's holdings as well as most of his neighbors and, as it expanded into the side of Sandrak's fief, the side farthest from Throne World, a planetary distress call appeared.

Eth let it continue for a few more seconds but then stopped the display. "Anyone care to place a bet?" he asked, opening the details for the planetary emergency. "Raiders. Five cruisers and six frigates. They destroyed the orbital patrol and bombarded three cities."

"Sounds familiar." Mishak gave Eth an approving nod.

"Just an economic disruption," one of the captains ventured, but his face colored at the obvious disdain he felt over his easy answer.

Eth was one of the assembled leaders who made no attempt to hide their feelings. He knew the safe course of action would be to keep silent but he hadn't been made for caution and he had an example to set for his two Human petty officers.

"Their objective had nothing to do with the economy of that world," he said politely but firmly. "Their goal was to elicit a reaction from our overlord, Sandrakwilu – may he outlive us all." He bowed his head as he named their overlord, the noble who ruled their lives in the emperor's name. The assembled captains did likewise, bowing and murmuring the traditional blessing.

"Small wonder they went to such lengths to protect their identity," Eth continued. "They attacked one of the most powerful lords in the empire, one with a reputation for his love of the old ways. Few lords would dare to anger him and *none* would consider doing it on their own."

Mishak raised an eye ridge at him and Eth nodded affirmation. "My Lord, whoever carried out this attack has a powerful backer. Someone strong enough to balance the scales against our own lord."

"If we found them in this sector," Rimush mused, looking over at Mishak, "they might have been planning an attack on your uncle's holdings as well.

Mishak nodded. "We'll need to be much more careful. From now on we come out of path farther out from our destinations than usual. You never know when they might try to ambush an arrival corridor."

This was met with grunts of approval.

"Thank-you, gentlemen." Mishak's tone managed to convey that the meeting was now at an end. "Warrant Eth," he called out as the group began moving toward the exit. "A moment, if you please."

"I'll see you down in the hangar," Eth told his two protégés.

Mishak waited until the hatch snapped shut. "You said a strong lord was backing this incursion, but you were holding something back. What are you reluctant to say?"

Despite having shared intoxicants with Mishak, Eth hadn't quite expected this level of consultation, though he suspected old Ab had enjoyed their lord's confidence in the past.

Perhaps this was how such an unlikely relationship began. Eth had undoubtedly gotten his lord out of a very sticky situation, not only against Chiron, but with his father as well.

He looked Mishak in the eye. "You know there are no lords with the power to risk your father's wrath."

Mishak shrugged. "This is true, but a coalition…" he trailed off, sensing Eth's response.

"Strength, Lord, lies half in your mind and half in your people. Even the most brilliant fruit of imagination withers on the vine without people to carry it out. You can't form a coalition, even an undeclared one, without a lot of people getting involved.

"Certainly you can negotiate a pact in secret and only muster your forces at the last moment, but too many people will still know."

"And any three might keep a secret," Mishak said grimly.

"Providing one of them has murdered the other two," Eth finished the old saying. "A coalition is too clumsy. That leaves only one lord."

"Tir Uttur." Mishak waved the recording out of existence. "The emperor believes we pose a threat to him."

"Don't you?"

"Our very existence causes him to worry about the chances of his daughter being elected to take his throne. Usually, an heir apparent like Tashmitum is confident of ascension. She has all the requirements, brains, beauty and lineage, but we have a very strong argument in our own favor."

"Power," Eth said. "Raw, naked power."

"And looks," Mishak grinned as he gestured at himself but then his face darkened again. "If the emperor thinks this is the way to neutralize us, he's even more unhinged than I've heard." He shook his head and smiled. "Most nobles would give their third testicle to take his throne, so his paranoia isn't entirely unwarranted."

"You don't want it?"

Mishak seemed lost in thought for a moment, but he shook it off and grinned at Eth.

"I have more sense than that. Power isn't a plateau to rest upon; it's the tip of a dagger." He clapped a hand on Eth's shoulder and guided him toward the exit. "I have no desire to spend the rest of my days trying not to topple off."

Risk and Reward

A New Pattern

Noa stepped back beyond the demarcation line on the deck. Any nanites beyond that line were fair game for the regrowth of the *Last Chance's* new bridge but the system was prevented from using any other material. He'd placed a large block of the microscopic robots between the pilots' seats, though he expected the new design to actually use less material.

Still, no need to take chances.

"Already making upgrades?"

He jumped at the voice. The hangar was projecting a barrier around the scout-ship during the regrowth for safety's sake. Only engineering specialists could pass such a barrier.

He caught his breath and turned to face the intruder.

"Hello, Allatu." He should have realized she might drop by. She'd shown a keen interest in the development of the small ship, along with other things. Her help had moved its development along far faster than Noa could have done alone.

He'd had time to think about the other aspect of their interactions. She wasn't the first female Quailu he'd ever met, but he had never *noticed* one of them before. In the past, they'd always been aloof but Allatu had refrained from the engineering chief's abusive agenda toward the Humans even if she *did* steal Oliv's calibrators. Stealing kit was a time-honored tradition in the house forces.

It was during the race when he'd finally come to see her not just as a Quailu but as a *female* Quailu – a *very* female one. Her playful shove at the start of their race and her grace in beating him had changed his perceptions. Picking up on those feelings, she'd developed an interest in him as well.

It was the oldest story in the universe. Few things are more attractive in the opposite sex than a reciprocal attraction. It offers a heady mix of excitement and validation, and Noa was transmitting without any of the mental filters used by the Quailu.

Allatu couldn't help sensing his growing attraction and she seemed to forget what it was that she'd planned to say next.

Noa could feel his pulse pounding and, though his conscious mind didn't note it, his subconscious registered the flushed skin around her neck and the dilated pupils of her eyes. It increased his own response which she immediately felt.

In essence, it was a feedback loop that neither could have stopped on their own, though he knew there was a risk of being discovered.

Hands wandered, crew-suits were shed. Allatu turned around and pressed back against Noa, reaching back to guide him.

And he forgot all about being discovered.

Eth turned out of the side corridor from his quarters to find himself several meters behind Damkina, one of the engineering crew.

He was heading to the hangar bay. Noa was re-growing the bridge of their scout-ship today and Eth was already thinking of a few other holdovers from the old design that were better off left out of the new layout.

His eyes widened as he realized he was watching the subtle grace of Damkina's form as she walked ahead of him. It was more than grace. He was suddenly aware of a strong physical attraction.

He was designed to avoid fraternizing with his own subordinates but none of the Quailu on the flagship fell under that umbrella. They weren't so different from Humans as to preclude the possibility of attraction.

And he was feeling that attraction for someone with empathic abilities…

Ears red, he'd ducked into a side passage, looking for a chance to cool off. She'd stopped as well at a locker out in the main corridor as he was turning aside. He started, slightly, when she came around the corner.

She looked at him blankly, the usual face for the empathics on the *Dibbarra*, but she tilted her head forward aggressively.

Eth knew she could feel what was on his mind. *What do you do in a situation like this… apologize for mental lechery?*

"I've got the time if you do," she rumbled, leaning in even closer.

"What?" he blurted. *You know exactly what she's talking about, you idiot. Stop messing around and say yes or I'll stab our brain with a calibrater…*

A mental response serves as well as a spoken one with the Quailu. Damkina pressed one hand on the scanner by one of the doors and grabbed the front of Eth's suit with the other. She dragged him into what seemed to be her own quarters.

He'd sought refuge from his attraction outside her very door? *If that's not a sign from the Universe then I don't know what is.*

She guided his hand down the front of her suit, which had come open at some point. "A little to the left," she gasped.

Eth's relief at her willingness to ask for what she wanted wasn't lost on Damkina.

It turned out to be a very instructive encounter.

They were still lying together in her bunk when the door whispered open. Neither had thought about locking it when they'd entered the small cabin.

"Zaidu?" she growled. "What brings you here? Come again to tell me how you're willing to ignore your better judgment for my sake?"

Eth sat up to look past her. Zaidu, apparently, was the name of the rump-sniffing fool who'd tried to trip him in the senior NCO's mess.

And Zaidu was staring daggers at Eth.

"Do you have business with either of us, Surgeon's Mate?" Eth demanded negligently, refusing to acknowledge the Quailu's anger. "Business that can't wait till later?"

Zaidu's skin was dark below the eyes. He opened his mouth to speak, but nothing came out. His fists clenched.

Finally, he found his tongue. "You're beneath my station anyway!"

"Honestly," Eth replied   before Damkina could, "I didn't even realize you were interested in me."

"I..." Zaidu trailed off into a stream of guttural incoherence. Finally, he slammed his palms together and shook them at the couple, which must have meant something on his own home-world. He spun on his heel and stalked off, chased down the corridor by Damkina's rumbling laugh.

Eth eased back onto his elbow, grinning at her. "Sorry about that," he said with mock solemnity. "I had no idea the poor fellow was into me!"

She broke out laughing again, dropping back onto the bunk, one hand going to her belly. "Enough!" she said, still chuckling. "You're gonna give me hiccups!"

She gave him a nudge. "Go ahead and get dressed. It's pretty clear that you want to get somewhere important right now and I need to put the other half of my brain to sleep so I'll be ready for my shift."

Eth sat up, looking down at her face, one eyebrow raised. "You mean you've had half your brain asleep the whole time?"

"You're not fooling me with that tone of outrage," she mumbled sleepily. "I can feel your interest in the idea. You're probably wondering what happens in the sleeping half of my brain."

She rolled over. "Now go. Perhaps we'll fornicate again later…"

Eth climbed carefully over her legs and pulled on his suit. "So what *does* happen to the sleeping side?"

"Mmmh… Dreams," she mumbled. "The best dreams and, if I can fall fully asleep in time…"

She started making a low rumbling noise in her throat and Eth couldn't tell if it was snoring or some kind of purr. He watched her for a moment, smiling, before reaching down to pull the covers over her. He stepped out, setting the auto-lock on her door and resumed his journey to the hangar bay.

Eth stopped beneath the hull of *Your Last Chance*. Large sections were growing into place as he watched. He shrugged. Something was nagging at him and he figured a chat with Noa would shake it loose for him.

Noa was probably too busy with the scout-ship in the middle of a reconfiguration. There was little chance of distracting him right now.

Eth wandered over to the main hangar-bay door. Washed out whorls of color flew past the shielded opening. They were on their way to Ur – called in to consult with Mishak's uncle. News of the fight with the raiders had made a definite impact on the old fellow.

Eth turned, frowning at what sounded like a gasp but there was nobody in sight. *Not the only thing I'm failing to see,* he thought.

His eyebrows shot up. Why did that force stop in Uktannu's territory? There were two other minor lords along the path they'd taken after their raid. Did they want to pin this on Sandrak's own brother – get them fighting each other?

Eth shook his head without even realizing it. The other two holdings were relatively compact. A force hiding there could expect to be discovered by the lords who ruled them. A force hiding in Uktannu's space could also be found with relative ease.

Unless they had reason to believe they'd be unmolested.

Mishak had filed his patrol plan with the central authority on Ur before setting out but he'd never had any intention of actually following it. It was one of the many arcane practices that they still maintained in his uncle's dominion but which hadn't made sense in thousands of years. He'd simply made up a random route on the spot and filed it.

But a force with access to the local system's military database would think they knew where Mishak's forces would be at any given time. If they also knew where the rest of Uktannu's ships would be…

He turned and ran for the hangar exit, letting out an explosive curse as he raced beneath the re-growing scout-ship. Considering what was going on inside the scout-ship, his choice of words was doubly appropriate.

He skidded to a halt on the bridge just as they dropped out of path. Fortunately, they'd done so in accordance with their earlier resolution, giving themselves more distance from the usual arrival zone and, sure enough, there was a large collection of warships flanking the arrival corridor.

Rimush looked as though he wanted to turf him out but, no doubt in deference to Mishak's tolerance, allowed the unruly Human to remain on the bridge.

"Medium-sized Varangian force on our starboard flank," the sensor officer announced. "Reading an energy spike in their flagship but it's inconsistent with weapons usage. Multiple warships also present, transponders match the Lord Uktannu's order of battle."

"Computer," Eth hissed, opening a screen, "compare battle-damage assessment of enemy forces from our recent engagement to any ship now within sensor range."

His blood ran cold at the results. He turned as Mishak entered the bridge from his ready-room and his agitated mood easily caught the Quailu's attention.

"What is it?" Mishak demanded.

Eth looked around. His fear had touched every Quailu on the bridge. "Your uncle," he said, turning back to Mishak. "He was behind the attack. Two of the cruisers are sitting out there right now – the battle damage is a match for what we saw in that raiding force."

"Fornication!" Mishak's choice of words could have been a further tribute to the shenanigans in his hangar bay. "Whatever he's planning, it must have been accelerated by our fight. He's not even bothering to hide the evidence now!"

"And we're standing in the way," Eth added. "He'll want us dead, or you at least." He offered his lord an apologetic shrug. "Probably try to get you isolated from the rest of us. That way, he can cook up some kind of accusation, maybe even roll your ships into his own forces once you're out of the way."

"He'll have it all gamed out," Mishak realized, "and, here we are, stumbling right into his clutches like a pack of rump-sniffing cheal-hounds."

"We need to get out of here," Rimush said quietly, stepping over to join them, "but the instant we signal a path order to our ships, the situation will get… exciting…"

"We could pass the order on the sly," Mishak said, "using the fleet positioning beacon but the bandwidth is almost nonexistent. It's only meant to prevent collisions."

"I already have a fallback position selected," Rimush advised. He activated a link to the beacon, looking pointedly at Mishak in what passed for subtle Quailu body-language.

"Send it," Mishak ordered, "but my uncle isn't going to give us time to think our way out of this." He looked up at a blinking icon as Rimush started sending the new orders over the beacon. "And it looks like our time is already up. We've got an incoming comms request."

He sighed. "Any delay will simply convince my uncle that we're on to him and that we're cooking up mischief." He reached out and touched the icon.

Mishak and Rimush each took a half-step back in surprise and Eth nearly followed suit.

"I greet you, Mishak, son of Sandrakwilu," the Varangian in the holograph inclined his head politely. "I am Commodore Hrakkon of his Imperial Majesty's forces. It is… fortunate… that we find ourselves in orbit around Ur at the same time." He glanced toward Eth. "We have unfinished business between Hjalmar and one of your personnel. Might we have a moment to pursue it?"

"He means me," Eth explained to the two bemused Quailu. He didn't need empathic abilities to see that Mishak was now wondering what other secrets his pet Human might be keeping from him.

"This is a wrinkle in the proceedings," Eth advised, "that your uncle is not a party to. *He* won't be able to turn this to his advantage with any degree of ease."

Mishak nodded and Eth turned back to the holographic Varangian. "My Lord has given his consent. We will come aboard immediately." He waved away the projection and turned to an angry Rimush and curious Mishak.

"We?" Rimush demanded.

"Uktannu would never dare attack while our lord is conferring with the Emperor's forces, even if they're here to support his own plot. He can't kill you, Sire, if you're aboard a Varangian ship. He'll have to wait till we return to the *Dibbarra* before he makes a move."

"That buys us the time to coordinate our ships," Mishak said, "but how do you and I get back aboard? The instant our shuttle launches from the Varangian's flagship, my uncle will pounce."

"Shuttles, you mean, Lord," Eth corrected. "Surely you wouldn't care to travel in the same shuttle with a former slave?"

Mishak chuckled. "You expect me to sacrifice my personal shuttle?"

Eth grinned. "Loan might be a better way to phrase it, Sire, but, yes. I'm sure the Varangians would be willing to give it back, eventually…"

"So," Mishak began, "we take my easily identifiable shuttle and also the shittiest piece of flying junk we can find to the Varangian ship…"

"And return in the shit-mobile," Eth confirmed. "Your uncle will have to assume you're still with the Varangians and the moment we clear the landing bay shielding, Captain Rimush initiates the fleet-wide path."

It wasn't quite phrased as an order, so Rimush was able to overlook Eth's presumption but just barely. "We'll be ready," he assured.

"And my uncle is clearly eager to get the proceedings underway," Mishak added as he opened a new call icon.

Uktannu's visage appeared before them. "Nephew!" he boomed. "Well done. Well done indeed! You showed those filthy cowards the cost of attacking our family, neh? Come to my ship and tell me all about it."

"I will, Uncle," Mishak replied cheerfully, glad that Quailu empathy didn't reach through electronic communications. "But first, I've been called to the Varangian flagship, no doubt for the same purpose, though they've also requested a chance to meet with this creature." He nodded toward Eth. "You can find your own way over there," he told the Human, voice dripping with scorn.

He turned back to his uncle. "I'll take my shuttle directly to your location as soon as I'm done with the Emperor's busybodies." He waved the image away.

"Nicely done, Sire!" Eth knew he didn't need to voice his approval, but his brain was wired to recognize good performance. "You've made it clear we're traveling in two shuttles and that only one of them will be expected to return directly here. It should create just enough confusion to get us away from here."

"It's a lucky break, alright," Mishak conceded, "but what brought it about in the first place?" He looked keenly at Eth. "What's their interest in *you*?"

"Just that, Lord, an interest in a relatively unknown species." Eth knew better than to hide anything from a Quailu. Even if he hadn't been conditioned to see them as his natural superiors, he'd still have known better. "They suspect me of being luckier than the average citizen."

"Lucky enough to have been a slave?" Rimush couldn't resist the jab.

"I'd say *have been* makes my point for me, wouldn't you?"

Rimush clearly didn't care for that but he kept it to himself. "I'll have your shuttles prepared," he said crisply as Mishak led Eth off the bridge.

"How did you manage to attract Varangian attention?" Mishak asked as they began descending the port-side ramp to reach the hangar deck.

"Ran into one of them on the station at Kwharaz," Eth replied. "He seemed to think I was good at getting away with risky behavior."

Mishak grunted an inarticulate reply but remained silent for a few more paces. "What was it like, the station?"

Eth let his confusion reach out. He wasn't quite sure what the question was driving at.

"The station," Mishak reiterated. "It's one thing to be a newly freed man around the same old people, but to walk through the midst of anonymous crowds who see you as just another mushkenu… To have that kind of implicit acceptance…"

Eth was surprised. He'd mostly attributed his enjoyment of the station to the temporary freedom it had afforded him from the responsibilities of his small command. No crewmen expecting him to provide victory.

Mishak had put his finger squarely on feelings that Eth had only barely acknowledged. He didn't think it was his lord's empathic abilities either, not if Eth didn't even feel it openly.

"This insight surprises you?" Mishak chuckled – a deep gravelly rumble. "We're not so different, you and I. My whole life has been spent in the shadow of my father's crushing dominance."

That actually explained a great deal for Eth. "Now that you're out here," he said, "away from Kish and commanding a fleet of your own…"

"My father suddenly seems much smaller," Mishak said. "And my uncle, who was supposed to keep me under his own heel in my father's absence, has graciously exposed himself as a traitor to the family. I'd love to deal with him right now but…"

"…but he has us at a disadvantage here," Eth finished for him.

151

Mishak nodded. "First we run, then we find a way to deal with him."

"Figuring out what his game is would go a long way toward that goal," Eth asserted. "I just wish we had more time to sort out what he's up to. If he's not even bothering to hide his false-raid forces, then he must be planning to make a big move very soon."

"Immediately, I'd say," Mishak insisted as they rounded a corner and entered the hangar bay, nodding to a startled young Quailu who stood beneath *Your Last Chance*. She reached up to check the fastenings at the front of her crewsuit.

"Our fight with his false-flag team probably leaves him with no choice but to proceed now, whether he's fully prepared or not."

Noa dropped lightly out one of the belly hatches of the newly regrown scout-ship. He raised an eyebrow at the young female Quailu before following her gaze to see Eth following their lord and looking back at him. His eyes drifted out of focus, as they always did when he was processing new information, and then he shrugged and turned away.

They boarded their respective shuttles and took the short flight over to the deadly looking Varangian flagship. The hangar was far more utilitarian than its Quailu counterpart and it was empty, except for two officers.

"I'm Afvaldr," the Varangian with the greatest number of red lines on his collar announced, "the executive officer. Welcome aboard, Lord Mishak, son of Sandrak." He gestured to the forward exit hatch.

"If you'll come with me, I will take you to the commodore."

Eth turned an inquiring gaze on the Varangian lieutenant as the two more senior officials left.

"This way, Warrant Officer," the junior officer indicated, waving to a large hatch at the aft end of the bay.

Eth followed him, not bothering with questions, as he assumed the lieutenant was simply there as his guide. The corridor outside the hatch led them aft until they reached a ladder set into the wall. The Varangian descended without a second glance at Eth.

He felt vindicated as he stepped onto the ladder and began following his guide down. The Varangians were the foremost military power in the HQE and they had ladders, just like the ones Noa had convinced Mishak to add to his own ships. He felt a fierce flush of pride at being an arboreal species.

They stepped off the ladder in an engineering space and he recalled the sensor officer's remarks about a power surge in the area. Perhaps Eth would find out what it was all about.

They turned at an intersection and moved toward the centerline of the ship, coming at last to a door guarded by four armored Varangians.

The lieutenant stepped up to the door, leaning forward for the optical scanner in its center. The heavy armored door slid down into the deck and Eth followed his guide into the room beyond.

Roughly five meters square, it was unremarkable, possessing only one other door on the far wall.

"We would appreciate if you could step through the next door as rapidly as possible," the lieutenant explained as the heavy door slid back up into place. "The less time you spend in actually passing through the door, the less energy we have to expend."

"Well, I'm certainly glad that wasn't at all cryptic," Eth said dryly.

The other officer didn't react in the slightest. He simply looked at Eth with continued, earnest expectation.

Not to worry, Eth thought sarcastically, *nothing dangerous or mysterious – just a power draining portal of mystery, that's all.* He shook his head. *Might as well expect poetry from a Zeartekka.* The thought almost made him shudder.

He stepped up to the door and it snapped open with blinding speed. He looked through to the short hallway and, just as he lifted his right foot, the Varangian gave him a firm shove.

He stumbled through and the door snapped shut before he could turn to glare at the officer.

A sudden, formless dread began picking at the edges of his consciousness. His inability to identify the cause did nothing to ease it.

The short hallway was entirely unremarkable, so why was he suddenly so ill-at-ease? He considered the mysterious nature of the heavily guarded door and the shove that had propelled him through but discarded both as possible causes.

He turned back to the door but it refused to open when he approached. Having no other options available, he turned and moved toward the door at the other end, unexplainable fear growing with every step.

By the time he reached the door, he was almost jogging in his desire to leave the hallway and find answers.

This door opened and he stepped through, gazing ahead in awe, his fear momentarily pushed to the back of his thoughts.

The space ahead of him was large – impossibly large. It was also very different from the parts of the ship he'd seen so far. This area looked more like a cathedral, with a central nave, a hundred meters wide, running for at least three hundred meters away from him. Arched bays ran down both sides of the nave, adding at least another forty meters to the width and balancing the soaring, hundred-and-forty-meter-high arched ceiling.

It was far too big for the ship he'd landed in. There simply wasn't room enough to accommodate it inside the hull.

So where was he?

The fear reasserted itself and he spotted a group of Varangians in one of the bays to his right. He moved their way, feeing a sudden, desperate need for their reassurance but still having no idea why.

He looked into the first bay on his right as he passed it, seeing that its outer wall was a shielded window.

And the view…

Human

He could see a massive black orb in the distance, shrouded in streaks of light that coalesced into a wide glowing accretion disk.

It wasn't, in itself, frightening but it seemed to confirm his fears somehow. It almost seemed to be taunting him, laughing at a false sense of security that he'd never be able to regain.

Fully terrified now, he broke into a run, aiming toward one of the Varangians who'd left his group to come toward him, a look of concern spreading on his angular features.

Five meters away from the approaching Varangian, Eth's mind finally gave it all up for a bad job and decided that a nice shutdown would be just the thing.

He didn't even feel it when his face slammed onto the floor.

Eth didn't quite wake up, but he was at least half conscious. He was in a maturation chamber, the same kind that had been used to grow him, to heal his wounds…

…to train him.

The fear was still there but it had somehow lost much of its power. He still couldn't identify its cause but he could at least think in a more-or-less coherent manner.

He felt exposed. Even inside the gravity-free, womb-like environment of the chamber, he felt as though he had no protection from the vagaries of the Universe.

Come to think of it, he didn't quite trust the Universe to play nice anymore. Was it even real? Was the chamber real? Was the chamber's link to his mind real… ?

Hold on.

He was linked to the chamber's system as though a training module had been implanted on his brain. The exit command was available and, real or not, he wanted out of the damned thing.

The door slid up and his feet settled to the floor of the chamber. Like the end of a warm embrace, the neural interface let go of his mind and he stepped out, oddly off-balance.

"We thought you'd be ready to come out soon," a voice said.

He turned to find a Varangian sitting in one of the low lounge-chairs that faced a large window, looking back over his shoulder with a friendly smile, or what passed for a smile among his kind.

The same black orb was visible through the window. It was impossible to tell how far they were from it but it looked like a black hole. Eth moved toward it, and the chairs, on unsteady feet.

"I'm Jabir," the Varangian offered. "In your language, I might be described as a psychophysicist."

"A what?"

Jabir grinned. "We believe reality is an artifact of observation, so it would be quite hypocritical of us to study physics and psychology separately, don't you think?"

"Well, that sounds great for you," Eth said, easing into a chair next to Jabir. "Maybe you could explain why I was crammed into that chamber?"

"You suffered quite a shock when you crossed over," Jabir explained. "Your mind had to shut itself down to prevent a complete psychotic break."

"I suppose that sort of news would sound comforting to a Varangian," Eth mused. "Let's stick to something more concrete for the moment. *Where* have I crossed over to?"

Jabir gazed out the window for a moment. "Technically, you're no longer in your universe, at the moment."

"Technically?" Eth looked out at the black orb, frowning at the use of 'your'. "Where *am* I, *technically* speaking?"

"Between your universe and ours."

"Alternate universes?" Eth darted a glance at Jabir's reflection in the window, hovering next to the black orb. "Hasn't that concept been thoroughly disproven?" He turned to Jabir as the Varangian chuckled.

"Disproven by the Quailu, yes," Jabir agreed. "But do you really think they know everything there is to know?"

Eth opened his mouth but then quickly shut it again. He suspected that he might be out of his depth here and that was, more often than not, a good time to shut up and hear what others might have to say.

The Varangian offered a conciliatory smile. "You know, your kind are on the verge of eclipsing the Quailu, at least in theoretical thought."

Eth tried to imagine some secret research lab on Kish, run by renegade Human slave-scientists. The image was too preposterous to sustain itself.

"If the Quailu are so wrong," Eth retorted, "why are the Varangians their subjects instead of their masters?"

"You can't rule every universe," Jabir said airily, "and besides, we're just visiting here."

"Just visiting..." Eth raised an eyebrow at him. There were billions of Varangians in the HQE and they were the emperor's personal military – quite a large presence for a species that was only 'visiting'.

The Varangian shrugged. "We find you interesting."

Eth looked back out the window, heaving out a deep breath. He shook his head, very slightly. "Anyway, what caused the shock?"

"When you passed through, your perceptions underwent an... evolution."

"My perceptions? Perceptions of what?"

"Everything," Jabir said with emphasis. "How you see the universe around you." He paused for a moment, frowning at the wall behind Eth. "Stepping away from something," he began, turning his eyes back on Eth, "and looking back at it can open new perspectives. This tends to be true at all levels, at least for those who are able to truly perceive what's around them.

"Imagine a two-dimensional being in a two-dimensional space. If it were restricted to a single, two-dimensional plane, it would see only the edges of its friends. It would assume that they were all line segments. It wouldn't even realize that it lived in two-dimensional space.

"If it moves in the x and y axis, it might perceive one of those axis as *time*, not really understanding it's true nature.

"If it were to suddenly step out into three-dimensional space and look back at its friends, it might be shocked to learn that they weren't just line segments. How would it feel to learn that they were circles, squares and triangles – that they're creatures of far greater depth than ever suspected?

"The shock came when you stepped out of your universe and into the interior of this super massive black hole. Frankly, we didn't expect it, especially when the young female that Hjalmar sent to us had no such experience."

"She's here?" Eth sat up, staring intently at Jabir, hands on his armrests.

A shake of the head. "No. We spent some time with her but she was returned to Uktannu's station several months ago."

That nagged at Eth. He'd only seen her taken from that station a few weeks back.

Jabir leaned over toward Eth. "Your comfortable belief in the physical world has taken a bit of a beating, I'm afraid."

Eth shuddered. It had the ring of truth to it but he still didn't trust what he was being told. Still, coming here had triggered *something*, wherever *here* was… "Where *am* I?" he demanded.

The Varangian chuckled. "In denial, if I'm not mistaken."

"Fine!" Eth threw up his hands. "My perceptions have been altered. That's why I'm feeling this fear?"

A nod. "Almost every life-form creates a view of the Universe that's largely informed by its own biology. Most of us train ourselves not to see beyond it."

He gestured to Eth. "As an example, *you* continually move physical mass through the power of thought."

"I'm… pretty sure I don't do that," Eth replied.

"You see? This is a perfect example," Jabir insisted. "If you don't do that, then how did you reply to me just now?"

Eth rolled his eyes. "My brain sent a signal and my lungs moved air past my vocal chords. My mouth did the rest, also under orders from my brain."

"And what caused that electrical impulse to race from your brain to the rest of your body?"

Eth squinted at the Varangian, who now seemed dangerously close to making a point.

"At some point," Jabir continued, "you have to accept that your desire to move muscle tissue is causing a polarity change in your neurons. Following the entire process back from muscle movement, you end up reaching the point where your own wishes *are* causing something physical to happen, even if it is only initiated at the sub-atomic level."

"Unless my wishes are merely a product of that same electrical activity," Eth observed.

"A very inelegant view of existence," Jabir reproofed him gently, "and one that fails to explain much that my people can do. It also fails to explain why you're suddenly so unsettled. Our expectations really do create our reality."

"Are you saying I've been turned into a superhero or something?" Eth joked. "I can move things with my mind…?"

"I wouldn't do that," Jabir said urgently. "Even if you *could* control such a thing, it would exact a heavy toll on you. The Universe is no longer what you thought it was, but it still favors balance. Nothing comes for free."

"So, no throwing enemy ships into the corona of a nearby star?"

Jabir was holding his hands up, palms toward Eth in a shushing motion. "Gods, no! You get away with moving your own body because it starts at the sub-atomic level but to move whole atoms or," he shuddered, "a ship…"

"Bad?"

"Very." The Varangian nodded emphatically. "It would probably mean the end of you, maybe even the end of all around you as well."

"Alright," Eth spread out his hands to placate Jabir. "I'll try to avoid smashing planets into each other but you're gonna owe me for that." He kept his expression serious despite the ludicrous subject. "How about you just drop the soft-sell and tell me what you're driving at? Why have you brought me here?"

"A comedy of errors, actually," the Varangian said frankly. "Your future raises many questions for us, so we decided to bring you here in an attempt to find out what it was that set you on your path." He chuckled ruefully. "As it turns out, the act of bringing you here was the cause we were looking for."

He shook his head. "Talk about 'expectations creating reality'. One of the basic tenets of Varangian science and we failed to anticipate our own role in your future."

"My future?" Eth was about to make a sarcastic remark but, given the metaphorical beating he'd taken over the concept of alternate universes, he held his tongue.

"We know you have a role to play," Jabir said, "because we've seen what happens."

"So you have the ability to peer into the future?" Eth asked. His eyes grew wide. "Will I be able to do that, now that I've been through your damned portal?"

The Varangian held up a hand to stall Eth. "As individuals, we have a slightly improved ability to feel our way through the tangle of causality. It looks like 'luck' to outsiders." He paused, looking straight through Eth as he collected his thoughts.

"As a species," he continued, "we already know the future of your universe on the larger, political scale because we've already lived through it."

Eth stayed silent. Such a statement was so preposterous as to beg interrogation. Jabir had to be expecting an outburst or a string of questions but that merely proved they weren't needed. It was blatantly obvious the Varangian would have to provide some sort of explanation, so Eth merely tilted his head to the right a little, raising his eyebrows a fraction.

Jabir looked mildly disappointed but it was hard to tell with his species. Finally, he nodded to himself and continued. "Where we come from, time – for lack of a better word in Imperial Standard – *flows* in a different direction. We first broke through to your universe ninety thousand years ago in *our* frame of reference which, of course, is in *your* future."

"How does that even work? Do you only come for a few years and go back?"

"Some do, in order to maintain the connection with the rest of our people," Jabir said, "but there are still a few Billion of our kind living permanently in your universe. We do have a planet to populate, after all. The vast majority of our presence here is descended from settlers sent from our own future, which required some pretty strict rules about what those early settlers could tell their own children."

Eth frowned. "How is this not common knowledge? billions of Varangians living in our universe and none of them have let the secret out? None of your 'settlers' passed on knowledge of disasters or wars in your own universe?"

"Oh, thousands have blabbed," Jabir conceded cheerfully.

Eth leaned toward him, shaking his head slightly. "And... so?"

"So?" Jabir grinned. "Our past is your future... sort of... Look, it's a simple matter for us to maintain a group of enforcers who scan history for such leaks and trace them back to their origins.

"If I were seriously considering the betrayal of our secrets, one of them would show up and give me a stern warning. Might even wave a gun in my face or something. If that didn't take, he'd come back and blow my head off."

Eth made a show of looking around the room. "Jabir, you're telling me everything right now," he said, eyes coming to rest on the Varangian. "Where's your enforcers?"

Jabir flicked a dismissive hand. "This has already been approved. You won't betray our trust."

"How can you possibly know..." Eth trailed off in the face of Jabir's exaggeratedly-patient expression. "Right. Of course you'd know."

"Right about now," Jabir resumed, "you're probably wondering why we didn't establish more of a presence here, even take over the HQE while we were at it..."

"Well, yeah." Eth scratched at the back of his head. "I am wondering that – now."

"For one thing, it's damned difficult to overthrow an existing empire when your time frames are opposed. We'd be fighting constantly as we went back in time. For another, there are plenty of other universes out there.

"We were looking for one that had no multi-galaxy empires in it. Someplace where we could put our feet up. A universe to save our species."

"Save it from what?"

"The end of time." Jabir shrugged. "Not trying to panic you or anything but they don't last forever, you know."

"They?"

"Universes." Jabir turned his gaze back to the window. "They're born with great fanfare, grow for billions of years, but a moment comes when the expansion stops and it's all downhill from there.

"We found this universe while searching for our own new home. We'll eventually have to evacuate our current Universe. When we find it, we'll ride the new one back in time for all it's worth and then find another headed in the opposite direction."

"You don't just return to your original universe?"

"Why would we want to do that?" Jabir looked at him in mild alarm. "Do you have any idea how crowded it would get if we kept jumping back and forth between two universes? Remember, our ancestors would still be there."

He shook his head in amazement. "Imagine if we accidentally interfered in the discovery of the bow and arrow or the fleem or even the pointy stick. It could set us back by thousands of years, and we barely got out of there in time as it was."

"Yeah, that would be problematic for you." Eth sat up. "Thanks for the chat and for messing up my brain, but what do we do from here?"

"Well, we promised you'd know what our questions were once we had our answers," Jabir said. "The question we wanted answers to was *what set you on your particular path*, and the answer, as it turns out…"

"Is you," Eth finished for him. "I get the irony, but what exactly is this *path* you speak of? What is it that I'm going to do?"

"You'll learn the answer to that as you go," Jabir said guardedly, "unless, of course, I actually told you right now and changed your future as a result."

"Well…" Eth looked around the room again. "… looks like you're not going to do that, so what's next?"

"We send you back," Jabir replied. "We'd intended to send you back after a quick chat, but then you collapsed on us so we had to put you in stasis – give your mind time to adjust to the changes."

Eth felt the hairs rise on the back of his neck. "How long was I in there?"

Jabir considered his response for a moment. "About seven months."

Eth leapt out of his chair. "Seven months? We were facing off against Uktannu's fleet when I came here. What happened to our people? Where is Mishak?"

Jabir sighed. "Firstly, if you've missed a battle by seven months, there's no real need for urgent histrionics so could you please stop pacing around like a gralloch who's caught a scent?"

Eth unclenched his fists and, after a few deep breaths, forced himself to sit again.

"Much better," Jabir said, smiling reassuringly. "Now, as far as your friends are concerned, they're still there. Remember, that door you stepped through was a portal in space-time – time being the operative word in the current conversation. Months have passed on this side but, with the portal held open, no time has passed on the other side."

Eth was impressed. "That must take an incredible amount of energy – holding open a space-time portal for seven months!"

Jabir raised an eyebrow and looked as though he were about to say something but he stopped himself and leaned forward slightly, an expectant expression on his face.

"Ah!" Eth felt mildly foolish. "No time has passed on the other end. *That's* where you hold the portal open from, yes?"

The Varangian heaved an exaggerated sigh of relief as he stood, gesturing Eth toward an exit door. "They told me you were supposed to be clever. I'd have given them a merciless ribbing if you'd failed to sort that one out."

He led the way to the portal. "The reason we wanted you to get through so quickly was that we didn't want you colliding with yourself on the way back out."

Eth stepped through the portal. The Varangian officer was still straightening up from having shoved him through, seven months earlier.

"All finished?" the lieutenant asked.

Eth nodded, standing there while he waited for another wave of crippling fear to assail him. Nothing happened, except for the officer's polite gesture toward the heavy outer door.

The fear was still there, at the back of his mind, but he understood it better now and, frankly, he was far too tired to care.

The outer door slid down into the deck and he followed the officer back to the hangar bay. He had to wait for Mishak who, after Eth's seven-month absence, was still just arriving on the bridge of the Varangian ship.

He walked up the back ramp of the barely serviceable shuttle he'd arrived in and, ignoring the disgusted shudder of the Quailu pilot, stretched out on one of the benches that ran down either side of the small craft and fell asleep.

He was awakened by the arrival of Mishak and his personal pilot as they clumped up the ramp.

"Well," Mishak began, nodding to Eth, "that didn't take very long! Hopefully, Rimush has had enough time to send the coordinates for our fallback position."

He gave Eth's feet a friendly slap to get them out of the way as he dropped his own posterior onto the bench. "So what did they want with *you*?"

"It's hard to say," Eth answered honestly enough. "I…" He leaned away from his lord, ever so slightly, feeling a wave of revulsion. "What? What's wrong, Lord?"

Mishak had turned to face him, his left hand on the bench as though ready to push back from the Human. "What did they do to you?" he asked quietly. "I can't read you anymore."

"What?"

"All I'm getting are jumbled fragments, like hearing sound from underwater."

"He's right," Mishak's pilot agreed. "It's like you've turned into one of those Zeartekka. Creeping me out."

"Were you attacked?" Mishak demanded. "Did one of them hit you in the head or inject you with anything?"

"No. I just had one conversation," he said, again, more-or-less truthfully. He was reasonably certain the Varangians had known this was going to happen. If they knew the future, then they knew he'd be able to keep secrets from the Quailu.

Mishak shuddered. "Well, we can't sit here forever trying to figure it out." He got up and headed for the cockpit. "We need to get the fleet out of here."

They flew back to the *Dibbarra*, leaving Mishak's personal shuttle behind on the Varangian flagship. It was worth the sacrifice of one shuttle, if it meant that Uktannu would think his nephew was still aboard the imperial vessel.

The moment the shuttle touched down in the hangar-bay, Mishak's ships leapt away, shaping path to the rendezvous.

Mishak headed straight for the bridge, not bothering to give any indication to Eth as to whether he was required there as well.

Instead, Eth wandered over to *Your Last Chance,* resting a hand on her landing strut.

The Varangians had clearly planned to meet him back at the station and, given what he'd just learned, it wasn't surprising. He turned at the sound of footsteps.

"So what did the Emperor's thugs want with you?" Noa asked. He held out an apple, only slightly desiccated on one side. He gave a shrug. "The food-cycler does meat well enough now, but the fruit is still a little hit-or-miss. It's a side-effect of the tandem drive arrangement we're using. The interference patterns are hard to isolate because they shift with the power settings. It's messing with a few of our systems."

"That's all it is?"

Noa nodded. "Small price to pay, when you consider how well our engines reinforce each other."

Eth started to nod but he froze, skin tingling. "Birdu's balls!" he whispered in shock. *Reinforcing to make something greater than the sum of its parts...*

Without even a backward glance at Noa, he raced for the exit hatch. He skidded around the corner and ran up the ramp toward the bridge, bellowing at crewmen to make way for him.

He no longer cared if Mishak wanted him on the bridge. He had good reason to go there. For the second time in the same day, he burst into the command center, but this time at least, they weren't shaping their way into another ambush.

But the future of Mishak's family was.

"Heiropolis," he announced breathlessly before Mishak or Rimush could say anything.

Even without the ability to read Eth, Mishak was quick to pick up on his meaning. He turned to the holo display and brought up the mapping function.

"Your lord father led eight squadrons through the Heiropolis system two days ago," Rimush said, scrolling through a list.

"Anyone who knows my father will realize that he'd respond to a raid on one of his worlds with overwhelming force." Mishak zoomed out his view and began stalking around the projection to the left to get a better sense of the picture in three dimensions.

"There are few in the empire who don't know that about your father," Eth confirmed, "but that raid would make an excellent opening move if you're hoping to bisect his holdings with his forces trapped on the wrong side of Heiropolis."

"Given how many systems we've taken from rivals in this region in the last century," Mishak muttered half to himself, "there'd be no chance of anyone granting him military access, especially if they scent imperial involvement in an attempt to cut us down to size."

"Which brings us to the Varangians," Eth stated. "If they wanted to speak to me, they could have sent just one frigate. Nobody in their right mind wants to tangle with the Varangians. The Emperor would excommunicate anyone who tried. Anyone could attack them, regardless of pretext. They weren't waiting with your uncle to help deal with *us*, we were just a complication."

"The Varangians are sitting there waiting for Uktannu to seize Heiropolis Prime." Mishak's fists clenched. "They'll wait a day or so, then show up to 'investigate' the veracity of Uktannu's claim on the system. A massive shift in power resulting from relatively small expenditures of force."

"The claim will already have been fabricated for him and registered at court," Rimush growled. "That slimy little pile of…" He started suddenly, glancing nervously at Mishak. "Your pardon, Lord. I forgot myself for a moment there."

Mishak waved off the apology. "It's nothing I haven't already thought, uncle or not. I can hardly fault you for cursing him when I'm expecting you to open fire on him in the very near future."

"Your uncle will already be on his way there now," Eth insisted. "He just watched us consulting with the Varangians and he has to be wondering what we may have learned from them. He'll launch whatever plan he has and he'll do it immediately, before we have a chance to cook up any mischief against him."

"But if he assumes his plot is compromised," Rimush cut in, "why go through with it?"

"Because my father will already kill him for the plot," Mishak said. "Far better to be killed for taking the Heiropolis system. That course of action at least holds out the chance of survival if he can still get the Varangians to run interference for him."

"And he'll have to use whatever plan he's already developed and disseminated to his captains." Eth zoomed out the display a little. "There's no time to adjust anything and coordinate it. He has to roll the dice. Probably come at them with a small force, real friendly-like.

"Just friendly old Uktannu, brother to the lord who owns the whole damned place. He'll get in behind the security patrols and wait."

"And then his main force comes blazing out of path," Rimush growled. "Fornicating cowards! How do we stop them?"

Eth shuddered. He could feel the thought bubbling up in Mishak's mind somehow. "We don't," he said, pre-empting his lord who raised a surprised eyebrow. "Say we got there first. We see the Lord Uktannu come out of path with his small advance force and we do what? Open fire?" He shook his head. "That makes us renegades. Do we warn Heiropolitan Orbital control?"

"Baseless allegations." Mishak sighed. "Or rather, they're baseless until my uncle opens fire."

"Which he'll do if he doesn't know we're there," Eth said, grinning. He looked at Rimush, sensing his understanding of the plan. "We get to the rendezvous, pass out our new destination and get going for Heiropolis Prime."

Rimush nodded, liking the idea. "And we follow our new SOP."

Meanwhile, at the New Ranch...

"Lady Bau!" General Tilsin turned to greet the Quailu who'd sent him to incorporate Arbella into her holdings. "This world is not yet safe! There will be rebels here for years and, if they learn of your presence..." He gestured toward the heavy doors leading from the governor's office to the planetary council chamber.

"Enough, General!" she replied tartly. "Would you have said such a thing to my husband?"

The general bowed his head in acknowledgement of the point.

"If it were so dangerous," she asked, "then why have you already sent back half the fleet?"

Surprise at such a question.

"Ships cannot stop a determined fanatic with a bomb, Lady," Tilsin replied. "I kept the soldiers and they'll need to stay here for quite some time, at least until the citizens get used to the idea of living under your rule."

"You seem upset, General Tilsin." Lady Bau's open smile encouraged him to speak freely.

Tilsin had served her husband, Nin-Girsu for decades and, though her husband wasn't the most inspiring leader, he could have been far worse. It hadn't been until after his death, when the Lady Bau took the reins, that people understood just how much she'd done to protect them from the full effect of his 'leadership'.

She'd taken over a house on the verge of losing elector status. Three of their nine worlds were on the edge of ecological and economic collapse. That would have demoted them to colony status and colonies didn't count toward the eight systems needed to make a lord into an elector.

She'd brought in a slate of reforms, putting all nine worlds back on the road to recovery and agricultural output had skyrocketed. Most of the profit had been poured back into development, leaving little for her military, but she'd at least listened to Tilsin's plea for new equipment templates.

The general nodded again at the heavy doors that led to the council chamber. A steady bubbling of voices could be heard beyond it. "They had terrible management here. The previous governor fled with half the records, though the half he didn't have time to take already implicated him in enough corruption to get him lynched.

"How could any other lord be worse than what they already had? Why should they care who rules them?"

"Why indeed?" She chuckled. "When one lord's the same as the next, the only thing that changes during an annexation like this is that they're *reminded* of just how hopeless everything is. That's why they can find young males willing to throw their lives away on desperate attacks. It makes them feel like they're serving something greater."

Frustration.

"Even if it's just a return to serving the same horrible overlord they had before?"

"*Especially* if," she insisted, "because it gives them the feeling that they're taking a hand in their own destiny, choosing, if not the flavor, then at least the *brand name* of their oppression. Don't forget it's the branding that lets an ineffective governor stay in power.

"How many factions are there in this planet's council? Five?" She tilted her head back. "Have you looked at their social media feeds? Every single policy discussion degenerates into factional insults and memes – the adherents of each brand posting their views and shouting down opposition. The citizens of this world were too busy squabbling with each other to notice the systematic looting of their economy by their own officials."

A mental shrug. "That's politics for you." Tilsen sighed.

"Politics!" Bau sneered. "The single greatest marketing success in recorded history. It's still just feudalism. The only difference is that the peasants are too occupied fighting each other to turn on their masters."

Loyal confidence. "If you're finished with the lecture, ma'am, perhaps you could go out there and sort the council out."

She laughed, turning for the doors. "I'm sure you could have done this, General, but sorting out my own holdings has given me a taste for this."

Tilsin just managed to catch up as she reached the doors, opening them for his lady. They moved forward into a loud wash of voices that quickly grew quiet as she approached the rostrum.

She spent a moment looking out at the assembled leaders of this system. Arbella was the only world in this system to hold full planetary status. Two nearby worlds had colonies and they would have representatives here as well.

She let them see her.

She was well into what might be called her twilight years and there were some who whispered that she should step down in favor of her young son, but he hadn't yet reached the age of majority. He still lived at Askuza, fostered to the great lord Ashkazum.

Those who whispered such things tended to change their mind after meeting her. There was no weakness in her stride and certainly no weakness in her spirit.

The room was massive, those sitting at the far side taking several minutes to notice the wave of quiet descending on the assembly. Finally, with the room nearly silent, she cleared her throat.

"I've just seized this system by right of conquest, so I won't insult you with pleasantries and self-deprecating humor. I *will* tell you that we don't intend to displace any of you with our own people. As long as you don't give us cause to do so, you will not be removed from your positions.

"I would have told you this as I stood next to your governor but he seems to have fled the system. This is almost certainly for the best because it seems that much of the profit from this world has flowed into his personal accounts.

"I *will* serve warning to you all that I don't tolerate corruption. If you were lining your pockets at the expense of your citizens, you will be dealt with severely *if* you fail to stop doing so immediately."

Mild alarm flowed around her. She nearly laughed but this was too serious.

She had seen, during her husband's administration, the true cost of 'looking the other way'. Too many officials had taken bribes and all nine systems had been systematically looted, bringing the family to the verge of collapse.

A corrupt administration passed very little tax revenue to its overlord.

"From now on, half of all tax collected from Arbella will be spent on improving the local infrastructure. This world is falling apart at the seams and your military was nearly non-existent. Even *our* meager forces were able to overwhelm you in less than three hours!"

She made a mental note to expand her forces.

"I ask you to consider this – as one of the worlds belonging directly to an electress, you no longer have an intermediate lord in your tax hierarchy."

She paused, enjoying the exited murmur that ran around the circular room. Minor lords who didn't owe fealty to an elector were required to pay their taxes into one of the many consolidated taxation authorities. Those authorities needed funding to support their bloated bureaucracies and that funding came from the taxes they handled.

"You pay your taxes to me," she continued, "and I pay the emperor directly. From this day onward, Arbellans will see their tax burden reduced by a third."

She'd had one of her personal bodyguards standing at the chamber entrance on the far side, waiting to applaud at the tax announcement but she was gratified to see it hadn't been necessary.

Several Arbellan representatives within earshot sprang to their feet and immediately began clapping. It spread quickly, bringing most of them to their feet in a slow moving wave that wrapped its way around in both directions, meeting at the far side.

She let the positive feelings wash over her. Many Quailu just wanted a quiet life but they had no idea how it felt to take an angry, fearful crowd like this one and turn it around.

Getting Ahead

"That's good, Hendy." Eth looked out at the blackness. The biggest thing in the sky was the pinpoint of light thrown back at them from Heiropolis Prime and, yet, this counted for close in naval matters -- especially in relation to the planetary approach corridor.

The rest of the fleet was farther back, out of detection range and waiting for the signal from Eth and his scout-ships.

"Nothing out of the ordinary in the chatter," Glen announced. "No sign of marauding enemies or anything."

"So who are we expecting?" Hendy asked.

"It's… sensitive," Eth replied, wondering at the frustration he felt from the pilot. Whatever had happened when he stepped out of this universe, it seemed to have left him with abilities similar to those of the Quailu, but it also made him a blank slate to the ruling species.

He wasn't sure he wanted it.

"Look," he began, "if it happens, then you'll know who it is. If I tell you now, we risk rumors getting out that could harm relations with an otherwise friendly lord."

He got up from the co-pilot chair and stretched. "I'm going to see Noa about your wild idea."

Hendy let his gaze drift meaningfully to the assault rifle racked on the bulkhead behind his chair. "If you thought it was so crazy, why bother bringing infantry weapons aboard?"

Eth grinned. "Maybe I'm crazy too? You're not the only one tired of sitting around at a console all the time."

Eth was sleeping when the call came in or, rather, trying to sleep. It was getting easier to drift off but not by much. He could feel all his crewmen in the close quarters of *Your Last Chance* and their hopes and fears weighed even more heavily, now that he could feel them directly.

Oliv was throwing off an aura of surprise and excitement tinged with that sharp edge of fear that Eth knew only too well.

The enemy had come.

"Same ships we saw in Uktannu's space," she told Eth before pointing at one of the cruisers. "You can even see the repaired damage on that one from the raid they pulled in Sandrak's territory, and they're running with hulls open to space."

Eth could feel his pulse quicken. He'd been right. They were coming in rigged for combat.

"Keeping pace," Ed announced, nodding to Hendy as the lead pilot strapped into the co-pilot's seat.

"Let's hope the others are doing the same," Eth said with a glimmer of pride. Even knowing that *The Last Thing You'll Ever See* and *The Reason You Don't Have Friends* were out there watching the enemy ships, his own sensors were having a hard time finding them.

They knew the plan and they knew, roughly, where *Your Last Chance* was posted. The damaged cruiser was the closest one to Eth so she'd serve as their target.

"Glen, eject a message drone with the enemy composition and current course."

The drone shot out from the side of the small vessel, waiting until it was far from the ship and well along on its tangential course before sending a unidirectional burst back to Mishak and the rest of his fleet.

"The thief is in the house!" Rimush exulted.

"And now we just wait for him to grab the valuables first," Mishak muttered. He needed Eth to succeed in his plan if they were going to have a chance, but he wasn't sure he liked all that success would entail. Sighing, he gestured to the captain who gave the order to start moving in.

And their small fleet, the only chance to preserve the family's power, began falling toward Heiropolis Prime.

"I think I'm picking up a faint return off one of our sister ships," Oliv advised. "Looks like they're moving closer to our target."

"Good," Eth said with more restraint than he thought he possessed. If the other scouts had gone after the wrong targets, the chances of success would be drastically reduced and the costs of victory greatly increased. Oliv's news had come as a massive relief.

His head came up, frowning at the sudden impression of alarm and then he felt the confirmation through Oliv a heartbeat before she spoke.

"Reading spikes in all targets!"

Eth grabbed a stanchion. "Ed, standby to take us in!"

He didn't need to hear it from Oliv when the enemy fired on the orbital patrols. He could see the brilliant plumes of plasma ejecting from the front of the attackers. "Now, Ed! Get us in there as fast as you can!"

He kept his eyes open as he watched the sickeningly fast approach to the targeted cruiser, but he was sorely tempted to squeeze them shut and pretend they weren't a minor course-correction away from a spectacular death.

The inertial dampening was so well adjusted by now that he could have pretended nothing terrifying was happening but, if the two pilots could stand it, then so could he.

The enemy hull now filled their entire view and it was only a matter of heartbeats before they swung around and came to an abrupt stop at one of the open spaces in the enemy hull that revealed a companionway inside.

The energy shield protecting the cruiser was designed to let any friendly craft through and, thankfully, Uktannu had been unable to switch his fleet's alignment indicators, given his need to catch the local defenses off-guard.

Eth reached up and pulled down a short assault rifle from its mag-clamp on one of the overhead supports. "Line up!" he shouted, feeling more at home by the minute.

This was what he was made for. It was on a ship in space, but it was infantry combat and his Humans were very good at it.

He checked his ammunition loadout. He'd checked it before sticking the weapon onto the support and he'd pulled it down at least twice since then to check it. The rituals of a man waiting for combat to begin…

He touched a finger to the grenade dispenser on his chest and a holographic window appeared in front of his left eye, showing a full load of stun, smoke and flechette grenades. He resisted the urge to look down again at the readout on his assault rifle.

He breathed a sigh of release as his helmet snapped shut. The wait was finally over.

In front of his team, a section of *Your Last Chance's* hull flowed out of the way, showing them an empty corridor leading to the center of the enemy cruiser. Free now to channel his nervous energy into action, he moved forward, leading them into a ship that probably didn't even know it was being boarded.

The Quailu weren't complete strangers to the concept of boarding actions, but then they didn't tend to get close enough in combat to make it feasible. By the time a warship was that close to an enemy it would have had to run a gauntlet of missile and railgun fire that would probably have reduced the attacker to a cloud of nanites and central core fragments.

They sometimes ran drills in which their fierce resistance always ended up repelling the 'boarders' but they didn't carry troops specifically for the task.

And this ship wouldn't even know it was carrying professional, enemy infantry until the first crewmen started dying.

They moved down the corridor toward the centerline. Ten meters away from the central companionway running from bow to stern, Eth noticed a shadow appear in the open, far end of the transverse corridor. One of their scout-ships preparing to land more troops.

He held up a hand, signaling for his team to take up defensive positions at the main intersection.

Noa and Oliv moved up to the corners bordering on the central, fore and aft companionway and, when Ed and Glen touched their shoulders, they swung their weapons around to aim down the central hallway; Noa facing aft and Oliv facing forward. Ed and Glen flowed past them, crossing the hall to take up similar positions, while Eth led the remaining four across to link up with the crew from the other scout-ship.

It turned out to be Carol, the warrant officer in command of *The Last Thing You'll Ever See*. She flashed a grin at Eth, reminding him that he wasn't the only one who felt the relief that comes with the end of the long waiting phase.

"We're still killing whatever tries to resist us, right?" she asked.

"Native or Quailu," Eth confirmed. "You gonna have any problems with that?"

"Had a long talk with my crew," she said. "They won't hesitate. They know we're playing by a new set of rules."

"Good." Eth nodded in Ed's direction. "Take your crew aft. Clear out whatever you find and take engineering. We'll go forward and seize the bridge."

A cold chill ran up his spine as a rail gun shrieked a few decks below them. He shook it off and led his team forward.

They came to the main ramp before encountering anyone. With the entire crew at action stations, there wasn't a great deal of wandering about going on, but a large work party was moving an ammunition pallet onto the ramp.

Eth and his team cut the native Durians down with a flurry of short bursts, leaving only one Durian and their Quailu petty officer on the far side of the pallet.

The Durian stayed behind cover, being an unarmed rating, but the Quailu, seeing that he faced native Kish troops, stepped boldly out from behind the pallet, drawing his sidearm with a nasty smirk.

"Didn't think ahead, did you?" he said, lifting his weapon toward Henkenu.

Eth could feel the arrogance of the petty officer. He was Quailu. He was in no danger, aside from a stray round. No native would dare harm a Quailu, regardless of rank or provocation.

And he was going to enjoy executing the impudent Humans, starting with Hendy.

Eth wished he could stop what was happening. The Quailu was going to die but he didn't realize it yet. His bold decision to come out and kill them all had been somewhat unexpected and he was going to get a shot off before his own wounds could stop him.

Eth's mind rebelled. This couldn't happen. The Quailu had to stop.

And so he did.

The enemy petty officer stopped raising his sidearm, a look of confusion quickly changing to fear as he sensed the intent of the Humans. Eight rounds slammed into his torso, throwing him back onto the tangle of dead Durians.

The terror and outrage faded into nothingness and Eth stood there, staring in shock. The Quailu was going to kill Hendy but he stopped. Eth stopped him, just by thinking it.

He snapped out of it as his team flowed past him and up the ramp. He fell in with them, now consciously reaching out to look for trouble ahead. The immediate area seemed to have a few echoes, but he got only faint impressions until he was close enough to carry on a conversation.

Noa was walking backward up the ramp, aiming up at the gallery that overlooked it. He squeezed off a burst. "Got him," he said laconically.

They left the ramp at the next deck and moved toward the bridge, slowing slightly as they encountered the occasional enemy. There wasn't even time for the five Quailu they eliminated to feel surprise at their predicament. Eth's people were showing no compunction at killing members of the master species.

They came to a stop outside the bridge. The enemy had finally realized that they were rapidly losing their crew to a hostile element and they'd set up an armed presence in front of the bridge entrance.

"No flechette grenades," Eth ordered, sidling up next to where Oliv was pressed against the curved wall, just out of the enemy's arc of fire. He slid a concussion grenade from the dispenser on his chest. "We're too close to critical systems here. We'll stun-and-gun."

Oliv nodded, holding up her own concussion grenade. "In three, two, one…"

They both leaned out and tossed the small discs toward the knot of enemy crewmen. The brilliant flash and the shockwave were both attenuated by the enemies' crew suits but it was enough to disorient them.

Eth and Oliv led the team around the curve to find most of their targets aiming more at the floor than at them. Some were even trying to examine their suits, searching for breaches in the mistaken assumption that they'd been attacked with flechette grenades.

Starting with the ones who seemed the most alert, they put them down with precisely controlled bursts and moved to the entry hatch leading into the bridge.

"No grenades," Eth insisted. "The concussion might be enough to input a touch-command on one of the consoles. We don't want to veer into another ship while we're trying to take *this* one."

They lined up, four on each side of the door but it was secured from the inside. Noa managed to talk the locking mechanism into seeing things their way and the team began pouring inside.

Eth was the third one in and he went left aiming at a crewman with a sidearm who was drawing a bead on Oliv. Before he could fire, she put three rounds into the Quailu's chest. He wondered, as he put a three round burst into what appeared to be the captain, whether he could stop a Quailu consistently enough for the ability to be reliable in combat.

His eyes grew wide as the last of the enemy bridge crew fell.

Could he do more than simply *stopping* them in their tracks?

"Not hard to track them." Rimush stared at the holo display where the attacking force was lit up by the plasma discharge from their railguns.

"How close can you get us?" Mishak asked.

"With all the ionized gases they're trailing," Rimush scorned, waving a hand at the display, "we could get close enough for our secondary batteries to engage, assuming they haven't left a screen behind to look for us."

That gave Mishak pause for thought. "No," he finally declared, "this is an all-or-nothing gamble for my uncle. He needs to grab this system as quickly as possible, so he'll throw every single gun he has at the defenses. Let's get in as close as we can."

It wasn't easy – watching allies get shot at while you snuck in with your guns silent, but he wanted to give his scouts a chance to deliver on Eth's plan and they wanted it to be very clear that Uktannu had committed to an attack on Heiropolis.

"At least there'll be no doubt about your uncle's intentions," Rimush said, his thoughts falling into the synchronicity that used to bother Mishak far more than it did now.

He sighed, watching the projection of the probable enemy locations, waiting for the cruiser nearest to Eth's planned location to send a signal.

Something had happened to Eth when he was aboard that Varangian ship, but he was reluctant to discuss it and, even more unsettling, his mind had closed to Mishak and all Quailu.

Mishak had gained a great deal of confidence in his own abilities lately and that had changed his own aversion to Quailu empathy. Did he trust Ethkenu any less now that he couldn't read his feelings?

He owed the Human for his *own* transformation. The information gained by his Human team had allowed him to face down a hostile coalition that may well have had the enthusiastic blessings of the Imperial court. More importantly, he'd been able to face down his own father.

He'd rewarded Eth and his entire unit with freedom, strengthening the reciprocal bond between lord and follower so there should be gratitude on both sides. Should he trust him any less just because he couldn't feel his thoughts?

"Carol," Eth smiled at the holo. "Glad to see you made it to engineering in one piece."

"Only to find Thane and his boys already here," she groused. "We're ok, except for Kan who took a wrench to the head because he didn't clear behind the comms modulator."

"How is he?"

"We'll know when he wakes up," she said with a shrug. "Did I mention the comms modulator's in a bad way as well? Full of holes, seeing as how we all cut loose on the Quailu that smacked Kan."

Eth suppressed the outburst that came immediately to mind, turning to Ed who'd heard the exchange and was now glaring at him from the comms console with an I-told-you-so look on his face.

He usually thought faster when he wasn't cursing angrily anyway. He looked past Ed to where Henkenu waited at the helm. "We'll have to send our message back to the fleet without the comms system.

Hendy, bring us around so our mains will bear on the nearest enemy cruiser. Oliv, fire as your guns bear and then let 'em have a salvo of missiles as well."

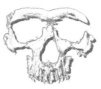

The fleet was close enough now to make out the individual enemy ships rather than just their firing signatures. Mishak's force remained undetected, though, thanks to the trailing haze of gases that blinded Uktannu's aft sensors. Mishak realized he was clenching his fists and forced his fingers open.

He was ridiculously conscious now of his hands. They were dangling oddly at his sides and so he stuck them behind his back, forcing his left hand to clasp his right lightly enough not to break any bones.

The very picture of military leadership, he derided himself.

Rimush grunted in amusement and Mishak could clearly feel, not derision, but commiseration. Of course the captain had been through countless battles and he'd most likely started out his first fight, as captain, in much the same state as Mishak.

Even serving on the bridge at one of the stations wasn't the same thing. Those crewmen and officers all had something very specific to do and it demanded their full attention.

At a moment like this, Rimush and Mishak were faced with the prospect of battle but with no physical tasks to occupy their hands.

Mishak stepped closer to the holo and pulled out a secondary projection of the cruiser that was closest to the scout-ships and, therefore, the most likely target for boarding. He held his hands on opposite sides and rotated the view, rather than walking around it to get a better feeling for the three-dimensional view.

He almost didn't notice when the vector display began to change. "It's turning!" he shouted in surprise.

Rimush cursed. "They spotted us? Must have had a frigate holding back to watch for us."

Mishak was nodding in agreement but then a huge plume erupted from the cruiser's bow. "It's firing on one of the other cruisers," Mishak said excitedly.

"Why didn't they signal us?" Rimush groused, then caught himself. "Well, I suppose they just did, didn't they?"

"Signal weapons-free to the fleet, if you please, Captain," Mishak ordered. "And also remind them not to fire on our newest cruiser!"

Much of that opening salvo was directed toward the enemy frigates, seeing as they were the most maneuverable class in the action and they'd be far easier to deal with while they were still cruising along in ignorance, firing down-well at the Heiropolitan security forces.

"Have a signal sent to the Heiropolitans when you have a moment, Captain." Mishak was watching the progress of the outbound weaponry as he spoke. "Advise them that we're here to assist."

The missiles began ejecting clouds of cluster-munitions, each with a tiny pitch drive and enough reactant to last for several minutes of target-pursuit. The heavy railgun projectiles, lacking the constant acceleration, would eject the second wave of cluster missiles, using the force of separation to adjust the trajectory of the heavy casings.

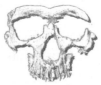

"First target is crippled," Oliv announced.

"Good," Eth said, still caught up in the adrenaline rush of infantry combat, though now he was fighting with a ship instead of a combat team. *Perhaps that's not so different.*

"Spread the next salvo among the ships we can hit from here," he ordered, "then, Hendy, I want you to get us in close to that crippled cruiser. Keep her between us and the rest of the enemy forces."

He could feel Oliv's desire to concentrate fire on another target but she kept it to herself. "We need to distract them away from their attack on Heiropolis," he explained. "Knowing one of your ships has taken heavy damage in a fight is easy enough to put aside but knowing your *own* ship is taking damage from an unexpected flank is far more insistent.

"We want them turning away from their surprise attack and concentrating on us while our fleet comes in on them from behind."

"Let's hope *our* fleet shows a proper sense of urgency," Noa added quietly.

Eth turned to the damage control station where Noa raised an eyebrow, daring him to challenge his mistrust of the Quailu. "They're more than happy to let us take all the risks while they sneak up from behind – they've only sent us natives. None of their ships are up here. I'm just hoping they don't plan on sneaking along till they finally get detected."

Eth didn't really want to reprimand Noa for voicing a concern that he'd been struggling with as well. Fortunately, he could feel Oliv's sudden elation. "Of course they're going to come to our rescue, Noa," he said, with a mischievous smile.

"Massive wave of cluster-munitions inbound!" Oliv announced. "They're targeting all ships except ours."

"This ship *is* quite valuable to our lord, after all," he told his engineer, still smiling.

"Firing," Oliv said. "Dispersed targeting enabled."

The rail guns howled beneath their feet and the holo displays of the enemy fleet froze in place for a moment while the sensors were temporarily blinded.

"Moving us into cover." Henkenu's fingers flew across the navigational display.

The forward motion left most of the ionized gasses behind and the tactical holos jumped ahead to show the latest data.

"Multiple hits!" Oliv exulted. "The fleet hit 'em hard. Looks like they went after the frigates first. They've only got two left that can answer to their helms from the look of it!

"Looks like we've got their attention," she added. "Their countermeasures were concentrated on what the planetary defense threw at them and they didn't count on an attack coming from one of their *own* ships! We've hurt three cruisers and knocked out one, maybe two – there were secondaries going off...

"They're turning!" she shouted.

"Our way?" Eth asked.

"Two ships turning our way but most are trying to face the fleet," she replied. "Bad timing for them. A wave of missiles from Heiropolis is just starting to separate."

They had to find a way to coordinate with the local defense forces. Eth didn't want to take this ship only to lose it to friendly fire. When it came to him, he nearly smacked the faceplate of his helmet with his palm. "Glen," he turned to the useless comms console where Glen was running diagnostics.

"Get back to our ship and get us linked up with the defense forces."

Glen looked startled for a moment, then shook his head ruefully. "I should have thought of that myself," he muttered, jogging toward the exit.

Eth started to tell Hendy to get the shattered cruiser between them and the Heiropolitan missile barrage when Oliv shouted again, this time in elation tinged with an edge of frustration.

"They're running!" Rimush said in surprise.

Mishak understood his fleet-captain's response. For a Quailu force to flee an open battle was to lose face before the entire empire. The same ships had run from him before, but they'd been on an underhanded false-flag operation and, therefore, had accrued no dishonor to their house.

This force was clearly fighting for his uncle and that meant his uncle was fleeing from battle.

"We've made contact with our scouts," the communications officer added. "They passed on a report from Orbital Defense forces indicating the small force attacking their flank has run as well, "Looks like the attack is over!"

Cheering broke out on the bridge.

There was no chance of Uktannu seizing this system now. His attack was in tatters, his people dying. His own future was sealed, as Sandrak would not take this betrayal lightly. If he fell into his brother's hands, Uktannu would die stretched, face-down, between four posts with his lungs pulled out of his back to deflate in the cold air.

That he would consider running from the fight, escaping an honorable death in combat, only to die the traitor's death…

Mishak shook his head and Rimush grunted agreement with his lord's feelings. Uktannu's retreat spoke to the very lack of judgement and forethought that had gotten him into this mess in the first place.

He wasn't even thinking clearly enough to realize that he was trading a quick death in battle for an excruciatingly painful and humiliating death at his brother's hands. His house was finished.

Mishak stared at Rimush, his shock reaching out.

"Gods!" Rimush exclaimed. "You have the strongest claim on your uncle's fief! You defeated the traitor. If you can get to Dur before anyone else gets wind of this battle, you can assume control of Uktannu's government – purely in the interest of stability, of course."

"Of course," Mishak agreed drily, but he couldn't hide the exultation. Kish was still his, but his uncle had held seven planets and Mishak had every right to claim them. He was of the same dynasty, being Uktannu's nephew, and he was the one who'd defeated his uncle's traitorous scheme.

He reached out to grab a stanchion as the realization hit him.

It flooded across to Rimush. "Your uncle held seven worlds," he breathed in awe. "and you still hold Kish…"

Mishak's head was reeling but he forced himself to concentrate. He needed to act quickly and decisively. "Get me Warrant Officer Ethkenu on this holo," he ordered, suddenly feeling very generous.

And he owed much of this current situation to Eth.

"My Lord," Eth bowed to the holographic image of Mishak. Such formality was expected over open communications and, frankly, their relationship had veered away from the growing familiarity of the last few weeks.

"Warrant," Mishak nodded in acknowledgement of the honor. "Is your cruiser operational?"

My cruiser? Eth nodded. "All but for communications. A firefight in engineering damaged a critical component. I have a team fixing it right now." He saw Mishak frown but he couldn't *feel* it. He supposed that was how his lord now felt about talking to *him*.

"Then how are we talking?"

"I have a man relaying our conversation through *The Last Thing You'll Ever See.*"

"Ah." Mishak nodded absently. "Very resourceful but not why I called you." The hazily projected Mishak straightened. "You will retain command of the cruiser as well as overall command of the scouting force. Liaise with the Heiropolitans, give them whatever assistance they need to get their defenses back on their feet. If nothing else, an extra cruiser and some scouts should lend some weight to their forces."

"Me, sir?" Eth's mouth dropped open but he quickly put it back to work. "A warrant officer in command of a cruiser?"

"Good point," Mishak agreed. "I'd better register a full commission for you. Computer, as a member of the Awilu class and under my authority as a planetary governor, I hereby confer the rank of lieutenant upon Ethkenu of Kish. I also confer the rank of second lieutenant upon Olivkenu, Noakenu, and Mihenkenu of Kish. I hereby declare patents of dispensation for all personnel being advanced by this order. Record and transmit to Throne World."

He grinned at Eth, whose mouth had fallen open again. "Well, you need some officers to stand watch on the bridge, don't you?"

"Lord," Eth stammered. "You do us a great honor! We never expected this."

"Nor did I," Mishak admitted. "It just came to me a moment ago, when I realized I had a strong claim on my uncle's holdings, seeing as how he's been caught in rebellion against his overlord. I've got seven systems to seize and I can't dally around here to accept the praise of the Heiropolitans."

"You'll have to stay here and 'wave the banner' for me."

Seven systems. Eth's eyes grew wide. "Nergal's bones! That makes you an elector!"

Mishak laughed. "From a one-province minor to an elector in the HQE in the course of a few hours. If I ever find the person who put this idea in my uncle's ear, I don't know if I'll kill him or reward him!"

He shook his head. "Well, you see why I need to leave immediately and with most of my forces?"

"I do, Lord, and congratulations!"

"Same to you and I'll endorse any warrants you wish to write for your people." The projection shut off.

Eth took a deep breath and blew it out between pursed lips as he set the system to page Noa to the bridge. He turned to look at the others, catching Oliv and Hendy's gaze in particular. The two new officers were grinning broadly. "I suppose you heard that?"

He wagged an admonitory finger at them. "Nobody talks to Noa till he can get back up here from engineering. I'm the captain," he said with a sudden thrill of realization, "so it's my prerogative to tell him about his promotion."

That brought him up short. Till now, he'd been the only Human with rank, aside from the two warrants in command of the other scout-ships. He now had the authority to rate his people. He could make and break petty officers as he pleased.

He caught his breath. Mishak had also promised to endorse any warrants Eth wanted to make as well. Not only could he create new warrant officers, he could *promote* his existing warrant officers to higher grades as well.

And he'd have to if he was to run this cruiser on a skeleton crew with a mere lieutenant at the top of a very flat pyramid.

Noa burst onto the bridge, breathing heavily.

Eth stared at him for a moment. "Did you run all the way up here?"

"Yeah," Noa wheezed. "I'm trying to make some improvements before the new captain shows up to take over. He'll probably bring some of our folk along and they'll thank me for a few ladders, at the very least. I don't have time to stroll back and forth between engineering and the bridge so…" He gave Eth an expectant look.

Nobody said anything but he could feel Oliv fight the urge to blurt out the news.

"Well?" Noa demanded. "What is it? Spit it out before the new captain gets here."

"Too late," Oliv told him. "The new captain's already here."

At least she hadn't spoiled Eth's fun.

Noa looked around the bridge, cursing softly. "Where?"

"Right here," Eth told him.

"What, you?" Noa blurted, grinning. "Gods, but they're scraping the barrel, aren't they?"

"Well," Eth amended, "I have the *title* of captain but I'm actually just a first lieutenant by rank."

"You're serious?" Noa looked back to Oliv.

"It gets worse," she teased.

"Mishak made her a second lieutenant," Eth explained.

"And Hendy's one as well," she added.

"You're not kidding!" Noa exclaimed. "So our lord just started handing out commissions to whoever he saw in the holo? Wish I'd been here."

"He commissioned three second lieutenants," Eth corrected him. "One of them wasn't on the bridge at the time, so we had to call him up to the bridge to tell him."

He could feel the guarded hope in his old comrade and it was Oliv who finally let him off the hook.

"Congratulations to our new engineering officer," she said.

"Huh!" Noa took a moment to mull it over. "Well," he said, turning for the exit, "if you'll excuse me, I've got a lot more changes than I'd originally planned waiting for me down in engineering."

Under New Management

"We have the beacon from Dur Orbital Control," the communications officer announced. "They sound a little squirrely, but they're giving us a standard approach vector. Lots of chatter going on with the ships in orbit."

"Are the Varangians still here?" Mishak demanded.

"They are, sir," the sensor officer confirmed. "Same holding-orbit they were in when we were last here."

"Good!" Mishak was throwing off a mood of enthusiasm like a message-drone set to omnidirectional, boosting the bridge crew's morale. "They're exactly what we need right now."

Because they'd now do for him what they'd intended to do for his uncle. Uktannu's plot had turned in Mishak's favor so neatly he'd be tempted to believe a claim that he'd arranged the whole thing himself.

"Most of the planetary defense forces are here," tactical advised, "minus a few frigates that the Lord Uktannu took with him and which we disabled at Heiropolis. Two of the cruisers from the attack are here as well, but neither one has ever been known to carry your uncle."

"Very well." Mishak took a moment to calm himself. He'd rehearsed this moment dozens of times while they shaped path to Dur. He'd spent hours talking it over with Rimush.

"Let's get this party started. Open an unencrypted holo-channel, omnidirectional." He was ready.

"Attention, all points – Dur. I am the Lord Mishak, only son and heir of the great Sandrakwilu, may he outlive us all." He placed a hand over his hearts, bowing his head in accordance with the forms.

"I have just come here from Heiropolis where Uktannu the traitor has attacked that peaceful system in an open act of rebellion against his lawful overlord. In attacking his liege, he attacks the very fabric of the Holy Quailu Empire and, therefore, the emperor himself, may His

194

Imperial Majesty outlive us all." Again he bowed his head and covered his hearts.

"Calling upon the authority given by the emperor to our overlord, I now declare Uktannu of Dur to be a renegade. Every hand shall be turned against him and any who give him shelter or aid shall see their genomes wiped from existence.

"As you have lost your lord," he continued, "I shall shoulder the burden in his stead. I am of the same dynasty and, as heir to Sandrakwilu, your systems would have come under my authority eventually. Accordingly, I shall serve my noble father in the administration of Uktannu's former holdings."

Rimush stepped forward into the pickup zone for the holo-reader. "All captains currently present in orbit will now declare their oaths by order of seniority."

This was the tricky moment. The forces in orbit were shocked and, perhaps, desperate enough to do anything. It had been Rimush's suggestion that he give the call for oaths, demonstrating to the others that he was very much behind Mishak and serving as a subtle reminder of the terrible revenge that only Mishak could protect them from.

For Sandrak would happily destroy every single ship in Uktannu's forces, if they didn't see the light and double-quick, at that.

"Captain Meerak is signaling us on an encrypted channel," the communications officer said.

"Decrypt it and make the conversation open to all channels," Mishak ordered, forcing himself to stand straight.

Meerak shimmered into view, his features proclaiming his anger clearly enough to make up for the lack of readable emotions. "You arrogant young gelding!" Meerak raged. "I'll be damned before I ever swear an oath to the likes of…"

"Mass separation!" tactical shouted. "Missile launch from delta four-five-seven! They're targeting Meerak's ship!"

Mishak had been fighting the mix of rage and apprehension triggered by Meerak leading the proceedings off with an act of outright defiance, but this new news brought his spirits back up.

Meerak, in the ship designated by tactical as delta four-five-six, and Chusain, in four-five-seven, had both taken part in the attack at Heiropolis. Meerak had probably assumed his role in the attack would doom him anyway, but perhaps Chusain saw another option.

Meerak had broken off in mid-rant and was now looking to the left, at crewmen Mishak couldn't see, but the captain's wild gestures spoke volumes. Then his arms came up to guard his face and the image faded away.

"We've lost the signal," the communications officer said. "Incoming hail from delta four-five-seven – unencrypted and in the open." He looked back at Mishak.

"Connect us."

"I believe I'm next in the seniority list," Chusain drawled.

Mishak had only seen him a few times and they'd never had occasion to talk with each other. He had a feeling he'd get to know a great deal about him in the next few moments. "You have my thanks, Captain, for dealing with an unrepentant traitor."

Unrepentant had been a deliberate choice of words. He wanted to signal to the assembled captians that clemency was on offer to those who saw the light.

"As for me and those who serve me," Chusain began, using the same phrasing that the Quailu had used for thousands of years, "we will serve you and those whom *you* serve. We shall live and die at your pleasure..." he bowed his head, "... My Lord."

"By the authority granted to me by my lord and, through him, by our noble emperor, I accept your service."

Mishak had decided to leave his father in the formalities even though, as an elector, he was now considered a primary lord himself, answering directly to the great Tir Uttur. As Sandrak's son, he still owed a level of fealty to his father and he knew it would raise Sandrak's wrath to see eight planets carved so completely out of his own holdings.

With Chusain's deadly support, any other captains who might have been considering defiance lost heart. Every one of them, from warships to freighters, swore allegiance and promised to pass the word to every ship they encountered.

Commerce would slow in the weeks to come as ships diverted to one of the seven worlds for the oath. Defense forces from the other six planets would swear to the planetary governors, who would then come to Dur to serve as proxies for their respective worlds.

The last of the uncertainties was dealt with when the Bashar in charge of the local defenses appeared in front of Mishak and bent the holographic knee.

This had all happened at Kish when he became governor, more than a decade ago, but it had carried little meaning for the younger Mishak. He'd merely been taking over an unfashionable posting so his father could keep him out of the way.

This time, he was savoring the fruits of victory.

And they were sweet. He was an elector by his *own* efforts, a prince of the realm. He would have become one eventually, on his father's death but it was a rare achievement to actually *take* that status by the sweat of one's own brow; by right of conquest.

His uncle had tried and failed.

Uktannu could conceivably manage to scrape together enough ships from his other six worlds to cause problems for Mishak. If he moved quickly enough, he could bring a large force to Dur and, if he managed to kill Mishak, he'd be able to muddy the waters over his renegade status.

That still left the powerful rage of his brother, Sandrak, but nobody ever got ahead in the empire by assuming they were out of options.

Uncertainty about his uncle made the Varangians doubly welcome aboard the *Dibbarra*.

"We meet again, Great Lord." Commodore Ingolf bowed his head this time instead of the polite incline he'd offered to Mishak, the one-system minor lord, who'd so recently visited the Varangian flagship.

Mishak returned the honor to the Varangian officer who'd come to *him* this time. He held out a hand toward the ready room. "Please, join me for coffee."

Though Mishak saw the value in keeping stewards around to handle some tasks, he didn't hold with cluttering up a warship with servants. There was a steward who had brought coffee over from the mess but he was likely off sleeping or gambling at the moment, which suited Mishak just fine.

Mishak poured two mugs, sensing approval at this act of humility from a newly minted elector. The Varangians tended to be harder to read than most, but they were nothing like the Zeartekka. He frowned.

Or Eth…

He shook his head, clearing the thought away for the moment. "It's fortunate to find your force still here, Commodore," he said as he set the mug down in front of Ingolf, near the end of the long table.

Mishak waved the Varangian commander to his seat and dropped into a chair at the same end so they'd face at an angle rather than opposed across the table. "A new claim, especially one with no prior registration, can be very tricky."

Ingolf took a sip and shuddered with delight, a reaction that most citizens would never expect to see from a Varangian but Mishak had spent much of his youth at court. He'd seen these nearly invincible warriors drink, joke and prank one another, just like any species.

He also knew there was no rushing them in a meeting. They always seemed to get things done but they rarely got concerned about how quickly it was accomplished.

There always seemed to be *just* enough time.

He smiled. "The coffee is to your liking, I see."

"I had twenty kilos aboard the *Visundr* but cheevers got at it."

"Cheevers?" Mishak chuckled. "Been having a quiet cruise, Commodore?"

"We had to rig for combat twice on the way out here from Throne World," Ingolf countered, his tone mild, "but you know how it is. The damn things have learned that spare suits make for good nesting. We went into a fight near Isriria – driving off some raiders – but a sizeable number of the little vermin survived.

"We rigged for combat again when we got here and cleared out the suits but..." he spread his hands, "...they got their damn mold all over my coffee beans."

Cheevers, small semi-sentient six-legged mammals, were the constant bane of all ships. They were nearly impossible to eradicate and they had the ability to communicate effective hiding spots among themselves.

Their survivability was commendable but their biology was problematic, to say the least. They relied on a symbiotic relationship with a highly specialized mold that produced several vitamins the cheevers were unable to make on their own. They licked the secreted vitamins from their fur. It kept them healthy but tended to leave mold spores on everything they came into contact with.

Mishak chuckled as he brought up a holo interface. "I'm just sending a quick message to the quartermaster," he told Ingolf. "I'm having a forty-kilo case of coffee delivered aboard your shuttle."

"Ahh! Coffee straight from Kish!" Ingolf practically beamed. "I sincerely hope I haven't brought any of the little vermin over with me. I'd hate to see *your* stock spoiled."

"Unlikely," Mishak said. "We have rats on most of our ships. The galley staff does several good dishes from rat-meat but we always have enough to kill off any cheevers that get aboard."

"Really?" Ingolf stroked his chin. "Perhaps we could have a few?"

"I'm sure the galley would have a few in cages. We capture them alive so they stay fresh. We can give you a couple of breeding pairs." He raised his mug but stopped and set it down.

"Commodore, a friendly warning; you do *not* want to get bitten by a rat. Our Humans bleed for an hour or so if they get bit but Quailu need a coagulation booster or we bleed for several days, even from new cuts. They have powerful anti-coagulants in their saliva."

"Small but deadly? No wonder they're so effective against cheevers."

"It's a little scary to see them in action. I pity the cheever that gets aboard one of my ships." Mishak took a sip and sighed. "You should definitely test their effects on Varangians before you turn them loose on your cheever problem."

Ingolf nodded. "I have a crewman in the brig for repeated incompetence. He's an idiot, but he has connections. I'll toss a couple of rats in with him and see what happens."

Mishak laughed. "I would dearly love to see that!"

"For forty kilos of fresh coffee, the least I can do is send a copy of the holo-recording," Ingolf raised his mug in a toast before taking his next sip. He grunted his approval of the flavor.

Mishak set down his coffee. "What twist of fate took you away from palace security?" He asked.

The Varangian looked at him, surprised, pleased but also a little guarded. "I wasn't sure you would remember me," he said carefully. "I was just one of the protection detail back then."

"But you were guarding the princess Tashmitum so I saw you every day," Mishak replied, "until the Emperor decided she and I were growing too close and sent her away to her mother's home-world."

"And most of us were transferred to ship-board duty for not keeping the Lord Marduk properly informed. Though I've managed to advance, nonetheless." The Varangian said, with a grin. "And that brings us to the present. You'd like for us to stay and review your claim?"

"I would," Mishak confirmed. "Though we'll need some time to prepare our case in the proper form..."

The Varangian chuckled. "A phrase that has become a part of the 'proper form' through its own frequent use." He inclined his head, a show of friendly respect.

"We will stay, young prince, and gladly."

So Mishak would have the time he needed to collect the oaths from his outlying systems. Once that was completed, there would be no point in Uktannu trying to reclaim his lost territory.

Heiropolitan Hospitality

Heiropolis was a more advanced world than Kish. The natives had been far more technically advanced and they'd managed to avoid enslavement when they were annexed into the empire. They were known for their expertise in sensors, among other things, and half the sensor suite in Eth's new cruiser had come from this world.

They also seemed to lead the empire in smug mushkenu business owners.

"Kish has only had mushkenu natives for a few cycles, hasn't it?" a portly Heiropolitan native asked him.

Eth was glancing around at the reception being thrown in their honor, though there was little honor in evidence here.

"Yes," he answered without inflection, as though he were talking to a computer. He didn't like the posturing circuitry magnate, especially when his wife's amusement gave the lie to his barbed politeness.

He, of course, could feel their disdain for their wardu-born visitors but they thought they were hiding it.

"And what was your job, before you were raised to mushkenu status?" the Heiropolitan inquired silkily. "Agriculture? General labor, perhaps?"

The wife actually had to turn her head to hide her amusement at that one, but Eth felt it as plainly as if she'd broken out laughing.

"Combat," he said, turning now to stare into the other's eyes directly. "I killed the natives of other worlds, mostly mushkenu, and I'm quite good at it. Would you like to arrange a demonstration for the other guests? I believe you've given just enough provocation for me to escalate this conversation."

Fear feels so much better than contempt. Eth smiled at the Heiropolitan as he bowed and muttered an apology. "Perhaps another time?" he called to the retreating couple.

"You too?" Oliv came to stand next to him, drink in hand.

"Somebody give you a hard time, Oliv?"

"A hard time's exactly what he had in mind," she answered darkly. "Evidently, they have a small wardu class here and prostitution is one of their 'career paths'."

"You can't expect these sphincter-burglars to get action on the basis of their charming personalities, can you?" Eth asked. He glanced at her. "You mean that…"

"Offered me five hundred ducats to service him behind that pillar over there," she nodded to a far side of the large reception room.

"What did you say to him?"

"Not much sense wasting breath talking to him at the moment." She looked at him with defiance. "He'd need to be conscious first…"

"I didn't notice any commotion…"

"That's because I smiled at him and went behind the pillar before I gave him my answer."

"Just a friendly thumping, right?"

She paused. "Might be a broken bone or two."

He took a deep breath. He could hardly blame her, especially when he'd just offered a duel to an influential local. "I think we've had enough of the local 'hospitality'. Why don't you go round up the rest while I make our excuses to the governor?"

The governor saw him approaching and hastily concluded a conversation with one of his courtiers. "The hero of the hour!" he announced grandly.

Eth could feel that the Quailu noble was unconvinced that his world would have fallen into hostile hands and that he was hosting the Humans for fear Sandrak would think him ungrateful for his son's efforts.

Perhaps Mishak and his forces should have let the locals take more of a beating before they'd intervened.

"With your leave, Governor," Eth began politely, "I'll take my people back to our ships now."

"But we have just begun," the governor waved a hand about the hall, his relief at this request at clear odds with his words. No doubt the inability to read Eth was weighing heavily on his attitude toward him.

Eth was tempted to tell the governor to compile a list of insults from his guests and send it to him in orbit to save time. He resisted the urge, knowing it would only make the Humans seem touchy.

"We have much work to do if we're to be battle ready," he said instead, "and I should let you know that you'll need medical staff for one of your people." He was about to point toward the pillar but the governor had already glanced in that direction.

"Yes," he replied, tone growing colder. "He was cruelly assaulted and…"

"He fell," Eth said forcefully.

"Fell?"

"Against a pillar," Eth insisted, iron in his voice, "repeatedly."

The governor gaped at him.

"With your leave, Excellency…" Eth turned and stalked out through the crowd.

He glanced over at Noa as he fell in beside him. "What's that thing on your face?"

Noa brought a hand up to touch a red bump on his cheek. "Remember that security officer on Chiron?"

"I seem to recall meeting a *lot* of security officers the last time we went there…"

"I think you'd remember this one," Noa said. "Bad manners. Exploded all over me?"

"Oh yeah. He was funny."

"Funny like a blood-borne parasite."

"You don't mean…"

Noa nodded. "Posthumous revenge. He had a binary infection. The spores spread out in the neighboring muscle tissue until the 'queen' node achieves critical function. Then it comes together to build a spore-production cyst. Any day now, she'll be releasing new spores into my blood."

Eth shuddered. "Then why don't you cut the damned thing out?" he growled.

"I only get one chance at this. If I act too soon, the remaining spores will scatter throughout the body and start over in a thousand locations. If I wait too long to cut, then it's essentially the same problem."

Noa licked his lips. "Believe me, I want to pull out a knife and slice into my cheek like you wouldn't believe but that's *exactly* why there are so many carriers in the empire. I programmed my medical nanites to deal with this. They're surrounding the cyst, waiting for the first hint of a hormone shift."

Noa fell silent, reading the anger in Eth's face.

His expression was enough to deter further conversations as they moved through the crowd. He was thinking about how good it would feel to shoot a few of the attendees, perhaps even that idiot of a governor.

Abdu had died for a Quailu just like him and he'd received no thanks for it. He'd even died a wardu for his troubles.

And now these comfortably lazy fools were looking down their noses at their saviors because *they'd* been born to the mushkenu class. They missed no opportunity to point out their perceived superiority.

Eth almost stopped walking as he realized what that meant. The Quailu rarely bothered with such games, except for those who were near the bottom of their own hierarchy – that cargo handler when they first came aboard the *Dibbarra*, for example.

No matter how wealthy or well-dressed these Heiropolitans were, they still ranked beneath the lowliest Quailu. The governor was Quailu, of course, but he was probably just some extra son, sent to this boring little dustball. Barely a member of the awilu classs.

That was why they were such a pack of assholes.

He laughed out loud, not caring what they thought of him. He left through the same side door they'd used when they'd arrived an hour earlier – had they really been insulted that many times in only an hour?

Your Last Chance was bobbing gently at the edge of the pedway. Oliv already had the rest of their crew waiting at the boarding ramp.

"What changed your mood so suddenly?" she demanded. "I thought we agreed to be pissed."

"It was more an understanding than an agreement," he replied cheerfully, waving them up the ramp.

"Hold on!" a loud, deep voice yelled.

They all turned to look, seeing a Quailu in oracle robes running toward them. The robes were stained with what looked like an atlas of at least a week's worth of meals. The filthy garment fought a valiant but ultimately doomed holding-action against his large belly which had parted three of the toggles near his navel.

"Gods!" he wheezed, coming to a stop in front of Eth. "I look away for half a heartbeat and you all disappear!"

"Didn't see that coming, did you, Father?" Eth needled him, not exactly well disposed to non-Humans in general at the moment.

He'd meant to be churlish but the disheveled oracle seemed imperturbable. "You can't insult me!" he declared with an angry face he couldn't hold for more than a few seconds before it dissolved into a friendly grin. "Believe me, others have tried!"

Eth couldn't help but laugh. He wanted to hate this Quailu but he suspected it might entail more work than it was worth. "What do you want with us, Father? We're about to lift off."

"That's exactly what I want," the oracle exclaimed, reaching inside the fold of his robe and pulling out a strip of fermented fat, which explained the oddly shaped bulge above the braided leather belt.

Eth had no trouble imagining this holy man racing after them but stopping to grab a tray of fat from a waiter and dump it into the fold of his evil-smelling garment. "Father?"

"Lift-off," the Quailu said. "I'd like very much for you to take me with you – to get me off this shit-heap of a planet."

"No customers here?" Oliv asked, one foot on the ramp.

"Oh, plenty of those," he did a double-take at her before taking a bite of the fat, nodding in appreciation at the flavor. "No end of folk wanting to know their futures, but I see the same thing in every one of them: they scheme until some other schemer out-foxes them and they end up starting over from square one.

"You know why a Heiropolitan gives you a pat on the back?" he asked the Humans. He turned to shout at the crowd standing near the exit, taking the night air. "Because they're looking for a place to stick the knife!

"All they stand for is themselves," he said, turning back to Eth. "In all seriousness, if I could unleash a terrible plague on this world, I'm not certain I'd be able to refrain."

"I'm not certain you *have* refrained," Eth said, leaning back from the odor.

"I don't know if you've noticed," the oracle continued, apparently missing Eth's comment, "but the little darlings don't have the highest opinion of you Humans, even though you helped save them from a nasty tax hike."

"Why tell us that?" Eth demanded.

A shrug. "Common enemies... Look, I'll work for my passage. I'll serve as your personal oracle, if you like."

Eth certainly had questions about his future, especially after learning of the Varangians' interest in him.

And he just couldn't help but like the fellow. He didn't act like a member of the ruling race; he was just a person. "What's your name, Father?"

"Sulak," he replied, leaning forward slightly. "Sulak the traveler, perhaps?"

Eth smiled. "What does your sight tell you, Father?"

Sulak belched mightily. "I'm afraid the sight tells me little about myself," he admitted, "but it doesn't take the sight to know you make for better company than the locals."

"Well, we aren't going anywhere at the moment," Eth told him. "We're supposed to help secure Heiropolis."

"You'll be moving on soon enough," Sulak assured him, "and I'd rather not miss it."

It seemed Eth's fate to be the last to actually *know* his fate. "You're welcome to join us," he said, "but keep your predictions to yourself. You'll have us running into all sorts of harebrained schemes."

"My weary ears thank you!" Father Sulak scrambled up the boarding ramp. "And thank you," he said to Oliv as she passed him on the way to her tactical station, "for improving Marenko's personality. Unconsciousness becomes him!"

"And don't dwell on that mouth-breather," he told her solemnly. "His attitude, like all the others, comes from jealousy, if I'm not much mistaken."

He dropped into Glen's unoccupied comms chair and rooted around in his robe until he found a large piece of smoked fish.

Hendy dropped into the pilot's seat and began the pre-flight check, while Eth stopped at Oliv's tactical station, casting a quick glance at the Quailu and his snack.

"It's worth remembering," Eth said to her quietly, "that the weight behind our commissions advance or decay with the fortunes of the lord who issued them.

"Our lord is most likely an elector by now, a prince of the realm. The only way our commissions could hold more backing is if he replaced the emperor himself."

Seniority counted for much in the imperial house militaries but the power of an officer's lord carried a great deal of weight. A lieutenant of seniority who served a *minor* lord would be wise to defer to a junior lieutenant commissioned by an elector.

It was a complicated system and it applied to civil matters as well. "Your word carries more weight in court than anyone in that reception, except for Quailu, of course," he told her. "And you've only been freed for, what, a couple of months?"

The space above her nose wrinkled. "Are you telling me they're just jealous?"

"Well..." he paused, "... if they are, then they probably don't consciously realize it. Then again, they might just be assholes!"

She laughed. "I don't see why it can't be both."

Bad Timing

Bau sat at the governor's desk. Three faces were projected in front of her, their backgrounds listed beside each. She turned to General Tilsin. "I see no great differences between them. Do you have a preference?"

Tilsin sat behind a second desk, brought in to make room for the new governor. It was meant as a sign that he was there to work with the soon-to-be-appointed leader.

And also to keep a close eye on him.

"Sumugan seems the least shifty," Tilsin offered. "We can work with him better than the others."

The three candidates had been selected by the assembly and put forward for Bau's decision.

She closed the projection and got up from her seat. "Good. Let's go find him. The sooner we park his backside behind this desk, the sooner I can get home."

They left through a side door that led to a long, descending corridor. It took them under the public square and back up into the assembly offices.

They found Sumugan's office on the two hundred fifteenth floor. He practically jumped out of his seat when they walked in.

"Assemblyman Sumugan," Bau said, coming straight to the point, "you will be my representative, here on Arbella."

Tilsin cursed violently, radiating alarm.

"General?" Bau turned to face him.

Tilsen held up his forearm, showing a small holo interface. "A horde of refugee ships are falling out of path in our approach corridor. Their registries list them as being from Gimmerai."

Gimmerai and Arbella. The two worlds were heavily agricultural and cut into Bau's profit margins. Marduk had assured her the imperial court would stay out of this and Shullat, the minor lord she'd taken them from, didn't have the forces to face even *her* small military.

She had pacified Gimmerai in much the same way she was now winning over the Arbellans. Gimmeraian refugees meant someone had snuck in behind her and taken it over, most likely Shullat, but he didn't have the forces to do it nor the reputation to win allies to his cause.

Who would be willing to aid someone like him?

"Governor," Tilsin said, looking up from his holo, "congratulations, and my apologies for this immediate crisis, but…" he turned to Bau. "My Lady, you have to leave. They're likely headed this way as we speak. No sense taking half the territory back and leaving us here to prepare for a fight. They'll want to hit us here while we're still scratching our heads."

"Absolutely not!" she flared. "You'd insist on sending my escort with me and you'll need those ships here."

"But the danger…"

"…Is something I decided to accept when I began planning this venture."

"Those ships may be needed at home," Tilsin suggested, feeling her disagreement. "They might head straight for our heart, counting on an attack at Gimmerai to trick us into thinking the next fight will happen here at Arbella."

"I've had new ships grown," she told him. "The crews are green, but an attacker won't know that when he sees a mass of cruisers and frigates facing him. And besides," she leaned in, "you and I both know the attack's most likely to be coming here next."

"They'll throw whatever they have at us," Tilsin warned.

"All the more reason why you *need* my ships, General." She reached out to put a hand on his shoulder. "You should start planning our defense, old friend."

Tilsin paused for a moment, his discontent clearly felt but it changed suddenly to acceptance. He nodded and left the office.

"So," Bau said conversationally, turning back to Sumugan, "how's your first day as governor going so far?"

He offered her a wry smile. "Well, I've seen one important improvement over our previous situation, at least."

"And what is that?"

"Leaders don't run away when trouble threatens."

Moved by the clear respect she could feel from Sumugan, Bau's usual gift for sharp banter failed her. She gestured to the door. "Perhaps you should continue this crisis from your new office. Any announcements will carry more weight if they come from the capitol building."

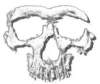

Tilsin was tempted to review his deployments but he knew it was just nerves. He'd already set up his forces to the best advantage for this initial engagement. It would do his bridge crew no good to see him obsessing over his plans. "Commander Bilia, you have the bridge".

He walked into the ready-room, just aft of the bridge, and poured a mug of coffee. He took a seat and sipped at the stale brew, gazing up in surprise at the holo display of his ambush. He smiled, shaking his head.

Despite his firm resolve not to keep going over his plans, he'd opened this screen without even realizing it.

The plan was a good one. Despite the obvious good sense one might see in bringing in an attack force from any other location than the designated arrival corridor, it wasn't advisable.

Shullat would have to assume there would be mines to deny him a sneaky approach and there were, though they were sparsely deployed.

Still, they had incredibly long ranges and their effective areas were just barely overlapped to provide full coverage.

Upon sensing an enemy ship, a mine would engage its small pitch drive and 'fall' toward its target.

Imperial conventions prevented the mining of approach corridors, so just about every battle at a planet took place in the corridors.

Shullat could try an unexpected approach, but he'd lose ships, maybe even the one carrying his own precious hide.

Tilsin had all of his frigates with him, leaving the cruisers, minus his own flagship, to stand between the attackers and Arbella. Like all worlds, the approach corridor was between the planet and the sun to simplify the gravitational effect calculations used in the transition out of path.

It meant the attackers would be coming at Arbella with the sun at their backs, making them harder to detect but Tilsin was waiting even further out.

He'd provide the enemy positions to his cruisers, ensuring his own force was off-axis before opening fire. He didn't want to hit his own ships.

He frowned. That still left the local defense forces who were in orbit. They were ready to fight, knowing now the difference that the Lady Bau would make in their lives, but they were a last line of defense and a thin one, at that.

And all those refugees crowding the orbitals were going to get plastered. He knew from bitter experience that telling refugees they were in danger and actually getting them to move were two completely unrelated things.

And he'd also learned how to work around that. He got up from his seat. "Lieutenant," he said, stepping back onto the bridge and turning to the communications officer, "Send a message to Captain Mearwhal aboard the cruiser *Cremani*. Tell him he's to *prepare* to inspect the refugee ships and requisition any supplies that may prove useful to us during the fight to come. If we drive them back, we're still going to be in for a long siege.

"Also tell him he's not to leave his defensive sector. Any refugee ships moving to the departure-standby queue will have to be ignored for the time being." He nodded to the officer. "Send that in the open."

"Aye sir," the lieutenant replied, grinning. Though he didn't know exactly what his general was up to, he could sense his confidence.

There was still the defense forces. Tilsin knew he could make better use of them. It would be irresponsible of him to simply leave them in orbit.

That departure corridor was about to get crowded…

"Tactical, get me a list of all the freighters in orbit, quickly!"

Shullat thought he was going to surprise them. He'd learn what it meant to tangle with an experienced warrior.

Cut Loose

Eth stared at the small coin laying on his ready-room table aboard the *Mouse*, the cruiser they'd seized from Uktannu's forces. He was feeling a coldness, deep inside himself.

That coin could be anywhere. Movement in any direction came with a corresponding probability tied to the surrounding location coordinates. Those coordinates were tied to matter and it explained why Eth stayed in his seat rather than floating up to the ceiling.

He wasn't sure the explanation was entirely right but it gave him a framework for understanding, so it would do for now. The ship's grav plating mimicked the same coordinate gradient one found on a planet. The closer you got to the plating, or to a planet, the more locations you could move to.

Sure, you could move in the opposite direction, but not for long. The odds were always in favor of falling down-gradient. Like a casino, gravity always won out in the long game.

Eth brought expectation to bear on the coin. The same absolute confidence that started impulses moving in his own neurons now created potential to the right of the coin. Just enough to overcome the friction between the coin and the smooth table.

And the coin moved.

Somehow, he'd found a way to rig the game.

It had only moved a finger's width, but he'd done it with his mind. He shuddered, grasping for his coffee mug and draining it of the last of the hot liquid. The effort had cost him some of his heat energy.

"Sir, contact!" Oliv shouted from out on the bridge.

He got up, forgetting about the coin and the chills that came from moving it. He raced out the door onto the bridge. "What do we have?" he asked, eyes taking in the large fleet of warships, showing on the holo, now approaching Heiropolis.

"Eighteen cruisers," Oliv replied, "three of 'em heavies, thirty-two frigates and a 'lick & stick'. Looks like they all ping friendly."

"Keep us at General Quarters," Eth ordered.

The 'lick & stick' was a hastily grown cargo vessel, based on a long range shuttle core, used to carry supplies or personnel. They were usually the barest minimum vessel to do the job, no weapons and horrible maneuverability. He enlarged the holo of the utility ship. It had two landing bays with signatures for six shuttles inside.

"Incoming hail," Glen said. "The Lord Sandrak orders you to report aboard his flagship immediately!"

Eth's body temperature was back to normal by the time he reached the Mouse's hangar deck. He took one of the scout-ships with Ed as pilot and they approached at high speed, stopping hard at the entrance to the forward landing bay. They slid inside, scattering a team of handlers who'd frozen in terror at their brutally fast arrival.

Eth started opening the side ramp as soon as they passed the navigational shielding and hopped down as his ship's landing struts touched the deck.

The crew on Sandrak's ships were entirely Quailu and, not having been stationed at Kish like Mishak's crews, couldn't care less that he was Human, but they still showed open revulsion for him anyway. The cause was no mystery: they couldn't read him.

But he could read them so it almost evened out, though he had to live with the disgust they broadcast his way. He walked up to the officer of the deck, who showed only a little surprise at seeing a native officer – it *did* happen from time to time – but his unease at talking to a blank slate was plain.

"The Lord Sandrak is waiting for you to report," the commander told him. "He's on the bridge." He gestured toward the obvious exit, such was his eagerness to get rid of Eth.

Eth walked to the bridge, feeling the mental shudders as he passed crewmen on the ramp. It was going to be interesting to see how Sandrak handled this.

He stepped into the bridge and waited quietly as Sandrak finished a conversation with one of his officers. He turned to Eth, frowned and then abruptly affected a perfectly natural attitude.

Eth could feel the faint distaste from Sandrak, who he'd never met before this moment, but he also had the distinct feeling that he'd decided not to let his reaction show.

He may well have assumed that Eth had always been impossible to read. Whatever he'd assumed, he wouldn't be demanding to know why Eth was different from other Humans.

"Well?" he said curtly. "What's the status here at Heiropolis?"

Business then. Eth resisted the urge to let out a sigh of relief, especially since he still wasn't out of the woods. "Stable, Lord – especially now that you're here." He felt anger from Sandrak and knew he'd screwed up.

"Get your lips off my rectum! I have courtiers for that, probably locked away somewhere unpleasant." Sandrak wanted honesty and the more brutal the better.

Eth felt it clearly. Quailu knew how to moderate their emotions during confrontations like this one but Sandrak didn't know that Eth could read him. "The Heiropolitans don't really believe they were in any danger," he told him. "The governor himself refuses to believe that the Lord Uktannu almost seized control of the system."

"So nothing has changed?" He radiated astonishment.

Eth shook his head. "Aside from *our* presence, Lord, very little. I've tried to convince his defense forces to step up their patrols, to push farther out, recruit enough crews to man all of their warships, but they laugh us off. We're fighting an uphill battle here." He nearly reached for his weapon, such was the anger he felt coming from his overlord.

"You let them laugh at you?" Sandrak said quietly, though the depth of his feeling was hitting Eth like a punch to the gut. "I don't know what my son was thinking, making you an officer, but your commission has the backing of two electors, if my information is correct, and laughing at you is laughing at both me and my son!"

Eth felt Sandrak's sourness at the mention of two electors and, perhaps, a little concern. Was he feeling threatened by his own son?

"The civil administrators in charge of recruiting are beyond my authority," Eth insisted, "but the lieutenant commander in charge of local defense-planning isn't. He's in my brig."

Sandrak drew slightly straighter, amusement evident in his mind. "You locked up a superior?"

Eth shook his head. "Lord, I locked up a local security officer, commissioned by a governor who refuses to see his own peril. I'd hardly call him a *superior*..."

Sandrak let out a sharp bark of laughter. "Send him to my ship. I'll deal with him. I'll have to deal with all of them, most likely.

"In the meantime," he continued, "we have the latest draft from Kish with us – more than five hundred of your kind. They've been crewing that l&s bucket," he said, waving at the 'lick & stick' ship in his holo-display, "and they managed to get here in one piece, so I suppose their training sessions were worthwhile.

"I was going to leave them with my son but, since you're here, I'll hand them over to you. I'll be too busy here to go chasing after Mishak just to hand over a pack of... Humans. Take them and go."

Eth had caught the slip. Whatever word Sandrak had held back was less polite, most likely 'slaves'.

Eth could understand why Mishak didn't like his father. The old bastard looked down his nose at everyone. They'd done well to anticipate Uktannu's scheme. Eth and his Humans had even taken one of the enemy cruisers but now Sandrak was here, taking over without a word of acknowledgement.

And he now had over half a thousand new recruits to worry over. He frowned. "Lord, if I may make a request?"

Sandrak stifled a response, though whether it was annoyance or surprise, Eth couldn't tell, not with the limited context he had on his lord's father.

"The request itself will determine the answer to that question," the Quailu rumbled.

It was, in Eth's opinion, a weak way to deal with a subordinate. Either allow a question or not. Nonetheless, Sandrak was a prince of the realm and Eth was a lowly mushkenu. "I'd rather not leave orbit with a pack of half-trained recruits. If you have no objections, I'd like to remain in orbit for a few days and put them through a few exercises, maybe even have some of the more promising candidates try stalking some of your ships?"

He didn't need context to recognize the curiosity in Sandrak's mind.

"You'd like to try some attack runs on my ships?"

"Only if it won't disrupt your operations here, Lord."

"Disrupt?" Sandrak blurted in surprise, clearly expecting little more than amusement from such Human antics. He mastered his reaction and waved a dismissive hand. "Do your worst, Lieutenant. We'll be ready for you."

Eth returned to the *Mouse*. He walked onto the bridge and opened a channel to Noa. "Get over to the brig with a couple of your guys and grab that gasbag lieutenant commander. Put him on *Your Last Chance*. Glen's waiting for you."

"You're cut loose from Heiropolis, Captain?" a deep voice asked behind him.

Eth turned. "We are, Father. Free to head for Dur. We'll leave in a couple of days."

"But not exactly *ordered* to Dur, now, are you?" The oracle's intonation had no question in it.

Eth looked at him for a moment. "I suppose you're right, but where else *should* we be going other than back to our own lord?"

"I saw the attack on Heiropolis coming," Father Sulak told him, "three months ago. Do you think that fool of a governor would listen to me?" He shook his head in frustration.

"I also saw the next bit of mischief that Uktannu will get himself into," he continued, pulling out a strip of over-dried fat and gnawing off a corner. "He'll be stopped by native troops, three days from now."

"Are you saying *we* are going to stop him?"

"Hard to say with visions." Sulak sniffed at the strip and shuddered, disgusted by the odor but not enough, apparently, to get rid of it. He shoved it back into his robe. "Vague things, visions, and *you* are particularly difficult to see through the veil. You seem to cloud things somehow." He shrugged, not very bothered by it. "Technically, even *Varangians* are native troops, and they often cloud visions, so…"

"Well, Father, since we don't even know where this takes place, I might as well sort out our new crewmen and then head for Dur." He looked to the door in the aft bulkhead.

One of the warrant officers from the 'lick & stick' ship (it didn't even have a name) was standing to one side, regarding Eth with a quiet awe that he'd felt from the moment she stepped into the bridge.

"Now *that* I can tell you," Sulak said with a grin as the warrant officer approached.

"You don't know what species foils Uktannu but you know which planet?"

"I can recognize the world of my own birth."

"That was the reason you came aboard, isn't it?" Eth demanded, though he wasn't upset. It was hard to get angry at Sulak.

"Well," Sulak waggled his head, "that and the fact that Heiropolitans are a pack of window-licking jackasses!"

Eth felt the nervousness of the warrant officer. She was standing next to one of the first Humans to earn a commission and he knew the stories on the voyage out here would have made far too much of his accomplishments. She was also shocked at how familiarly he spoke with a Quailu oracle, even a filthy one like Father Sulak.

He was surprised to realize he felt some resentment toward this new influx of Humans. They came with inflated expectations, looking to him for leadership and continued success.

As far as Eth was concerned, half of his success to date had been due to luck. Maybe more than half.

You couldn't plan on luck. You could only try to place yourself in luck's path and hope for the best.

He turned to her.

"Warrant Hela, sir." She came to a position of respect. "I have five hundred twenty-three personnel on our l&s."

"Your timing couldn't be better, Warrant," Eth said. "We've recently seized this cruiser and we're trying to run her with three scout-ship crews." He tilted his head. "What are your backgrounds?"

"Five small-unit raiding teams, like the one you led, sir, though two of them are still pretty green. The rest are grown to the same pattern but without actual combat experience. We've all been imprinted with the fleet training modules as well."

It was no surprise that Eth didn't recognize her. Mishak had always skirted the fine line between noble and pirate and he had dozens of teams to carry out his raids. He couldn't even say for sure whether his own team had been treated any differently, though it seemed that way.

"Equipment, Warrant?"

"We have the l&s that we arrived in, as well as five shuttles, six hundred side-arms, six hundred fifty assault-weapons as well as the standard pressurized combat-suits."

"Rigged for infantry combat?"

She nodded. "They're rated for shock suppression and they all have grenade dispensers."

"Five shuttles," he mused, opening a channel. "Second Lieutenant Noakenu, please report to the bridge."

Sulak grinned.

"You've seen what I'm going to do, Father, or do you have gastric distress?"

"Can't really say no to either option, Captain," Sulak replied cheerfully. "Do you have coffee aboard, by the way?"

"What does that have to do with anything?"

"It has a lot to do with me drinking coffee," the oracle explained helpfully.

"Uktannu must have been getting a good bulk price through his brother," Eth said. "The main locker behind the galley service counter has about three hundred pounds."

"And now you know the main reason why I asked you for a ride!" Sulak beamed.

Eth looked at him. "But you're not rushing off to the galley, I see."

"I said *main* reason," the Quailu shrugged. "There are other, lesser things one might wish to stick around for…"

"Vagueness seems a good quality for an oracle," Eth mused.

"Indeed?" Sulak prompted, darting a playful wink at Hela.

Eth smiled, feeling her consternation at this undignified attention from a member of the master species. *She'll have to change her attitude toward the Quailu double-quick if she wants to stay alive out here. I don't want her freezing up when she needs to kill one of the bastards.*

The corners of his mouth dropped a little as he realized how quickly he'd acquired the habit of thinking freely in the presence of the Quailu. "Vagueness lets an Oracle claim knowledge of just about anything that comes to pass."

"Hah!" Sulak gave Eth a thump on the shoulder. "You know why I like you Humans so much more than the Heiropolitans?"

"Because they're all assholes?"

"Well, there is that." Sulak shrugged. "But it's more about the soup, as they say…"

"Soup, father?" Hela asked, curiosity overcoming her awe.

"An old saying among my people." Sulak turned the full force of his random charm on her. "But it applies here. If the lieutenant here were to piss in my soup, as the old saying goes, he'd climb up on the table and do it right in front of me. A Heiropolitan would sneak into the kitchen."

Noa arrived, taking note of the new warrant officer as he approached Eth. "Sir?"

It was a little odd to hear that from Noa. Even though he'd been their leader for a while, he'd only had his commission for a few days. Now with a new influx of crewmen, he'd have to get used to a little more isolation.

He nodded toward the holo display. "That L&S ship – how many scout-ships do you figure you can make from its nanites?"

Noa grimaced, bringing up the datasheet for the ship. "Maybe two, if we're lucky but we'd want some cores and we only have four shuttles aboard this cruiser."

"This is Warrant Officer Hela." Eth gestured, waiting for them to exchange polite nods. He could feel her getting used to the idea of dealing with Human officers. Noa was far less intimidating than meeting him and Sulak at the same time.

"She has five shuttles aboard."

"Ah! That changes things! We could manage three easily and still have plenty of nanites left over."

"That's what I figured." Eth considered for a moment, then opened a channel. "Warrant Carolkenu to the bridge." He turned to Hela. "Warrant, how would you like a ship of your own?"

"A scout-ship?" Hela's eyes were shining. "I'd like that, sir!"

"I'll keep Carol in command of the *Last Thing You'll Ever See* as well as being the senior scout. The other two of the original scout-ship crews will stay aboard the *Mouse.* We can't crew this beast without some experienced people. We've all had the fleet training implanted but it's a far cry from actual experience.

"With three new ships, we'll need another four crews beside you. Do you have any recommendations, Warrant?"

He watched her as she thought it through. He felt an honest effort to identify the best of the new warrant officers. If he sensed any cronyism from her, he would have politely ignored her suggestions.

"To start with, sir, I'd definitely recommend Colm and Fink, the two with combat experience. It was mostly infantry work, of course, but I don't need to tell you it involves some pretty dynamic situations and we often end up taking fire while flying in or out of a target zone."

She frowned for a moment. "I think Henrik and Bel would be the best choices from the rest."

"Good! Thank-you, Warrant. Now, let's get started on moving the new recruits over to the *Mouse.* I want those new scout-ships built before the Lord Sandrak remembers you have shuttles aboard that heap of nanites and tells us to shift them over to his flagship."

He felt mild alarm from Hela at his irreverent attitude toward a prince of the realm.

Had he been that innocent when he left Kish? As far as the rest knew, they'd only been away for a couple of months but he'd spent a lot of time in a semi-conscious state while under Varangian care.

Noa hadn't experienced more than a couple of months of this life and he showed not the least concern. Then again, he'd killed a few Quailu himself.

The myth of the master species grew thin surprisingly fast when you were ordered to kill them.

"We'll be training against Sandrak's fleet before we move on," he told them. "Warrant, the sooner you can get that L&S emptied out, the better. Head over there and get everyone moving."

She turned and left, passing Carol at the bridge's main entry hatch.

"Reporting as ordered, sir." Carol came to a stop in front of Eth.

"Your scouting force is going to get a lot larger, Warrant."

"My force, sir?" *A definite thrill of anticipation.*

"I'm making you our senior scout," he confirmed, "and I'm registering a new warrant for you." He opened a system holo and accessed the personnel menu. "As of this moment," he said, inputting a change and watching that record turn from red to green, "you are Master Warrant Officer Carolkenu."

"But," she spluttered, staring at the file, which was clearly green and not the intermediate orange of a pending file, "confirmation from our lord…" *Shock, guarded exhilaration.*

"Was entrusted, *pro tempore*, into my hands until we return to the fleet," he explained. "It's done and you'd have to give a damned poor performance to make our lord rescind it.

"Moving on to new business, I have some new crews pre-picked for you to start with. Use the existing scout-ships and start training them. We have permission to stalk the Lord Sandrak's ships for the next two days, so don't waste any time."

Grinning, she nodded in agreement. "Yes, sir. Thank-you, sir!" She made for the exit hatch at a pace that could almost be called a sprint.

He still hadn't decided where they'd be going, two days from now, when they left orbit.

Eth wasn't eager to get back to Mishak's fleet. Sulak might not be bothered by his inability to read the Human officer, but the other Quailu in the fleet certainly were. Even Mishak seemed to be more distant, now that he didn't have his empathic advantage.

He was faced with a rare opportunity to get away from the stultifying environment of a Quailu fleet, even if only for a few days. It was a bit of an over-reach for his limited authority but, if he could pull this off, all would probably be forgiven.

Probably…

There was no way he'd be able to stop Uktannu's mischief if he went back to the fleet. There wouldn't be time to get to Dur, convince Mishak and then get reinforcements into place. More than that, Mishak would be far too busy consolidating his new position and he'd need all of his forces to pacify his new holdings.

Sulak seemed to think Humans would come to the rescue, so why not?

Hot From the Forge

"If you're trying to kill yourself," Carol roared at Hela, her voice crackling as the helmet speakers attenuated the volume, "then do it on your own gods-damned time and make sure I'm not on the same ship! Close with them, damn your worthless hide! Don't just sit out here with your pants down, waiting for a thermonuclear suppository!"

"Eve," Hela began, her ears burning, "take us…"

"Belay!" Carol overrode her. "We're already dead by now. Take us back to the jump-off point and reset the exercise."

Hela knew her skin was flushed, showing her mingled shame and rage but her only real outlet at the moment was to obey orders and try to redeem herself. At least they were rigged for combat and her helmet hid her flushed skin.

It didn't stop her suit from filling with the rank scent of stress from her sweat.

She nodded to Eve. "Take us back."

Carol, the master warrant officer in charge of scouting, wasn't done. She glared around her at the rest of the crew. "If any of you walking organ-banks think I'm just yelling at your captain, think again!"

She jabbed a finger at Hela. "She's taking the heat on your behalf, like a good leader should. A poor leader might have offered up excuses."

"Eve," she barked, without turning to look at the pilot, "what do the SOP's tell you to do when you're lit up during a stealth approach?"

"Close and board."

"Because the enemy," Carol growled, "has missiles and gunnery and you have what exactly?"

"Infantry weapons and ration breath," Gleb offered with an unreadable smile.

Carol considered reprimanding him for answering a question he wasn't asked but it showed, at the very least, initiative under stress. It was also possible that he was attempting to draw heat from his crewmates.

Either way, it was a good sign.

"And you can't always count on your breath," Carol emphasized, "so you nuzzle up close, get aboard and make the little darlings fight our *strengths*, rather than our *weaknesses*."

"So I shouldn't wait for the order to…" Eve trailed off, ears turning red, probably realizing that her question was pushing responsibility for their last failure onto Hela.

"If Hela has some other plan in mind," Carol explained, "it's up to her to communicate it. Otherwise, when Gleb says you've been made – and he doesn't wait until someone asks about it before passing that on – you should get this shit-wagon moving without having to be told. If your captain has to tell you, she might as well just be the pilot herself and cut one link out of the chain of command.

"A crew that survives is a crew that acts without delay, cooperating in a pre-arranged plan without needing their hands held the whole way.

"Every second you waste looking for orders that confirm the obvious," Carol continued, raising her voice as if the crew in the engineering space couldn't hear at her previous level, "is another second for those dim-witted ass-sniffers in the enemy ship to notice you, get over their shock and remember that they actually have weapons."

Those *dim-witted ass-sniffers* were Quailu but nobody objected to Carol's choice of words.

"Gleb, you should be highlighting insertion points based on coverage from other ships in the enemy formation – the ones that are in a position to fire at us. As Eve takes us in, both she and Hela should be able to use that data to formulate their next steps. Eve, you need to pick an insertion point on your own initiative and make for it.

"This is knife fighting, people. Your captain has a dozen things to prioritize so she can't be holding your hands. You handle the obvious so she can deal with the *clever*."

"We're back in position, MWO," Hela advised.

Carol nodded. "You may commence a new stalking run when you're ready, Warrant."

Hela took a deep breath and put on a calm demeanor like she was putting on an EVA suit. A sweaty, stinky EVA suit.

"Aye, ma'am. Meesh, dump what we have in the heat capacitor and reset emission-management systems to full tactical. Gleb, plot us an approach course for the Lord Sandrak's flagship."

There was a momentary pause, the kind that usually follows something completely unexpected.

"Aye, Warrant," Gleb finally responded. "Passing a course to the helm now."

Carol gazed at Hela for a few seconds as the small scout-ship got underway. "You've got some minerals but, if you're going to stalk the elector, you'd better not bugger it up or I'm gonna enjoy breaking my foot off in your ass!"

"No unnecessary talk during the approach, if you please," Hela snapped. She could have sworn she saw a ghost of a smile on Carol's face before she turned away.

"Target is keeping station over the planetary capital," Gleb advised. "Her engines are running at sixteen percent."

"Understood," Hela replied. "Bring us in astern, keep us in her baffles."

The area behind an active engine was relatively opaque to sensors due to all the heat and radiation. It would ease the load on the scout-ship's emission management systems.

"Keep in mind," Carol advised, "that the Quailu mind is hard-wired to pay more attention to the rear than we Humans tend to. Their vision is nearly three-hundred-sixty degrees so they don't like blind spots in their sensing suites."

"Understood." Hela nodded.

They cruised along, approaching the ship's blind-spot from behind at a velocity that balanced speed with the need to manage the waste heat from their own pitch drive.

Carol was pleased to see that Gleb was already putting up recommended insertion points as they moved in.

"Take us up to the dorsal edge of the baffle," Hela ordered. "Let's see if there's any Sig-Int to pick up while we're here."

Carol nodded to herself. Hela had definite potential. After a dressing down that would have left some small unit commanders too shaken to perform, she'd not only approached to within the designated approach-phase distance undetected, but she had the presence of mind to think of signals intelligence as well.

Now, if only…

"We're lit again!" Gleb announced. "I think the bastards are towing a sensor array. They're rigging for combat. Recommend the dorsal engineering insertion point."

"Belay!" Hela cut in. "Eve, take us dorsal, but all the way up to the bridge. We'll go after the command center."

Carol frowned. "The chances of seizing critical systems are higher in engineering," she offered diplomatically, noticing, with approval, that the crew were still executing Hela's orders despite the interference from the training officer.

Hela smoldered for a half heartbeat. "My chances of seizing a prince of the empire are far higher on the bridge of that ship. I'll trouble you not to interfere in the exercise of my command again!"

Top marks! Carol thought as the flagships turrets flashed past them at bowel-loosening speeds.

They left Eve at the helm and moved to the weapons rack in engineering. They were ready to fight just as the hull began melting out of the way on the port side. Hela led the way through and Carol, her heart in her mouth, followed the last of the boarding party.

Sandrak may have given his permission for the Humans to train against his fleet, but she doubted he'd had this in mind when he gave the go-ahead. He might not be entirely pleased about having weapons pointed at him.

She had no trouble picking him out on the bridge. He was the one whose armor was worth more than a heavy cruiser.

And his state of mind was a complete blank to Carol.

"You've taken the bridge?" he demanded. "Why would you waste the element of surprise to seize an obvious but still minor objective? From engineering, you could have taken control of the entire vessel and turned her weapons against the rest of the fleet.

"You've shown some skills, approaching us so closely, but you've thrown your strengths away to take a useless target and you'd be lucky to escape an enemy ship in one piece, once you'd realized your error."

Hela grinned, though Sandrak wouldn't notice. "A useless target, My Lord? I respectfully disagree. Now, if you'd step this way…" She waved her assault rifle toward the opening that connected their two mismatched ships.

Sandrak stepped back, head rearing up in surprise and Hela suddenly feared that she'd gone too far. She wondered if she should offer an apology but she felt that would only make things worse.

And then a deep rumbling laugh sounded in her helmet.

"Exercise complete," Sandrak rumbled. "You've seized a prince of the realm. I'd call that a successful result! Perhaps my son knew what he was doing after all."

He paused, after mentioning Mishak, as though reading their responses. Hela wondered what he was looking for.

He must have come up short, whatever he was up to. "Dismissed," he said curtly, turning back to his captain.

"That's about as lucky as I want to get for one day," Carol's voice said from a point higher up in Hela's helmet, indicating the crew-only channel. "Let's get out of here and celebrate your confirmation as a scout captain!"

The Quailu Life

Eth shuddered. The coin fell back to the table with a dull clatter.

Despite the Varangian's warning, he'd been moving matter but it was only a small coin, not a cruiser or a planet.

Still, the effort had drained a lot of heat from his body.

Coffee would help.

He reached out, feeling the presence of the hot liquid, understanding it… His eyes narrowed.

He could feel the warmth. He could feel the heat flowing into his own body but he was clear across the ready room.

He could pull heat energy out of an object? In the flush of realization, he turned his attention back to the coin but the doors hissed open and he looked up guiltily.

Father Sulak walked in, throwing Eth a friendly nod as he steered for the coffee pot. He pulled it from its housing, lifting the lid and putting his face directly over the opening.

"Cold," he said in mild reproof, looking over to Eth. "You know, the problem with you Humans is that you take coffee for granted."

Not anymore, Eth thought, the corners of his mouth turning up as he watched the oracle dump the pot down a reclamation chute.

Sulak activated the control holo and initiated a new pot. "Just because you live on the only world in the empire that's allowed to grow the stuff, you think you can treat it with disdain. Are those kibbrim still warm?"

"It's cheap for us," Eth told him, tossing the oracle one of the barely warm Quailu pastries. It bounced off Sulak's chest and landed on the table. "Sorry, forgot about the depth perception…"

Sulak chuckled. "Aye, we're great at running an empire but absolute shite at catching anything, even if it's edible." He picked up the kibbrim and stuffed it into his mouth.

233

"Something tells me you're already comfortable with the concept of cheap coffee," he added, nodding at the brewer, which was still grinding, well beyond the time needed for a normal-strength pot.

"Abusing hospitality is a time-honored tradition among oracles," Sulak said as loftily as he could around a mouthful of pastry. He leaned in to breathe the scent of fresh ground beans.

"Did you wear out your welcome on Arbella?" Eth asked. "That's your home-world, yes?"

"Yes and no." Sulak shrugged. "We've been there for three generations now, but I'm the only one to call it home."

"Your family disagrees?"

"My oldest brother would tell you that Bir Jebra is our home. He sees himself as a potential replacement for our cousin, who rules there with an iron fist and less-than-productive loins."

"You're Awilu?" Eth blurted, startled to learn in such a cavalier fashion that he was talking with a noble.

"Barely." The oracle made a negligent gesture with his right hand, his gaze still on the coffee pot. "Minor lords breed 'beggar emigres' almost as fast as the rats on this ship reproduce." His eyes drifted from the pot to check the corners of the room, though rats tended to stay on the lower decks.

"Only the eldest inherits. The rest of us must make our own way in the empire. Military service is popular but there's entirely too much exploding for my taste."

Eth smiled. "There's not enough room in the fleets to accommodate all of you, though, is there?" There was a small horde of penniless nobles sheltering at Mishak's palace on Kish.

"Not even close," Sulak agreed, snagging one of the steel mugs that sat on a tray next to the brewer. "Frankly, I think a patent of nobility should expire in three generations, unless you're the one to inherit the original title."

"You think that would ever pass in the assembly?"

"With the right persuasion." Sulak poured a mug, then set it down and filled a second cup.

"Most Awilu would be open to the idea of clearing out the clutter. Not only does it cheapen the idea of nobility to have so many beggar emigres wandering around, but it's a bothersome strain to have a horde of indigent relatives eating you out of palace and pantry." He sat opposite Eth, sliding the second mug across the table.

"Kind of like hosting a convention of oracles, I suppose." Eth took a sip of the deliciously hot beverage to hide his grin. He could clearly feel the oracle's disdain for his own social class. That couldn't help but isolate the poor fellow.

Eth could certainly relate.

"Even worse, if you can believe it!" Sulak drained half his cup in one gulp. "Oracles can't stand each other. Hard to claim you're the one with your finger on the Universe's pulse when there's a dozen others making the same claim but with different results. Makes us look bad so we'd all bugger off pretty quickly." He set the mug down, staring into it contemplatively. "Relatives never leave. They just keep breeding."

He looked up abruptly. "What about you?"

"What about me?"

"Breeding. You're entitled to have your steri-plant unlocked…"

"Are you nuts?" Eth shook his head. "Can you imagine me having offspring?"

"Why not? You'd let that high-priced genome go un-replicated?"

"Can't imagine the Meleke Corporation would be very happy about me creating copies of their intellectual property."

"Not like they'd have a say in it," Sulak said. "And they'll be winding down the Human product line pretty soon anyway. Word is your lord will be pushing to turn Kish into a Mushkennu-based economy soon anyway. He'll have to offer Meleke a pretty large compensation package to take over the rights to your species but freeing them will pay back his investment in the first decade, assuming he takes an energetic hand in the economic changes."

"And where did you get wind of this, Father?"

"Would you believe it's because I have my finger on the pulse of the Universe? No? Well, perhaps I hear things while I'm scratching its armpit. Nobles like to show off what they know…"

Eth gazed steadily at Sulak, unable to tell if he was aware of the irony of his statement. "Yeah… evidently…"

Raising the Stakes

Hit and Run

"Multiple contacts!" the tactical officer announced, looking up at the general. "The full picture is still firming up, but we're seeing at least a fifteen ship advantage over us."

Tilsin projected an aura of calm. He knew they'd probably face heavy odds, but that would have meant more to a commander who planned to simply dash in and slug it out in a straight battle of attrition.

In the grand scheme of things, this counted for little more than a border skirmish, not worth even briefing the emperor. This was not a clash of massive fleets at a key system where the empire itself was at stake.

But losing here would see his lady captured and his own line disgraced. His fists clenched in anger. A suitable emotion to display to his crew.

"They're already firing at the defense forces."

Tilsin shook his head, letting the act emphasize his disdain, making it obvious to his crew. "Wasting ammunition," he growled.

At their distance, missiles would have little fuel, if any, left by the time they closed with their targets and needed to vector in on their nimble enemies.

"Do they expect our ships to simply sit still and wait for death?" the tactical officer wondered aloud.

"Whoever's leading them has let himself get over-excited," Tilsin said. "I heartily approve. The more he wastes on his way in, the less time he can stay and fight without re-supply. Let me know when he starts moving parallel to those refugees at the departure line."

"There goes another salvo from the enemy," Tactical said. "You'd think he'd at least notice our people aren't firing back."

"Not if he's the excitable type," Tilsin replied, "which would help us greatly. Once *we* start surprising him, he's likely to scamper off and try to regroup. Helm, start bringing us in. I want to be close when we open up on them – as close as we can get without our shadows giving us away."

"Might be hard to hit some of them from back here, sir," Tactical advised. "They're advancing in three staggered planes."

"Staggered?"

"Yes, sir, and they're tightly packed. Only the front plane is firing."

"What in hells are they playing at?" Tilsin demanded. "Either this is something very clever or we're dealing with an absolute idiot." He supposed that, if this force served Shullat, he might have been so embarrassed by the loss of this planet that he'd assumed direct control.

But where had he gotten the extra ships?

"There's the third volley, sir, and they've got the refugees on their port side."

"Just a little closer," Tilsin muttered to himself. "Let 'em see we're right up their back passage before we fire…"

A chime sounded.

The tactical officer looked up at him. "Sir, we're lit up. They can see our force."

"Fire!" Tilsin roared.

A distant hissing sound of ejecting missiles accompanied the soul-rending howl of the rail-guns. Tilsin felt alive, every cell tingling with the madness of the fight. The long wait was finally over.

As soon as his cruiser fired, the frigates on her flanks opened up as well. They were so close that the outbound ordnance had an incredibly short travel time, giving the enemy almost no time to react.

Only a heartbeat after the enemy point-defense systems had opened up on the first set of inbound missiles, the remainder of Tilsin's opening salvo struck home. The general tilted his head forward, lips sliding back to expose his teeth as he watched the chaotic eruptions of fire and debris coming from his opponent's hulls.

It was a strong opening move but they couldn't hope to smash such a large force in one go.

"We made mincemeat of the rear plane," Tactical announced. "It's down to less than twenty percent combat effective but the other two layers are intact and turning our way."

"Now would be a good time, Baden," Tilsin said under his breath. The freighters mixed in with the refugee ships were now directly to starboard of the enemy force.

It was a hard enough thing to trust subordinates in independent commands but it was taking years off Tilsin's lifespan to trust Commander Baden of the Arbellan Defense Forces.

"ADF ships are emerging from the freighters," Tactical announced, to Tilsin's great relief. "They're firing…" He pounded a fist on his console, startling the rating who sat there. "Lots of hits! Baden's boys were far closer than us; I don't think their point-defense managed to knock out a single missile! The enemy don't know which way to turn!"

Grim satisfaction. Sometimes, when you have the smaller force, you have to play a stronger hand. By hitting back from multiple directions, one after the other, he was pushing an attacking force into reaction-mode.

The stronger enemy was now dancing to *his* tune, though his sheet music had just run out. He had no further tricks to play.

"Picking up multiple capacitor signatures," a sensor tech called out. "They're heating up their path-banks!"

"It's about time for them to realize they blundered into a bad position," the tactical officer said.

"They're going," his tech added.

"They'll be back," Tilsen warned, "and not all of them are leaving. Give me a channel to those crippled ships."

"We're sparing the crews on those ships, sir?" the tactical officer asked.

"The conventions must be observed," Tilsin insisted, "*all* the time, not just when it's convenient. If we start firing on disabled ships after an action is completed, then they'll start doing the same to us."

Three captains shimmered into view and a fourth showed an audio feed but no image was available.

"I'm clearing this battle-space for the next round," Tilsin told them. "You have two standard hours to evacuate your ships. If we see anything other than shuttles moving, we open fire on all of you. Is that understood?"

He got the sullen agreement he was looking for and so he terminated the call.

The Lady Bau must have initiated a call in the few seconds he'd been talking to them because her image appeared as soon as they faded.

"My congratulations, General! The people of Arbella owe you a debt of gratitude."

"Don't thank me just yet, Lady," Tilsin said. "We drove them off but they're still lurking out there, probably out near the gas giants. They've taken a lot of damage, but they'll come back in four or five days."

She raised an eyebrow. "Four or five days?" she asked archly.

Tilsin nodded, showing a confidence in his estimate that he wasn't entirely sure he felt. "They could use more time than that to effect repairs, but they'll know it takes our ships two days to get back home, a day to mobilize our forces there, and two days back. They'll use what time they can to repair their battle damage but, if they don't beat us in five days, they'll never beat us at all."

"I've sent couriers," she told him. "As you said, two days for them to deliver my orders. I should have had a signal-pair ready so we could link this world to our own. We should purchase *several* pairs."

"They're more expensive than a cruiser," Tilsin said, loyally defending his lady, even though he *did* feel she'd been too stingy with his forces.

She gave him a rueful smile. "And yet, we'd force the enemy back to the fight much earlier if we'd had immediate communications here. They'd have been fighting us with most of their damage unrepaired."

She sighed. "I should have increased military spending the moment we heard of the emperor's meddling. I knew I'd be using the unrest to seize this world. I might have been able to hang onto Gimmerai."

"There's no changing the past, My Lady. We'll just have to beat them here in the present."

Run and Hit

"No contacts," Oliv announced. "This area reads clear."

They had taken their SOP to extremes, dropping out of path, not just beyond the approach corridor for Arbella, but outside the entire system.

"Gleb?" Eth stepped over to the communications suite.

"Getting chatter from Arbellan orbit. It's a couple hours old by the time it gets out here." He began pulling up files from his panel. "Lots of data-files whizzing around – order of battle estimates, tactical projections based on a previous engagement which... happened..."

He enlarged a report. "...eighteen hours ago. They're not being very circumspect about comms."

Eth nodded. "Anyone arriving is either an enemy who'll get the same data from their allies or they're here to help, in which case they'd probably just go straight in and say hello."

"Probably," Oliv muttered, chuckling.

"We're here to help," Eth said, "but not by *their* rules. We're not Quailu, no offense, Father..."

"None taken!"

"...So we don't give a monkey's fart about the prestige of a stand-up battle or the disgrace of a retreat. We'll slip in, slap 'em on the side of the head and then slide away before they hit back.

"They're bound to be hiding, licking their wounds from the first round but they'll stay close. They want to repair as much battle damage as they can before heading back in and they'll want to do that before reinforcements arrive."

"That'll take four days at least," Sulak said. "The Lady Bau is a great administrator but she's never been one to spend funds on an item that she *might* need some day. Given how quickly she moved on Arbella, there's just no time for her to have gotten her hands on a signal-pair."

242

Eth looked at Sulak. "You're surprisingly well-informed, Father, even for an oracle."

He could sense Sulak's suddenly heightened feelings but it was hard to read the Quailu, given their natural reaction to his own unreadability. It was a variable that complicated matters for him.

"So she'll have to send a ship," Eth reasoned. "That gives us three days to work some mischief." He nodded to the scout-ship captains as they filed onto the bridge. Carol must have had them meet out in the corridor and enter together.

Eth approved. It might seem a small thing, but it was good to get them used to acknowledging her authority now, when it was over minor issues. It should reduce friction later, when she was directing them in combat.

"The Lady Bau's forces have already engaged the enemy less than a day ago," Eth told them, "and she gave them a nice friendly beating. They've gone to ground but they're still a force to be reckoned with and they'll be back in the next three days because they have the shame of a withdrawal to answer for. Your task will be to sneak in close and slit a few throats."

"Do we know where they are?" Hela asked.

Eth could still feel some apprehension from Hela. It was good to see she wasn't keeping her concerns to herself. "No, we don't," he admitted, "but it's unlikely they'd simply leave this system and run out into the black. It puts them too far out to make repairs and still get back in time for another assault.

Eth paused to consider his thoughts. "I might be putting more weight on that because it relieves me of the need to search an impossibly large area," he admitted with a smile. The faces remained mostly serious but he could feel the mild amusement hiding behind them.

"They'll want to stay in system, but hidden. That leaves only three possibilities – the three gas giants in the outer system. The innermost giant is the biggest and, therefore, the hardest to search. That's probably where they're hiding. I'd bet Father Sulak's entire supply of fermented fat on it."

"Given where he keeps it," Carol said, making a face, "I'm starting to question whether you want to be correct on this!"

Sulak frowned, sniffing at his robe.

"Seems like a bit of a stretch," Carol continued, shrugging, "but I don't have a better theory. What's our play?"

Eth brought up a holo of the gas giant. "This band, near the equator, has relatively low turbulence compared with the rest of the atmosphere. It's the most likely place to hide a partially damaged fleet. They'll be staying close together, given the sensor and comms challenges in that dense gas.

"They'll be reasonably certain that Lady Bau won't strip Arbella of defenders to come after them but they'll be in the outer atmosphere, just in case they're wrong. They want to spot any incoming frigates and cruisers."

"But they won't be able to spot us!" Hela said. "Our scout-ships should have no trouble closing with them in that soup."

"You'll have twenty additional crew in each scout-ship, two ships in each hunting party. Working together gives you a decent sized boarding party and barely enough of a prize crew if you manage to seize anything.

"I want three frigates. Don't come back with cruisers; the damn things need too many crew for the punch they deliver and they move like a fat-raised water buffalo. The automated systems on the frigates will let twenty serve as a decent crew, just barely, but you can't operate a cruiser without a *lot* more people."

Everyone nodded assent, though he could feel the strong desire to take a larger ship. He sensed they'd let their training and common sense override their desires.

"Alright," he nodded past them to the exit, "off you go, and good hunting."

He watched them file out, wishing he was going with them. It went against the grain to send them off to risk their lives while he sat in the relative safety of his cruiser.

He'd expected to spend the rest of the current turmoil in his little scout-ship but then he had to go and seize a cruiser. He grimaced. If he'd thought it through, he might have simply scuttled it and gone after another target, but it was too late for that now.

And now he was attempting to take more ships, frigates to turn his little fleet into a force he could use to aid the Lady Bau in Mishak's name. He laughed as he realized his own hypocrisy. He was feeling sorry for himself – the victim of his own success but he wasn't a victim.

He was an active co-conspirator.

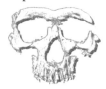

Hela sat up in her bunk, feigning a yawn for the sake of the crew. She hadn't slept but she didn't want them knowing that. In a small scout-ship, trouble spread fast and hearing your captain was a nervous wreck wasn't good for morale. "Contact?" she asked her tactical rating.

"A ghost of a contact," Nils replied, leaning against the doorpost of her sleeping cubicle. A ghost was what they were looking for. Hunting in a gas giant was a chancy business.

She touched a tab in her collar and her under-suit closed up as she stood and backed into the suit armature attached to the wall. The nanite-plate mix flowed into place around her body, fully closing and pressure-testing before opening up again to leave her head and hands exposed.

Fifteen hours and they were finally getting a contact. She'd been starting to doubt Eth's read of the tactical situation.

"Are we closing on the ghost?"

Nils nodded. "It's firming up. I'm betting fifty ducats it's a frigate."

"Who's taking that bet?"

"Just Gleb."

She walked out of her cubicle and led Nils back forward, threading their way between the seated and sleeping forms of the prize crew who had no room to store their suits and so had to stay in them round the clock. They walked through between the two pitch drives and into the bridge.

At least it didn't take long to get to work in a little ship like *Your Last Chance.* She was pleased with her new command, especially since she'd inherited the ship from the first Human to gain a commission. It felt like a vote of confidence.

Gleb, Nils' shift-relief, sat at the tactical console. He gave her a nod. "We've got a cruiser ahead of us."

Nils muttered a curse.

"Someone owes you fifty ducats, Gleb!" She grinned at her tactical specialist.

"I'd gladly give up the money if I could just know why we're seeing cruisers first," Gleb groused.

"Maybe we just missed their frigate screen?" Hela offered, her tone innocent.

"Miss frigates?" Gleb exclaimed. "This may not be the clearest of conditions but there's no way we'd miss something the size of a frigate trying to fight against all this gravity. Twenty-eight times our mass and with only three pitch drives? They'll be lit up like pulsars, red-lining those drives for all they're worth."

The Quailu preferred size and firepower over mobility. Their species was heavier and less agile than most of their subjects, their design philosophy tended to favor their own strengths. Most of them saw the scout-ships as extravagant toys, a waste of two perfectly good pitch drives.

Hela had to admit to a certain respect for Quailu design as she snuck up behind one of their cruisers in a mostly unarmed little scout. Still, she'd been on her share of operations against stronger enemies and she knew the value of stealth and agility.

"Should we go around them?" Eve called from the pilot's seat.

Hela considered that. *Don't come back with cruisers.* That had been Eth's orders. He said nothing about *attacking* any cruisers that got in their way.

And she didn't want those weapons aimed at her backside.

"Bring us up under their hull," she ordered. "Ventral, center-line. We'll link up to them in one of the un-pressurized engineering spaces."

She pulled a holo-display down from an overhead emitter, ignoring the exclamations from her crew. She stripped away the outer hull on the standard cruiser overlay and did a search of the critical systems file.

"Here," she said, clenching a fist and throwing a copy of the projection up to where Eve could see. "Right under the main power shunt in the central core. We'll open a boarding link on our starboard side and toss in a few grenades."

"Ok…" Eve looked back over her shoulder. "I like where your head's at, but please tell me we're all keeping in mind that we're gonna be attached to the *bottom* of that thing while we're fixin' to drop it to crush depth?"

"That's why grenades have delay settings," Hela replied. "Gleb, close all suits and rig the ship for combat."

"You got it, Boss." He activated a command in the system and thirty suits closed up. He looked up at her. "Aren't we supposed to be all formal in our orders, now that we're in the house fleet?"

"Screw that," Hela said. "They need that on a cruiser where they have an overblown hierarchy. We run lean. I can talk to every crewmember on this dinky little boat without taking a single step. It's working so let's not screw with it."

She grabbed her holo display and dragged it aft. It flickered as it jumped from emitter to emitter until she stopped and released it to starboard of the two drives. The main core flashed in red, showing her the shapes to look for once the enemy hull was breached.

Meesh came over from behind one of his beloved pitch drives. "We're gonna make their core go boom?" He unspooled a safety cable from his chest and clipped it to an overhead support.

Hela did likewise. "HE grenades on a five-minute delay."

"I'd recommend synchronizing them," he offered. "Explosions in non-pressurized compartments are always so underwhelming. We want to get the max bang for our buck. I'll toss in a few-shaped charge grenades as well, if you don't mind."

"Thanks for the advice," she said. "Throw whatever you think will work best. This is more your area of expertise."

She knew she couldn't be an expert on everything, so she made sure she showed appreciation when her subordinates filled in the gaps for her. She'd seen how officers in the house military would snap at NCO's for volunteering information that they probably needed. It didn't make for the most effective teamwork but, then again, they hadn't been *grown* for this work.

The last of the cabin atmosphere disappeared into storage and the side of the hull opened in front of them, letting in the roaring winds of the upper atmosphere. She had to resist the urge to jump back as the cruiser's hull filled their view, coming closer with alarming speed.

They came to a stop, or rather, matched course and speed with only a finger's width between the two ships. The strength of the wind, rushing between the two hulls, compressing in the gap and then buffeting against her whole body, was unexpected. The atmosphere was thin up here but it was still blowing along at a hell of a velocity.

Gas giants looked so peaceful from outside.

Somehow, perhaps because the atmosphere was too thin and toxic to be breathable, she hadn't expected to hear so much noise when the hull opened up. Still, gasses were compressible and, therefore, capable of transmitting sound. The compression waves buffeted against her suit, transmitting through to the air inside and battering at her eardrums.

The noise rose to a high-pitched shriek before cutting off entirely as *Your Last Chance's* hull flowed out from the edges of the opening to connect with the nanites forming the enemy hull.

Once the seal was complete, the enemy hull activated a subroutine designed for maintenance access and split open in the middle of the gap, flowing out of the way.

Hela and Meesh both aimed their weapons through the growing gap. If some enemy crewman happened to be mucking about in there, they wanted to be the first to shoot.

There were no enemies in sight and Hela stepped up to the edge of her own decking. She slid a high-explosive disc from her grenade dispenser, tossing it toward the core. She cursed as the planet's gravity took hold of it and slapped it down against the inside surface of the cruiser's hull.

She'd forgotten that these spaces didn't have grav plating to counteract external forces. She pulled out another grenade and threw it with all her might. The disc hit one of the shapes she'd identified as critical and she breathed a sigh of relief.

She'd hate to go through all this trouble only to slink away without doing what she'd proposed. She made a mental note to keep more to herself. That way, her crew might not realize it when she failed to carry out all of her plan.

They got more than two dozen grenades placed before Meesh deigned to offer another opinion.

"That ought to mess them up," he grunted, voice sounding slightly deeper over the comms. "Shall we activate the countdown?"

"Yeah, let's get on with it." Hela used the pad on her forearm to synch the timers and start them. Now there was no stopping them.

"Let's go, Eve," she ordered.

"Roger that," came Eve's relieved reply.

But nothing happened.

"Let's GO, Eve!"

"We're not separating!" Eve said. "I can try to tear us loose but I don't know if that's even possible."

"It's not," Meesh confirmed. "The bond between nanites is stronger than the engine mounts; we'd just knock the drives loose."

"Well, why the hells are we stuck?" Hela demanded. "We're gonna have a front row seat for an explosion in about three and a half minutes." She'd managed to keep her voice calm, but she could feel the sweat collecting on her skin.

Meesh was scrolling feverishly through lines of holographic code. "Wait, Eve, what the hells are you doing inside the code interface?"

"Trying to break the seal!"

"Is that how you originally tried to break us free?"

"Yeah, why?"

"'Cause Noa programmed a lockout to prevent accidental separation while a boarding team might be crossing over. You can't separate from the coding screens. Get out of there."

"Three minutes," Hela warned. She was starting to think they were about to disgrace their species in the eyes of the empire and the lord who'd given them this chance.

And dying would also really suck.

"Ok, I'm out."

"Give me a second to put the code back in the right sequence."

"Hurry up," Hela growled. "We still need to get clear without being detected."

"Got it!" Meesh nearly shouted. "Ok, Eve, if you bring the drives up to anything more than point-five standard grav-units, the separation subroutine will kick in."

The sound of shrieking wind was the sweetest Hela had ever heard. The racket grew louder and deeper as the seam between the two ships widened and then they were completely free.

The small ship lurched away from the cruiser and they had just cleared the starboard side of the larger vessel's hull when she saw the eruption of debris from the underside.

The cruiser still had its forward momentum but, with power cut to her pitch drives, she could no longer hold out against gravity. The emergency capacitor bank cut in but they couldn't supply the power needed to keep her drives running at their designed maximum output.

The huge ship started dropping down into the atmosphere and the bridge windows slid past the little scout-ship. Hela could see the terrified Quailu at their stations, the captain gesturing wildly and she realized, for the first time, that the result of her own orders would be the deaths of every Quailu aboard.

She shivered, keenly feeling the coldness where the suit's airflow was evaporating sweat through her under-suit. Her whole life, up till now, had revolved around service to the Quailu. To harm one of them or even to fail to protect one had been unthinkable.

And now she was deliberately sending hundreds of them to their deaths.

"Bye, folks," Meesh said, waving. "Next stop, metallic hydrogen!"

Clearly, he wasn't as struck by the moment as she was, but then this was on *her* authority, not his, and, frankly, he was a bit of a sociopath. She wondered what it must have been like for the Humans boarding the *Mouse*. They'd killed Quailu in close combat, shooting

251

them from so near, their victims would have felt their attackers' emotions.

She shivered again. That was exactly what she'd be doing if they found a frigate.

It seemed stupid to put a bridge so close to the outer hull – so close they actually had *windows*. She shook her head as she stepped away from the closing hole in the scout-ship's hull.

Kill a few hundred Quailu and suddenly she's allowing herself to think they're less than magnificent. There were no Quailu aboard to catch her at it but it was a dangerous habit to get into.

"Gleb, any more ghosts?"

"Nothing right now," he replied, his voice changing in pitch as her helmet snapped open. "Just our original contact and it looks like she's starting to lose her hull integrity."

Even their path drive would be useless, though some deck officer had likely suggested they jump out of their predicament, raising hopes for a brief moment. Someone would have pointed out that the path drives needed power just as much as the pitch drives, which would have depleted the capacitor bank far too much to allow even the shortest of jumps.

"Is *A Waste of Time* still out there?" She hadn't even considered what reaction her hunting partner might have had to their unexpected approach to the enemy cruiser. She cursed her own foolishness.

What if they'd thought we were trying to seize that ship and moved in to back us up? She could have sent a lot of Humans to their deaths if that had happened.

"Pretty sure they're right here," Gleb pointed into the holo.

She suppressed a sigh of relief and made a promise to herself to think things through a little more thoroughly next time. She'd gotten lucky this time but she wouldn't be trying anything like that again, unless she could predict what the other scout-ship might do.

She took some small measure of comfort in the talk she'd had with Eth before leaving his cruiser. She'd been apprehensive about letting him down and, almost as if he could sense it, he sought her out.

"Every good leader has their fair share of dumb-assed blunders in their past," he'd told her, "myself included." He held out a hand to forestall her protest. "It's true. I've been behind some monumental screw-ups. I'm only alive because of luck and a damn good team. Rely on the second more than the first. Do everything in your power, and a few things beyond it, to look after them."

She was too keyed up from the action to stay around on the bridge. "I'll be in my bunk," she told Gleb, ignoring the look of awe on his face.

They'd just taken out a cruiser, killed hundreds of Quailu, and now she was going to grab a quick nap?

She kept the grimace off her face as she wove her way through the crowd of extra prize crew in the engineering spaces. She wasn't the imperturbable leader he thought her to be. She just didn't want to deal with her post-action jitters and recriminations in front of the crew.

She flopped down on her bunk. She'd take a half hour or so to sort out her thoughts and then head back out.

She was still lying in the same position, six hours later, when Meesh gave her foot a shake, waking her up.

"Frigate," he said simply.

Hela sat up, realizing as she did that she still had her suit on. It was probably the smart thing to do, really, given that they were lurking around in a gas giant's outer atmosphere, looking for trouble.

She had an easier time getting through the middle of the ship now that the prize crew were all on their feet, checking suits and weapons.

"Talk to me, Gleb," she said, leaning over to see the holo from something approximating his own perspective.

"A frigate here." He pointed. "A faint ghost over here that looks like a cruiser. I think *A Waste of Time* is moving in for the assault but she's even harder to see than the frigate."

"They're matching our approach," she replied, nodding with approval at their vector-icon in the holo.

It had been worked out in advance. They couldn't use communications without alerting the enemy, so the junior scout-ship in each hunting pair would try to mirror the leader, approaching at the same time.

Assuming they could even see each other. It was nearly impossible even when they *knew* that friendlies were out there. For an enemy ship to spot them, it would take a minor miracle.

"Almost there," Eve called over her shoulder. "Two minutes out."

Hela stuck her head around the bulkhead. "Line up!" she shouted at the prize crew. "Two minutes! Get your fingers out of your noses; it's time to button up!"

She turned back to Gleb. "Rig the ship for combat."

"Rigging for combat!" Gleb confirmed.

Their helmets snapped shut and gloves grew into place. The background sounds of the ship, the ones she never noticed until moments like this, became muted, though an alarm was sounding in her ears and a red icon flashed in front of her left eye.

Cursing, she ran back into the engineering compartment, seeing a corresponding red icon over one of the crewmen of the prize crew. She strode over to the helmetless man who was hammering, ineffectually, at the collar of his suit.

She grabbed his collar and dragged him over to her cubicle door. You can come out if you get it working," she snarled, shutting him in her sleeping space. One improperly suited crewman could hold up the rigging process, unless the captain authorized an override or that crewman was sealed in a space with air to breathe.

As soon as the cubicle door closed on him, the atmosphere was sucked out of the little ship and what little sound she had still heard from the ship faded, carried now by the thin upper-atmosphere of the planet.

She shoved a few crewmen into line as she moved toward the growing hole in the starboard side of the hull, directly opposite the pitch drives. The frigate was rapidly growing to fill the view.

She grabbed a stanchion and leaned out to look along the length of the frigate. She would have jumped out of her skin, if there had been enough room in the suit, when Meesh grabbed her tie-cable.

She looked back inside where he held up the mag-clip at the end of her cable.

"Best time to hook up is *before* you fall out of the ship."

Before she could reply, Eve interrupted.

"Hammurabi's nads!" she shouted, overloading the channel with a layer of static. "Gas harvesting platform, dead ahead!"

Hela turned to look ahead. A massive complex floated ahead of them, suspended by a series of large balloons. It was coming up fast.

The scout-ship swerved upwards and to port, understandable with a frigate preventing escape to starboard, but Hela was hanging partially out of the starboard side and *Your Last Chance* was an incredibly nimble ship.

The inertial dampeners weren't meant to cover things outside the hull. Their effects did bleed out past the plating for a few feet but the fall-off in the effect was pretty sharp and Hela's left arm suddenly felt as though some invisible giant was trying to pull her out of the hole in the hull.

She looked back into the ship, her breath catching in her throat and she saw Meesh standing there with a look of shock in his eyes and the mag-clip still in his hand.

Hela was pulled out of the opening, accelerating as her body left the dampening field.

Meesh finally snapped out of it. "Belay maneuvering!" he yelled, slapping the clip up onto the thicker stanchion that radiated out from the top of the engine mountings.

Hela hit the end of her tether less than a second after Meesh had attached the clip and it felt like she'd been hit with a speeding ground-car. Her back was screaming protests to her brain and her left shoulder might have been dislocated from the violence of the unexpected acceleration.

They'd managed to clear the harvesting platform but Hela, straining to reach her cable retract, was a good twenty meters closer and headed straight for the lowest of the four balloons that held the platform up.

She managed to get her right hand up to her retractor and she started inching toward the ship but not in time to miss the lower balloon.

It was big enough to hide a frigate inside and the material had to be tough but, thankfully, her suit was tougher and she punched through, her tie cable slicing a rent along the side as she flew in toward the center. A staircase wound its way up from the base of the balloon, leading to a gas generator near its center. A startled Quailu stood at the controls with some kind of tool in his hand and she managed a casual wave as she sped past.

She looked down and her blood suddenly ran cold. A second, narrower staircase worked its way up the inside of the balloon wall, leading to a hatch near its equator. She had no idea what it was for but she was heading straight for it; the retractor was working too slowly.

She grabbed the cable with both hands, ignoring the searing pain in her left shoulder, and pulled for all she was worth. She saw no slack in the cable at her chest but her hands were moving toward her as she tried to climb back along the cable, hand over hand.

Either her retractor was automatically taking up the slack or her hands were slipping on the cable. Either way, there was nothing to do but keep trying.

Her breathing froze as the stairs raced toward her but she slammed through the fabric of the balloon with just over a meter to spare.

"Gahhh!" she opined as her head struck an antenna and her ass tore a signal light loose. All things considered, she felt it was an appropriate comment.

But she was clear!

And the scout-ship was closer than she would have expected, so her desperate scramble had been worth the effort. She twisted to look for the frigate.

"Oh my various gods!" she exclaimed softly.

The harvesting platform had been slightly to port for the frigate so she'd sheared off to starboard. It was a sensible course of action, except there had been a scout-ship closing in on them from that side.

The bulk of the frigate would have masked the platform from the scout-ship's view so the enemy's emergency course-change would have been completely unexpected.

She couldn't see *Waste of Time,* but she suspected they were embedded in the starboard side of the frigate. Its crew would almost certainly be dead. A cloud of debris was spinning away from the enemy ship's side.

The Quailu would have been partially incapacitated by the sudden drop in pressure. The hull would have sealed itself around the scout-ship by now but a lot of air would have been vented in the relatively thin atmosphere of the gas giant. The large central ramp would have spread the pressure change very rapidly.

Hearing loss, temporary or permanent blindness and a general feeling of terror would be infecting the Quailu crewmen and at a time when quick action would be needed to save their ship.

An explosion tore a new hole in the hull on the port side. It might be from a damaged system or maybe even from one of the small mines the scout-ships had received from the *Mouse*. Whatever the cause, the frigate began to drop her bow toward the planet.

The *Waste of Time* and the frigate were both doomed.

She brought her breathing under control but she couldn't wipe the moisture from her eyes with the helmet closed. Nineteen good people gone due to shitty luck.

She remembered Eth's advice.

You can't count on luck. It'll turn on you but, if you look after your people…

Meesh and someone from the prize crew grabbed her arms and pulled her in.

And Then the Murders Began

Eth had to force himself to look away from his holo and open up the queue of status reports he'd been ignoring. They didn't make for very exciting reading but, if he continued to ignore them, every department head would notice and they'd know exactly why.

He resisted the urge to open and close each file. They'd end up with a set of timestamps that would have proclaimed his distraction even more eloquently than simply ignoring them.

He grunted in surprise. His gunnery officer had located a large cache of anti-ship mines in storage and he'd parceled them out to the scout-ships.

Not that he would have stopped him, but Eth wished he'd told him about it. He grimaced. Technically, he was telling him in his report, but this was an important detail. Too important to leave in a report that might be ignored.

He'd have to have a quiet chat with him. Initiative and exceeding authority got up from opposite sides of the same bed. The idea was sound, but a quick call up to the bridge would have been welcome.

"You were pretending to be absorbed in your reports and then you accidentally started doing some actual work, didn't you?"

Eth looked up. Father Sulak stood there, one hand holding a steel coffee mug and the other scratching absently under his robes. The Quailu grinned widely at him.

"Look sharp!" Eth called out to the bridge crew. "Our oracle's suddenly on the bridge, trying to act casual. Something's about to happen!"

"Am I that transparent?" Sulak asked.

"Even more transparent than that old robe of yours," Eth told him. "You just make a fresh pot of my coffee?"

Sulak chuckled. "It was Uktannu's coffee not so long ago…"

"And I took it as the spoils of war," Eth said, sounding as though he were explaining it to a child. Mostly, he liked Sulak because he didn't seem put out by his inability to read him, but his refusal to take himself too seriously helped as well.

"Perhaps I've seized the galley," Sulak suggested.

"Good!" Eth grinned at the oracle. "I haven't really sorted out who's going to run the place. I like my eggs over easy. Something should squirt out when you bite into them."

"Carnivores!" Sulak shuddered, though Eth felt nothing but amusement from him. The Quailu were mostly vegetarian but they did eat the occasional bit of dead animal. "I'm already looking after the galley staff."

"Then why haven't they started on the second-shift main meal yet?"

"Reading multiple distortions!" Oliv said. "Looks like they're opening paths from inside the atmosphere. They must have just had a timer counting down so they'd all jump out at the same time."

"That would be why," Sulak said casually. He noticed Eth's look of confusion. "I hate to waste food, so I had the galley hold off on…"

"Any sign of our people?" Eth asked, cutting off the oracle.

Oliv shook her head. "Not yet."

"That's a day earlier than we expected," Henku said, sounding as though an agreement had been broken.

"First smart thing they've done so far." Eth waved at the holo. "They know what we're likely to expect from them so they're changing the tempo, trying to catch the defense off-balance."

"Here come our people." Oliv began tagging ships as they emerged from the atmosphere. "That gas might make comms difficult but there's no hiding a distortion effect. Our hunting teams will know the quarry's run off."

The thick gasses that had made it possible to approach the enemy undetected also wreaked havoc with sensors and communications. That was why the scouts had been advised to watch for distortion signatures.

It was the one sure sign that the enemy was leaving. It ensured Eth would be able to consolidate his small force in time to have an impact on the second battle for Arbella.

He came out of his chair, seeing only two of the hoped-for three frigates, each with two scout-ships attached to their flanks like parasites. A single scout-ship signaled from the far side of the gas giant.

He opened the channel. "Warrant Hela, report."

"We lost the *Waste of Time* to a collision with a frigate," she told him. "So we spent the rest of our time hunting down cruisers. Managed to knock out three before the rest pathed out."

"I'm sorry to hear about the *Waste of Time*," he told her, "but well done, Warrant. Dock with us until we get back to Arbella."

Three cruisers knocked out of the fight before it even began! Warrant Officer Hela would bear watching. He'd have to get his captains together after the fight, assuming they were still alive, and have her explain what she'd been doing for the last few days.

He designated two channels to the frigates, bringing up holograms of their captains in front of him. "Carol, Fink, your ships are ready for action?"

"As ready as we're going to be," Fink shrugged. "We're running with a skeleton crew here."

"We're ready," Carol confirmed, "but I'm not going to pretend I like this."

He knew she didn't mean running a short-handed frigate. "I need you on that frigate," he told her. "I've got someone in mind for lead scout but she's going to have to lean on you. We don't have a lot of experienced leaders to choose from."

"And by 'a lot' you mean 'any'?" Carol chuckled.

"It's a steep learning curve," Eth admitted, "but we have good people to work with – lots of combat experience, just not combat in ships. We've been relatively lucky so far, but we need to get our shit together before that luck runs out.

"For now, just go with the plan I just sent over."

"Sir," Hela interjected, her holographic image appearing next to Fink, "I haven't had a chance to go through the whole thing yet but isn't this a violation of the conventions?"

"Only for a defensive deployment, Warrant. I believe this qualifies as an offensive usage."

"*Your Last Chance* is docked," Oliv interrupted. "We're ready to go."

"Any inspiring words, Lieutenant Eth?" Carol asked, smirking.

"Yeah, um… This is a make-or-break moment for our people. The whole galaxy is gonna be rehashing what we do in the next couple of hours so, what do we say?"

Carol rolled her eyes. "We're not at home to Mr. Screw-Up?"

"Damn straight." Eth nodded. "Let's get in there, murder some of the bastards and see if we can scare them off.

"Hendy, confirm path-destination with our two frigates and coordinate the jump."

The path back to Arbella was a short one, taking less than five minutes, and they came out well back from the standard approach corridor.

"Enemy appears to be in two echelons," Oliv advised. "One facing down the approach to the planet and one facing out toward us."

Eth glanced at the holo showing his own ships, pleased to see his scout-ships already separated from the larger ships and racing toward the enemy fleet. "Clearly, they're expecting an attack from behind. The database describes Tilsin as a sharp tactician. He's probably got them dancing to one tune or another.

"Waypoint one," he ordered. "And watch out for incoming."

The cruiser and the two frigates began heading in, but they were angling heavily to starboard, aimed for a course that would skirt that side of the opening in the planetary minefield.

The enemies' sensors would have detected their arrival waves and now they'd be watching the small force as it moved over…

Away from the approaching scout-ships.

"Incoming," Oliv said calmly.

"Altering our velocity by two percent so the slugs will miss us," Hendy said.

"Missiles?" Eth asked.

"We're nowhere close to their maneuver range so they'll be purely inertial by the time they miss us," Oliv scorned. "It's almost like they're just trying to scare us off."

"So Uktannu isn't in overall command," Eth mused. "He'd have more sense than to waste munitions like this."

"How the mighty have fallen," Hendy offered dryly. "At least that increases our chances of success."

"Maybe we *should* return the gesture." Eth squinted at the holo. "Fire off a few rounds, kick up a ruckus to keep their interest, let 'em know it's mutual…"

"We'd have to turn back in," Hendy cautioned.

"Yeah, our mains can't traverse that far on this course," Oliv added.

"I don't see how that's a problem," Eth countered. "They'd *expect* us to fire back at them. It might even reassure them. Why not just fire a few slugs in whatever random direction we're currently headed? That'll hold their attention for a while – wondering what the Hells we were shooting at…"

"Well, we *are* decoys," Oliv conceded. She began feeding power into the capacitor banks for the main rail-guns.

"What in the hells are they shooting at?" Hela peered out the starboard side cockpit window.

"Absolutely nothing," Eve said. "Just the minefield over there."

"I suppose if we're scratching our heads, then so are the enemy, which is probably what the lieutenant had in mind." Hela turned back to her display panel.

"Should be coming into detection-range any second now."

Dark as the scout-ships were, they still reflected enough light to get picked up at just under a thousand kilometers. Their infrared signature was managed by the same system found in the shuttles they'd cannibalized to make the newer ships. It captured the emissions in a multi-layered system and channeled them back into the reactor.

That didn't stop external light from bouncing off the hull, though, and the small flotilla of scout-ships were fast approaching the point where the enemy would start noticing them.

"Accelerate to release velocity," Hela ordered. "Gleb, standby."

"OK!" the weapons specialist called back with a wicked grin. "All weapons confirming their targeting."

Eve pushed the throttles full open, the two pitch drives synchronizing their gravity waves, reinforcing each other. "We're at release velocity."

Hela felt the blood pulsing in her neck. This was more than just combat; this was an attack on Quailu, specifically on Quailu. She'd taken out several ships filled with the master species but that didn't mean she was numb to the implications.

Not quite yet.

"Gleb," she called over her shoulder, "execute!"

He touched a holographic sphere in the middle of his weapons display. "Mines away!"

"Slow us down, Eve." She wanted as much distance between *Your Last Chance* and the mines before they activated their proximity detectors.

"Time to impact?"

"Three minutes, give or take."

They'd fly on inertia alone for two of those minutes before going live. They'd gone over the numbers twice – nobody wanted a repeat of the grenade incident – and she had to force herself not to re-open the calculations.

The manual target selection had been the legal work-around saving them from war-crimes prosecution, or that was the theory, at least. It was still a dicey business, deploying mines in an approach corridor.

She fervently hoped the mines would survive impact. At more than forty thousand kilometers per hour, their small shield generators might not be up to the task, despite Noa's assurances.

They'd soon know.

"It doesn't matter what they're shooting at," Tilsin said calmly. "They aren't shooting at us, but *those* bastards," he growled, pointing at the tactical holo, "*are,* and they're doing a lot more damage than last time, seeing as they're right in our faces."

The Lady Bau shimmered into view. "What's our situation, General?"

"Grim," he said curtly, knowing she hated anything other than the unvarnished truth. "My ventral flank is starting to crumble. We won't hold them out for much longer. I strongly urge you to leave Arbella while you can. Get out to the gap in the minefield on the anti-sunward side. I can hold them off long enough for you to…"

"It baffles me, General, why you'd even waste breath on such a suggestion," Bau cut him off. "These people have shown a great deal of overt support for us. I'm not going to reward that by running off and leaving my best general to die with them.

"Now, pull up that ventral flank; I'm coming in rather fast and we're going to start firing in less than two minutes!"

Grunting in surprise, Tilsin enlarged his display and rotated it to show the region behind his defenses. Sure enough, his lady's personal cruiser was coming up around the planet's southern pole, leading a formation of orbital defense gunboats.

She must have collected all the remaining defense forces from around the planet and now she was going to use them to plug the growing gap.

If he'd known about it beforehand, he would have given serious thought to having her confined aboard her ship and sent home. He sighed. Tilsin doubted her crew would allow it, despite the horrific impact her death would wreak on her holdings.

Now, all he could do was comply and hope she could turn the tide. He used his hands to drag a box around his ventral-most ships and he shifted their markers up toward the center of the formation.

They began trying to disengage and move to their new positions but it was a slow process. A ship in combat can't simply turn and head straight for a new position, it had to keep its bow facing the enemy. The strongest shields were there as well as the main guns, built inside the ship along the center axis.

"Bring us along that lower edge, Captain," Bau ordered. "We'll give 'em a salvo as we come in and then it's just going to be a good old-fashioned slugging match and the gods help whoever steps back first!"

"Aye, ma'am," Captain Muz replied calmly, as though he were agreeing to meet someone for lunch.

"Coming up on optimal firing range," the tactical officer announced.

"Signal weapons free to our team, if you please, Captain."

"Aye, ma'am," this time with a hint of enjoyment. As the captain of her personal ship, he never got to fight anymore. When she'd told him what she intended to do, he'd agreed instantly.

There was no real use in leaving orbital defense units around the planet. If Tilsin failed to keep the enemy out, the small gunboats would be easy work for a coordinated force of cruisers and frigates.

If the Lady Bau ran for home with only one cruiser, the enemy would likely pursue her. Despite the new ships and crews at her home world, the only seasoned forces were here at Arbella.

If she didn't win here, she'd no longer be a great lady. If she didn't stop the enemy at Arbella, she'd no longer be an electress.

It was all or nothing.

The enemy ships in the growing ventral gap were still in disarray and hadn't moved yet to take advantage of their opening. Some were turning to aim at the receding defenders, while others were hanging in strange orientations, not yet sure if they should go after the ships or push through and try to roll the enemy up.

Bau's force came in at an angle, their axis of approach aligned along the edge of the retreating flank and they opened fire on the newly disengaged enemy.

Missiles streaked out, seeking targets that had almost no time for point defense systems to acquire and engage them. Kinetic rounds, largely immune to point defense fire, slammed into hulls that had no chance to maneuver out of their way. Ships flared as they vented plasma, hull fragments and crew, turning away from the fight.

They'd hit a lot of ships with their sudden attack but they'd never have the time to fly past and come around for another run. That flank, even if Tilsin hadn't pulled up his socks, would never last that long.

All of her makeshift squadron began braking, turning in to join the fight but it was still a very lopsided equation. The enemy had been hurt and thrown into confusion but they still had overwhelming numbers and they were all frigates and cruisers while Bau had only one cruiser and a few dozen gunboats to face them down with.

Grim finality.

"It's looking serious, ma'am," Muz said conversationally.

"I can think of nowhere else I'd rather be right now," she replied calmly.

The bridge flooded with an air of desperate, hopeless pride.

The enemy started pushing them back, their second echelon finally committed to the assault. Gunboat after gunboat blossomed into a cloud of energy and debris.

Better to die here with honor, she thought, *than to run back and die a coward in front of my own people.* She frowned. Would her husband be there, waiting to spoil the afterlife for her?

And then it happened.

"The enemy's taking multiple warhead impacts!" the sensor officer shouted. "It's like nothing I've ever seen before. They're detonating deep inside the enemy hulls. We're picking up brief traces before impact… their inbound velocities are incredible! They're coming in at near path velocities."

Shock, cautious hope…

"Enemy formation is losing cohesion," the sensor officer added.

Sure enough, the enemy didn't know which way to turn, but at least half were now trying to face the sudden threat from the rear.

A non-Quailu shimmered into view, a native in house-uniform. He gave a polite bow.

"Lady Bau." The hologram straightened. "I bring you greetings from your noble cousins, the princes Sandrak and Mishak. I apologize for taking liberties with your enemy, but I trust our intervention is not unwelcome?"

Cautious hope gave way to pure elation.

Cheers rang out on the bridge. The enemy, suddenly assailed by a new force and hearing feared names invoked over an open channel, began shimmering out of sight as they opened paths to their emergency rendezvous point.

Help had come.

The enemy were gone from Arbella.

Bau peered at her savior. He wore the uniform of a lieutenant in Sandrak's house military. She was unaware he'd promoted any of his natives to officer status, though such a thing wasn't unheard of in the empire.

"Any who serve my noble cousins are welcome in my dominions," she said graciously.

Of course, there was no blood relation between her and Sandrak but it was the way electors talked. As princes (and princesses) of the realm, they affected a common royal bond.

"And to whom, aside from our royal cousin, do we owe our gratitude?" she asked.

The hologram inclined his head politely. "I am Lieutenant Eth from Kish, one of Prince Mishak's worlds."

She noted that he didn't bother to tack on the 'kenu' suffix, even though Kish's native population had all been wardu, last she'd heard. His rank had to mean he'd been freed and that he'd done something deserving of promotion.

Many freed slaves would make full use of their new name suffix. Indeed, many at the lower end of the mushkenu class were very deliberate in its application, icily correcting those who left it off.

This young officer seemed to understand that it was implied by his position and, therefore, needed no mention. In her experience, those who gave little thought to such distinctions were the ones most likely to see an even better future for themselves, the ones with the ability to rise above their current conditions.

"So, young Mishak is now an elector?" she asked. The last time she'd seen him, he'd been playing children's games with the crown princess, Tashmitum, on Throne World. "Has his father assigned him more systems to rule?"

General Tilsin shimmered into view but refrained from interrupting.

"Ah, no, My Lady. The Lord Uktannu had turned on his brother and my lord was the one who discovered his plot and prevented it from weakening the family.

"He exercised his right to declare him an outlaw…"

The native officer didn't insult Bau by explaining any further. She knew the law of fealty as well as any in the HQE.

The rest fell into place quickly for her. Mishak had become an elector by his own hand and his treacherous, dispossessed uncle...

"Did Uktannu flee from his nephew?" she asked. "With a respectable force of warships, perhaps?"

A nod of respect. "Indeed, ma'am. We had reason to believe he'd come here and we happened to be nearby..."

"So," she mused, "Uktannu's gotten his hands on Shullat and shoved a temporary spine up his back-passage...

"Where will they go from here? Gimmerai, which they've already taken back from us, or my own capital?" She looked at Tilsin.

"The only possibility we care about, right now, is the second," the general said. "Gimmerai's already lost, for the moment, but if they take your home world..."

"Then I'm nothing but an unemployed awilu," Bau finished for him. She had no intention of becoming one of the penniless nobles that infested the empire. "Take your forces home immediately, General. Just leave me a couple of frigates to shore up the defenses here."

"I can't leave you here alone!" Tilsin exploded.

"I thought you didn't want me getting into battles," she countered reasonably. "I'm not sending you home for rest and relaxation, you know.

"And I want to keep this world. They're warming up to us and I'm not about to run off on them when things get a little problematic."

Tilsin looked as though he was going to continue protesting, but he must have seen the sense in her argument. He bowed his head and faded from sight.

She turned back to the native. "Lieutenant Eth, how many ships did you bring with you?"

"A cruiser, two frigates and six... no, five scout-ships."

"That's all?"

He smiled. "I only had the scout-ships half a cycle ago and, frankly, they're the ships that did most of our damage. We used them to take our larger ships from the enemy."

She was impressed but also increasingly apprehensive. Had this creature truly used… whatever scout-ships were… to take three ships from a Quailu lord? Such a thing went against the accepted natural order. How long had this fellow been serving in house uniform anyway?

To speak so casually about getting the better of his *betters*…

Realization dawned.

"You're one of Mishak's pirates!"

"That's right, ma'am," he replied cheerfully, taking no apparent offense.

Though it went a long way to explaining his tactical abilities, it still didn't make her feel much better. Native troops weren't supposed to be this efficient.

Nevertheless, he'd been very useful to her at a crucial moment. Had he not brought his ships into the fight when he did, she might now be dead or a captive.

"You have my thanks, Lieutenant. I would be very grateful if you could linger here until we know where our enemy has gone. As you've seen, I ordered General Tilsin home with most of my local forces."

The hologram bowed his head. "Your request does us great honor, Lady Bau." He straightened, grinning now. "As to our enemy, I might be able to shed some light on his current disposition."

"And how do you propose to do that?"

"We believe that Uktannu hasn't yet killed Shullat and taken over. He's coming off a string of defeats and Shullat's crews would refuse his leadership.

"Shullat shows a penchant for repetition. He attacked the same way twice, essentially, and I would suggest that he's used the same rendezvous a second time as well.

"And you know where he went after the first attack?"

"Indeed, ma'am. That's where we took two frigates from him and destroyed three of his cruisers."

Again that irritatingly confident manner. He'd inflicted heavy losses against a Quailu force and he mentioned it in such an off-hand manner.

What was Sandrak thinking, turning these creatures loose on the empire?

A Leap of Faith

Eth leaned forward, ever so slightly, to gaze at the tactical holo as their combined fleet came out of path near the gas giant. He'd look a complete fool if he'd read the enemy wrong. Still, no sense in assuming failure.

"Rig for combat, all ships." It felt as though such a simple step would make him look even more foolish if the enemy weren't here.

After having decided to keep his wild-ass hunches to himself in future, he'd gone and blabbed to the Lady Bau – all but promising her they'd find the enemy. That was on top of the nagging fear that Uktannu and Shullat *had* come here but then left while Eth and Bau got the Arbellan gunboats joined to the hulls of their larger path-capable ships.

He clenched a fist, waiting for the plasma-wash of path-drop to fade so the sensors could tell him if he was an idiot or not.

"Contact!" Oliv called out as the enemy ships started appearing. They were in a loose gaggle around the giant's equator, just outside of the massive rings. "They're spread out a bit, but we can at least hurt the ones near to us."

"Separate the smaller ships," Eth ordered, "and let's get after the bastards before they can run again."

There was no making this look good for their enemy. To run from a battle was disgraceful for a Quailu. Uktannu had run from Heiropolis, but he was about to become an outlaw anyway. Now he could at least spread the shame, claiming that it had been Shullat who ran from Arbella, once in losing it and twice more in trying to retake it.

That would mean that both were desperate to regain some of their honor and that wouldn't happen in a meaningless, indecisive skirmish on the fringe of the Arbellan system. This would be a very short engagement.

They were going to run again. The only question would be where and nobody doubted what that answer would be.

"We're inside missile range," Oliv advised.

"Not yet." Eth was counting on confusion, hoping it would let them get closer before firing that crucial first salvo. The enemy would still be reorganizing and a few cruisers and frigates, some of whom had, until recently, been a part of their own fleet, might be mistaken for friendlies.

"Silly bastards," Oliv muttered to her screens. "They might not be certain about *some* of our ships, but the scout-ships are close enough to bounce all kinds of visible spectrum back at them and those gunboats don't even have any emissions management systems at all. It's like failing to notice a forest fire headed right for you."

Several of the ship-icons suddenly displayed new vector icons in blinking red.

"I'd say they're on to us!" Oliv said, looking urgently at Eth.

He nodded. "Weapons free!"

The deck shuddered as a full salvo of missiles were ejected from their launch-tubes throughout the ship.

"Reloading in twenty seconds," Oliv said. She frowned at the displays. "The old bat's going in for all she's worth," she commented, highlighting Bau's cruiser which was leading a flock of gunboats straight for the middle of the loose enemy formation.

Eth enlarged his display. "Could be she's got intercepts or pattern-analysis that shows the command ship. Hendy, follow her in. Glen, make sure the others know to stick with us. Let's back her play."

"Salvo up," Oliv called out.

"Target the ships trailing her apparent target," Eth ordered. "Concentrate on the ones whose course she'll cross on her way in. They're the biggest threat right now."

"How's this?" Oliv asked.

Eth took a quick look and nodded. "Give 'em a salvo of missiles and then carry on as you see fit."

The vibration of the second salvo tingled in his feet.

"You gotta admit the old gal's got guts," Hendy said, putting their ship into a sideways drift to port.

"So do I," Oliv muttered, "and I'd like to keep 'em in my belly, thanks very much!"

Eth grinned, despite the stress of the moment. *If Bau were traded into Oliv's shoes, she'd probably spill her own guts – going from an electress to some jumped up native officer…*

Oliv reached up to drag the second swarm of missiles together and redirect them. "Diverting the second salvo. I think they're trying to ram her!"

The new target reticules centered on a frigate that did indeed seem to be heading straight at the port side of Bau's cruiser. The gunboats were turning to protect her but they wouldn't have time to burn through the enemy's shields.

The deck vibrated as the third salvo ejected.

The missiles of the first two salvos arranged themselves into a pair of waves, the first overwhelming the frigate's shields, the second obliterating the unfortunate warship.

"She's onto something. They're definitely trying to protect their leaders." Eth enlarged the area of the hologram around Bau's ship. "Oliv…"

"I see it."

There were now two frigates bearing down on Bau. It seemed extraordinary that the crews would sacrifice their lives for a lord who'd lost so much prestige. Though he'd reclaimed Gimmerai, Shullat had lost Arbella and he'd lost two fights trying to take it back.

It was why Uktannu had left Shullat alive. Mishak's traitorous uncle had been involved in the recent defeats, as well as the one at Heiropolis, but Shullat already had the oaths of his captains and crews.

They might not be happy about that but they had no conceivable option but to obey.

There was no chance, if Shullat were killed, that they would willingly bend the knee to a dishonored leader like Uktannu.

"We could do a lot more damage if we were able to spread out our missiles, rather than using them to protect one hard-charging Quailu," Oliv groused.

The two frigates changed course to avoid one of their own cruisers.

"Just keep her alive," Eth ordered. "If we end up getting her killed…"

They had no orders to be here. Their only justification was in protecting an electress who happened to be on good terms with Sandrak and, therefore, Mishak. There *was* the fact that that they'd created this problem for her by driving Uktannu in her direction in the first place.

Of course, that would be an unpopular argument in Sandrak's eyes, as it laid a sizeable portion of blame on his family.

It was a sketchy excuse and it hinged entirely on bringing her through this debacle alive and preserving her status. She'd be worse than useless if she lost her power and influence. The presence of Eth and his Humans would tie Sandrak and Mishak into the story of her fall.

Damn that oracle and his hints.

The two frigates turned back in toward her vessel.

Eth remembered how he'd stopped a Quailu from raising his weapon when they'd taken the *Mouse* from Uktannu's forces at Heiropolis. He wondered if he could stop Father Sulak from talking...

He shuddered. It was bad enough picking up the feelings of his own people, like a spy in their midst, but it would be worse to actually force his will on someone he respected.

And, even worse, he might accidentally kill Sulak in the process of trying to shut him up. He shivered.

What if he killed someone without trying...

"She's scoring hits on the suspected command ship," Oliv said. "The redirected third salvo is closing in on the two rammers..."

Just then, an Arbellan gunship threw itself bravely into the path of the closer frigate but the enemy ship shifted upwards to avoid it, effectively shielding the farther enemy ship.

Bau's cruiser was taking hits and Eth's stomach felt as though it were being punched every time her shields took an impact.

But her shields were holding.

So far...

Oliv's missiles slammed into the nearer frigate, again in two waves. Most of those designated for the farther ship assessed that they wouldn't be able to maneuver enough to hit it after flying around the closer target and so they re-designated themselves to the nearer one.

Only five of the weapons reached the farther frigate and they only struck glancing blows along the dorsal shielding. Eth watched in horror as it bore in on Bau's cruiser, leaping out of his chair as the enemy frigate fired a last salvo of missiles and kinetic weapons before impact.

He knew he was watching the end of free Humanity as the frigate displaced the already-weakened shielding of the cruiser. The glowing silhouette of energy was pushed back against the ship's hull extending out from the far side before the shield generators, torn loose form their mounts, lost reserve power and failed entirely.

"No!" he said softly as the frigate plowed into the large cruiser, massive electrical discharges jumping between the jagged edges of the two doomed warships.

Eth was filled with adrenaline he couldn't use. His audacious plan was falling apart before his very eyes and all he could do was watch. The Lady Bau was as good as dead. Her cruiser's engines must have taken damage because the two ships were slowly spinning their way down into the atmosphere of the gas giant.

The frigate's engines might still be sufficient to defeat the planet's gravity but not with the dead weight of an entire cruiser hanging from her bow. Even the shuttles, designed for use on habitable planets, would have too much to deal with at their current depth.

"Ho!" His eyes suddenly grew wide. "Gods curse me for a fool! Glen, get me a channel to Warrant Hela."

The scout-ships had been dancing around the enemy, dropping mines in their paths, but now was the moment for their underlying design philosophy to really shine.

A holographic Hela appeared in front of him, hunched over someone he couldn't see, probably Gleb in tactical. She turned to him in surprise. "Sir?"

"Warrant, you're to make for the Lady Bau's cruiser at best possible speed, dock your ship directly to her bridge and take her off. Is that understood?"

"Ahm…" Hela frowned but cleared her expression almost immediately. "Yes, sir!" She stood and turned. "Eve, you heard?"

Eth heard Eve's affirmative over his helmet speakers.

"Get us moving!" Hela ordered.

"Keep this channel open, Warrant," Eth ordered. "We'll try to clear the road for you." He gave a slight upward nod to Oliv as he said this and she returned the gesture before turning her full attention back to her weapons.

Center Stage

Hela felt like cursing. A widely varied range of pithy comments came to mind but she refrained. She even had a few thoughts on the lieutenant's mental capacity, which surprised her. Only a few days ago, she'd been in awe of him.

Being ordered on a probable suicide mission had a way of updating your outlook.

Your Last Chance had two pitch drives but they'd be pretty deep in the gas giant's gravity well by the time they broke contact with Lady Bau's cruiser. It was going to be a near-run thing and with her boss listening the whole time.

With that in mind, she decided that cursing him out was probably not the wisest course of action.

Eve was already racing their scout-ship down to the stricken cruiser at top speed, so Hela turned and headed aft to arm herself, still limping from her encounter with that communications array. She found Meesh standing at the starboard opening in the hull with a tactical holo in front of him and a mine in his right hand.

"How's your ass?" he asked with a grin.

"Still sore."

"My offer to massage it still stands…"

"No thanks," she said, watching as he dragged an enemy icon from the holo and slipped it into the mine's interface screen. "We all know where those hands end up."

"Your loss," Meesh tossed the weapon out the side and turned to grab another from a locker that sat up against the forward wall of her sleeping cubicle.

She'd somehow managed to forget that she was sleeping next to so much destructive power. She shook her head, clearing it of the irrelevant thought as she grabbed two pistols and moved over to attach her tie-off next to his.

Meesh looked up from his next mine as she slapped a sidearm onto the mag-plate at his hip. "Expecting trouble are we?" Then he chuckled darkly. "Of course we are. We're about to waltz into the midst of a panicked Quailu herd-mind and pull their leader away from them."

He targeted his mine to a frigate and tossed it out. "They don't really care about our little scout-ships," he said. "They can see we don't carry guns or missile launchers so we're minelayers, at best. I figured 'why not?'"

There was a brilliant flash and the last ship he'd targeted showed a trail of debris coming from its stern.

"That one's free!" he shouted, fogging the visor of his suit for a heartbeat before the life support system recovered the moisture. "Doctor Meesh's micro-singularity suppository – guaranteed results!"

"Heads up," Hela snapped. "We're coming alongside."

'Coming alongside' sounded so graceful and stately. The reality was anything but.

She'd been through a few close approaches now but it was still unnerving to stand there, at a hole in her hull, as a massive cruiser burst across her field of vision, blurring into place so quickly that the mind rebelled at the change in perspective. Her knees flexed as though she were going to leap away but she mastered her instincts and stepped closer.

The hulls came to within a hand's breadth of each other and they flowed together, creating an opening onto the bridge of Bau's flagship.

Hela stepped through and found close to a dozen helmeted faces looking back at her. Angry with herself for not having already thought to do so, she switched on a proximity channel, regretting the lost seconds. "Lady Bau?"

One of the suited figures stepped forward. "I'm Bau," she confirmed. "And you are?"

281

"I'm the one who's here to take you off before it's too late," Hela replied, not even noticing how rude she was being to a princess of the realm. The Hela of two months ago would never have believed herself capable of such an answer.

Bau didn't seem to take offense at the tone or the deliberate misinterpretation of her question. She merely came toward Hela and didn't argue when both Hela and Meesh took her by the arms and hustled her through the opening to *Your Last Chance.*

"Eve, we've got her. Break off and get us back up to the fleet!" She was just telling herself that things had gone surprisingly well when she was shoved out of the way and pushed against the stanchions that surrounded the two engine mounts.

She turned to see the small engineering space crowded with Bau's bridge crew. Three more of them were still pushing their way onto *Your last Chance* when the hulls separated and the small ship pulled away as fast as she'd approached. Two of the last three Quailu fell into the gap while the third backed away into his own bridge to get a running start.

He raced out the hole in his hull but the nimble little scout-ship had been out of his reach from the moment it had started moving. He drifted down, out of sight.

Hela pushed her way through to the bridge, seeing Bau on the way and dragging her along with her. She tied off Bau's suit next to Oliv's station before stepping over to Eve. "Can we climb out?"

"Just barely," Eve replied in clipped tones. "Another ten seconds and we'd be on a one way ride."

Both women flinched as a large piece of warship tumbled past them. The gas giant was pulling down the debris as fast as the combatants could create it.

Hela came to the executive decision that now would be a very good time to not get hit by falling debris.

The Universe, however, thought it knew better.

A suited figure, moving too fast to identify, flew down through the top of *Your Last Chance's* hull, smashing the power couple to the starboard pitch drive and killing the Quailu who'd been sitting with his back to it.

The hull began flowing back into place but couldn't find the mounts for the power couple. Alarm holos flashed to life above them, pulsing in emergency colors.

"If anyone's been sitting on a clever idea," Eve shouted, "now would be a great time to share it 'cause we're going down!"

Eth brought his clenched fists up as though ready to fight. His belly felt like it was filled with glass shards.

His desperate gamble had worked, but then the vagaries of combat had snatched salvation away once again. The scout-ship would never be able to lift all those people, not on one engine.

The rest of the enemy were blinking out of sight as they opened paths. Vector analysis indicated Bau's capital as their likely destination.

But the victor had already been named.

He glared down at the decking before him. Every face on the bridge was looking his way. *Damn them!* "What are you all staring at?" he demanded, not looking up. "I don't see any of you coming up with a way to salvage this fornicating mess!"

That wasn't entirely fair, he knew, but he was weary of their constant expectations. Still, it wasn't *their* fault he was grown for a leadership role.

How would they fare if I just jump off the ship and give myself to the gods? he thought morosely. *That, at least, would solve all of* my *problems because...*

The sour face turned to a reckless grin as it came to him. "Sometimes," he whispered, "the gods must bring you to your lowest point in order to raise you up..." He got up, waving off Oliv's inquiring look as the adrenaline took its grip.

"Oliv, take command," he said, walking past her. "Follow the enemy to Bau's home-world and help Tilsin. If she loses that planet, we might as well kill her ourselves."

"Take command?" She turned to him in shock. "Where the hells are you going?"

But Eth was already running. He raced past her and straight out the port-side opening in the *Mouse's* hull.

The HUD in his suit showed the location of the stricken scout-ship and he angled toward it with small nudges from the thrusters on the backs of his hands.

The system had been designed for getting around the outside of a ship in space, not for flight in an atmosphere but he figured he stood a decent chance of reaching *Your Last Chance.* He almost laughed at the name he'd chosen for the scout-ship.

It truly represented his current situation.

He could see the hull now, growing rapidly as he approached in free-fall while she was straining against gravity with her single remaining engine. He rotated his body and used the thrusters to begin braking.

It wouldn't do any good to smash into the side of the ship, though it *would* mean an end to his worries.

"I suppose I should be grateful," Eve said, peering up through the upper windows of the cockpit, "that the Universe is treating us to a properly bizarre death."

Hela looked up and her mouth fell open. "Minor gods preserve us – who the hells is that?"

The figure slipped out of view behind the upper hull and Hela turned to run back to engineering. She was just in time to see the suited figure slam into a trio of unsuspecting Quailu.

The figure stood. "Where's Bau?"

"Bau?" Hela echoed, still amazed at what she'd just seen. She barely recovered her wits in time to avoid looking like a fool. "She's tied off next to the tactical station." The Lieutenant was here? He'd *jumped* to her ship?

"Good!" He waved her over. "Give me a hand here."

She took a step forward but froze when he grabbed a Quailu and shoved him out the opening in the hull. The others must have felt the sudden, brief flare of terror before he fell too far away to be sensed. They began edging away from the opening.

Eth grabbed another and hauled him over to the gap, shoving him out as well, and that was when Hela shook off the horror at what he was doing. He'd come because the scout-ship was too heavy to climb back into space.

It probably didn't stand a chance anyway, not with an engine knocked out, and the other scouts were too far off to reach them in time. Still, he was determined to do whatever it took to give them a chance. She pulled out her sidearm and deactivated the safety.

Eth had come because he didn't think she would have the resolve to kill a dozen Quailu in cold blood. She couldn't say for sure she would have thought to do it herself.

And she couldn't say she'd have acted on it. She'd killed Quailu but that was combat. Killing *allied* Quailu was another thing entirely.

Now that he'd gotten the ball rolling, however, she realized these Quailu were doomed either way. There was no need to screw her own chances and, more importantly for the eventual inquiry, those of the Lady Bau.

She shot one of them and the others, feeling his pain, decided she represented a worse danger than the less immediate peril of falling to the core of a gas giant.

In the end, they killed at least half their own number as they crowded away from the Quailucidal native with the handgun, pushing those who were closer to the opening until they began falling out. Eth shoved one of the last three while Hela shot the other two, watching them fall back and out.

After a maturation and a lifetime of conditioning, it felt terribly wrong…

…and, yet, there had been no other option.

Eth came over to where the Quailu Hela had shot lay holding his shoulder, desperately trying to keep the atmosphere inside his punctured suit. The lieutenant grabbed a foot and she rushed to grab the other one.

Without a word, they dragged their struggling victim to the hole in the hull and tossed him out.

"Are we still losing altitude?" Eth asked.

"Not as fast as we were," Eve's voice crackled, "but yes."

Hela followed him back to the bridge where Bau sagged against a stanchion, glaring at them. She would have felt the terror of her doomed comrades.

"You killed my crewmen," she said, weakly.

"We came here to keep *you* alive," Eth said. "Those crewmen were weighing the ship down, killing you faster. That makes them the enemy."

"I don't see *you* jumping out," Bau observed tartly.

"That's because I bring more than dead weight to the equation," he snapped back.

Hela should have been shocked to hear a Human talking to a princess of the HQE like that, but she was looking death in the face.

That tended to claim one's attention.

"You said there were harvesting platforms down here," Eth said, turning back to Hela. "They'd have to use pretty powerful beacons in this soup; are we picking up any signals?"

Gods! She turned to the comms station. "Caleb, do you hear anything?"

Caleb's eyes grew wide. "Anshar's itch! I've been hearing a signal but I thought it was coming from the cruiser beneath us. Now that you mention it, though, it's getting closer and it's not losing altitude…"

"Where is it?" Bau demanded.

"About a thousand meters off our bow and roughly eight thousand meters down."

"Eve, make every effort to get us to that signal," Hela ordered.

"They used to have condensing platforms at that depth," Bau said. "I was planning to have them reopened if any were still afloat."

"Well, ma'am," Eth said lightly, "we might as well drop in for an inspection while we're in the region. How big would you say it is? Large enough to accommodate a crash landing, perhaps?"

Bau suppressed a shudder. This creature was a blank to her. How could she trust him if she couldn't read him? Still, he'd risked his life and the lives of his people repeatedly for her, and he was doing it again in an attempt to save her from what she'd seen as certain death.

"They were supposedly the size of small cities," she said, "but you can't trust everything you read in a gas mining prospective."

"I've got visual on the platform," the Human sitting closest to her said. Bau looked at the holo.

A large station, roughly two kilometers cubed and hanging from a long string of massive gas bladders, was growing more detailed as they flew closer. Two smoking gouges on the upper level were punctuated by shuttles.

"Looks like someone managed to have the same idea," said the Human next to her, his apprehension reassuringly clear to Bau.

Was their leader the only blank slate?

"They might be friendlies," Eth mused, "but we won't take chances. As soon as we touch down, I want everyone to switch headspace. We're back to fighting in built-up areas, just what we were grown for.

"If you make contact and you're unsure of their intent, put a hole in them."

Bau wanted to protest, but she didn't have a better plan to offer. Those two shuttles could easily have come from the enemy. Given that she'd brought only the one cruiser and the enemy had dozens of capital warships, it was probable that there were no allies to be found down here.

Still, she was unsettled by his easy ruthlessness, even if it *was* in her service. A few cycles ago, no native citizen would have dared to even think of harming a Quailu. She doubted that even Eth would have considered it.

Now natives drafted into house-forces were killing Quailu all over the empire and some of them were disturbingly good at it. She watched Mishak's pirate as he organized their next desperate gamble.

He, certainly, was one djinn that could never be put back in the bottle.

"Getting an automated approach signal," the pilot announced. "It's sending us to a shield gate about five hundred meters from the upper level. I can make the target but not the recommended velocity. If I slow down, we'll have dropped too far before we get there. This is gonna be a rough one, folks."

Bau looked down at the hand on her elbow. "This way, ma'am," the darker-skinned Human said. "Rigged up a nice seat for you, aft of the engines." He grinned at her. "Don't want one of the pitch drives tearing loose and smashing you to a pulp, now, do we?"

She let him lead her aft, surprised at the calm resignation in his mind. The pilot's news must have been far direr than her tone and her feelings implied.

With a Quailu crew, the fear would bounce back and forth, feeding back on itself until they were all amped up on adrenaline. It wasn't so extreme in a well-trained crew but it was still impossible for any single Quailu to ignore a dangerous situation.

She sat in the chair he'd apparently grown for her and the restraints closed.

He sat in another chair facing her, smiling cheerfully as it closed up. "No engineer with half a brain in his head sets up his crash-seat in front of the engines," he explained. "Since you and I are the two most important people aboard, we owe it to the others to make sure we're secured."

"You and I?" Bau tilted her head to the side, though she suspected the movement was lost in the glare of the overhead lighting on her visor.

"Oh, sure," the engineer chuckled, "our Eve's a crack pilot, Gleb is a murderous little bastard but he's got a great visual sense, which makes him great for filtering out the sensor data, and Caleb... well, he opens channels I suppose...

The Human frowned for a moment. "And Hela's the best combat-leader in the empire, but they'd all be useless if I don't find a way to fix our ship and get us off that platform we're about to crash on.

"And you're the reason we're here in the first place," he finished. "Time to go limp."

She relaxed her muscles. It was interesting how she was the reason for their presence in this system and, yet, he sounded far more indispensable...

The light coming in through the two holes in the hull above them went from a steady dull blue to a darker scheme, punctuated by brilliant flashes as they entered the floating city and roared down the approach tunnel at many times the recommended velocity.

She fought the urge to tense up. The engineer's advice was correct; she'd break all of her bones if she didn't go limp.

Still, she was terrified. Thankfully, none of these natives would be able to tell.

There came a shrieking noise and the deck under her feet began shuddering. The noise died abruptly, only to be replaced a moment later by more of the same, though this time they were hitting the tunnel roof. A cascade of debris fell through the holes above, which were growing steadily larger.

They fell away from the roof, bouncing now along the floor as the scout-ship flexed alarmingly. The timbre of the shrieking changed as their progress along the tunnel slowed suddenly.

Bau began to feel a shred of relief growing in her mind but she could feel the engineer's apprehension and she followed his gaze to where one of the pitch drives was leaning drunkenly, its two forward mounting points sheared off.

The pilot must have thought to use the drive to slow the ship. Now that they were held up by the tunnel floor, using the drive's power to brake would no longer cost them altitude.

It also meant that, if it tore loose, it would come tumbling aft, crushing her and the engineer. She smiled despite the danger.

Perhaps the Human wasn't as clever as he'd thought.

Fortunately, something gave out inside the engine or, perhaps, in its power source, because the deceleration suddenly ended and the engine dropped back down onto its torn forward mounts.

The impact came as a surprise. One moment they were sliding along at twice a running pace and the next her brain was bouncing off the inside of her skull. She sat there, flexing her neck, but the Human engineer was up immediately and heading forward.

She realized there might be a fire risk and followed his example but he wasn't simply evacuating. All five crewmen and their piratical leader were pulling weapons from a locker and strapping on ammunition pouches.

And they'd just crashed, not five seconds ago.

She stepped closer and Eth turned to her, holding out a pistol. "You've used one of these, ma'am?"

She shook her head.

"Point it at the enemy and pull this trigger. Safety's in the trigger," he said. "And there's atmo here, so…"

Perhaps the crash had shaken her up more than she thought because she realized, for the first time, that she was the only one with her helmet still up.

Sighing ruefully, she opened it.

"So, what's the plan now?" she asked.

"One of our engines is beyond repair," Eth said. "The other is heavily damaged and we need two to get us back into space."

"So, we're spending the rest of our lives here?" She asked, grimly amused.

"Well, we did see two shuttles up topside. We might be able to salvage one or both of their engines…"

The engineer cursed so vividly it was obvious that he'd forgotten all about Bau in his distress.

Eth turned to him. "What is it, Meesh?'

"Our damn PLC module is damaged! Of all the gods-damned luck! We can't build *shit* without a logic controller!"

"The patterns are lost?"

Meesh kicked at the module mountings. "They're probably intact but half of the bus emitters are smashed. We can't transmit the whole pattern to the nanites. Certainly not enough to keep two pitch drives operational…"

"Let's hope we can replace all of that topside." Eth cocked his weapon. "We've got a long walk ahead of us and two shuttles can land a lot of enemy crewmen, so stay sharp!"

They had to backtrack slightly. The crash had driven them deep into a secure storage system and the access doors were all locked down, so they were obliged to leave through the tunnel they'd created in the walls.

Bau had seen Quailu training for infantry operations, mostly in connection with her own security detail. She'd seen them line up to breach a room or close in to protect a principle, all the while, their commander had provided a running commentary for her.

These Humans seemed different to her. Their movements seemed to have a furtive grace that her own security team lacked and they moved with a near-silent harmony. Each seemed to know where they should be looking and aiming at any particular moment.

They flowed through the pierced rooms and into the open space of the arrivals platform without a word, spreading out to cover the area as well as might be expected of only six people.

The only exit from this secured zone was easily guarded and the pilot took up a position that gave a view along the approach. The warrant officer moved to a spot opposite her to cover the hallway from a slightly different angle.

She saw the engineer was already working to tap into a security console at the scan-gate.

A long row of bags and cases lay along the elevated platform and Bau wandered over to get a closer look. They all had name-holos that sprang to life as she approached, projecting the owner's names above each item as she approached.

She reached down toward a small hard case but a hand clamped around her wrist, pulling her hand firmly away. She looked up, glaring, but Eth was impassive, unreadable.

"Unless you've got a chip that matches that bag, ma'am, it's gonna get pretty loud in here," he told her.

"I doubt their owners are still around…"

"We aren't the only ones to find this platform's beacon in the last thirty minutes," Eth cut her off firmly. "We've got two shuttles crashed topside. They're almost certainly enemy and they'll probably have seen us on our way down.

"We need to give their brains a good airing out but that's gonna be harder to do if we advertise our location."

She sighed, nodding acceptance of the rebuke. He might only be a native, but he *had* saved her life and seemed inclined to continue in that vein. "I was just drawn by the story that must lie behind these possessions, just abandoned. It didn't occur to me that they'd have alarms on them."

"Not much to tell," the Human shrugged, gesturing to the holographic tags hovering above the cases. "All native names, mushkenu workers.

"It's nothing new. When the Quailu-run company says the last shuttle's leaving at a certain time – that's it. If there are too many workers left for the last ride off a closing facility, Quailu luggage is the first to go and natives are a close second."

"No!" The word exploded out of her before she even knew it was coming. "I would never allow such callous waste of lives in my dominions…"

"This has only become a part of your fief quite recently," Eth reminded her curtly. "Not all system-lords show the same sense of… efficiency."

She noticed, not without some irritation, that he'd attributed her outrage to economics, rather than morals.

"I'd wager that we'll find some Arbellan corpses between here and the shuttles," he added, "but such blatant fraternization would be overstepping my bounds."

He said it calmly enough but she felt as though she should be picking up resentment along with the words. She fought back against the chill creeping up her spine.

This was worlds worse than dealing with a Zeartekka. Humans were *known* to have emotions and the thought of what might be lurking inside the Human officer's head, out of her reach, was deeply disturbing.

He seemed to notice something and he stepped over to a scattered pile of baggage. "Looks like someone didn't want to be left behind," he said softly.

She looked down at the cases and he pointed to a dark brown stain. "That's not coffee," he said.

"They shot someone?"

"We've just seen how desperate people can get when there's only one way out of a bad situation," Eth told her. He pointed to a series of brown streaks, punctuated by less distinct smears.

"Dragged away, probably by the victim's child, given the inability to move them more than a couple paces at a time."

He stood and met her gaze. "I killed your bridge crewmen, when I came aboard that scout-ship, but they were in the process of killing you with their self-interested panic. You'd be dead right now, otherwise.

"They knew they were in a high-risk occupation. They'd signed up to work on a warship and they owed you their oaths." He waved at the smear that led out past his two sentries. "The natives here were just on a mining contract. They thought the company would do right by them."

Bau had never spent so much time with natives before in her life and this was proving a very uncomfortable encounter. She owed this team her very life and every moment in their company increased her debt as they continued to protect her.

She'd never given much thought to the lives they led, except for the occasional pat on the back for having improved the conditions of those she ruled. Here, though, was incontrovertible evidence of natives having been abused and of a simmering hatred for her kind.

The engineer saved her from having to comment by waving for them to join him at a projection above the security console.

"Pretty much what you'd expect," he told them. "Pre-nanite construction so we have no nearby source of repair material. The separators and the condenser farms are in this area," he said, pointing to the middle of the upper half of the platform.

"Vulnerability to small arms fire?" Eth asked.

"Moderate to high," the engineer replied. "Lots of caustics still sitting in those pipes and pressure vessels. Not the sort of place I'd want to fight *us*, let alone a pack of amateurs who think fire-control is a setting on their hearth…"

"You'd rather go around, Meesh?"

The engineer shrugged. "We start taking fire in that mess and I can't guarantee our suits would stand up to the kind of stuff that'll start spewing from the pipes."

"Then we'd better go around," Bau decided, but she frowned at the impudent finger Eth held up.

"Let's think this through properly," he said, apparently oblivious to the implied insult or simply not caring. "Our enemy is probably going to stay topside, hoping for some improbable rescue operation to take place. They aren't likely to patrol in any depth. In fact, I'd be surprised if they patrol at all."

Meesh nodded. "They'll likely put sentries on the approaches and stare up at the sky until hunger drives them to foraging."

"We have till the end of the day before they start thinking about looking for stabilized foodstuffs," Eth said, nodding. "Their training for a scenario like this is probably pretty minimal. We'll likely meet up with some of them a level or two beneath their crash site and that's far enough from the gas-separation plants."

"How long will our people wait for us?" Meesh asked.

"They're gone by now," Eth told him. "I ordered them to help General Tilsin defend the Lady Bau's home world. That means we want to take off in five days."

"Just one day to beat them?" Bau asked, affronted by the certainty she felt from the engineer in response to this bold statement.

"Two days each way," Eth confirmed, "and one for the fight. They shouldn't be much trouble, not after being slapped around three times. The crews are probably on the verge of mutiny."

"And you're sure your ships will be out there looking for us after three days?"

"They weren't happy about leaving me behind," Eth assured her. "They'll be back."

Even if her conscious mind hadn't managed to notice that his crew was concerned for him but not for her, her ego certainly caught it and it crowded in against the earlier issues, such as his casual overriding of her decisions.

"You take too much upon yourself, sir!" she snapped, gratified, at first, by the feelings of alarm now radiating from the engineer. The gratification faded quickly as the unreadable lieutenant stared back at her.

The uncomfortable silence grew between them and, just before she was about to speak again, he replied.

"My apologies, ma'am." He tilted his head in a gesture of acquiescence that didn't *feel* at all like acquiescence. "I sometimes forget my station. I have taken drastic measures without your consent, forcing our services upon you without first ascertaining your wishes.

"And, in so doing," he added, "we have been remiss in our duty to our own lord, the Prince Mishak. We are long overdue at Dur and should return there with all due haste."

He bowed. "We shall remove our offending presence, My Lady." Straightening he turned to the engineer, who was distinctly surprised at this turn of events. "Come, Meesh. We need to get moving."

She nearly spluttered in shock. The jumped up native was proposing to abandon her? Would he dare leave a Quailu behind to die?

She took a half step backward as she realized that these Humans had already killed hundreds of Quailu crewmen to take their ships and hundreds more in the recent fighting.

She took a full step backward, crouching slightly as she remembered the Human officer throwing her bridge crewmen to their deaths in order to lighten the scout-ship. Killing Quailu presented no barrier to these people.

The angry threats she'd been formulating died unspoken. She'd seen only opportunity in the emperor's vulnerability. Now she was coming to realize how short-sighted her people were being.

Many Quailu had drafted natives into their house-militaries, mostly to make up numbers in their under-crewed warships. A few, like Mishak, were giving them far too much latitude, turning them loose on their own, letting them kill their betters…

These Humans should never have had the nerve to abandon her, no matter how politely they'd stated that intention. She would never have dreamed of needing to ask them for help and, yet, that help was walking away even now.

And she was being forced to admit to herself that she had no idea how she was supposed to get off this station.

It was galling. It was humiliating. And it was completely necessary to her survival.

She opened her mouth, but Eth turned just before she could speak.

"Though I'm sure your ladyship has matters well in hand," he said respectfully, "we would, nonetheless, be honored if you decided to accompany us."

Aside from vague curiosity, she got very little from his engineer and nothing at all from the blank-minded lieutenant, but she knew when she was being played. She could give in to anger or she could survive, which meant leaning heavily on her sense of humor.

The bastard had been toying with her, making sure she knew who was *truly* in charge on this moldering platform. She had to admit he'd done a decent job of it.

She allowed herself a chuckle. She could either act the petulant fool and lose their respect or show her appreciation for how well she'd just been manipulated.

No use in fighting a lost battle. "Lead on."

They moved down the long corridor leading out from the transport zone. It opened onto a large public concourse lined with abandoned shops.

Rows of residential balconies lined the hundred-meter-high atrium, enclosing what amounted to an artificial canyon. A network of fountains and streams had once graced the vast open space but they'd long ago run dry. The water was still present, however, because it was dripping from girders, far overhead.

The light pattering of rain fed the wild growth of what had once been carefully tended green spaces. Weeds and wild grasses had found their way out onto the decking, slowly building on their own decayed ancestors as they worked toward the eventual overthrow of the orderly humanoid habitat.

The blood trail led to the main empty fountain. Two skeletons were there, a larger one propped up against the low wall surrounding the fountain and a smaller one, less than half the size, curled up next to it.

"It *was* a child," Eth said, turning to look at Bau. "Probably too young to figure out where to find food."

Bau was radiating anger and shame at the idea that Quailu could behave this way. She was not a champion of native rights by any stretch but this was beyond the pale.

She was saved from commenting because they had to keep moving.

"The industrial section is over there," Meesh pointed. "There'll be ramps and elevators…"

"No elevators," Eth growled. "We're not going to trap ourselves in a noisy box."

"Then we'd better do this right," the scout-ship captain said. "Half a click straight up on a ten-degree ramp; that's nearly a full click and potentially hostile territory the whole way."

She turned to the engineer. "Meesh, how badly is our PLC module damaged? Can it hold a secondary pattern and control our nanites if it's not too complicated?"

"Probably." He shrugged. "Only one way to find out."

"Good!" She turned to Eth. "Sir, if we need to go topside for engines, we should bring along everything we can salvage from our own ship. No sense in making this trip twice."

He nodded. "So what's the pattern you have in mind?"

Hela cast a look sideways at Meesh and Bau could feel the captain's uncertainty fading. "I want our grav plating flipped to make us a simple ground effect vehicle. We can angle the forward and rear plates to give thrust.

"The nanites will hold the plates together, just like in a ship, but the rest will just form a simple box with firing slits. We should be able to load everything inside and take it topside with us."

Eth made no response that Bau could see, but she could easily feel the scout-ship captain's pleasure at his apparent approval. *Were they all empaths and we just never knew?"* She discarded the idea. Surely, it would have been noticed before now.

The captain's respect for the lieutenant, however, was unmistakable. These Humans all seemed to revere him.

"Meesh," Eth turned to the engineer, who was mildly startled to be drawn back into the discussion, "can you do it?"

The engineer paused. *Not uncertainty, but a desire to be precise.* "Yes," he finally agreed, "but we might have more nanites than the plates can carry. Those grav plates were never meant to do more than keep us stuck to the deck and hold our dinners down."

"That's fine," Eth said. "Remember, there are two shuttles worth of nanites topside, minus crash damage, and we only want enough to give us our work stations, and a couple of engine mounts. Any more than that and we might not get out of this gravity well."

Meesh nodded and raced back to their crashed ship.

"Will something like that be able to fit through the passenger departure corridor?" Bau asked.

"Not a chance in all three hells," Eth replied casually.

"Shouldn't you call him back? Plan how to deal with the problem?"

Eth reached in through the neck of his suit, scratching at his shoulder for a moment while apparently considering her suggestion. "No."

Hela watched him for a moment before turning to Bau. *Mild amusement.* "Initiative can't be grown in the chambers," she told Bau, "and it can't be instilled from without. Each of us must develop it on our own."

"Warrant Officer Hela chose Meesh as her engineer," Eth added. "I trust her judgement, which means I trust Meesh to do what needs to be done."

Bau's crews were far more regimented and these Humans sounded chaotic by comparison. Still, the feeling of pride coming from Hela was unmistakable.

Meesh came running back and, at first, Bau thought he'd come to mention the impossibility of moving a large vehicle through the corridor, but he had a module in his hands.

Behind him trailed a swarm of nanites and he led them to the left of the corridor exit, stopping in the middle of the largest area of unencumbered floor-space. He set the module down and pressed a control.

A holographic image of the scout-ship appeared in front of him and he made a copy before stripping away the flight control systems as well as the engine mounts and workstations.

He reshaped the hull into a simple box, just large enough to carry them, with a single workstation for a driver. The sides were sloped out from top and bottom, meeting in the middle.

The non-nanite parts of the ship – gravity plating, inertial dampening emitters, life support and workstation emitters and the high-density capacitors – came flowing out atop the horde of nanites and stacked neatly next to a growing cube of the microscopic machines.

"How's this?" Meesh asked, gesturing at the holo.

"Looks good," Eth said, glancing at Hela, who nodded, a gesture Bau congratulated herself on noticing. These Humans were annoyingly dependent on physical cues.

"Of course, the capacitors would never fail us," Eth nodded gravely.

Bau was mentally patting herself on the back again, seeing his emphatic stance despite her inability to read his feelings. Meesh put an end to that.

"You doubt my capacitors," he countered his leader. "I don't trust them any more than you do…" His face changed, teeth showing. "… At least, not until I've pulled them apart and reconfigured them."

Bau bit back an angry exclamation. How had she read the officer so incorrectly?

"So these have been worked on?" Eth asked.

"Wouldn't keep Anshar-408's in my ship, otherwise," Meesh insisted. "I've only been at this a few weeks but I know garbage when I see it."

Strong disdain. Bau looked sharply at the engineer but kept silent. *Anshar?* The company was Quailu, of course, and they operated from Throne World, which meant they only hired Quailu.

And this native felt their products were garbage unless he could take them apart and *fix* them?

The engineer pressed a control in the display and the nanites started carrying parts into place. They held up the grav plating until a capacitor could be connected and then they released the plates and began flowing into place at the sides.

Bau knew this was how ships were grown but she'd never watched the process before. It was mesmerizing but not quite mesmerizing enough to stop her from coming back to what she'd just heard.

Did the other natives of the empire feel the same lack of respect as these ones? It would never have occurred to her before today but she'd seen more than enough in the last hours to shake her views to the core.

"Right," Eth said, pulling her back to the present. "This is still your ship, Warrant Hela. I'd be obliged if you could get us topside."

Hela turned to look around the small group. "Eve, take the controls. Meesh and Gleb, get out ahead and walk point for us." She turned to Eth. "Sir, I'd appreciate if you could bring up the rear while I walk flank with Caleb."

She seemed to take his head movement as agreement because she turned from him with a feeling of relief, looking now toward Bau. "My Lady, the safest place for you would be inside the vehicle. We didn't come all this way just to lose you now."

It wasn't quite phrased as an order but her emphatic feelings were clear. Bau knew when argument was wasted and, frankly, she didn't relish the idea of climbing a half kilometer on foot.

Using the nod she'd seen earlier, she climbed aboard the newly grown vehicle, relishing the surprise she'd generated using the Human head-gesture. She found an open-topped turret, just to the right of the driver's position and she pulled herself up into its seat.

An assault rifle had been mounted in the front of the turret. Bau smiled. If she was going to sit in this thing for gods only knew how long she could at least be ready to fire back at any enemy.

She felt a flush of irritation and looked left to see Warrant Hela quickly looking away from her. It was all Bau could do to hold in a chuckle. She was willing to defer to their expertise, but she wasn't going to sit meekly in this contraption when she could still contribute.

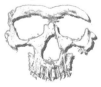

303

They'd been walking for at least two hours when Gleb suddenly exhibited a feeling of alarm. Eth actually started moving forward before the scout signaled a halt. He came to a stop next to Hela, beside the vehicle.

They looked forward to where Meesh crouched at the next turn in the ramp, some twenty meters up. He was looking forward to where Gleb crouched at the next turn but he didn't seem to know what had spooked his colleague.

Eth, however, had been practicing – reaching out to the other team members. He'd felt the moment when Gleb heard movement.

"Someone's coming our way," he whispered to Hela.

When Meesh looked back, Eth gave him the rally signal with two fingers extended, telling him to pull back and to bring Gleb along with him.

He looked around, confirming that this section of ramp didn't differ from the dozens he'd already seen over the last few hours. The same side corridor still branched off from the middle of each level and another connected at the switch-back where the ramp turned back on itself.

"Get the vehicle back to the last turn," he told Hela, pointing at the last switch-back they'd taken. "I'll take one man and hide up there where the corridor branches off from the next switch-back. You'll take the rest into this side branch," he said, chopping a hand at the corridor that led away from the middle of the ramp.

"Let 'em come around that corner up there and, when they've gone about five or ten meters past it, you start firing on them." He turned as Meesh and Gleb came to crouch next to them. "Once you've made them commit to your attack, Gleb and I will hit them from behind."

He nearly shuddered at the vicious glee coming from the young specialist. He'd already suspected that Gleb's nearly angelic face concealed something dark, but this was far more than Eth had imagined.

Still, they were here to kill their master's enemies, not to sell them insurance. He had no regrets about choosing the vicious little bastard.

Hela began moving her people into place while Eth led Gleb back up the ramp. They went right at the switchback, finding what appeared to be a traffic monitoring station at the back of the wide, curving turn. Eth was first in and he saw, to his surprise, that what he'd taken for a blank section of wall from the outside was, in fact, a one-way mirror.

The mirror would have given officials inside a perfect view of ramp traffic and, because it could only be seen through from the inside, those using the ramp would consider themselves under observation whether the room was staffed or not.

He gave serious thought to running down a level and finding out, if there was a similar room there, whether the viewport was breakable. He'd hate to count on firing through this one only to find out it was unbreakable. It would waste the element of surprise.

He'd just have to come out of the room when the time came to fire. It was still a solid vantage point as Gleb's pleased grunt confirmed.

"Can we shoot through it, d'ya think, sir?"

"Can't count on it."

Gleb nodded thoughtfully. "I'd armor it," he mused. "If I was putting enforcement staff in here, I'd definitely expect them to take a bit of light-hearted gunfire from time to time."

Eth was about to point out the lack of similar armor concerns on Kish but the first shadows started wavering across the wall opposite the next switchback.

"Here they come," Gleb muttered, clearly radiating his eagerness to start shooting.

The first to turn the corner and start down the ramp in front of them were a pair of Durian natives. That marked them as crew from one of Uktannu's ships. They were followed by three Quailu who didn't seem particularly concerned about their surroundings. They were talking heatedly, only occasionally glancing at their lackadaisical native scouts.

They were perhaps four meters behind the two Durians and seemed to be following their scouts blindly. It was shaping up to be a fairly simple massacre until a second, larger group came into view at the switch-back.

"Shit!" Gleb said softly.

Eth agreed. That second group wouldn't be caught up in the same ambush. To complicate matters, they'd be on Eth's flank if he tried to come out and hit the first group from the rear, as planned.

Even worse, they'd be able to fire down into Hela's side corridor from the middle of the upper ramp, turning the ambush on the ambushers.

Even as he thought this, the first group triggered Hela's ambush and the two Durians went down in the opening seconds. The Quailu, surprisingly fast for their species, dropped behind their dead scouts and laid down suppressing fire on Hela's position.

It would have been so easy to step out of the room and shoot the three in the back, but the second group was arming their weapons and advancing to the edge of the ramp. One of them was reaching for the grenade dispenser on his chest.

Eth caught Gleb by the elbow. "Not yet," he hissed.

He concentrated on the Quailu with the grenade disc in his hand. He could feel his enemy's anticipation, understand his desire to wreak maximum havoc on his opponents. He stilled the Quailu's hand, the six-second fuse just activated.

How exactly could he make him open his fingers? Could he then keep him from simply kicking the grenade over the edge? His body was growing cold.

Then he found the Quailu's primary cranial artery. He pinched it. He wasn't sure how, but he was constricting the flow of blood.

It took far more than interrupting an electrical impulse in the brain. He was actually moving physical matter and he was feeling the cost. His core temperature was dropping more quickly, just like when he'd lifted that coin.

He watched his target intently, sensing the moment when he lost consciousness. He let go of the artery as the Quailu began to fall, the grenade slipping from his fingers.

Those around him noticed him falling but they failed to notice the small disc on the ramp next to him.

Until six seconds had elapsed.

The blast sent out a cloud of tiny dense shards that killed or incapacitated two thirds of them. The rest were stunned and bleeding.

Eth let go of Gleb's arm. "We finish the advance group first, then we hit the guys up the ramp."

They burst out into the corridor, moving forward enough to finish off the three prone Quailu who were now more concerned with what was happening up-ramp than with the enemy to their front.

After putting several body-shots into each target, they turned their attention to the larger group, putting down three of the four standing enemy before the last one managed to try aiming back.

A burst of rounds hit the wall to Eth's right just as Gleb put a three round burst into the Quailu's chest. They both pulled their weapons up as Hela led her group up the ramp to finish off the survivors.

Eth was shivering slightly from the energy transfer used in pinching a single artery. He chuckled to himself. No wonder the

Varangians had advised against moving anything large. Throwing a cruiser into a star would probably be impossible, or fatal.

"Over here," Hela called to him, gesturing to a Quailu on the floor who was struggling to sit up. His insignia marked him as a captain.

Bau came jogging up behind him as he reached the captain, so Eth spoke before he had much chance to think about whether they should even bother. He didn't want her taking the initiative away from him.

"Who are you?" he demanded.

Anger.

"I'm Captain Hesh of the *Larsa*,." he growled, "and what business do you have, asking impertinent questions of your betters?"

He rose to his feet, glaring at Eth. "If you think I'm handing over my weapon to the likes of you, then you're even stupider than you look." He turned to address Bau.

Eth spoke again, before Hesh could say anything to Bau. "The *Larsa* was one of Uktannu's ships, was it not?" he asked mildly.

"Yes," Hesh snapped. "I serve the *Lord* Uktannu." He placed a heavy, admonitory emphasis on the word 'lord', radiating clear anger at a native using Uktannu's name in so familiar a fashion.

Eth smiled. "*Uktannu* was declared renegade, along with all who serve him."

Hesh showed the first hints of fear, but before he could even contemplate the idea of a mere native killing him, a mere native did just that. Eth's right hand snaked out, his knife-blade slicing the back of the captain's neck in what almost seemed a friendly gesture.

Eth felt Hesh's disbelief followed quickly by understanding and, finally, horror. As Hesh's horror faded into darkness, Bau's grew to take its place. He felt little else from the others, aside from mild approval, but Gleb was harder to read.

He turned to look at Hela's tactical operator and the young man's gaze slid, meaningfully, down to the mangled corpse of the Quailu who'd dropped the grenade.

He had no desire to stand here and get drawn into a discussion. "Warrant, I'll take Gleb forward and scout. There may be more up there. Police the available ammunition and follow us as soon as you clear these bodies."

"We should have more than enough ground clearance to get our vehicle over them," Meesh offered.

"Fine." Eth waved a negligent gesture. "Let's not waste any time. If we want off this platform, we need to keep the initiative over our enemies."

He ignored Bau's outrage and nodded Gleb up the ramp. It was a safe enough bet that the electress had expected better treatment of the Quailu dead. For that matter, she'd probably expected them to take Hesh captive, rather than slitting his cerebral arteries.

Gleb took up a firing position at the inside of the next turn, aiming up the ramp, and Eth glided past him, moving over to the far side to avoid blocking Gleb's field of fire.

After a couple of turns, Eth called a halt so Hela could catch up. Gleb came to a stop across from where Eth was looking up the ramp.

The younger man's curiosity was almost overwhelming. Eth wasn't sure what to do. If he talked about it, word would spread like wildfire. If he *didn't* talk about it, word would spread even faster.

But at least it would just be a rumor and Eth was fine with rumors. He could dismiss it if confronted by Mishak.

He could try to steer the issue, while it was still settling into Gleb's long-term memory.

"Did you see that idiot with the grenade?" he asked the younger man. "So much for the superior Quailu constitution! They crash land on a deserted platform and he quaffs down the first strip of fermented fat he can get his hands on."

"He was drunk?"

"Barely walking when he came around the corner. I'd lay a week's pay we find a pool of vomit between here and their crash site. Good thing for him he didn't need to have his helmet closed up."

Gleb grinned. "He would have *Glenned* himself!"

Eth glanced at him. "So that story's already made the rounds, has it? Well, Glen only ralphed in his work-station. His helmet saved him from smelling it while he cleaned up."

"It's funnier the way I heard it," Gleb said. "And far more likely to become an enduring part of the language that way."

"I'm sure Glen will be thrilled to learn of his contribution to Imperial Standard," Eth retorted dryly, secretly pleased to detect no further curiosity from Gleb.

He leaned right, holding up a hand to quiet his comrade. "They're almost caught up. Let's get moving again."

Six hours later, they reached a pavilion, one level down from the top, forty meters square and open to the swirling sky above. A lattice-work tower reared up from the middle of the pavilion supporting a small office block that probably served as a local traffic control point.

Meesh and Gleb jogged off to opposite sides of the opening, climbing staircases to the upper level where they could check for immediate threats.

Eth almost ordered Eve up to the offices on the tower but he didn't want to take over Hela's team. It could be bad for a unit's morale if their trusted leader was suddenly cut out of the loop.

He stepped over to Hela. "Traffic control, d'ya think?" He nodded upwards to where the structure sat a good twenty meters above the deck of the upper level.

She nodded. "Good vantage point." She turned. "Eve," she called softly, "trade that sidearm for my rifle and get up there. Scope out what the enemy are up to."

She took the pistol from the pilot, handing over her own weapon, which had better optics and a link to the holo emitter on Hela's wrist.

Eve jogged over to the tower and started climbing as Bau approached Eth. The Quailu noble seemed fascinated at Eve's quick progress.

"No arboreals in your dominions, My Lady?" he asked.

"The Arbellans were the first," she replied, still watching Eve. "I never gave much thought to the efficiencies it could open up. Your pilot is very agile."

"And hard to spot, we hope," Hela added.

"I was surprised to see the ladder on the tower," Eth admitted. "I suppose the efficiencies weren't lost on the local lord either."

He could feel Bau's temptation to claim Quailu tolerance, but she must have remembered the scene down below because it faded.

Eve reached the office section in the tower and began moving around the surrounding catwalk, rifle aiming around the upper surface of the platform.

Hela activated a holo display from her wrist unit and a three dimensional image of their surroundings began to appear as Eve swept her scope around.

Eth frowned. The crash sites for the two shuttles were clearly visible but he'd expected to see activity near the downed craft. There should have at least been work going on to salvage what they could, organize and care for any wounded…

"I see no detection equipment deployed," Hela said, a clear suggestion in her tone.

Eth nodded and she activated a control in her holographic interface. Three small discs ejected from a mounting on her shoulder, tiny counter-mass engines spooling up to speed before they started to fall back down.

The miniscule drones hovered until she drew a rough circle around the crash site and put their icons into it. They sped away, disappearing over the lip of the pavilion wall.

The details on their holo map sharpened dramatically as the trio sped towards their target. Just before they entered the assigned zone, one heartbeat was detected, enveloped seconds later by the heat signature of a Quailu.

Two other signatures held the standard Quailu shape but the average temperatures were far too low and still falling.

"Two dead in the crash," Eth mused, "and they left only a single sentry on the shuttles?"

"We were lucky no one died when *we* crashed," Bau muttered.

"To an extent," Eth allowed, "but Eve, like the rest of us, was designed with an enhanced neural architecture. Even by Human standards, we have fast reflexes."

Bau was gratifyingly affronted by this but Eth refrained from smiling. Instead, he affected the air of one who has no idea he's given offense.

Then he forgot about tweaking the Quailu noble as the two crashed shuttles came into sharp focus.

"Damn!" He looked over at Hela.

"That damage doesn't leave much room for hope," Hela said. "I wouldn't expect to find more than fragments of their engines."

He looked back at the ramp they'd been climbing. "That group we ambushed – they were heading somewhere and I don't think it was to attack us. They left one sentry on their gear and took everyone else. They must have been so impressed with their *own* landing on this heap that they didn't believe anyone *else* would find it."

"But there's no ships on the station manifest," Meesh's voice advised.

Though he was up at the top of the stairway to Eth's right, he was still tied into the proximity net. His suit projected the conversation to his inner ear, varying the volume for each side to give him a sense of direction. The projection of his voice was also tuned to appear to Eth as though it were coming from his own right.

"Yeah, well, they definitely seemed to have something in mind," Eth countered. He looked back at Hela. "Warrant, I want to speak to that sentry." He could feel relief at this demand for action. Hela definitely wasn't one for sitting around and telling sad stories when faced with difficulties.

"Eve," she said, looking up, "stay on over-watch. Gleb and Meesh, you both see the shuttle and the live target?"

"Seen."

"Seen."

"Secure the target and bring him down here, and, Gleb… bring him alive. None of your half-assed attitude toward instructions."

"When have I ever…"

"Remember that high oracle you got an audience with?" Hela looked over at Eth. "A junior cleric in the anteroom told him he had to prostrate himself before the seer. Our Gleb must not have heard the second 'r' in prostrate…"

"Early detection is key," Gleb insisted. "I just thought he was concerned about my health."

"Shut your hole and keep moving," Eth ordered. He reached out, feeling Bau's reaction as she watched the two men move in on the holo display. She understood that the two operators were moving with a lethal efficiency. They didn't need to stop and sort out who would move where.

One man took up a position to cover his partner who then moved past to the next vantage point. Their steady, fluid advance was borne of long experience.

"Captain Hesh…" he ventured, feeling the mental shudder the name conjured in her. "You feel I should have kept him alive?" He

313

wanted the memory to remain fresh in her mind. It would come in handy when the prisoner arrived.

Bau cast about for something weighty to say – he could feel it – but in the end she sighed and spoke her mind plainly. "He'd surrendered. He was Quailu."

"He didn't surrender, ma'am. He was stunned by a grenade but he was refusing to relinquish his weapon. Do you think he would have accepted *my* surrender?" He felt confusion from her for a brief instant, then the feeling that he was asking her unfair questions.

"What kind of question is that?"

"A fair one, My Lady," he replied gently. "If I'm to fight my master's enemies, then I must do it to the best of my abilities. There are no laws separating the treatment of combatants according to species.

"If Hesh was free to kill me out of hand, then I must be free to do the same, or I fail in my duty to the Prince Mishak. I've come here to aid you, and I'll do whatever I must to achieve that objective. If it means killing an enemy captain or throwing your own crewmen off a ship to improve your chances of survival, then so be it."

She believed him. How could she not, after all she'd seen him do? It was important that he reinforce that belief before Gleb and Meesh brought their prisoner to him.

And they were already on their way back, the sentry stumbling along with his hands bound behind his back. They led him to one of the four points where ramps led down into the sunken area and jogged him down to where Eth, Hela and Bau waited.

"You sent these creatures to accost me?" the Quailu demanded of Bau.

"Mind your manners!" Gleb kicked him in the back of the knees, driving him down hard onto his knee caps, making a sound that would have made Eth wince even if he hadn't already felt the Quailu's pain. "You're addressing an electress of the Holy Quailu Empire!"

Eth could feel his alarm at Bau's identity but also further anger at this continued harsh treatment from a lowly native.

"We didn't bring you here to answer your questions," Eth said mildly, sensing the alarm that his closed mind now instilled in most Quailu. "I want to know where the rest of your party has gone."

"*Ugkh drasil ish past!*" the Quailu spat in the ancient tongue.

Eth didn't know the language but Bau's angry shock made it clear that it wasn't a compliment.

He needed this man to start talking and he was willing to use torture but it was a less-than-perfect way of getting information. Once you start slicing off bits, most folk will say whatever they *think* you want to hear, just to make you stop.

If he could make his enemy *believe* he would be tortured, he might just hand over the truth to avoid it. He could start the ball rolling with a harsh beating, but he'd rather keep the fellow's wits clear enough to discern between truth and desperate lies.

"Ties," he demanded of Gleb, stepping behind the prisoner and shoving him down onto his face on the deck. He took the first tie and put it around the Quailu's lower leg, just above the boot, cinching it very tight.

"What are you doing you filthy savage?" his victim snarled.

"I'm going to start by cutting off your feet," Eth replied conversationally, "and I'll toss them down that grating over there. I don't want you bleeding to death, so I'm using the ties to keep you alive."

The outraged disbelief flared and died out like a fire built only with tinder. He was Quailu, after all. These natives wouldn't dare harm him.

But then he became aware of Bau's horror, her absolute certainty that she was about to witness a sickening spectacle. She clearly believed these natives were dangerous.

"You can't allow this!" he shouted, no doubt talking to Bau, though he was unable to aim his head in her direction at the moment. "I was only…" His eyes narrowed, focusing on the bot-knife Eth had pulled from a sheath under his arm.

Made of nanites, the cutting edge was incredibly thin and it vibrated, easing its passage through the target. It would slice through a leg like a hot knife through air.

Eth grabbed a leg and brought his knife close.

"Tenders!" the Quailu screamed.

"You'd rather he start by cutting off your tenders?" Gleb asked, gleefully confused.

"No! The orbital tenders that carried the harvested gas from this platform out to the freighters in orbit," the prisoner said.

"Bullshit," Meesh insisted. "There's no tenders on the manifest. I looked for 'em after we crashed."

"They wouldn't be, would they," the Quailu retorted, his desperation fading now that the knife was no longer coming closer to his leg. "Gas tenders operate on a separate charter. Imperial law. Prevents a monopoly forming."

"And they're still here?" Eth frowned down at his blade. "I think you're just trying to cheat us out of a little fun. Why leave expensive heavy-grav tenders behind?"

"Because there's no use for 'em elsewhere in the system," the Quailu insisted. "You'd have to pay to ship them to another system. Our tactical officer found maintenance records for a heavy-grav tender in the system."

"My gut's telling me this guy's serious," Gleb offered.

Hela snorted. "Where exactly do you stick your head when you're listening to your gut?"

"How long's this shit-hole been closed?" Meesh asked.

"A century and a half," Bau said stiffly.

"Pre-nanite era tenders?" he groused. "Sitting idle for that long? If there's a single control crystal that hasn't grown wild, I'll eat this guy's feet."

Eth nearly winced at the fresh wave of horror coming off their prisoner. "Those old engines were built to last, Meesh," he offered helpfully. "If we had nanites and a PLC module, could we jury-rig something?"

He couldn't tell whether Meesh's surprise was at the idea itself or at Eth's ability to come up with a technical suggestion.

"We just might," Meesh admitted, "but we'll need all the material we can get our hands on." He pulled out two PLC modules and set them on the deck, activating both. He then used his arm-pad to bring up the programming from the damaged unit controlling the remains of their scout-ship cum ground vehicle.

He copied the program into the two units he'd harvested from the crashed enemy shuttles and then moved them to an open space, roughly fifteen meters away from each other.

"How long?" Eth asked.

Meesh tilted his head, looking down at the two units. "About an hour for everything to migrate down here and assemble."

"Put some bunks in them. We're close to falling asleep on our feet here. We can take turns driving while the rest rack out in the vehicles." Eth turned to Bau.

"My Lady, I have a request to make of you…"

Despite her horror at Eth's casual threat to torture and mutilate their prisoner, Bau found she was warming up to the Humans. The simple fact that they needed sleep had taken some of the edge off her unacknowledged jealousy.

She'd watched them take out a medium-sized party of Quailu with relative ease and she'd seen evidence of their suitability for combat, a suitability that seemed to outstrip her own kind.

They were showing up the Quailu and it made her uneasy.

But then Eth had approached her, asking if she could man the turret on the lead vehicle, as she had on the way up. At the time, she knew she'd been put in there to keep her safe and out of the way.

This time, he'd asked her because his team was near exhaustion from lack of sleep. It was a gratifying thing to hear. He was tacitly acknowledging a physical advantage of her species. She could rest her brain without losing consciousness.

She couldn't achieve anything complicated with one of the hemispheres of her brain asleep, but she could spot an enemy and shoot him well enough.

They were entrusting their lives to her hands and it had sown the seeds of a bond.

She drew in a sharp breath as the lead vehicle, in which she rode, grazed against the heavy railing that separated pedestrian and vehicular traffic.

Bau dropped down from the turret and scuttled forward to the driver's station, grasping Eve by the shoulder and shaking it.

"It's been two hours, Eve," she told the exhausted Human. "Stop the vehicle and get into a bunk."

Bau waited while Eve slowed them to a halt, confirming that the two newly grown vehicles trailing them came to a stop as well.

Auto-follow was a useful algorithm but it had been known to fail at the worst of times. It was a risk they'd decided worth taking if it meant they could bring along the useable nanites from the two crashed enemy shuttles.

As the Human slid into one of the bunks lining the side of the vehicle, Bau moved over to Gleb, looking down at the sleeping Human.

She knew these creatures were all trained killers, but this one seemed to be an actual *enthusiast*. She'd felt his eagerness as Eth spoke of torture and she couldn't have missed his glee as her crewmen had been tossed from the descending scout-ship.

Keeping as much of a distance as she could, she reached out and poked him in the shoulder. His eyes opened and focused on her. "Your turn to drive," she told him when his thoughts had settled.

The trip down to the off-loading docks took several hours and three more drivers, none of whom had been Meesh. Eth had been very clear. Polite but clear.

Meesh needed to get as much rest as possible if they were going to trust their lives to a jury-rigged ship of his making.

Bau understood that. Even the Quailu knew better than to attempt such a feat on hemispherical sleep shifts.

The first thing Meesh did, on arrival at the docks, was to take charge, sending everyone off to scout the area for equipment. They all did so, though not without a fair amount of grumbling. They'd all had less sleep than him, after all.

He'd even asked Bau to join the search and, seeing as Eth had agreed to his own search sector without demur, she agreed to play along. This sudden devolvement of authority was interesting.

A Quailu would have seen it as a threat to authority but these pirates seemed to have no qualms about putting an expert in charge when the situation warranted it.

She'd been assigned an area at the far end of the docks and she chose to take that as a nod to her species' ability to cover long distances quickly. She felt a certain smug satisfaction at not taking it as an offense to a princess of the empire.

Even at her advanced age, she made it to her area before half the other Humans reached theirs. There wasn't much there, except for a cargo sledge, a few pallets of some kind of fluid and a locker against the wall with an elaborate security panel.

She chuckled, asking herself what a Human pirate would start with. The fancy lock was the obvious answer. She almost fired a shot into the security panel but, on a whim, placed her hand in the scanner.

She was obscurely disappointed when the panel gave out a friendly chime and the locker door slid down into the floor. She'd wanted to shoot the blasted thing open.

This pirate life was growing on her.

The object inside looked like some kind of gun but it had a strange, articulated head on it, long and narrow. Whatever it was, it was worth locking up, so she pulled it out and set it on the sledge.

She stepped on and activated the sledge's grav-plates, lifting it off the decking. She turned it back toward where Meesh waited and rode along to where Hela was tossing items out onto the main travel concourse.

The Human turned to find Bau stacking her loot onto the sledge. "Good thinking, My Lady," Hela said with another of those incomprehensible facial tics the Humans used to accentuate their communications.

Perhaps it was simply a function of her shared dilemma with this small group, but the casual praise gave her a warm glow.

They loaded up and moved along the concourse together, loading up as they passed the others.

Meesh was standing by what appeared to be a large shuttle when they got back. He waved them over.

"Food, water, whatever the hell these are," he muttered as he pulled items off the sledge. He stopped for a moment.

"You gotta be kidding me!" He grabbed the strange-looking gun that Bau had found. "Do you realize what we have here?"

"I would if you'd just tell us," Eth replied, getting chuckles from the others.

His tone must have implied something that Bau wasn't hearing but she was too intrigued by Meesh's reaction to care.

"It lays down a coating of carbon nanotubules." Meesh pressed a control and the thing hummed into life. He turned to the shuttle behind him and aimed the gun up at a protruding sensor blister.

With a slightly deeper hum, the gun sprayed a black material, edged with a crisply defined force field.

"The field keeps me from overlapping edges," Meesh explained. "Otherwise we'd get hundreds of random, visible seams. They use this to coat the replacement heads in the cryo-distillation separators. Newer systems don't need the coating because the heads project their own force-fields."

He stepped back, his face unreadable to Bau, but his hand gestured to the sensor blister. "Tell me that doesn't represent a tactical advantage!"

Bau could make out no details on the blister at all. She knew there'd been bumps and protrusions all over it, but they'd all disappeared into the black, shapeless lump of the blister itself.

Only by moving to the side could she see the protruding silhouettes of the various parts.

"The nanotubes stand like blades of grass," Meesh said. "There's no surface that light can bounce off from. It just ricochets down between the tubes."

"What about emission management?" Eth asked. "All that trapped light will add to your thermal signature."

Meesh's head bobbled up and down and Bau could feel his agreement. "Should be manageable," he replied, "but it might take some extra gear."

"Worth trying," Eth allowed. He nodded at the shuttle. "Do we have something worth putting it on in the first place?"

That head-bobble again, which Bau now realized to be a gesture of agreement. She was starting to understand these creatures.

"Should be able to get those engines to work," Meesh said. "We'll have to use our nanites to pull the shuttle apart, though; the main bus is corroded beyond repair."

"How long are we looking at?"

"I can get the nanites busy on disassembly right now." Meesh scratched at the back of his head, which Bau took to be a gesture of concentration. "Best part of today to finalize the details of the design, two days for assembly and a day to test..."

"We're cutting it close," Eth warned. "If we miss the rendezvous with our forces, they might move on to Arbella to look for us there. I don't want to go traipsing across the system in this piece of garbage."

Meesh chewed at the inside of his lip, staring up at the shuttle's hull. *Some of these gestures are incredibly subtle,* Bau thought.

"I'd have my reservations as well," Meesh admitted. "Best to assume a little extra risk in the short term, if it gets us out into orbit in time to find our friends. Greater chance of dying if we try to take this thing all the way back to Arbella."

"Well, let's get at it," Eth ordered. "This thing ain't gonna build itself."

Meesh made another face, his mood mischievous. "Technically, using nanites..."

"Just shut your pie-hole and get started."

Middle finger extended, Bau noticed, sensing the engineer's feelings. *Gesture of good-natured acknowledgement.*

Search & Rescue

Oliv waved away a holo of the gas giant where she'd been forced to leave Eth. Unlike a rocky planet, this monster hid its secrets well. The fifteen-hundred kilometer per hour winds below her flotilla left no traces of what had happened here while she was fighting alongside Tilsen at Bau's home world.

She resisted the urge to step over to the tactical station she usually shared with Lil. She was anxious to find Eth and get him back to running their growing forces but it didn't do to show anxiety when you were in command. "Still no sign of our friends, Lil?"

"Nothing on wide-survey," Lil replied, "but our scout-ships have a very narrow EM cross-section. It's going to take a while to find them – assuming…" She trailed off, face red.

"Hard, not being able to send out an omni-directional call," Glen said.

"Yeah," Oliv agreed, glad to avoid discussing the probability that their old friend was dead, "but we don't know this area's truly clear. Uktannu might have left some stay-back units. We start calling for our people and those units will realize we're here to rescue a high-value target."

They were 'regrouping' as far as any intercepted signals between their ships were concerned. The smaller ships provided a security screen while the *Mouse* sat with her forward hangar shielding down. A plan Oliv had started referring to as pulling a *Coronado*.

It was how they'd tended to recover their teams from raids, back before joining the house military. A freighter, usually the old *Coronado* in the case of Eth's team, would sit in parking orbit with their hangar shielding down, waiting for the team to slip inside.

Oliv fervently hoped there was someone to pick up though hopes were dwindling fast after the first half hour.

Maybe it was time to consider a more active search?

"Attention on deck!" a voice rang out, startling Oliv out of her seat and into a position of respect. She still possessed the presence of mind to come to attention facing the voice and what she saw nearly made her abandon discipline altogether.

Eth's grin bordered on the idiotic. "All hands, render respects for a princess of the realm!"

Oliv realized she'd been on the verge of saying something because she was drawing breath for it. She had no idea what it might have been and now she'd never find out because the entire bridge crew snapped to immediate immobility.

He'd managed to save the Lady Bau!

"Please," Bau demurred, "I'd say you've earned the right of familiarity by now."

The electress approached Oliv as the crew erupted into celebration. "General Tilsen?" She asked.

"We caught the enemy over your capital, My Lady," Oliv told her. "We scattered them but the general believes enough remain in the system to pose a serious threat. He wanted to come search for you, but he felt it was necessary to stay and hunt down the remnants of the enemy forces."

She handed Bau a small headset. "The general recorded this for you before we left."

Bau put on the headset and activated the polarized holo that was viewable only from a narrow field of view.

Oliv turned her attention back to Eth. "Very glad to see you," she said warmly. "Now, how the hells did you get aboard without my knowing about it?"

Eth called up a video feed from the forward hangar, one that looked out the hangar door. "We found an old piece of equipment that, though it has obvious uses, is no longer being made in the empire. If they still made them, we'd have heard of it by now."

Human

Oliv looked at the video feed. "What am I supposed to be looking at? All I see is stars."

Eth indicated an area to the right side of the opening.

"Less stars?" she asked him.

"No stars at all." He grinned at her. "There *should* be stars there…"

Isolation

"Making the Ashurapol Bombings the only such 'terrorist' attack in the sector for the last five centuries," the holographic reporter asserted with breathless excitement. *"This intrepid reporter finds it far too convenient, especially in the light of a recent meeting held in the neighboring Chusak system."*

Mishak chuckled as a holo of a hotel lobby appeared, focusing on a sign advising that a meeting of infrastructure conglomerates was being held in the Imperial Room. He'd been quite pleased with himself, arranging for the meeting to take place in such a suggestively named room.

Two security goons approached the camera drone, swatting it down but not before it captured a good dataset from their faces. The news cooperative rewound to a decent still of the two and the biometrics populated the screen, identifying them both as Buchnadel employees.

"You might wonder," the reporter mused dramatically, *"why a company that makes fifty-eight percent of its revenues from war-zone reconstruction is suddenly attending a meeting here on Chusak. You might also wonder why their delegates, and those of most other attendees, came here via Ashurapol."*

"Unless you know that Chusak's too small for its own path-hub and has to route most of its traffic through Ashurapol," Mishak gloated.

"I, for one, find this all to be more than a simple coincidence."

"It certainly is," Mishak agreed, though the reporter, of course, couldn't hear him. Nonetheless, he was enjoying this little half-dialog immensely.

"The attack on Ashurapol may seem insignificant, but I believe we're seeing the early stages of imperial pretext planning here. In the days to come, we can expect to see a massive over-reaction by outside forces, arriving to 'help ensure the safety of Ashurapolitan citizens'."

The reporter leaned in. *"Make no mistake. If I'm correct, this will spiral into massive violence, leading to the need for lucrative reconstruction contracts. How 'fortunate' for the Ashurapolitans that the emperor, may he outlive us all, has his cousin, an executive vice-president of Buchnadel, a short hop away at Chusak..."*

"One wonders what the Lord Anos could have done to bring down our sovereign's wrath, but this reporter will ponder that question from another system. I have no intention of being here when the fighting starts in earnest. This is Zaidu, reporting for the Galactic Constant – telling truth to power for seventeen centuries."

The image faded into a commercial and Mishak sat back, pleased with his results. Anos, a moderately powerful elector, was marshaling his forces and it seemed likely that he'd be positioning himself as a bulwark against Mishak's father.

His apparent support for the emperor and his expected opposition to Sandrak, who the public viewed with growing unease, might be his own ploy to edge closer to the throne. When Tir Uttur died, he might be hoping to gain enough votes to succeed the emperor over his daughter.

However you sliced it, Anos was a potential threat. Far better for him to start looking over his own shoulder, to start wondering if the emperor was coming after *him*.

The best thing about planting a story for a reporter to find was that they could be counted on to miss the deeper story. Reporters only wanted enough information to prove they knew more than the general public. Few of them actually did any investigative work.

Mishak could arrange for a headline-getting attack and a conference, and someone like Zaidu would never bother to find out the smaller details such as who booked the room for the conference. It would have been an alias and that meant a lot of work to find the *truth*.

The light playing across his face from the holo-commercial suddenly dimmed and he looked up to see a small image of his father sticking out of the engine compartment of a small luxury runabout that a group of sexy models were trying to sell.

Mishak had to force himself not to laugh. It looked, for all the worlds, as though his father was being adored by the sales models.

The mood quickly faded as the recorded message played.

"You've had enough leisure time in your uncle's palace. It's time for you to make yourself useful. Meet me at Kwharaz Station as soon as you can get there." The image disappeared from the middle of the ad.

"Uktannu's palace?' Mishak reared his head. "It's *my* palace, *my* damn systems, you old ingrate! I took them while saving your rump, thank-you very much!"

He sighed, sitting back in his chair. What use was there in raving at a commercial?

He missed Abdu. The old Human had been a valuable, if secret, source of counsel. The old fighter had taken Eth under his wing and it showed. Mishak could use Eth's steadying influence now, but he'd left the Heiropolis system and never shown up at Dur.

Had his loyal Humans deserted him?

Royal Duty

Marduk slowed slightly, picking up the warning in his aid's mood. Someone was in his office, but it was someone friendly, or relatively so.

The door snapped open for him, revealing the crown princess, Tashmitum, standing in the middle of an elaborately connected holographic map of the empire.

"Highness," he greeted her, not-so-secretly pleased at her boldness.

"You've been naughty, Uncle," she admonished, her feelings taking any insult from the words.

"Well, I *am* your father's chief of staff," he allowed, "so that's a pretty safe assumption for you to make." He came to stand beside her, noting that the lines in the holo ran between, among other things Arbella, Heiropolis and Dur. "Can you be more specific?"

"Your attempt to weaken Sandrak."

"Were we that obvious?" He felt mild scorn.

"Having the Varangians nearby, on whatever coincidental pretext you must have cooked up, was a touch heavy-handed."

"Not to mention the fact that it backfired on us," Marduk groused. "Still, it was worth a try."

"Sandrak *is* the most potent of our potential threats," she agreed, "but Sandrak *and* Mishak, both electors now, might just represent the beginnings of a voting block that could keep me from my father's throne."

"That was… unfortunate." Marduk sighed. "One possible avenue would be to portray Mishak as power-hungry. We might scare other votes from his cause." He spun his head, confused by the surprised amusement he felt from her.

"Uncle, am I really ahead of you in this?" She radiated mischief. "Have I truly learned of something before you?"

Marduk didn't know whether to be proud of his young protégé or insulted. He chose to let it play out on its own. "You may have, Highness, but we won't know unless you tell me."

Tashmitum gestured to the holo. "After his fight at Heiropolis, forces loyal to our old friend Mishak were dispatched to Arbella where the Lady Bau had found herself up against rather more ships than she'd been expecting.

"It seems that the now-renegade Lord Uktannu had fled in that general direction and he's inserted himself into matters at Arbella.

"The Lady Bau is not going to be very pleased when she learns that *our* failed scheme has blown up in *her* face. If Sandrak and Mishak intend to vote against me, she'll be likely to join them now, and nobody who wishes to eat will dare to cross her."

"There's no proof of our involvement…"

"I don't care about proof, Uncle," she said, cutting him off. "I care about votes and votes have nothing to do with evidentiary rules. Votes follow rumors, threats and bribes."

"Indeed." Marduk allowed his contrition to be felt. "It's been several decades since I've had to think in terms of the succession but your father's still healthy. We have time."

"You always have time until the moment when you don't and the transition is usually faster than expected," she said sharply. "It's time to stop scheming against Sandrak. We must work, instead, to turn his strengths to our own advantage."

"Indeed, Highness." Marduk focused on the admiration he felt for her in the hopes that his discomfort would be less evident. Nonetheless, the subject had to be broached.

"We must make amends," he said.

"*I* must make amends, you mean." She closed the holo.

Marduk was at a complete loss. He'd practically raised her himself, after the death of the empress. He'd also served the same role for Mishak.

He knew Sandrak's son to be a decent enough fellow, but was he good enough for Tashmitum?

"Don't be so morose, Uncle," she said, offering feelings of gentle reassurance. "It has always been the duty of royals to give their subjects peace and it's done far more often in a bed than on a battlefield." There was a degree of coy teasing, now, in her mood.

"And the Prince Mishak will make me a better husband than most."

"Husband?" Marduk took a half-step backwards, unable to conceal his alarm at the idea. "Highness, it wasn't our intent to hand the throne over to them. Your father might be willing to make Mishak your royal consort."

She laughed, her amusement genuine but tinged with mild derision. "Men! Uncle, you're the one who raised him and, yet, you have no better understanding of who he truly is than *he* does himself!"

Marduk could say nothing to this. The consort offer that had seemed so sensible, an hour earlier in the Emperor's morning-room, now looked foolish and half-hearted in the full light of Tashmitum's scorn.

He felt that scorn relent.

"I grew up with Mishak," she said with perfect calm. "I know him better than most."

He felt a negligent acquiescence from her.

"Send your offer as it currently stands, Uncle. You will be refused, but it's a necessary first step, nonetheless."

She moved toward the door but stopped just before the scan-line that would have opened it, spilling their conversation out to where the aide would hear.

"I shall have my *Gilgamesh* on my own terms, but first he must be awakened. Only then will the empire be secured."

Marduk couldn't hold back the swell of pride he felt for her as she left. She refused to be a simple pawn in her father's games. She had her own agenda, as any future ruler-in-waiting should.

Making the Leap

Back in the Fold

It seemed like a lifetime had passed since Eth had been to Kwharaz Station. Much had been done since then that couldn't be undone, even if he'd wished it.

Their adventures and subsequent rescue at Arbella would have seemed the product of a fevered imagination only a few short weeks ago. Now, he was bringing his master a message of thanks from one of the empire's most influential nobles.

He stood at the railing near the same barge port he'd used the last time, feeling the emotions of the flowing crowd. Folks here were, for the most part, happy to be at Kwharaz Station.

Gleb and Eve, standing behind him, were unmistakably eager to explore. No such stations existed near Kish and, if they'd ever been to one on a raid, they'd never had time to stop and try out the local amenities. Father Sulak was just happy to be off the ship for a change.

"We'll report in to the prince first," Eth said, turning to glance at them, "and, if we have time for it, we'll arrange a shore-leave schedule."

It was hardly what they wanted to hear, but the last thing Eth needed was to go searching for these two, in the event Mishak wanted to dispatch them on an urgent errand.

"We'll take this barge," he said calmly, pointing down into one of the ten-passenger vehicles that he'd ridden in on his previous visit. It was just finishing the debarkation of a group coming from the central section.

Without needing further instructions on the matter, both Gleb and Eve began herding the line of waiting passengers back from the gate.

Three of the waiting passengers were Quailu and the one at the front of the line, dressed in a manner that indicated some middling member of the mushkenu class, the same class as the Humans, sputtered in protest.

"Do you have any idea who I am?" he finally managed to ask, giving Gleb what must have been his fiercest scowl.

Gleb glanced at him, looking him up and down, and the Quailu must have felt the same thing Eth was feeling from the young tactical specialist because he shuddered.

"No," Gleb said simply and turned to shout abuse at the barge operator. "Not another word out of you," he warned the complaining Kwharzian. "An officer in your lord's service has need of your barge, so shut your noodle-hole and wait for instructions!"

That was the moment Eth felt the waiting passengers' attention slide from the scene at the gate and settle on him. Without their uniforms, they would have been mistaken for contraband. Still, even *with* the uniforms, none of them had thought to notice the officer's stars on his collar.

Such a thing was almost inconceivable and, yet, here was a Human with one large and one small star, a lieutenant. The astonishment felt good.

He stepped into the barge, this time *openly* not paying for the ride. He leaned over the gunwale on the starboard side, quickly spotting the large armored barge below them, several kilometers away.

"Take us there," he ordered. "We need to report to the Prince Mishak."

The Kwharzian touched a knuckle under one of the eyes on his chest and swung the small craft away from the docking platform. He deftly rotated the barge toward their target and dropped the nose, putting on a burst of speed.

They were only a few hundred meters away, just approaching the security screen of small, two-man cruisers, when Eth suddenly stiffened. "Stop!" he shouted, lurching forward as the Kwharzian complied.

He stared up into the cloud of traffic, reaching out to identify something he'd never felt until now. Someone up there was in the grip of an absolutely single-minded purpose. He had no idea what it might regard but there was a finality to it that frightened him.

Then he found it. A woman – a Human woman – was up there, preparing for something very serious. He pointed. "That green and orange runabout," he hissed at the driver. "Get us up next to it. We need to board it."

Having said that, he concentrated on her, much as he did with that Quailu officer when he'd boarded the *Mouse*, a lifetime ago. He forced her to stop what she was doing but, this time, he was drawing heat from *her* body instead of his own.

They came alongside and, as they sidled in closer, he risked his hold on her to warn his people. "Gleb, Eve, get over there and grab her but be careful. I think she's got some sort of weapon on her, like a bomb."

It was her. The same woman he'd found here on his last visit. The Varangians had taken her and then they'd just put her back on the station to fend for herself.

Apparently, she was here for some dangerous purpose and the Varangians were glibly assuming that *he'd* be here to take care of it. It was working out but it seemed a shoddy way to manage risk, in Eth's opinion.

Eve hesitated. "She's not moving." She looked back at Eth. "Why is she not moving?"

"Because reasons!" Gleb said, knowingly vague.

Eth could feel the young man's certainty. He knew that his officer was somehow doing this.

The young man stepped closer and ran his hands over the woman's torso, frowning. He pulled up her loose over-tunic to reveal a black vest. "High-explosive frag-vest," he confirmed.

The vest contained a layer of high-explosive topped with a layer of fixatropic gel. On detonation, the energy would solidify the gel, shattering it into thousands of tiny shards that would remain hard as steel until they finally came to rest.

Gleb pulled out a knife. "I don't see any tamper switches," he advised. He sliced up the right side of the vest and through the right shoulder.

Eve took the back half, helping him slide the vest off the still-immobile woman's left arm before dropping her tunic to cover her up again. She took a restraint from a dispenser on her suit's forearm and secured the woman while Gleb began searching the vehicle.

The woman's mind had suddenly gone quiet and she stood absolutely still, no longer making any attempt to resist. Eth shuddered. "She's gone blank," he said.

Eve looked at her but Gleb darted a sharp glance at Eth, one with more questions than they had time to go into at the moment. Eth gestured at the prisoner's face, glad to have physical evidence to back up his statement. "Just look at her face," he explained.

Gleb looked but Eth could feel that he wasn't entirely off the hook. Suspicions had been aroused during the firefight on the gas platform and they had to be wondering how he'd noticed their current prisoner in the first place.

"Self-erasing conditioning?" Eve blurted, her outrage quickly taking over from her curiosity.

To do such a thing to a living, sentient mind was unthinkable. The techniques were far too roughly defined to prevent the subject losing a piece of themselves along with the destroyed programming.

It was one thing to send someone out to die in combat – they were all comfortable with that concept – but to trap someone inside their own ravaged mind like this…

"Who would do this?" Gleb asked, the quiet in his voice sending shivers up Eth's spine.

"Couldn't have been Uktannu," he replied. "He would have been foolish to turn her loose on this station, seeing as he owned it."

He had a pretty good idea who was behind this, though. He couldn't tell Gleb or Eve about the Human genomes his original team had found while raiding Chimera, but it had probably been for something just like this.

"Sit her down over there," he said, pointing to the back bench. "We'll take this runabout the rest of the way to our destination. It's sportier."

Gleb guided her to the seat and turned to Eth, staring at him for a quiet moment.

"We need to talk," he said quietly.

"We will," Eth assured him, ignoring Eve's curiosity. "Later."

He turned back to the barge. "Father Sulak, we're letting that barge go, so hop aboard, there's a good fellow."

Showing more than a little concern at the gap between the two vehicles, Sulak made a desperate leap. He shot over the gunwales of both craft and nearly went clear over the far side of the runabout.

Eth grabbed the oracle's filthy tunic and hauled him back from the brink.

They passed the cordon without incident. His implant was coded with the rank of a full lieutenant in Mishak's service and that was enough for Mishak's security forces.

Eve brought them to a stop at the docking gate, next to a nondescript but clearly expensive runabout. It would have been unremarkable but for the two Varangians standing in it.

Perhaps the Lady Bau had been wise to urge haste.

After their narrow rescue from the gas giant, she'd taken up Sulak on his offer of a personal reading. When they'd emerged from the ready room on the *Mouse*, she'd handed a data chip to Eth and advised him to return to his master with all due haste.

He patted the pocket on his tunic. "Gleb, stay here and keep an eye on the prisoner." He stepped off onto the deck of the huge barge. "Eve, Father Sulak," he gestured to the single entry portal to the large, domed enclosure that took up nine tenths of the barge's deck space.

He approached the portal and one of the two Quailu petty officers guarding it stepped into his path. "Our master is busy," he said, tilting his head forward in the Quailu gesture of threat. "He has no time to amuse himself with natives."

He was clearly of the school of thought that felt that any native, even an officer, was still inferior to any Quailu.

"You can't say you didn't bring this on yourself," Sulak warned the guard with indecent relish.

The guard looked at Sulak and Eth could feel the mild disgust at the oracle's filthy state mingled with confusion about his statement.

Eth held up his left hand. "Do you see this hand?" he asked menacingly.

"What of it?" the guard demanded, then staggered as the Human slapped him hard on his left ear-aperture. He crashed down to his knees, his mind reeling from pain and outrage. He almost missed the answer.

"Well, for a starter," Eth told him though the high-pitched hum, "it wasn't the hand you should have been keeping an eye on, now, was it?"

Eve whipped her weapon up from the friction-plate on her hip, pointing it straight at the second guard's forehead. The guard's right hand fell away from his weapon's handgrip.

"Now," Eth resumed calmly. "Let's try this again. I am *Lieutenant* Ethkenu of Kish, in service to the Lord Mishak, a prince of the realm, may he outlive us all."

"May he outlive us all," Eve and Sulak repeated.

They stared at the two guards until the second one gave his still-kneeling comrade a rough nudge. "May he outlive us all... out live us all," they muttered in sullen, ragged discord.

"I come with an urgent message for our lord from the Lady Bau." He waved off their attempt to repeat the phrase again for Bau.

"You don't need to say it for her," he told the two guards, who now looked like two sullen, scolded children. "Our master is her equal."

"We have brought her message, which we will now deliver." He looked down at the first guard, who still had a hand over his left ear-aperture. "Shift your thick skull out of my way," he suggested helpfully.

They stepped inside to find Mishak, his father Sandrak and a third Quailu, richly dressed, staring at them from a circle of comfortable lounge chairs.

"Father Sulak?" Eth inquired quietly as they began their slow walk over to them.

"That'd be Marduk," Sulak advised him.

Eth suppressed the urge to let out a low whistle. That certainly explained the two Varangians in the expensive barge.

So what was the emperor's chief of staff doing here? Eth wondered. Everyone knew that Uktannu's betrayal of his brother would have been utter folly if he didn't have reason to expect imperial support afterward.

Was the imperial court now abandoning its efforts to weaken Sandrak's family? Had they come here to secure peace?

Mishak stood as they approached and the other two followed his lead. He'd grown weary of their insistent opposition, attenuated only by their focus on arguing between themselves rather than with him.

Both had a course of action planned out for Mishak and each seemed to be operating under the misapprehension that they only needed to convince the other before they could put it into practice. He'd been listening to them for over two hours now, knowing that he'd have to step in and make his own wishes known.

He'd hoped to delay that moment for at least a few months, giving him time to solidify his plans, but this meeting was bringing things to a head far too soon for his taste. This interruption by his Humans, though he would never admit it, was a welcome distraction.

He stepped toward the small group as they approached, wondering at the presence of a disheveled oracle in their midst but he checked his pace as their emotions came into range. The gap where Eth's mind should have been was still noticeably there.

Then Eth grinned at him.

Mishak was better than most Quailu at reading Human expressions, due more to his casual relationship with Oliv than to his lordship over the species. Most Quailu tended to ignore such things, after all.

What he saw on Eth's face was a genuine pleasure at being back in his lord's presence and it elicited a reciprocal feeling in Mishak. He was glad to have him back, even if only as a distraction. The presence of the same loyal Human who'd helped to elevate him steadied his nerves.

If anything, Eth's grin got even more pronounced. Mishak supposed he must be displaying some of the Quailu micro-expressions that Oliv had been pointing out to him.

In a way, this was superior to having a readable subordinate. Eth wasn't readable to either Sandrak or Marduk, but there was the potential for subtleties to pass between Mishak and his Human officer that others would miss.

It was a great relief to finally make peace with whatever changes the Varangians had made to his most trusted retainer.

Eth brought his facial expression back under control, surprised at how good it felt to see his lord again. He could feel the tension in Mishak's mind suddenly melt, almost as if the young Quailu had recognized the friendly facial expression. There was no trace of his earlier discomfort at Eth's unreadability.

"Lieutenant," Mishak greeted. "It's good to see you, even if this isn't the best time."

"I apologize for our lack of subtlety, Lord." Eth pulled the data chip from his pocket. "But the Lady Bau insisted that we deliver her message to you with all possible haste."

Mishak's head moved back, tilting upward in surprise. "Bau?" He stared at the Humans. "You have a message from Bau? Did she come to Heiropolis after I left?"

Eth allowed himself another grin, feeling the gesture register in his master's mind. "She told me that she'd anticipated such questions, Lord, and that she included an answer in her message." He glanced at Marduk briefly.

"Considering who you are currently meeting with, My Lord, the haste she pressed upon us seems to make a great deal of sense."

Mishak gazed at him for a moment, then sighed. "You'd better have something important on that chip, Lieutenant."

Eth drew a deep breath. "Oh, I do, Lord. You'll either be very pleased by it or you'll be ordering my execution for overstepping the bounds of my commission. Frankly, I'm hoping for the first option but..." He trailed off with a shrug.

That was enough to hook Mishak. He turned to Sandrak and Marduk. "Will you both please excuse this interruption?" he asked, though he clearly had no intention of altering his plans based on any response from either of the two.

"Privacy," he commanded, waving a hand to indicate where he wished to create a partition.

A wall of shimmering energy split the lounge into two roughly equal halves. It would prevent sound from passing, though Eth could clearly feel anger from Sandrak and mild annoyance from Marduk.

How strange. He'd been a slave only a few months ago and here he was feeling the emotions of the emperor's chief of staff.

He slid the tiny locking clip off the data chip and the barge's system read the data, activating a life-size holographic image of Bau.

Eth now felt curiosity from Sandrak and... alarm from Marduk. He glanced over, noticing the Emperor's chief advisor was now at least a full step back from where he'd been standing.

Mishak, of course, was immensely curious. Why was an influential noble like her sending a message to *him*, rather than to his father?

"Greetings to my noble cousin the Prince Mishak," the holograph said with as much warmth as a shimmer of light could muster.

"I wish to convey my gratitude for the small force you sent to assist me in my recent difficulties at Arbella. Though they were few in number, they were able to have an impact beyond all logical expectations." She bowed.

Eth could feel the surprise from Mishak. It matched Sandrak's and both were wildly accented with curiosity. Marduk, however, had gotten his reactions under control and now simply presented mild disinterest. *Did he actually have to convince himself in order to project such feelings?* Eth wondered.

"Suffice it to say," Bau continued, "if not for your timely intervention, your uncle would most likely have killed off Shullat by now and would have been busy consolidating his new position as lord of my *own* holdings and as an elector of the HQE.

"I won't bore you with the minutia of it all, but I am alive, thanks to your assistance, and will certainly support you in *any* endeavor you might wish to undertake."

She held up her right hand and, with great solemnity, extended her middle finger as the image faded.

"Did she just give me the finger?" Mishak turned to focus both his eyes on Eth.

"Ah…" Eth could feel his ears reddening. "She's a keen observer of… intra-species communication…"

"So you're saying she saw your people give *each other* the finger? Nobody extended that gesture to her? I need to be sure before I tell her the true meaning and that's a task best done while she's got a favorable opinion of us.

"And speaking of favorable opinion…" He gestured to where the hologram had been. "Hammurabi's ears!" Mishak looked back at Eth. "What the hell have you been doing since I left Heiropolis?"

Eth filled him in on the broad strokes.

"How did you know Uktannu was going to cause trouble for her?" Mishak demanded.

"An oracle gave us strong reason to believe it was going to happen," Eth said, seeing Mishak's eyes slide over to Sulak. He judged it was time to sort out the Sulak mystery for good or bad.

"And it was that same oracle who convinced the Lady Bau to record her 'urgent' message, wasn't it, Father?" He turned his own gaze on Sulak, who now took a step back, alarm radiating.

Eth grinned, though the expression was wasted on the oracle. "Didn't see *that* coming, did you, Father?"

"Wait," Mishak blurted. "What am I missing?"

"Well, Lord, if I had to guess, I'd say that the good Father Sulak, here, serves someone with an interest in your affairs."

They all turned to look at Sulak who, it appeared, was engaged in a valiant effort to pretend none of this was happening. He finally gave up a feigned search for something in his robes and sighed.

"If you must know," he said, resigned, "I serve your childhood friend."

"Tashmitum?" Mishak leaned forward. "What interest does the crown princess have in *my* affairs?"

Sulak chuckled. "Can you think of none, Lord? She told me of how you two used to play 'house' as children…"

"What of it?"

"Now she would like to make it a little more permanent. She knew of the plot with your uncle and, hoping it would be overcome by you or your father, she dispatched me to Heiropolis with a broad mandate.

"I was to take any actions I felt necessary to mitigate whatever damage her father's schemes might cause and, if possible, to advance your own standing in the empire.

"When I learned that your native troops were there, I attached myself to them and suggested that fate wanted them to help Bau." He waved a hand at Eth.

"I expected us all to die horribly, of course, but the *gesture* of support represented by your forces would have burnished your reputation, not to mention cooling the speculation that you would be as system-hungry as your lord father."

"Interesting," Mishak mused. "Marduk is waiting for my reply to an offer as we speak. I've been offered the chance of serving as Tashmitum's consort. It's a neat little way of neutralizing us as a threat, seeing as our first-born would rule after her."

"And yet, she seems to be grooming you to be her *husband* instead," Eth said, daring greatly to intrude on such a pivotal point in the future of the empire.

"Indeed," agreed Mishak thoughtfully.

Eth could feel a wave of relief come over his lord.

"If you had any idea who my father has in mind for me to marry…" he muttered. "I'd rather marry Father Sulak, here."

"You flatter me, Lord!"

"Not nearly as much as you think," Mishak groused, "but I need to improve my bargaining position if I'm to get a better offer.

"I've already started isolating the emperor from his more powerful supporters," he added. "That attack at Ashurapol…"

"That was your doing, Lord?" Eth asked, surprised. "It was clearly a false-flag operation. Real terrorists would never have placed the explosives in such a sloppy manner…" Eth trailed off, realizing he was criticizing his lord in front of witnesses.

Fortunately, Mishak didn't take it as criticism. "It's just the sort of sloppy machinations the imperial court gets up to, isn't it?" He offered Eth his own bastardized version of a Human grin.

"It happens all the time," Mishak continued. "Something that's clearly false but only to those who bother to connect the dots, and it quickly fades into the following news cycle."

"Then why…"

"Because I also had one of my people arrange a conference in a neighboring lord's system." Mishak chuckled. "Anos would have certainly realized the attack on his own capital world was a false-flag operation. Hearing that a conference of infrastructure companies was taking place nearby and that they were discussing possible contracts on Ashurapol…"

"Anos now thinks the emperor is plotting against him?" Eth looked around at the others. "Should we be hearing this, Lord?"

Mishak waved off the concern. "By the time Anos realizes he's been out-maneuvered, we'll have brought the entire matter to a conclusion. In the meantime, my position is stronger, especially now that you've brought your own news."

He straightened up.

"Well," he said briskly, "the obvious next step in this dance is to refuse Marduk's offer, though now I know Tashmitum won't take offense!"

"Your father won't like you refusing to make his grandchild an emperor," Eth suggested.

"Quite the opposite, I should think," Mishak countered. "He intends to take back our family's ancestral throne and serve as a king within the empire. He sees himself as becoming the permanent power behind the imperial throne."

He waved a dismissive hand, a gesture he'd learned on Kish. "He has no idea that I know this. His arrogance works against him far more than he realizes. He'll see my refusal as working to his advantage. Otherwise, there would be the uncomfortable tangle of being his heir *and* an imperial consort at the same time."

If indeed, Mishak was the intended heir to that kingdom. His father had been even colder lately, more distant, if such a thing were possible for Sandrak.

"The masses would need to believe there's a separation between his kingdom and the imperial throne," Eth said, feeling his master's agreement even before Mishak gave him a considerate, Human nod.

"Right," Mishak glanced toward his father and Marduk who were both trying to appear as though they weren't waiting on him. "I'll refuse to be her consort and offer myself up as her mate instead."

"And how do you do that, Lord?"

"We have to go to Throne World. I place myself at Tashmitum's mercy and hope I haven't read this situation incorrectly." He turned to Eth. "It would be best if I can get to the palace undetected."

Eth grinned. "I have just the thing, Lord. You recall our scout-ship program?"

"I'm afraid security around the palace is tighter than you'd find in a fleet," Mishak told him.

"Indeed, Lord, but we've made an interesting improvement to our scout-ships!"

Eve sighed.

"Up to our arses in it now," she muttered.

In Transit

Gleb nodded. "Makes sense," he said simply.

Eth, sitting opposite the younger man in his small stateroom aboard the *Coronado*, found it hard to believe his account had been accepted so readily. He'd left out most of the background information about the Varangians, knowing what would happen if he said too much.

Still, he'd just told Gleb that he could read emotions and move objects with his mind. Would it kill the little bastard to show at least a *little* incredulity?

"No, really," Gleb insisted, clearly reading the look on his officer's face. "The whole *stepping out of your current frame of reference* explanation makes sense. You can't remain unchanged after an experience like that."

He leaned in. "Can you *teach* me some shit?"

Eth leaned back a little, eyebrows raising.

Could he?

"You realize how dangerous this is?" Eth asked. "If the empire found out – even if our own lord found out…"

"This needs to be done carefully," Gleb said, nodding seriously, "but it *needs* to be done. You can't allow yourself to be the only one. If you die, our people lose an incredible advantage."

Eth reached out, feeling the sincerity. He also felt what he could only describe as a casual relationship with the beliefs and norms of their society. It made him a ruthless fighter but it might also make him a good student. He nodded, taking out his coin.

One Possible Solution

"Now would be a good time," Eth advised. "That freighter to starboard is masking our exit-point for the next few minutes." He turned to Mishak, who stood next to Gleb at the scout-ship's tactical station.

"Are you certain about this, Lord?"

"Certain?" Mishak laughed. "Of course not! She might just have me killed, but you can't go through life without taking the odd chance."

"The odd chance…" Eth looked at his master for a moment. "Very well, sir. Oliv," he called over his shoulder, "get us moving. You know where we're headed."

He stepped past Mishak to poke his head into the engineering space where Meesh was making adjustments to one of three new protrusions around the engines. Noa was watching a series of holo readouts behind him.

"How are we looking for emission management?" Eth knew there was little he could do about it if the answer were something along the lines of 'shitty', but he needed to know what the ship's weaknesses were.

"Better than our projections," Noa muttered, frowning. "That worries me."

"Uh huh," Eth replied. "Of course it does. I'd hate to see what you'd do if it suddenly achieved one hundred percent heat transfer or something."

"I wouldn't be happy about that, either," Meesh retorted. "The carbon nanotube coating we put on *The Reason We Can't Have Nice Things* is catching almost *all* the light coming our way."

"Which is generating an ass-load of heat energy," Noa put in. "Not such a big deal, out in interstellar space, but we're close to the local star, in orbit on the day-side of Throne World. Just imagine how hot this baby would get sitting in the middle of the central plaza, down in front of the palace. There's even more solar radiation hitting us up here where we don't have the atmosphere running interference for us."

"So, how long do we have before the new heat sinks lose containment and start frying us in our own juices?"

Noa shrugged. "About an hour."

"An hour?" Eth shook his head. "We'll be inside the palace in twenty minutes. You two are a couple of frightened old ladies. I was getting ready to be mildly perturbed about all this." He waved a hand at the three new heat sinks.

He stepped back up to the co-pilot's chair and strapped in. "Any sign we've been spotted?"

"Not yet," Gleb replied. "We're ghosts."

"Good. Once we've…" He glanced up at his holo displays. "… Why are we stopping?" His skin suddenly felt cold. "Damn!"

"Yeah," Eve said. "That exclusion zone just popped up on our screen. Some big important noble is descending from orbit and he's getting a hell of a big security cordon."

"Too big to go around?" Mishak asked, coming to stand behind Eth's left shoulder.

"About an hour, from the looks of it," Meesh offered, poking his head past Mishak and looking at the holos. He grinned at Eth. "Maybe you'd like to help this *frightened old lady* write her death poem now?"

"*Meesh had just one job,*" Eth replied,

"*Protect us with a heat-sink,*

"*And we all snuffed it.*"

Eth returned the engineer's grin. "Go babysit the heat sinks; we're not dead just yet." He turned back to the displays. "Computer, add lines inter-connecting each ship in the security cordon."

A dense network of lines crisscrossed the display and Eth activated a target reticule on the largest of the gaps. "Head through there, Eve. They can't see us and, as long as we don't get directly between any two ships in the cordon, they won't suddenly see one of their ships blink out of sight and start wondering what's going on."

They started moving again and Eth watched the shifting lines closely. "Noa," he called loudly, "will going faster be a net gain in safety margin, assuming that we're able to reduce our travel time?"

"If Eve decides to punch it and we get down there in ten minutes instead of lollygagging around at legal approach speed?" Noa went quiet for a few seconds. "Yeah, we end up with a twenty-minute margin on the sinks, especially seeing as we get into the night-side that much faster."

Eth grinned again. "Go wild, Eve."

Though the little ship fully compensated for the sudden acceleration, Eth could hear Mishak's gloves creaking as he grasped the stanchion behind him. He clearly felt his master's fear as the planet suddenly came racing toward their windows.

The ships of the security cordon whipped past them as the scout-ship darted through a gap in the lines of sight and Eve altered course to take them straight to the Imperial Palace.

"I forgot this was your first time seeing what our new scout-class ships can do," Eth admitted to Mishak.

The Quailu wiped sweat from his blunt forehead. "I was on the bridge of the *Dibbarra* when you pulled your little disappearing stunt during the shakedown. It was impressive enough watching my crew try to figure out where you'd gone." He shuddered. "Must have been terrifying from your perspective."

"Not something you'd want to try on manual control," Eth admitted.

"Coming around to the dark side," Eve advised.

Father Sulak came to stand next to Mishak. "Is it strange that I'm hungry at a tense time like this?"

"For most people, yes," Eth replied absently, scanning the holo. "In your case..." He turned to grin at him. "Who's to say what's normal?"

"Best to keep an empty digestive tract for now, Father," Mishak advised. "If this goes sideways on us, the Varangians might just slice off our heads, and you don't want your corpse to embarrass you in its last moments of life, do you?"

Sulak patted his stomach fondly. "It has spent a lifetime trying to embarrass me and with little success. I dare it to try – one last time..."

"We also don't want any non-critical systems, like the oven, creating heat right now," Eth muttered, highlighting a seven-ship patrol in the upper atmosphere.

Eve swerved them around the patrol and dropped down to tree-top level, skimming along toward the palace at twice the speed of sound. She slowed their approach as the glittering waters of the Sea of Akkadia slipped beneath them.

Even Eth grabbed at his arm-rests as the palace flung itself into view, entirely blocking out everything else. If not for the collision-avoidance algorithm, they would have crashed rather than simply stopping ten meters away.

Eth got up and led the two Quailu aft as Eve edged the ship up to the side of the palace wall, about a kilometer up from ground level. The side of the ship flowed open and Eth got his first lung-full of Throne World's brisk night air.

Meesh came forward with a cutting tool and started working as soon as he could reach across the narrowing gap.

"This feels mildly sacrilegious," Sulak said nervously.

"Yeah!" Meesh agreed happily. "It does, doesn't it?"

"Would you rather walk in the front door and ask the emperor for his help?" Eth asked the priest. "Our lord is not exactly in the emperor's good books at the moment."

Sulak's shoulders drooped. "I suppose I hadn't given this part of the plan a lot of thought."

A meter-square section of the palace wall fell down through the gap and spun wildly away, caught in the wind. The engineer stepped back and gestured with elaborate but mildly sarcastic politeness for Eth to lead the way.

They were on target. Inside the hole was a steel catwalk running around the elevator shaft that Marduk used to reach his subterranean office.

Eth stepped across, closely followed by the two Quailu. Noa hopped across next and moved to an access point on the far side, opening up several holos and working on them at a feverish pitch.

Gleb hopped across, eyes darting everywhere. He walked past behind the two Quailu, ignoring their shudders.

"We're in luck," Noa declared as they moved closer. "The elevator is already on its way to Marduk's office. We can bring it to a quick halt here. This saves us calling it remotely and triggering an alarm. Should buy us an extra three minutes."

"That should be enough," Sulak said. "Youthful enthusiasm and all that…"

Eth could feel the indignation build in his lord but it abruptly evaporated.

"Haste would be best in this case, I'm afraid," Mishak admitted, "though I could have taken more time if…"

"Yes, Lord," Eth interjected, rolling his eyes, "we're all sure you could have given the empire an event of epic proportions, but time is definitely not on our side."

The elevator arrived before Mishak could form a reply, the displaced air nearly blasting them all off their feet. The doors opened on a Quailu who started to step out before realizing he was faced by two unknown Quailu and a few armed native retainers.

There was also the small issue of this not being Marduk's office.

They all crowded in with the original passenger, Mishak staring intently at him. "Urhamsi?" he asked.

"That's correct," the other replied, "but who..." He tilted his head, leaning forward in amazement. "Young Mishak!" he blurted. "I haven't seen you since you returned to your father's dominions."

His feelings of concern filled the small compartment. "Throne World isn't safe for you," he warned. "The emperor has always feared your father's strength and, now that you've begun your *own* rise to power..."

"Are you concerned for me, old friend?"

"The emperor won't hesitate to have you seized on some trumped-up charge and use you as leverage against your father."

"He'd be a fool not to take advantage," Mishak agreed, flexing his knees as the elevator came to a stop, "which is why *I* must not hesitate in my own endeavor. I *am* glad to have you present for this, Urhamsi."

He led the way into Marduk's outer office, the bemused Urhamsi trailing behind the Humans, too confused at Mishak's cryptic manner to insist on proper protocol. Father Sulak broke from the group and moved toward Marduk's adjutant, the only occupant of the outer office.

"Not to worry," Mishak told the startled adjutant, "they're all with me." He swept on through the doors to the inner office where Marduk was closing down a large holo projection that he'd been standing in, back to the door.

The Emperor's chief of staff must have felt the unexpected presence. "Mishak?" He turned to face them, one foot moving back. "What in the name of the gods are you doing here?"

"Hello, Uncle." Mishak offered the polite honorific with more cheer than he dared to feel. "I've got a counter proposal that could bring stability back to the empire. Say, have you got any coffee?"

He glanced about the office hopefully. "We didn't pack near enough for the trip, you see, so I've been craving it for the last few days."

"Er… yes," Marduk leaned slightly to the left to shout around his visitor. "Nergall!" he shouted. "Coffee!"

He could, of course, use the proximity net to simply talk to his adjutant but he'd had it disabled. Mishak knew that shouting at his young assistant was far more satisfying for Marduk.

Eth could feel Marduk's mood, slightly improved by yelling, but it was now in danger of backsliding due to the lack of an immediate response. Just as he was filling his lungs to shout again, an affirmative was shouted back from the outer office.

Eth grinned to himself as the thwarted shout soured the chief-of-staff's mood to just the right level that Marduk enjoyed.

"How did you manage to reach my office with an armed party?" Marduk demanded. "Alarms should be sounding and Varangians should be destroying my office in an orgy of gunfire."

"We'd be happy to smash the place up for you," Mishak offered helpfully, "before we leave."

Marduk took an irritated half-step to the side, changing his angle on Mishak. "You may have found a way to sneak in here undetected but you'd have a harder time getting back out."

"Rest assured, Uncle, I've given very careful thought to what happens when I'm done here and I've narrowed it down to two likely outcomes."

"Have you indeed?"

Eth felt surprise from Marduk but also a willingness – an eagerness – to believe what he was hearing. It made sense, seeing as he'd had a hand in raising the young noble during his fostering to the imperial court.

"Admittedly," Mishak conceded, moving aside slightly for the adjutant and his tray, "one of the options ends with my decapitation, but I should point out that it's very firmly in the 'Plan B' column."

"So you weren't entirely asleep during our many discussions?" Marduk said, emanating amusement.

"Well, it *does* account for a major miscalculation on my part," Mishak explained. "One that doesn't feature in Plan A, so you see why I feel that Plan A is far superior."

"Oh, yes," Marduk agreed, taking a coffee from his adjutant, "a much better plan in all regards – an entirely sensible plan, if I may say so?"

"I should be honored." Mishak accepted a mug from the proffered tray, catching Sulak's nod as the priest entered the room.

"I could wax on about the brilliance of this plan," Marduk added, taking sip, "if you were to tell me what the *verpus collatus* it actually *is!*"

"Oh, have I not told you?" Mishak feigned surprise. "I suppose it's best that I not do so. If you were of a mind to stop me, then knowing my plan would be a great aid to you. Conversely, if you didn't try to stop me and the emperor finds out that you actually *knew* my plan…"

"This becomes tiresome, my young friend," Marduk warned. "Are we to stand here exchanging foolish pleasantries until you end up falling back on Plan B?"

Eth and his two Humans were standing closest to the anteroom door and he turned when Gleb put a hand on his elbow.

"I feel someone coming," he warned. "I think it's the princess. She's confident, whoever she is."

Eth's *talk* with Gleb had been an eye opener for both men. Gleb was inherently violent, but he also possessed a singular capacity for intense focus.

He made a surprisingly good apprentice.

Crown Princess Tashmitum stepped out, followed by three of her Varangians and two scensors. The Varangians saw the armed Humans inside the main office and began to raise their weapons.

"Hold your fire!" Eth hissed to his Humans. He reached out to the three Varangian minds, finding their motor control centers, and he willed the three of them to stop, drawing energy from their pericardial regions in order to do so. He felt Gleb's mind slip into the one on the right and let that one go.

The complex of pump muscles that circulated the Varangians' blood was the best place for the Humans to draw heat from. They had the advantage of a continuous flow of hot blood.

Tashmitum glanced back at them and he could feel her mild confusion at her guards' sudden sense of alarm.

The wisps of incense wove their way between the Humans, tickling Eth's nose with a scent like a rotting corpse. He wondered why such a disgusting odor was in favor at court. It must be perceived differently by the Quailu if…

A sudden small small movement from the left-hand Varangian warned him that his concentration was wavering. He put aside his musings on incense, returning his focus to the now-shivering imperial guardsmen. If this went on for much longer, they'd suffer permanent injury to their internal organs.

He held them there, ignoring the speculative look on Noa's face. His control was almost interrupted again as Mishak led Marduk and Sulak out into the anteroom, crossing his line of sight.

As far as the Quailu were concerned, the two armed parties were engaged in a war of threat and counter-threat. The struggles of insects had no bearing on matters of state.

"Your Royal Highness." Mishak bowed low. "I am your most humble servant."

"You've said as much before, in our youth," she replied, "though it's nice to hear it without the sarcasm for a change."

Eth was straining to hold the three guards. He was also using some of his own body energy for the demanding task of controlling two opponents. It was getting even harder to do, now that there was an important conversation to ignore.

"Your people knew this day was coming, Major," Eth hissed at the lead Varangian, noting the suddenly raised eyebrows of his opponent. "Lower your weapons."

Tashmitum turned to the guards and held up a hand. "Major Pilsen, stand down."

"But Highness," the Varangian ground out between clenched teeth, "we have very specific orders from your father…"

"Which you can only carry out by shooting through me," she replied, stepping between the guards and Mishak.

"Mishak, Elector of the Holy Quailu Empire and son of Sandrak, Elector of the Holy Quailu Empire," she continued solemnly, "you have placed yourself at my service. Will you accept whatever role I decide to offer to you?"

"I will, Highness."

She reached up to her throat, undoing the clasp on her cloak and Eth could feel the surprise of the others present.

Nudity, for most races of the HQE including the Quailu themselves, was entirely unremarkable. Nudity, however, in this particular context had a great deal of meaning.

The princess leaned slightly forward as Mishak approached from behind, removing his own cloak. Eth was grateful for Sulak's bulk as the oracle moved to take his place as an official observer of this joining of two noble houses.

Though Eth was able to avoid the distracting sight of his master mating with the imperial crown princess, he wasn't able to ignore the feelings coming from the pair.

He was aware that the two had grown up together but he was still surprised at the depth of affection they had for each other. Even though this was a matter of state and had to be appropriately witnessed, he felt as though this emotional eavesdropping was far more intrusive than simply watching.

He looked over to Gleb. The younger man's jaw was hanging open. Eth reached over and gave him a poke in the shoulder.

Gleb opened his mouth to speak but then shut it again with a guilty little shrug.

Eth wondered if the Quailu had the ability to not feel what was in the minds of others. He glanced at Sulak, noting the beatific smile on the oracle's face.

Of course, Sulak reveling in the couple's feelings meant nothing. The oracle was almost certainly a bit of a pervert.

It was around this moment that Eth realized he'd lost his grip on the three Varangians. They seemed to notice at the same time and they lowered their weapons, their eyes fixed on the act of statecraft being conducted in the anteroom.

It was far too late to stop proceedings at this point.

Mishak, true to his word, was commendably, if somewhat disappointingly, swift and the pair separated.

Eth, having felt the ultimate moment in his own mind, wished he could remove his own brain and give it a good rinse in a mildly acidic solution.

"It is done then," Marduk said, emanating an air of relief and resignation as Mishak stooped to recover the dropped robes.

"Indeed it is," Tashmitum agreed, accepting her robe from her new mate with a nod. "But it must still be *seen* as done throughout the realm before... opposed interests... decide to cover the whole thing up. We must register the *bannen* to every corner of the empire. " Tashmitum looked pointedly at Marduk's adjutant.

The only *interest* that could manage a cover-up would be the Emperor but she could hardly make such an open accusation of her father. Especially at a moment like this when the recordings would be viewed millions of times.

Eth saw Marduk follow her gaze and felt the chief of staff's surprise and delighted anger at the young Quailu who was busy calling for a media officer.

He must have been serving Tashmitum in secret.

That would have explained why Sulak went straight to the young fellow when they first arrived and why the princess had been so quick to reach the office.

"The crown princess is right," Mishak insisted. "Our joining will give the impression that the emperor has gained my family's support. We should be able to restore peace to the realm before any questions of my father's loyalty can be raised.

"We need to get out there," he added, looking to his new wife. "Both of us, My Lady. The intervention at Arbella would be a good template for us to follow."

"The crown princess cannot be risked for the sake of a few small border wars," Marduk insisted stiffly.

"It is exactly what the heir apparent is *for*," replied Tashmitum. "My father filled the same role, in his day, and I dare say he wouldn't have won the votes for ascension if he'd hid in the palace like he does now."

She stepped forward, closer to Marduk. "Uncle," she soothed, "I owe peace to our subjects. That duty extends beyond the bedchamber."

Mishak approached the chief of staff from the other side. "A wise teacher once told me that a noble who has never shared the hardships of those he leads is no leader at all."

Eth could feel the old Quailu's resistance melting.

"That's a dirty trick," Marduk groused, "using my own words against me."

"Well, I felt the moment called for wisdom," Mishak explained, exuding confidence, "so quoting you seemed a safer bet than just winging it."

"Hah!" Marduk surprised them all with his loud outburst. "You'd better get used to winging it. There's no manual on how to stop petty border disputes."

"I rather thought we'd just thrust ourselves into the thick of it," Tashmitum said lightly. "Dazzle them with our charm and wit, maybe threaten them, in the most polite of terms, and then accept the accolades."

"Worked for your father," Marduk conceded before turning to Mishak. "You let *her* handle the charm and wit. You may have grown up here but living on Kish has turned you into a back-galaxy bumpkin. Just back her up and try to look unpredictably dangerous or something."

"Now, there's a role I can excel at!" Mishak took his wife's hand and turned for the elevator. "Come along, Eth. We've got an empire to pacify."

Eth sighed quietly and fell in behind his lord. He kept his thoughts to himself as the Humans boarded the elevator.

It all seemed achievable.

He was fairly certain that very thought preceded just about every disaster in history.

Carving up Loose Ends

Eth returned General Tilsen's semi-bow, grateful for the public acknowledgement. Standing on the left bank of the Ghatra river, the imperial palace's main throne-room waterway, Tilsen was in a position of honor – the best location from which to view the proceedings, but he wasn't above recognizing a native on the far bank.

Especially when he owed his continuing employment to that native's actions.

Tilsen had only arrived the previous day, bringing with him Mishak's renegade uncle, captured during the mopping-up operations in Bau's home system. His gift for the prince-presumptive had earned him his current view.

The newly minted royal couple had been conducting a tour of major houses, speaking about the importance of peaceful coexistence. They'd rushed back from Lord Gil's capital at the news of Tilsen's arrival, leaving Gil with the distinct impression that he'd be facing the wrath of Sandrak's family if he made any moves on Lord Anos.

Mishak's false-flag ploy at Ashurapol had almost been *too* successful…

Mishak and the Princess knew they had to return and deal with Tilsen's *gift* before public opinion reared its ugly head.

Eth sensed the approach of focused attention and he turned to see a Varangian approaching. "Hjalmar," he greeted him neutrally.

"Eth."

"You could have told me before you turned that woman loose on Kwharaz Station," he admonished the Varangian. "She nearly killed my lord."

"She wasn't going to." He leaned in slightly. "What have you done with her?"

Eth raised an eyebrow. "You already know, don't you?" Varangians seemed to bring out his sarcastic side.

He refrained from insisting that he'd felt her intent. His current advantages, though caused by the Varangians, were nonetheless none of their business.

Unless, of course, they would eventually find out, which meant that they already knew. He drew a deep breath and blew it out.

Varangians were even more annoying to be around once you started to understand them.

"She seemed pretty determined to try," he hedged.

"Oh, she had *intent*," Hjalmar allowed with a slight incline of his head, "but it was never going to happen. You *know* what I meant by that."

What exactly did Hjalmar mean by 'you know'? Eth wondered.

"What if she *had* succeeded?" Hjalmar asked. "Or, more to the point, what if the empire was thrown into turmoil? If it ceased to be the great entity that it is now, what would you and your Humans do?"

Eth had been watching the approaching barge, an antique that traveled only on the surface of the water. He tore his eyes away from the small craft and its doomed passenger to meet Hjalmar's gaze.

"Your people don't engage in idle speculation, Hjalmar. Given the… nature of your society, you understand better than most where it can lead." He glanced around them.

Hjalmar chuckled. "Looking to see if anyone will come to 'erase' our discussion? Any correction would have occurred *before* this point, if you take my meaning."

So, this talk is sanctioned, Eth thought. "Isn't this a little reckless for your species? Warning me of future events…" He trailed off as Hjalmar leaned in.

"For all either of us knows," the Varangian whispered, "we may have had a dozen different versions of this conversation before hitting upon one that leads to a favorable outcome." He grinned. "Let's hope this new tangent doesn't send us back to the start again!"

"So you came here to warn me?"

A nod. "That and to watch your lord during today's *festivities*."

Mishak looked down at Uktannu. His uncle was chained to the ancient wooden deck on his hands and knees, the posture of an unevolved grazer a severe humiliation, especially here in the throne room.

They were almost up to the mooring posts and Mishak braced himself by putting his right foot up on his uncle's posterior.

The barge crew tossed their mooring lines with unerring accuracy and the heavy ropes snapped taut, arresting their forward motion. Mishak flexed his right knee before pushing hard against Uktannu's rump. The young prince recovered his balance and remained standing while the renegade at his feet, having taken on Mishak's momentum, sprawled onto his face, his backside still ludicrously elevated.

Sandrak was furious. He'd threatened, cajoled and even begged for the right to carry out this ceremony but Mishak wasn't about to waste diplomatic stature simply to please his father. As the noble who'd exposed and defeated Uktannu's treachery and as the noble who'd assumed the renegades holdings, the right fell to Mishak.

The prince-presumptive would execute his own uncle for treason.

Not that he was very enthusiastic over the prospect. He'd given the matter a lot of thought, knowing his feelings would be on display to those in the barge and he'd settled on an emotion he'd honed during a lifetime as Sandrak's son.

Cold anger.

He turned to Tashmitum who was better able to control her emotions. She emanated a firm belief in the rightness of the proceedings as she handed Mishak the axe.

Mishak had expected an epic struggle to get his family's ancient axe but his new bride had assumed responsibility for the matter, assuring him that he needn't worry any further about it. He looked down at the weapon.

The swirling cartouche, carved into the side-cheeks of the double-bladed weapon, indicated his wife's family, not his own. He would execute this renegade with the same blade used by the emperor, five decades earlier, when he put the infamous *Treasonous Trio* to death.

Frank admiration. He looked up at her.

She met his gaze. *Pleased acknowledgement*

"Can we get on with this?" Uktannu snarled, his face still pressed against the smooth wood.

Mishak allowed himself to display amused admiration. His uncle had gambled and lost, but he'd shown courage in taking such a chance. He reached down and grasped Uktannu's collar, pulling him back up to the all-fours position.

He brought the axe up and slit the tunic down the back, his eyes searching out the line where the back muscles bind to the spine.

A slow deep drum-beat began from the aft end of the barge and Mishak took a deep breath that was mirrored by Uktannu who could feel his nephew's resolve suddenly crystalize.

Mishak brought the axe down gently to rest at the top of Uktannu's spine on the left side. He drew it downward with a firm, forceful stroke and the thick muscle tissue of his uncle's back drew away from the spine, curling as the renegade's feet twitched.

He dipped the fingertips of his left hand into the bloody mess before he stood, facing the crowd around Tilsen. He dragged his fingers from the top right of his face down to the bottom left, leaving five diagonal red stripes reminiscent of the empire's long-gone, barbaric death-priests.

Uktannu made no sound but his breathing was becoming shallow and rapid as Mishak grabbed the loose muscle tissue and pulled upward as he sliced the axe into the gap between meat and ribs, exposing the ribs fully.

Now would come the hard part.

He turned the axe, exchanging the slicing blade for the serrated one. Placing it along the left side of Uktannu's rib cage, roughly two hands-breadths from the spine, he took a deep breath and then ground the serrated edge down and into the ribs, grunting with the effort.

It took him several tries before he broke through and he nearly botched the job when his uncle twitched, bringing the blade within inches of his cardiac pressurizers.

Mishak shifted his position, rotating the axe back to the slicing edge and he deftly sliced between upper and lower ribs to create a hatch in his uncle's back. He placed the top tip of the blade at the upper part, where the 'hatch' hinged to the spine.

The axe-tip was designed for this exact purpose, as well as for an even more important one. It was an extension of the upper edge of the blade and served as a rather awkward knife.

He worked the tip down, around the ends of each rib, severing the ligaments and connective tissue binding them to the spine until the entire hatch could be lifted free of the body. The condemned traitor grunted as his organs were exposed to the cool evening air.

Mishak straightened and tossed the bloody rack of ribs overboard with a loud splash. With a shudder he looked down at the hideous mess, the cardiac complex pulsating obscenely.

It was time to end this. The waves of pain coming from his uncle were torturing everyone on the barge; a salutary lesson to all would-be traitors.

He adjusted his grip on the blood-slicked weapon so that the point was now aimed downward. He took another deep breath.

And then he paused.

Uktannu was struggling to say something. Mishak lifted the weapon away, oblivious to the moan from the watching throng, and knelt beside his uncle, leaning down to better hear his last words.

"… doomed. Brother… will never support… you…"

Mishak sighed. Of course Sandrak would make trouble for him but…"

"No, fool!" Uktannu snarled, voice shaking. "*Your* brother!"

Mishak sprang back to his feet in surprise. He stared down at Uktannu's ravaged back without really seeing it. He'd always wondered if his father had another heir stashed away somewhere.

He looked up at Tashmitum as she touched his elbow. This delay in an execution was unseemly. He brought the axe-head over Uktannu's body once more and plunged the tip into both of the cardiac pressurizers, the hot spray splashing wetly across his face.

His uncle was now irrevocably on the path to death. It was within Mishak's rights to leave it at that, but Uktannu had provided him with useful information at the end, even if it *had* been meant as a taunt.

He brought the weapon up and swung hard. Uktannu's head rolled away from his body, eyes blinking, and Mishak steeled his mind against the sudden surprise and terror coming from his father's brother. It wouldn't do for the assembled dignitaries to feel any weakness from a possible future emperor.

Then the thoughts faded and the head was empty, unreadable.

Mishak stepped back, returning the bloody axe to his wife and looked to the bank where the crowd, released from the silence of the spectacle, were building up a buzz of discussion. He saw Eth there, looking back.

Eth had to admire his lord's composure. The Human had no familial connection to Uktannu but that didn't mean he could block out the condemned's pain. He suspected he could reach out farther than the Quailu. The ones around him didn't seem so affected but perhaps they were more accustomed to controlling it.

Did the Varangians also have this ability? Would Hjalmar be allowed to tell him?

"Where are you going from here?" Eth asked turning to the Varangian. He frowned, scanning the crowd. "Hjalmar?"

Well that's just great. He shook his head. *Hint at an imperial collapse and then just bugger off while my back is turned.*

He sighed. *Varangians…*

Get Free e-Novellas

When you sign up for my new-release mail list!

Follow this link to get started:

http://eepurl.com/ZCP-z

From The Author

So… Eth has some interesting abilities. Using them comes with a cost and it's not going to give him an instant 'win' button because, let's face it, concentration is hard in a combat situation. Figuring out fields of fire and anticipating enemy maneuvers is still going to take precedence.

In book 2, Humans, the low level rash of brush-fire conflicts will intensify. The leading families of the Holy Quailu Empire will continue to grab what they can, taking advantage of the emperor's damaged prestige to press their own agendas.

And a new pattern will emerge from the chaos.

The prophecy, revealed to Uktannu, spoke of the destruction of a great house. Has it already been fulfilled with his fall? Is there more to it? Was the oracle just some drunken fool, spinning nonsense to amuse himself?

The fight isn't over for Eth and his people just yet. They'll be very busy in the next installment, though what exactly they're fighting for is less than certain.

Thanks for reading this story! If you enjoyed it, please consider leaving a short (or long) review. Folks talk about marketing strategies for Facebook or Amazon but the one thing that makes the most difference to a story's visibility is individual opinions.

Especially for a nobody like myself!

If you'd like to get some free novellas, you can get access to my freebie download page by signing up for my mail list. I don't send out a ton of spam (honestly, you'll probably forget who I even am by the time you finally get an email) and you can unsubscribe at any time.

Whenever I write a shorter story (anything under seventy thousand words) I load it at the freebie page for my subscribers. You can get your free stories by following the link on the next page.

A.G. Claymore

Human

Made in the USA
Las Vegas, NV
12 December 2022

62109374R00218